The Kalahar

The Kalahari Ferrari

by

Nick Dillon

METHUEN

1

First published in Great Britain in 2016
by Methuen
35 Hospital Fields Road
York, YO10 4DZ

Copyright © 2016 N F Pearson

N F Pearson has asserted his right under the Copyright, Designs
and Patents Act 1988 to be identified as the author of this work

ISBN 978 0413 777904

Typeset by SX Composing DTP, Rayleigh, Essex

Printed and bound in Great Britain by
CPI Group (UK) Ltd, Croydon, CR0 4YY

The view from the French window of the elegant house in one of Pretoria's wealthier suburbs could not have been more idyllic. Two dobermans sprawled in the late afternoon shade of the veranda, hungrily eyeing the shabbily dressed gardener as he pruned the bougainvillea hedge which grew alongside the length of the secure fence surrounding the villa. The scarlet flowers provided a dramatic backdrop to the well-manicured garden and the wicked thorns were an additional deterrent to trespassers who were a constant menace in this most violent of African cities. To the side a swimming pool dominated the garden and, under the shade of a small thatched rondavel, a quartet of attractive bikini-clad young women reclined on comfortable sun loungers. Another servant, smartly attired in a crisp white jacket, hovered in the background with a drinks tray whilst the women gossiped and flicked through the latest glossy magazines. The tranquillity betrayed no hint of the tense meeting which was taking place inside. Convened in utmost secrecy, the gathering comprised the founding fathers of the Rhodesia Homeland Army. This highly secretive group had been formed from among those within the white population of Zimbabwe who, from the 1980s onwards, had seen their land, farms and businesses seized by the increasingly rapacious government of Robert Mugabe and his ZANU henchmen.

At first the international community had shunned the evident cynicism and anger of these dispossessed people. However, it became clear that Mugabe was turning his attention and his violence to those among the black population who opposed him, and the white landless community could see there was an opportunity to make real something which had only been a wild dream for at least two decades – namely to wrestle control of their beloved homeland from the hated presidential dictator and to see the State of Rhodesia rise again from the ashes of Zimbabwe. They were shrewd enough to understand that Mugabe's regime of terror was at last opening the door for them to act incisively. Once again it would be they who would dominate the black majority and who would reap the rewards that this most bountiful of African countries had to offer.

The Rhodesia Homeland Army had been founded nearly ten years ago by Peter Esterhuize and Frederick Pretorius but, as a dispossessed group, they did not have the financial clout to mount an effective campaign to undermine Mugabe and his armies. Based in Salisbury, Esterhuize was a former multi-millionaire landowner and industrialist, who had owned majority shares in a number of large mines across Rhodesia. He had been declared bankrupt when the share price collapsed during the pre-independence sanctions era and abandoned the country of his birth when Robert Mugabe came to power.

As a young man, Pretorius had inherited a large prosperous farm to the south of Salisbury but he had left the country when his property was seized during Mugabe's programme of land reform. Many of his loyal black workers had been murdered during the land grab. His beautiful farm – now ruinously infertile – had been divided into separate ownership. Pretorius was now reduced to managing a lodge in the Witwatersrand Mountains, to the west of Pretoria in South Africa, which was owned by a prominent black member of the governing ANC. It ate into his soul that fate had dealt him such a cruel blow and he spent many of his waking hours dreaming of his former life on his now defunct farm.

Although the tide of world opinion was beginning to turn their way, a lack of finance restricted these embittered individuals. The majority of the discussions this sultry afternoon had focused on the issue and a solution had been found. Predictably for an organisation whose members had experienced violence first hand they did not opt for a simple, half-hearted, course of action. Instead they decided on a plan, which, if successful, would provide them with an unimaginable fortune which could be used to tear down the Mugabe edifice. Esterhuize, Pretorius and their colleagues had listened intently as a quietly spoken, but determined man, who worked at the diamond mine at Jwaneng in the south-eastern corner of Botswana explained his proposal. If what he said was true then it was just possible that the Rhodesia Homeland Army might be able to seize a quarter of the mine's annual production, which, if the government figures were accurate, was worth in excess of half a billion US dollars. Having put the proposal to a vote, the plan was set in motion, the meeting drew to a close and the group left the library and joined the other guests in the garden.

* * * * *

As the Comair commuter plane levelled out to a cruising altitude on the flight from Johannesburg to Botswana's Sir Seretse Khama Airport, Rusty McKenna stretched out his six foot frame. The long, ten-hour haul from Heathrow to Mandela International Airport in Johannesburg had been packed with a spirited collection of Afrikaners relieved to be escaping the onset of a British winter and to be returning to their beloved Africa. For some this would be a rare trip home and Rusty was unsure whether their high spirits reflected genuine pleasure at the state of affairs in their country or whether it masked an apprehension at what the recently elected government of President Zuma had in store. Certainly the relative calm and stability since the demise of apartheid had given those who had genuine ambitions for peace hope for the future.

The interior of the small aircraft was by no means full. The thirty-odd passengers who had transited through South Africa en route to Gaborone appeared to be a mix of smartly dressed European businessmen and casually attired development workers who still had a role to play in this complex country. For many, Botswana was viewed more as the playground of the businessman than the aid worker. The combination of well-managed presidential democracy, combined with the vast wealth which the discovery of diamonds had brought since independence, had led to the growth of a stable, prosperous country which was the envy of its South African neighbours. There were many adjacent countries such as Angola and Mozambique where the largesse of developed nations could have been spent productively. What was singularly lacking on this flight were the tourists who might be expected to be travelling to a country which boasted some of the last few remaining areas of wilderness on the continent. As the plane sped on its north-westerly course Rusty thought of the vast emptiness of the Kalahari Desert which lay ahead, still inhabited by a dwindling number of olive-skinned San bushmen. Beyond the desert lay the massive salt pans, remnants of age-old lake beds which, during the wet season, filled with a shallow film of water and attracted teaming multitudes of birds and spectacular herds of migrating zebra, wildebeest and gemsbok. Beyond the pans, to the north-west, lay the incomparable Okavango Delta. Here the river, fed by rains from the Angolan Highlands, headed into the interior to flow into the Kalahari Desert and evaporate. A huge swamp was formed which filled and emptied with the passing of the seasons, creating a multitude of changing and multifarious wetland habitats, and a home for countless thousands of insects, fish, birds and animals together with a number of diverse tribes which had adapted to live in harmony with this magical place.

As the plane began its descent, Rusty spotted the main road from Jo'burg to Gaborone and the distinct broad swathe of cleared land in the acacia scrub which marked the border. The lush green of the bush, the numerous waterholes and the large numbers of sleek and fat brown cattle served to impress upon Rusty the reality of what he had read in the British press: that the recent barren period of drought had been replaced by a period of plentiful rainfall. Rusty gathered up his belongings and, as he reached the exit, instinctively flashed his deep blue eyes, smiled and thanked the attractive stewardess for a pleasant and relaxing flight.

* * * * *

'Hey, Rusty, you old bastard! Good to see you,' a voice bellowed from behind the security fence. 'You look terrible!'

Rusty span round and caught sight of his old friend.

'Mats!'

As his eyes adjusted to the harsh glare of the sun he could see that Mats Tingstad was unchanged. His short, brown hair was sun-bleached and as unruly as ever and several days of stubble stood out on his thin, weather-beaten face. His tall muscular frame was encased in a colourful T-shirt and khaki bush shorts. He was wearing an American baseball cap and his feet were shod in Zimbabwean rafting sandals. Mats, brimful of energy and vitality, hopped up and down.

'Get yourself through Customs and I'll treat you to lunch and a couple of Castles in the Bull and Bush.'

'You're on. It's bloody good to see you too. You look great,' Rusty shouted, adding as he laughed. 'I hate you.'

'And I've got a surprise for you,' Mats shouted, before bounding off by the side of the airport.

Arriving in Botswana was usually a pleasure and it did not take Rusty long to get through immigration. The officials were efficient and courteous, particularly if visitors could speak a few words of Setswana. Rusty was pleased to discover that the old pleasantries came back with ease.

'*Dumela Ra, Lo Kae*,' he said to the smiling, well-dressed Motswana official.

'Good morning sir, I'm fine. How are you?'

'*Ke teng*,' Rusty replied.

The men laughed at the casual way at which they swapped greetings in two languages. In many ways this easy exchange reflected the way in which the black and white communities co-existed peacefully and sensibly, unlike elsewhere in this troubled part of the world. This happy position had been heavily influenced by the fact that the first President of the newly independent country, Sir Seretse Khama had fallen in love in his youth with an English girl during his years of study in Oxford and London. Despite the initial hostility of the tribal elders and the disgraceful attitude of the British colonial government who, concerned about the reaction of the racist South African Republic, had barred him from returning to Bechuanaland as it then was, Seretse had stuck to his guns, married the girl and eventually returned home in triumph. His subsequent election as first President of the new Botswana was the final good omen for the harmony that had come with independence and which had, so far, stood the test of time.

'I see from your application for temporary residence that you are to be based in Hukuntsi,' the Immigration Officer observed as he scanned Rusty's documents. 'With all due respect, Sir, Hukuntsi is a place to depart from rather than arrive at. I wish you luck.'

Rusty laughed inwardly, knowing how the Batswana, having achieved the status of a well-paid government job, were reluctant to leave the comparative civilisation of Gaborone. They were at a loss to understand why anyone would voluntarily take themselves off to live in the back of beyond on the fringes of the awesome Kalahari Desert. For Rusty, however, this was a heaven-sent opportunity to reacquaint himself with the desert wilderness.

'I'll survive,' he replied and walked through to collect his luggage from the carousel.

* * * * *

As soon as Rusty passed through the sliding doors which led into the main part of the terminal building Mats pounced on him.

'Come and see your surprise,' he shouted excitedly, grabbing Rusty's rucksack and heading for the car park.

Rusty followed at his own pace, the effects of the flight and the intense midday heat beginning to take their toll. As he passed through the rows of Japanese saloon hire cars and a variety of battered pick-ups and air-conditioned Toyota Land Cruisers – the favoured means of transport amongst the locals – he suddenly realised where Mats was taking him. Parked under the shade of one of the trees he could see the Kalahari Ferrari! She was just as Rusty remembered her, still complete with her rusty roof rack and an array of green jerry cans. Her bodywork – now faded from its original glossy, navy blue – still bore the scars of many a foray into the bush. The Kalahari Ferrari was a short wheelbase four cylinder petrol engine Land Rover County. Wanting to fly the flag, the British High Commission had shipped her out in the 1980s. When she had become so battered that she had become an embarrassment to the exalted individual at the Commission, the company which had first employed Rusty in Botswana had purchased her as a runabout in the bush. It was here he had begun his love affair with her. There was no company policy about using vehicles for private trips and many had been the weekend or holiday break when Rusty had stocked her up with fuel, water and provisions for an off-road foray deep into the wilderness that was the Kalahari. Sometimes these excursions had been in convoy with other vehicles and then the campfire parties had been long, boozy and noisy. On other occasions Rusty had escaped alone or with female companionship and these had been glorious episodes of peace, solitude and sometimes passion.

Although the central Kalahari was not renowned for plentiful animal life, thoughtful travellers such as Rusty soon learned the way of the desert and would often be rewarded with sightings of shy duiker, klipspringer and springbok. On rare occasions a leopard might be spotted giving the camp a wide berth and lions were occasionally heard at night but never seen. However the sheer emptiness of the desert and the immaculate beauty of the night sky were perfect encouragement for Rusty to make his regular trips.

It was not just that the Kalahari Ferrari was a 4x4 which had won Rusty over. It was her reliability and overall sunny character. During numerous excursions she had never suffered major engine failure and she had never got stuck. Of course there were broken shock absorbers, blocked fuel lines and punctures aplenty, but all of these were meat and drink to the experienced bush driver and added to the adventure's allure. She had never yet got bogged down in the deep soft desert sand. Rusty put this down to her rosy disposition and her innate magic. It was probably a combination of cautious driving, good quality sand tyres and, most importantly, her short wheelbase. It was a little known fact amongst even the most bush-hardened 4x4 drivers that short wheelbased vehicles were better equipped to get out of a tight spot than their lengthier, and often haughtier, cousins. There had been several occasions, during group trips with other V8 Land Rovers, Toyota Pajeros and Land Cruisers, when the Kalahari Ferrari had, with the aid of ropes and chains, come to the rescue of many a more illustrious and upmarket companion, saving it from the embarrassing embrace of the fine sand to be found at the bottom of a dry stream bed. The Kalahari Ferrari's ability to sail through these obstacles, and pull other vehicles from them had lost Rusty many superficial friends amongst the 4x4 owning community of Gaborone, who often found it difficult to stomach the fact that their extremely valuable heaps of state of the art Japanese engineering had been pulled, unceremoniously, up the side of a dusty stream bed by an ancient, battered twenty-five year old Solihull-built Land Rover.

Rusty was almost dumbstruck.

'Mats, I thought I was going to find you standing in the arrivals hall with some old flame I could barely remember and here you are with my lovely old Land Rover. I knew I should have trusted you. You always get things spot on.'

Rusty hugged the undemonstrative Swede. For a moment he could feel the affection pass between them before the big man bustled off across the car park.

In all his wildest imaginings Rusty had never thought he would see his Land Rover again. It had been nearly two years since he had last visited Botswana and at that time she had been rusting away in a locked yard, after the Government had cancelled the project he had been employed on, making everyone redundant overnight. The initiative had been launched as a pilot project to establish if there were recoverable levels of oil under the sands of the Kalahari Desert. The Government, mindful of the fact that much of the country's diamond wealth was being exploited by foreign business interest, predominantly from South Africa, had artfully collaborated with the United Nations Development Programme to ensure that not only would all profits remain in the country but that all expatriate workers would share their skills with a Motswana so, in time, such work could be undertaken without the need for foreign participation.

It was this which had interested Rusty when he had seen the advert whilst convalescing in Liverpool after a near-fatal accident in the North Sea. The United Nations had delegated staff recruitment to Skillshare Africa, a lesser known British aid agency which specialised in pairing professional people with a counterpart in Africa. They were looking for managers, geologists, engineers and rig workers. Rusty had applied, more in hope than expectation, and had been staggered to find himself explaining the finer points of setting up a truck-hauled oil derrick to a group of bemused Batswana on the edge of the desert a few weeks later. Although the exploration was unsuccessful, Rusty had been pleased with his contribution. He proved an able teacher and there were a number of proficient Batswana engineers in the making who had benefited from his tutelage. The government, disgruntled that they were not to be bathed in vast oil riches, nevertheless concurred that the style of the programme had been an unqualified success and soon introduced similar schemes. Rusty was devastated when his contract had been terminated for it meant he would have to leave the country, but he had been relieved at the outcome. Having grown to love the beauties of the desert he was certain that there were some elements in government who would have thought little about the effect that a major extraction programme would have had on the fragile environment of the Kalahari Desert had oil been discovered. Botswana was still very much in a 'get rich quick' mode and it would be many years before the administration learned the error of its ways.

So, with a wealth of happy memories, Rusty had parked the Kalahari Ferrari in the yard two years previously, boarded a plane home to Liverpool and a period of unemployment. At that time he had not anticipated returning to Botswana and even if he had he would have expected the battered Land Rover to have long since been driven to a well-earned grave on a scrapheap on the outskirts of Gaborone.

'How the devil did you track her down, Mats?'

'Oh, it was easy,' his friend replied. 'When the Board got the funding together for the expansion at the Youth Training Centre I knew we'd need extra vehicles. Money was short so I took myself off to a government auction and there she was, in all her glory. I picked her up for peanuts. Come on let's get to the pub and I'll tell you all about it.'

Over numerous beers and a couple of huge steaks on the pub's thatched veranda, Mats explained how, as a result of the small print in the original exploration contract, all the property of the doomed oil venture had fallen into government hands, so it was hardly a surprise that the Kalahari Ferrari had ended up at auction. Mats had driven the Land Rover back to Hukuntsi where he was now Senior Instructor and, since the Land Rover had good-sized, robust and relatively simple working parts which were perfect for trainees to cut their teeth on, she had become the centrepiece of the car mechanics' practical work. Over the course of a year she had been thoroughly reconditioned. Little had been done to the bodywork other than to knock out a few bumps. Despite her looks, she had slowly become a solid and reliable work-horse once again. It was while she was being reconstructed, Mats explained, that the Training Centre's Board of Trustees had been lucky enough to acquire substantial financial support from the European Commission. The agency was particularly concerned with providing solar power to the outlying Kalahari villages for the purpose of providing lighting and, in particular, electrical power to pump water out of the underlying artesian basin. Without the latter the outermost villages became not only unpleasant but decidedly chancy places to try to exist during a drought. Once the funds had been granted Mats had been given the task of recruiting the various engineers who would become the instructors in these new initiatives. The philosophy behind the centre was to train local people whilst the new facilities were being constructed so that in time they could maintain and erect them themselves.

Mats had first travelled to Africa from Sweden when he was in his early twenties. Like Rusty, he had fallen in love with Botswana and would have found it difficult to fit in back home in Europe now. Over the years he had become an old hand at surviving in this beautiful but remote wilderness and he was painfully aware that not only did he need instructors who were well-versed in their subject but reliable individuals who would be able to stick at it. Bitter experience had shown that, although highly-qualified, many people weren't suited to the isolation. Some would turn to drink, stay but become barely adequate and certainly no example to their trainees. Others would depart pronto with their tails between their legs. Mats had the foresight, therefore, when he had started the recruitment exercise to actively pursue people who were currently working in the desert or had a proven history of having done so.

'I'll be honest with you, Rusty,' Mats drawled after his third beer. 'I didn't immediately include an ex-oil man on my list of prospective employees. I was racking my brains to think of people who would do a good job for us here and who would not be likely to run out when I caught sight of the lads working on the Kalahari Ferrari. My mind went back to our trip to Deception Valley. Do you remember? You cleaned out a blocked fuel line in Paul's Pajero and then rescued my Hilux from that goddamned dry stream bed. I decided it might be worth getting in touch to see if you were interested. You might not be the most highly-qualified engineer in the business but you are a damned good teacher and I knew you'd honour your contract.'

The two old friends spent the remainder of the day sitting in the open air in front of the water-hole bar at the Gaborone Sheraton. One or two familiar faces wandered past but for Rusty the real enjoyment was the thrill of basking in the pleasant evening temperature and looking up at the beautiful African night sky. Mats had gone from strength to strength. Over the course of the last two years he had consolidated his position at the Training Centre and had secured a worthwhile niche for himself in Hukuntsi. Knowing how much he loved the country, Rusty was surprised that Mats hadn't settled down here and found a partner to share it all with.

'I'm too busy keeping the Centre from grinding to a halt to bother myself with running off into the desert chasing young women,' Mats had explained wryly when Rusty had plucked up the courage to broach the subject.

Knowing the way that Mats threw himself into any venture which he believed was worthwhile, this had not really surprised Rusty.

* * * * *

That night Mats and Rusty slept for a few hours at the Swedish Volunteer Service hostel in Gaborone. The following morning they were both up at the crack of dawn. Rusty had a leisurely breakfast which helped to shake off the effects of the flight not to mention his hangover. Mats had left the house long before Rusty was ready and he returned bright and breezy with his long wheelbase 4x4 Toyota Twin Cab stacked to the roof with food and other essentials. Fresh fruit and vegetables were particularly sought after in the remote villages. Everything had to be carefully selected so it would not be inedible after the gruelling trip along the desert road once they left the tar at Sekoma.

'Get a move on Rusty!' Mats shouted. 'Have you forgotten what time we get moving here? If we don't get there before sunset we'll have to lay up at the side of the road.'

He threw the keys for the Kalahari Ferrari onto the table and strode out of the room.

'Yeah, let's hit the road,' Rusty exclaimed excitedly. 'This is the business!'

He followed Mats out to where the two vehicles were parked in the compound. They were soon heading out of Gaborone towards Molepolole along the newly-tarred highway. Mats led the way in the faster twin cab. On this part of the journey the road was easy, traffic was light and Rusty was able to concentrate on the simple pleasure of reacquainting himself with the vehicle in which he had already driven countless thousands of miles. When they reached Molepolole they pulled over into a petrol station and made the proprietor's day by filling both vehicles to capacity. This included both main tanks, both long range reserve tanks and the ten jerry cans that they carried between them. This came to a total of almost five hundred litres. Despite the prodigious thirst of the Land Rover in particular, this gave them a considerable range. Enough to cross the desert if they needed to and if they did not get lost. On this trip they were sticking to the road and there would be no need for all of the fuel. It was prudent to stock up because as they went further along the desert road to Hukuntsi it became more difficult to find a garage which could be guaranteed to have any petrol in stock. What they could be certain of, however, was that if they found a place with petrol to spare the asking price would not be to their liking. Once the tanks were full and the weight of the provisions was shared between the two vehicles, they set off out of the village on the long, westerly leg through Jwaneng onwards towards Kang where the true desert began. As soon as they left Molepolole, Mats' mind turned to the many tasks that lay ahead of him when he reached Hukuntsi, and instinctively, without thinking, he accelerated ahead of the aged Land Rover.

* * * * *

Kurt Viljoen had worked hard since the Rhodesia Homeland Army Council had approved his plans at their meeting in Pretoria. It had all seemed so perfect from the moment, late the year before, when he had discovered the closely kept secret which he knew he could eventually use to both his own advantage and that of his adopted cause.

After leaving Rhodesia during the civil war he had drifted from job to job, never making any money and becoming increasingly bitter at the rotten hand life had dealt him. Up until the fall of Ian Smith's regime and the rise to power of the detested Robert Mugabe, and his murderous Zanu People's Party, everything had gone well for him. Kurt's father, Vincent, had owned a prosperous cattle ranch near Bulawayo, in southern Matabeleland, and the life had been tough, rewarding and enjoyable. He had attended an exclusive private college in the capital, Salisbury. His father had not stinted with funds and with his clean-cut blond good looks set in his tough wiry frame, Kurt had excelled at sports and led the life of a young squire amongst the prissy but willing daughters of the white community. For a few short years his father had groomed Kurt and Uli, his younger brother, for the day when they would run the farm. They had both become good stockmen and could manage the farm well, with or without the guiding hand of their father. Running a large estate in the relentlessly unforgiving bush also taught them much about the ways of Africa. They knew the myriad types of wildlife which frequented the farm. The many types of small antelope, warthog and ostrich that roamed and foraged with the herd were hunted and provided a rich and delicious harvest. Occasionally, during times of drought, families of zebra and wildebeest would range from the Hwange Game Reserve to the north in search of water. These were marvelled at but otherwise left in peace as they passed through. It was not uncommon for leopard and cheetah to follow the grazers and chance upon their cattle. Both boys had hunted and bagged leopard by the time they were in their mid teens and were crack shots with a variety of weapons. At school they had learned military skills with the cadet corps and with their lithe athleticism and hunting know-how could easily have found themselves recruited by the infantry regiment in Salisbury. They had both turned their backs on this opportunity, however, for the good, but tough life, on the family farm.

When disaster struck it came swiftly and savagely. The war of independence and the bitter civil war which followed were cruel and bloody. There had been no hope for the Viljoen farm. It had been right in the thick of things, particularly during the civil war when Robert Mugabe and Joshua Nkomo had struggled for power. For a while Matabeleland was probably one of the most violent places on the face of the earth. The estate workers were slaughtered by Zanu troops and the animals were carried away to feed the ever hungry troops. Vincent and Uli had foolishly tried to hang on to what remained. During the early fighting they had successfully defended the land and stock from several armed bands and, on other occasions, the crack troops of the Selous Rangers of the Rhodesian Army had routed and butchered those who had threatened to overwhelm everything in their path. However the troops had no answer for the hit-and-run tactics and the conviction of the freedom fighters of both persuasions and ultimately Rhodesia was lost and Zimbabwe was born. It was during the bitter factional fighting of the civil war that followed that the Viljoen estate finally succumbed. At the height of the conflict it was overrun on a moonless night by a marauding band of armed soldiers. It did not matter which faction they belonged to. They had come with one intent only and the deaths had been long, bloody and painful. Kurt had seen the writing on the wall and, sometime earlier, had quietly crossed over the border to the south-west into Botswana to find relative tranquillity. He had not stopped to consider if this had been an act of cowardice, taking the pragmatic view that his father and brother had got what was coming. Although he took pleasure in giving pain, he had no inclination to be on the receiving end of it. As far as he was concerned the first rule of thumb was to stay alive. He was thankful that his mother, who would have remained loyal to her husband to the bitter end, had died peacefully several years earlier when things had been at their best. He hoped that there was no afterlife because he had loved her deeply and would not have wanted her to know the awful fate that had befallen her husband and younger son and the sad state in which her surviving child now found himself.

Kurt had drifted in and out of various temporary and poorly-paid jobs in South Africa and amongst the displaced 'Rhodie' community in Francistown in north-eastern Botswana without ever settling anywhere or finding any particular satisfaction in life. The only certainty was that he would not return to the newly-emerged republic of Zimbabwe. He had heard through the Rhodesian grapevine in Francistown that his father's once prosperous farm had been commandeered by the new government and was now run as a village co-operative. Predictably enough there had been no investment, the workers sat around in the shade doing nothing, the borehole pumps were poorly maintained and idle and the cattle were weak and few in number. When Kurt thought of what it had once been this made his blood boil. It was really not a surprise at all that, after one particularly protracted period of brooding on this subject, he had travelled to Johannesburg and taken the step of becoming a member of, and committing himself to the beliefs and policies, of the Rhodesia Homeland Army. They had welcomed him with open arms. It was clear from his background that there would be no question of his loyalty to the cause. For Hendrick Nordmann, the recruitment officer, there was the additional bonus that his fit and healthy wiry frame combined with his evident hard streak, which became apparent during the induction process, would ensure that he could be put to good use as an active field agent when the time came. Nordmann was accustomed to violence and its consequences. He had been serving as a police officer in the small town of Mazvingo when his wife and two young daughters had been shot to death during a massacre perpetrated by Zanla, the military wing of Zanu in 1978. Nordmann had immediately joined the Rhodesian Army and soon had a well-earned reputation as a fearless and ruthless member of the Special Services. He was reputed to have single handedly dispatched more than a hundred guerrillas during the subsequent fighting. He had left the country immediately upon the transfer of power to Robert Mugabe. Of course, at the time of Kurt's recruitment, Nordmann was unaware how important their new member would become.

The path which set Kurt on the route to this destiny began, predictably enough, in Francistown, in a bar frequented by disaffected white émigrés from the now defunct Rhodesia. He had run into Tom Robertshaw, one of his father's old rugger playing chums who had been in town attending a business conference at the well-appointed riverside Marang Hotel. Tom was a large, jovial, ruddy-faced, beefy character who was entirely devoid of the spite which he saw in many of the men around him. He had been appalled at what had happened to Vincent and Uli and had always admired the wily older boy. When Tom had seen the depths to which Kurt had fallen he offered him a job and a place to stay until he could get back on his feet. The job in question was as a driver at the new giant diamond mine at Jwaneng in south-eastern Botswana. When the troubles had come to Rhodesia, Tom, a skilled mining engineer, had skipped off to South Africa and been lucky enough to find a position with DeBeers. Several years later they had relocated him to Botswana as part of the executive team which would administer the mine in partnership with officials from the government. Diamonds had been found suspiciously soon after Independence had come to the Bechuanaland Protectorate. The new Government of Botswana had been quick to realise that if they were going to exploit this new found wealth to its full potential they would have to work with the De Beers Cartel rather than against it. Botswana was only one producer, although admittedly an increasingly large producer, of both industrial and gemstone quality diamonds. A partnership had been arranged in which the profits were split equally between the government and Debswana, the new offshoot of DeBeers. Untold wealth had come to Botswana as a result of this decision and the country had been transformed in less than a generation from a dry and dusty outpost on the edge of the Kalahari, to one of the more vibrant African economies. Tom Robertshaw had prospered on the corporate ladder and felt it was only right and proper that he should help the son of an old compatriot. He had come to love Botswana. His open-hearted attitude to life had never entertained the notion of racism and he had never been happy with the way things had been organised in the old Rhodesia. He enjoyed cooperating with the urbane and quick witted Motswana officials who worked alongside him and appreciated the way the two races existed in reasonable harmony in his adopted country. If he had been aware of the bitterness that was to be found in Kurt's heart and the membership card of the Rhodesia Homeland Army tucked inside his wallet it is unlikely that Tom would have acted with the same unquestioning generosity.

Kurt had abandoned his dissolute life in Francistown and made the long journey south in his beaten up but reliable buff-coloured Toyota bakkie to the Jwaneng mine in the far south-eastern corner of the country. He had moved into Tom's place and was soon in the thick of it. The work was reasonably well paid. His job was to drive one of the huge tractor trailers which carried the diamond-rich dirt out of the increasingly massive open cast pit to the processing plant at the centre of the main compound, where the valuable gems were recovered from the tons of detritus. He never saw inside the processing plant. How many million of pula's worth he dragged up the slope in the belly of his tractor he never knew.

* * * * *

Tom Robertshaw had never married, and was, essentially, a very lonely man. Like many a middle-aged white man in Africa he had sought solace in the bottle. He drank a lot but he could handle it and he did not let it affect his work. As a result he was now in charge of many of the important administrative aspects of the mine. His one fault was that after a few too many stiff whisky sodas he was inclined to talk. As much of his drinking in the past had been done alone this had never been a problem. However since Kurt's arrival, Tom had discovered an extremely amiable drinking partner and they spent many a convivial evening chatting and boozing. Not being a particularly political man they had never strayed into areas where they might have found that they differed. Much of their talk was inconsequential. They were both interested in sport and the success of the South African rugby and cricket teams were a ready source of conversation, particularly as Tom had a satellite television so they could watch their fill of games from both across the border and from overseas. Apart from sport, Tom found Kurt was keen to learn how the mine was run, without showing any particular interest in the diamonds themselves. In his naive way Tom assumed Kurt was looking for a way to improve his prospects. He was pleasantly surprised that his protégé appeared to be showing such ambition and was keen to get him into the trainee management division. Debswana was growing as a company and there were always openings for enthusiastic qualified newcomers. So it was then that one evening Tom was thinking along these benevolent lines. They were sitting facing each other on the spacious veranda watching the sheer splendour of the southern skies. The Milky Way stretched in all directions and the occasional shooting star flashed across the heavens. In the foreground goats from the nearby village pressed themselves against the wire perimeter fence of the compound garden, straining to nibble the tempting lush grass that formed the centrepiece of the well-tended and well-watered gardens which were an integral but incongruous part of life in this pleasant oasis. As the splendid African evening turned to night Tom sipped at a generous whisky and soda in a tall ice filled glass and Kurt caressed a chilled bottle of Castle.

'You know, Kurt, that the place will be crawling with security and army people tomorrow.'

'Oh yes, so what's happening then? Is the President coming for an inspection of his loot?'

'Well, yes and no. It's not the President but it is to do with the diamonds. There's a shipment. I had forgotten this is the first time that you will have been here for one of these jamborees. It occurs every three months. A squadron of troops come down from the BDF Army Barracks at Mogoditshane with two armoured personnel carriers and a specially converted secure vehicle. All of the big-wigs put on a great show. Everyone gets very pompous and a big blue steel box is taken from the strong room in the administrative wing, and placed in the security truck. The BDF commanding officer then makes a big song and dance about taking responsibility for it. Then they depart in a mini convoy back to the barracks. The following day the same convoy heads off under escort to the airport in Gaborone. There the blue box is loaded onto an Air Botswana flight to Johannesburg and then on to London. What happens after that I have no idea.'

'It all sounds like pretty sensible stuff to me. I am damn sure that if I owned a fortune in diamonds I would take pretty good care of them myself.'

'Well that's the funny thing,' Tom suddenly blurted out and laughed. 'It's all a charade. The box is empty!'

Kurt thought that the beer was playing tricks upon him and he was losing his grip on reality.

'What do you mean? This whole mine can't be worthless. For someone to have gone to all this trouble, we must be sitting on a whole mountain of the little baubles.'

Tom was silent for a moment but the whisky had got the better of his reserve, and his tongue, and he pressed on.

'No, you've misunderstood. There are plenty of diamonds here and we're shipping them out every three months. It's just that we don't use the army convoy. We do it ourselves.'

Kurt listened with utter fascination as Tom recounted the history of this bizarre set-up. In the early days of independence there had been a tremendous amount of hostility between the newly democratic government in Botswana and the right wing regime in South Africa. This situation had worsened when diamonds had been discovered in Botswana. Firstly the presence of another large producer of diamonds in the region did little for the South African stranglehold on the commodity and secondly it soon became apparent that the pace of economic development in Botswana would outstrip that of South Africa. This was not something which the apartheid regime was happy with. They were keenly aware that their black neighbours were much less of a threat, both politically and militarily, if their economies were weak and mismanaged. This may have been the case with many of the front line states but Botswana was rapidly becoming the exception to this rule. For their part the government of Botswana had been concerned that it would take little for underlying hostilities to develop into outright aggression and knew that their border could easily be violated. They were equally aware that the Jwaneng mine was close to the border and there was much discussion as to whether the Boers would be able to resist the temptation to cross over and try to grab some of the profits for themselves. Steps were taken therefore to defend the mine using the military. Getting the diamonds off site remained a headache however. Any military resolution had the drawback that if it came to a firefight, the South Africans had bigger and better equipped forces and would swiftly gain the upper hand. Eventually it was decided the best solution was subterfuge.

'So you see,' exclaimed Tom, 'it's all down to history. The President was so unsure of his own forces that he allowed himself to be persuaded to put on a show of force whilst all the time the diamonds are taken to the airport in an unmarked vehicle, just like all the other routine stuff that goes to and from the mine.'

'And despite the changes that have taken place over the border since the end of apartheid no one has considered reviewing the system?' asked Kurt.

'That's right. I suppose it hasn't crossed anyone's mind. It's worked fine up to now so inertia has set in. Perhaps something will have to go badly wrong before a re-think is on the cards.'

Tom Robertshaw would have been surprised to discover that what he had just said was not wholly accurate and he would have been a little disappointed to find out that his seniors had not trusted him with all the facts. The simple truth was that the mine authorities were aware of their vulnerability this far out into the desert and used a number of different tactics to ensure that the diamonds reached the safety of the airport. Tom had been incorrect when he said that the army convoy was protecting nothing. There were diamonds in each of the shipments, such was the sheer weight of those which were intended for industrial use. It had become the norm for this type to go via that route. In addition, there were occasions when some or all of the gem quality examples also went that way. Two other strategies had been devised for transporting the stuff to Gaborone. Tom was right in that regular trips into town were made by unmarked vehicles. A pool of vehicles was used for both the transportation of the diamonds and to carry the security detachment that went with them. The rationale was that it could be kept more unofficial than the army convoy, which because of the internal mechanisms and bureaucracy of the military had to be organised and ordered in advance. This in itself had obvious security implications. Those who advocated the use of unmarked vehicles argued that they could be used irregularly and would ensure that the shipment would be in a secure location swiftly and in an unobtrusive way. This would put hurdles in the way of any would-be thief. In addition however they occasionally put into action the administrative procedures which were required to use this route but at the last moment the senior personnel who loaded the container would leave it empty. It was intended that this strategy would provide an effective way of testing the mine's own internal security. There was also a third method – using aircraft – which had been used in the past but which had fallen out of favour. It had not been abandoned as an option – there was a private landing strip at the mine – and it was still considered to be the most secure route in times of internal civil disturbance within Botswana and also in the event of hostilities with neighbouring countries.

'And who are the lucky characters who get to ride shotgun with a king's ransom in gems?' Kurt asked, trying to control a surge of excitement.

'Oh, it only happens four times a year so it just goes to whoever is on duty in admin on the day in question. No one makes a big deal out of it.'

'Do you ever get to do it, Tom?'

'No, thank God, I'm far too senior for such a dubious honour. It goes to the two most junior in the office.'

'I can't say I bloody envy them. There are some right unsavoury characters out there who would not think twice about applying a little muscle to relieve them of their burden.'

'Mind you, from what I've heard about the prowess of the BDF they are probably better protected with what's arranged. The senior security boys are in on the act and I think there would be a pretty nasty surprise for anybody who did try anything out of the ordinary with one of the shipments.'

Kurt decided not to push his luck any further and, despite being desperate to know what the security arrangements might be, made do with a quip about the BDF standing for 'Boys Don't Fight.' For the rest of the evening the two men chatted about this and that as they enjoyed a night cap. Kurt realised he had stumbled upon something which could be life-changing.

The following day the BDF arrived at the mine and – after a considerable amount of to-ing and fro-ing on the part of the senior figures – both army and mine – a large brightly-coloured blue box was loaded aboard one of the personnel carriers and, amidst tight security, was driven out of the main gates under convoy and at great speed in the direction of Gaborone.

* * * * *

From that day on, Kurt kept his head down, performed his job diligently and nurtured his friendship with Tom. This gave him access to all parts of the mine. He joined the rugby team, spent time in the staff club, and joined the darts and pool teams. He swam in the staff pool, ate mouth-watering sirloin steaks and drank copious numbers of Castle beers at the regular poolside braais which were a key feature of the social scene of this close knit community. He could lay on the charm so it was not long before he knew and was known by many of the administrative and technical staff. He became popular among the younger men, who were envious of his good looks and athleticism, while genuinely admiring his good humour and camaraderie. The single women who worked at the plant were also attracted to him. In a different life he would have given them reason to gossip. However he had more pressing matters on his mind and he did not find it difficult to forego the pleasures of the flesh. He did not attempt to find out details about the shipment of the diamonds, preferring to bide his time. If the system was so casual, then eventually some snippet of information would come his way. It became clear in time that the shipment system was not common knowledge. It was only known to a few in Administration and they were keeping the secret. As well as putting himself around at the mine he periodically tried to spot likely vehicles, particularly around the time that the army convoy was scheduled, although he had no way of knowing if the diamonds were shipped before or after this date or if indeed the fake shipment and the real shipment were in any way linked in time. He soon found however that there were so many vehicles leaving the site that it would be an impossible task to work out which contained the big prize but just when he was resigned to giving up he was party to an idle bit of gossip between two mechanics during a game of pool in the staff club.

'You know, Bill,' one of the younger mechanics was saying to his Scottish workmate, 'that white Stallion delivery van is coming in again for its regular check up tomorrow. Have you any idea why this one and that other small Honda station wagon get a priority service every three months or so and all the other trucks only get looked at every six months? They don't need such dedicated maintenance.'

'No idea mate. All I know is that the orders come down from that turd, Draper, in admin, and when he says jump, the likes of us jump.'

'True enough, pal, but it still seems weird to me. Even the Chairman's Merc doesn't get looked after so well. Anyway the Stallion is due in tomorrow, so like it or not, it will get my undivided attention for most of the day.'

'Tough shit. It's your shot, I believe.'

As he bought another round of beers, Kurt decided he needed to conjure up a good reason to visit the workshop and inspect the privileged truck. He had had precious few leads of late and this seemed like the opportunity he had been waiting for.

* * * * *

The next morning, Kurt arrived at the workshop. In his hand he held one of the heavy duty rubber hoses which powered the hydraulic controls on his tractor trailer. He had punctured it with the blade of his American leatherman pocket knife and the flow of oil had pumped out satisfyingly, leaving his vehicle with power but unable to steer itself out of the pit. He called his shift leader over the walkie-talkie and received the predictable response.

'Use your own wrench and remove the bust hose. Take it up to the garage and they'll give you a replacement. Don't piss about though. Leaving that bloody great thing on the ramp is going to make life tricky for everybody until you shift it. I don't want any of those kamikaze drivers going over the side and then claiming it wasn't their fault.'

'Sure thing, gaffer,' Kurt responded. 'I'll be back sharpish.'

'OK get to it.'

Kurt knew he was trusted so he wouldn't be missed for an hour or so. He hurried up the ramp and quickly made his way across to the area, some distance away, where the offices, tool shops, repair yards and equipment sheds were all located around the massive central compound. Amidst the day-to-day hubbub of this enormous enterprise he passed unnoticed across the brightly lit, and baking, concrete yard and into the cool custom built open-sided workshop where most of the mine's vehicles were repaired and serviced.

The garage was predictably large, given the number of vehicles which were needed to keep the place working. The main floor was divided into eight equally sized sections behind which, against the rear walls in the shade, were placed the mobile tool kits and the benches where the mechanics plied their trade. The left-hand bay was equipped with a hydraulic lifting ramp. The right-hand bay was bisected by a deep inspection pit.

Kurt sauntered down the central span of the workshop, checking the vehicles in each bay. They were all either standard saloons, used by the senior executives and middle managers, or bakkies, which were the workhorses of the administrative section. These brought food, fuel, toilet rolls, electric fans, beer and all the other myriad items which kept the place afloat and alive, from the government suppliers in Gaborone and from the flourishing private wholesalers in Mafeking over the border in South Africa. Second from the right he found what he was looking for. The nondescript unobtrusive box-like shape of the white Toyota Stallion that the lads had been chatting about in the bar was parked there with its bonnet raised. Under it a familiar figure in clean white overalls was methodically removing its spark plugs and placing them, one by one, on a hessian cover on the front wing.

'Hey there, Billy boy. I've bust one of the hoses on my rig. Can you get me a replacement?'

The ruddy-faced Glaswegian came out from under the bonnet and looked towards Kurt with an air of good humour and mild exasperation.

'No problem. We've got just about everything in stock and this little baby is not exactly taxing my mechanical skills. You were lucky you didn't get hit by the fluid, by the way. It's pretty nasty stuff.'

Bill took the ruptured hose and headed off to the parts room to look for a replacement. Kurt idly picked up one of the spark plugs and casually scanned the busy scene around him. Teams of mechanics were carrying out their daily routine. Some were changing oil from sump reservoirs, others were checking points, and others, perhaps more senior, were checking off completed jobs against the inventory. No one was taking the slightest bit of notice of him. It was normal for a driver to come and collect a finished job, or to deliver a breakdown or to come from the sharp end of the job, as Kurt had, to collect an urgently needed part.

Kurt was not sure what to expect from this little van. The engine compartment looked clean and tidy but then again, since it was company property, and given the methodical nature of the service routine, this was not unusual for a vehicle which never had to withstand the rigours of the mine itself. Kurt leant against the side of the cab and casually inspected the interior. As with the engine compartment, it was neat and uncluttered. But there was nothing here to arouse his interest. Kurt moved towards the covered rear end of the bakkie. This one, despite being Japanese, was equipped with a simple South African designed rear cab, with a maker's stamp stating, like many thousands of others, that it had been manufactured in Zeerust in Western Gauteng Province. It had a single narrow tinted window down each side. The rear door, which stood open, was windowless and there was a fairly hefty hasp and padlock to keep it secure. The rear cab, with its narrow side windows could be rendered secure by the simple expedient of locking the rear door. Whilst this would not be the slightest hindrance to a determined night-time thief with a few minutes spare, it provided adequate security during the bright African day time, while a package was dropped off or a quick visit made.

As he pondered the sheer ordinariness of this little runabout, Kurt sat in the doorway, unwrapped a stick of chewing gum and flicked the wrapper into the rear cab. As he did so, his mind started to think about other avenues to explore and other areas of interest within the mine which he had not yet examined. He had not found anything of interest to arouse his expectations here, but he had been through much, had learnt patience and was not about to give up. He watched one of the young apprentices meticulously cleaning out the inside of one of the company Mercs and had the merest twinge of guilt about the casual way in which he had discarded his litter. He glanced back and, sure enough there it was, nestling against the bulkhead behind the driver's seat.

And that was when something odd struck him.

The bulk head was unblemished, as were the interior wheel arches and the floor. The internal buff paint job was slightly dulled with the effects of the African sun but was not scratched and scored with the hard earned badges of the daily grind of deliveries. Indeed it was possible to buy rubber matting at Haskins in Gaborone to protect the cab from the inevitable bashing it would sustain. He also knew this model was at least three years old and was likely to have done some considerable mileage along badly-maintained roads. Kurt moved to the front cab and read the mileage. Less then six thousand kilometres. For a three year old van this was surprisingly low. There was nothing to explain why this nondescript little truck had been used so infrequently. It was just the sort which would be expected to undertake the minor day to day tasks which would soon add mileage, worn bearings and an early demise. Quite the reverse seemed to be the case however. To have been used so sparingly would suggest it was being held back for some other purpose. Kurt looked down at the used spark plug in his hand. He knew it had not suffered enough heat to warrant replacement but there before him on the front wing were four pristine plugs in their wrapping ready to replace the one in his hand and the others still secure in the engine block. Just then Bill returned from the dark recesses of the store room with a new hydraulic hose.

'So what do you think of this pampered little baby then? I wish she were mine. Every two or three months or so Draper sends her down from the large admin shed and yet she's hardly covered more than a few hundred clicks since I last cast my eye over her. It's a funny old life. I've come all the way from a damp flat in the Gorbals to this hell-hole in the desert and I end up looking after a motor that no one seems to want to use. Still they pay me well and the beer is good and cold. Here's your hose. And don't bugger it up when you put it on. They won't issue another one without getting a bit shifty. Run along now will you. Draper will be on my back if I don't get this beasty shipshape by the end of the day. You can get me a nice cold Castle tonight before the pool tournament.'

With a good natured slap on the back and a promise to be at the watering hole-in time for a sundowner or two, Kurt headed back to his beached tractor trailer. He had plenty of food for thought. He was not sure why his interest was so aroused, but, added together, things did look odd. The mine, although extremely profitable, was efficiently run and it was out of character for resources to be wasted on a van which was not being used to capacity. Bill was a methodical man and a good engineer and was bemused by the task allotted to him. It was an oddity and it was not in his nature to accept it without comment. In addition the interior looked as if nothing had been transported in it or, if it had, it had been very carefully stowed. Kurt resolved to investigate further before moving onto pastures new.

When his shift ended later that afternoon, and after a swift shower back at Tom's place, he was at the bar before the rest of the mine personnel had wound down for the day. He settled down in front of the large veranda window that looked out over the main compound and watched as the working day ground to a halt. Buses arrived and drove the local staff back to their home villages. Senior executives came out of the air-conditioned admin units and picked up their cars from the shaded car park and headed off to their palatial residences on the edge of the main mine land holding. Meanwhile the big tractor trailers wound their way out of the pit and were parked in an impressive line ready to be checked over and refuelled by the mechanics in readiness for the morning shift. Over at the vehicle maintenance shop there was also a predictable degree of coming and going. Bakkies and cars were parked up ready for the morning and others were driven away by their respective users. Kurt idly gazed in this direction as he sipped his beer. Eventually he spotted one of the junior managers from the admin section, a young English guy called Paul Miller, leaving the rear of the shop, deep in conversation with Bill. After a moment or two, Bill duly handed over the keys and the pristine Stallion headed out of the shop. Its journey was brief. Kurt watched it pass down the side of the main admin building to the windowless side away from the main compound. Here a large roll-up aluminium door was the only feature to break the monotony of the featureless brickwork. As the bakkie drew up, Kurt heard the sharp note of its horn. The door opened and it glided inside. The door immediately closed and shortly afterwards the African sun gave up its fight against the night and dusk descended. As it did the lights inside the admin section were extinguished. Kurt felt sure that little else would happen now and decided to concentrate on the evening's easy going entertainment. He was determined to find out what life had in store for the bakkie over the next day or two and to that end had already put in for a couple of days' leave.

'Hello young man. Bit early for you isn't it?'Tom joked as he entered the bar. 'I hope you're not getting into bad habits. How about a game of pool?'

'Don't worry about me Tom. I'm a clean living fellow. Rack 'em up and I'll go and get another couple of Castles.'

* * * * *

As the sun ascended into a cloudless blue sky Kurt was up and, despite having had a few too many beers the night before, felt refreshed. Tom prepared himself for another routine day at the mine and took time to enjoy his breakfast on the purpose built east-facing patio at the rear of the house. As Kurt drank his coffee and enjoyed his juice and slices of water melon, the goats from the nearby village meandered their way past the perimeter fence, some with bells clanking.They were off for another tough day foraging in the bush and greedily eyed the well-watered lawn in front of the house. Kurt waved Tom off to work having already told him that he was planning a couple of days up in Gaborone.

As soon as he was alone, Kurt went round to the double garage at the side of the house and drove his bakkie out. It was South African registered and a non-descript white in colour, like so many others on the roads in these parts. He wanted to see if the Stallion was going to be used and, if so, where it was going to go. His intention was to drive five kilometres or so up the road in the direction of Molepolole and Gaborone to the north-west and park up under a roadside acacia tree to see what would transpire. Molepolole was the nearest big town to the mine and a motor such as the Stallion would be an obvious choice for an errand there. It seemed logical to Kurt that the small truck would be used soon after its service. Setting out from the mine, he was not concerned that anyone would spot him at the side of the road and wonder at his presence. His bakkie was undistinguished and was unfamiliar to his fellow mineworkers.

The road he joined was new and had been purpose built to serve the facility. It did however provide a shorter tarred route between Namibia in the west and South Africa to the south and east. As such it now formed the most direct east-west crossing point through the southern Kalahari. Because of the remoteness of the land to the west, Kurt knew the Stallion would not turn that way when it came out of the mine's gates and thus evade him. It would be foolhardy to head off that way with such an inappropriate choice of wheels.

So a short while later, armed with a cool-box full of soft drinks and some other provisions to fortify himself, he set his car under a suitable tree and started his wait. When the Stallion finally emerged, Kurt almost missed it. He had only been waiting for a couple of hours but it was already unbearably hot despite the shade afforded by the tree. During that time little had occurred. A duiker, one of the smaller antelope which favoured this habitat had darted out of the bush right in front of him and, wary of the unaccustomed smell of the tar and the road, had bolted away into the deep cover provided by the long grasses and scrub acacias. Two government trucks had roared by, one in each direction, and the drivers had, as ever, looked alarmingly on the verge of falling asleep. Heading west in the direction of either the Fish River Gorge in Namibia or the Okavango Delta in the north-west corner of Botswana, a convoy of three South African Mitsubishi shoguns had flashed by doing at least a hundred and forty clicks, laden down with stores and camping equipment and, in one case, towing a neatly built flat-bottomed fishing boat. The most recent vehicle to pass had been an undistinguished Toyota Land Cruiser.

A ground hornbill had been the main distraction during the morning. This particular spot was the centre of its stamping ground and it was now so accustomed to the sporadic human visitors that it did not feel the need to wait for their departure before it would come for its share. Kurt spent a happy few moments flicking fragments of prawn cocktail potato crisps for the bird. Like all true Kalahari dwellers, the hornbill had shown its adaptability and despite never having come within a thousand miles of a prawn was happily tucking into the bounty on offer, from the relative protection of a nearby thorn bush. The bird so transfixed Kurt with its beady eye and its large comical banana-shaped bill as it gulped down the proffered crisps that he nearly did not look up when the little van whispered by. Unlike the government trucks and the off-roaders, which made their presence felt the Stallion passed by without a sound. Its 1300cc engine made hardly any noise at its leisurely cruising speed of a hundred kilometres or so.

They were past before Kurt had a chance to move and his own reactions were unnecessarily frantic. The hornbill screeched a cry of alarm and headed for the upper branches of the shade tree as Kurt gunned his motor and made off in hot pursuit. The Stallion, closely followed by another vehicle, was already several hundred metres ahead and fast disappearing into the heat shimmer as Kurt got off the dirt, bit the tarmac and hit second gear. As he changed up into third the tension suddenly dissipated and his foot eased back on the pedal. After all he reasoned to himself there were no turn offs for at least a hundred kilometres, no towns, no roadside bars or shops or any other place where the truck could evade him. All he needed to do was to keep it in sight in the far distance and track it as far as Molepolole. Then, when other vehicles were about he could draw closer without a hint of suspicion. For the moment distance was required.

As the sun continued to rise in the sky, Kurt tucked in behind and doggedly tracked his quarry. From this distance he could see the Stallion was accompanied by one of the unmarked Toyota Land cruisers which were a common feature at the mine and were the favourite means of transport for the senior security officers. It was clear what its role was in this little escapade and Kurt felt sure that if called upon the hard characters inside would make a pretty good show of things. What he could not see, however, was how many occupants each vehicle contained. He would need to know this, but, for the moment, was prepared to bide his time. The relatively short journey to Molepolole passed without incident. Nothing unusual happened until he was a few kilometres from the outskirts of town. He then began to notice a few people in the bush cutting wood for fuel and tending the increasing number of goats. He cautiously overtook a couple of donkey carts and a beaten up old bakkie wheezing its way into town laden down with cut hard woods. He became increasingly cautious of the untended donkeys which meandered aimlessly on and off the highway without a care in the world. As the tin roofed sprawl of the suburbs enveloped him the traffic increased substantially, making it safe for him to draw up to within a hundred or so metres of the Stallion. It was here in Molepolole he expected the journey to end, perhaps at some out of the way factory on an errand to collect something as mundane as a gasket for a pump.

Kurt felt the tension increase as he tracked his targets with a considerable degree of awareness and caution. They soon reached the main T-junction at the centre of town. The Stallion turned left onto the main street where most of the small town's shops, offices, warehouses and other businesses that held the place together were located. The Land Cruiser dutifully followed. Kurt drew up to within a couple of vehicles of his prey so he would not lose them if they took a quick turn left or right. He could see the Stallion had two occupants in the front cab and there were four in the Land Cruiser. He could not see if there was anyone in the back of the Stallion but he recognised the two in the front: they were from the middle management team as Tom had said they would be. He also knew the men in the Cruiser. They were all from security and all former South African military. Despite the fact he did not know them personally, from their reputation and their demeanour, it was clear they had been hand-picked, would be well-prepared and well-equipped and could not be dismissed. Whilst pondering this potential problem, Kurt continued to focus on the Stallion as it carried on steadily through the small town, until it reached the slow left-hand rise which signalled the end of the town centre and the beginning of the eastern suburbs. Even now there was still the possibility that their destination was the recently opened industrial park. The new turn-off soon passed by on the right-hand side and the Stallion continued on in the direction towards Gaborone. It began to look increasingly likely that Gaborone was going to be its final port of call that day. Once again Kurt decided it would be prudent to be discreet and tucked himself in amongst the growing stream of traffic that was heading to Gaborone. From this reasonably safe position he continued his stealthy pursuit. As they made their way towards the capital city, Kurt became aware that as various vehicles overtook both himself and the two vehicle convoy ahead, another Land Cruiser remained in front, always maintaining the same distance. It was then that he recalled the Land Cruiser which had passed him a few minutes in advance of the other two. As they passed the increasing number of small villages on either side it dawned on Kurt that he was following a three vehicle convoy.

The presence of denser settlement signalled that they were now moving away from the harsh, arid desert climate and had reached the more temperate zone which ran down the eastern side of Botswana, where there was just sufficient mean annual rainfall for it to be possible to grow maize and sorghum and scratch a meagre living. An hour after passing the Thamaga Hills to the south, the capital city came into view. Kurt felt sure that he would not be spotted as he tucked in behind the Stallion and its escort once again. He was still wondering which of the industrial estates they might be heading towards when he saw the BDF barracks – the headquarters and the main base camp of the bulk of the army – at Mogoditshane ahead, on the outskirts of the city. The volume of army registered vehicles increased considerably and columns of foot soldiers in combat fatigues could be seen exercising inside the perimeter fence. Despite what Tom Robertshaw had revealed, it still struck Kurt as if he had been hit in the solar plexus, when suddenly the Stallion turned left and drove straight through the main gates of the barracks. Not only that, it was waved through without hesitation and disappeared into the tree-lined avenue leading to the heart of the complex. The two Land Cruiser escorts continued on as far as the roundabout a little further down the road, did a U-turn and made off, back in the direction of Jwaneng, their job discreetly and successfully completed. Kurt pulled over in front of a bar nearest to the main entrance and watched the Stallion head off into the middle distance. In order not to draw attention to himself he sauntered into the bar and casually ordered a cold bottle of Castle. Several locals and a couple of soldiers were idly chatting at a grimy table but no one looked up. As he sat drinking he wondered what business the Stallion could have in the barracks and more particularly why it had been waved through with such apparent ease?

Kurt stayed at a cheap hotel on the African Mall that night but at dawn he drove back to his shady lookout post. Just before noon, the armed convey he had observed during his first week at the mine dutifully arrived and soon after departed again. Two hours later, with Kurt following at a cautious distance, it turned into the same gate at the Mogoditshane barracks. At six o'clock that evening, nursing an exorbitantly priced three pula bottle of Castle, Kurt sat in the viewing gallery at the Sir Seretse Khama airport in Gaborone and watched as passengers and crew boarded a four engine Air Botswana BAe 146–100, ready for the flight to Johannesburg. At the last moment, just before taxiing and take-off, a mini version of the army convoy he had seen that morning coasted onto the tarmac and pulled up at the side of the aircraft. Out of the very same armoured personnel carrier which had that day made the journey from the Jwaneng mine, a brightly coloured blue box was hoisted aboard the mobile conveyor belt and disappeared into the rear hold.

Without a moment's delay the elegant plane moved out onto the single runway, taxied to the far end, executed a neat hundred and eighty degree turn and made an apparently effortless take-off, then banked in a south-easterly direction which would take it over the South African border. Kurt had no doubt that a consignment of diamonds had been safely stowed aboard en route to the markets of Amsterdam. He was determined that things would be very different in three month's time.

* * * * *

Kurt was surprised at how calmly and methodically he approached his tasks over the course of the next couple of months. For a week or two he enjoyed the mine's lively social life, shooting pool in the bar, swimming and spending time with his work colleagues. Over drinks with Tom, he effortlessly established the routine of the diamond shipment, which, while not rigidly fixed, was always within a two week span, although the precise time of day and day of the week would change. The variation in the security arrangements was considered sufficient to outsmart anyone who might attempt to get their hands on one of the largest regular shipments of moveable wealth. Once Kurt was clear this was the case he was able to relax in the knowledge that it would be some weeks before he would have to be back on full alert. Despite that, however, he established a pattern of strolling home from work through the main compound. Occasionally he would stop off for a game of pool and a beer or two, but he would, without fail, check the vehicle maintenance shop to ensure that the little white Stallion did not suddenly materialise without warning. What he was also able to do, without drawing attention to himself, was use a route home right past the side door of the admin building where the roll-up door was located. On most occasions this remained resolutely closed. There were, however, more than enough occasions when it was open, enabling him to see the Stallion parked tidily in a bay on the left hand side of the internal loading area. As long as the vehicle remained there he would bide his time.

Kurt now had sufficient information to report back to his Rhodesia Homeland Army superiors in South Africa. Over a long weekend he took the opportunity to cross the border into South Africa via the Tlokweng gate and make the easy journey to Pretoria. Once there he reported his findings to the army council. Peter Esterhuize and Frederick Pretorious listened intently and were excited by the potential of the enterprise. At this meeting they had introduced Kurt to Jonathan Ballantyne, another of the senior council members.

Ballantyne had been a senior figure in the Treasury Ministry of Ian Smith's last Rhodesian government. He had studied Business and Accountancy at King's College London and the University of Toronto, graduating with first class honours from both. He had been responsible for the successful management of the Rhodesian economy during the sanctions era and was widely tipped as a future Prime Minister. His hopes were dashed when power transfer took place and, shortly afterwards, he left the country. He currently managed the modest finances of the Rhodesian Homeland Army. Despite his meagre funds Ballantyne still had many international contacts from his earlier life, including several in South Africa. Using this influence he could still obtain favours and in this instance had been able to get hold of a South African passport issued under an alias. This was an original government issue document which would stand up to all but the most inquisitive scrutiny. Ballantyne had instructed Kurt to visit a particular Mitsubishi dealership in Johannesburg where a vehicle of his choice would be allotted to him for the duration of his scheme, registered in the same false name. Similarly, two locally produced high velocity hunting rifles were supplied at his request. Kurt had plenty of experience using this type of weapon from his days on the family farm and although not a true marksman he was pretty accurate within a range of at least a hundred and fifty metres. That would be sufficient for what he had in mind. What was uncertain was whether he would have it in him to take a human life. That was not something he had done before. Still he felt strangely calm about this aspect of the job, and was certain that if he proved to have a shortcoming, it would not be in that direction. Ballantyne also told him that a bank account would be opened in the main branch of Barclays' on the mall in Gaborone and that reasonable funds would be made available to him. Kurt had also discussed strategy with several of the field team leaders including Alfred Bronkhurst who it had been agreed would lead the backup team. Bronkhurst had been a Brigadier General in the Selous Rangers of the Rhodesian Army. He had been stripped of his commission by Robert Mugabe at independence and had left the country after several attempts on his life. It was never established who perpetrated these acts but it was thought likely to have been ZANU security officials acting under instruction from Mugabe.

* * * * *

Kurt was fully aware that he would require assistance given the nature of the apparent security of the shipment. He and Bronkhurst discussed the plan at some length. The intention was to intercept the Stallion and its escort before it reached Molepolole on one of the long straight stretches of road where it would be easy for him to spot both his quarry and any one else who might happen to pass at the same time. They had discussed the precise details of the ambush with others who had undertaken comparable missions in South Africa during the apartheid era, when it was common practice to intercept one's enemies and mete out summary roadside justice. Everyone was in agreement that the plan had every chance of success. They had also discussed a strategy for the days immediately after the theft. Kurt had assumed that he would be expected to cross over into South Africa along one of the sparsely populated stretches of the border fence to the south-east of the mine. Esterhuize and Pretorius were vehemently against such a scheme, arguing that by the time he had reached the border there was likely to be heightened police and military activity on either side. Attempting to cross either legally or otherwise would be fraught with danger. They also pointed out with some degree of sense that the South African military, now under the control of President Zuma, would no doubt do everything in its power to attempt to return the diamonds to their rightful owners, such was the power of black brotherhood in these very changed times in this part of the world. What Kurt was unaware of was that, although the Army Council were more than happy to go along with his plan, they were also keen to distance themselves from it should it fail. To be involved with such an audacious plot and to be caught out would be nothing more than political suicide from their point of view. They therefore suggested that the vehicle which he should choose should be one of the up market 4x4 tourers and that he should equip himself as if for a hunting trip. After taking the diamonds their plan was that he should go off road into the southern Kalahari and then travel up through the western side of the desert through Deception Valley. He could then choose to cross to the north-eastern side of the country via either the Okavango Delta and the Chobe Plains or via the central salt pans. Whichever route he chose he would be passing through some of the most remote country on earth where he could avoid contact with the rest of humanity and allow the immediate hue and cry to die down and the pursuit to be called off. What was further proposed was that he should cross over, not into South Africa but into Zimbabwe itself at the unmanned border crossing at Pandamatenga. This operated on the bizarre premise whereby you were required to report to the local police station in order to have your passport stamped. Since the station was off the main road and the officers did not possess a vehicle, a non appearance was hardly likely to result in punitive action. After crossing into Zimbabwe Kurt was to discreetly make his way back to his family's old farm, just to the north-west of Bulawayo. In the old days there had been a short air strip which had been used when the farm had been at its most successful in the late 1950's and early 1960's. Kurt was assured it had been checked over by some of their supporters in the area and, with a little bit of clearance work, which the organisation would be able to easily set in train, would be able to receive a light aircraft. Once at the airstrip, Kurt was to make contact via satellite phone and would then be picked up. The intention was to take him to the east into Mozambique. Here along one of the many lengths of deserted beach it would be easy for him and the diamonds to be spirited out of the country and up to Europe by sea. Kurt was not really thinking beyond the end of his mission, but the assurance of riches aplenty and an exalted place in the future military history of the Rhodesia Homeland Army was enough for him. Of course if it all came to nothing or to a messy end there would be nothing to link it with a right wing political organisation. In that event it might even lead to ill will or worse between the black governments of Zimbabwe and Botswana. For the Rhodesia Homeland Army even that would be a minor victory. For Kurt though the big prize was the main motivation.

After his meeting in Pretoria, Kurt returned to work at the mine but two weeks later he made an additional trip back to South Africa, in order to make further preparations. On this occasion he dropped his bakkie off at the airport in Gaborone and flew down to Johannesburg on a Comair commuter flight. Here he picked up a superb V12 Mitsubishi Pajero station wagon with long range fuel and water tanks and Yokohama sand tyres. He had quoted the name of his contact in Pretoria and all that he had requested was his. The vehicle was fitted to his specification which included bush bars, sand ladders, a three ton high lift jack and an impressive winch fixed to the front bumper. Most importantly of all was a neat little satellite navigation system integrated into the dashboard. This was state of the art and would tell him exactly where he was in the middle of the desert to within a couple of metres. With this impressive array of equipment it was unlikely that he would break down irretrievably, get stuck or get lost when he was out on his imaginary hunting trip. He also requested and was given a top of the range tool kit, a full range of spares and an Iridium satellite phone. During the lengthy sales pitch he endured, the salesman had done his best to sell him the latest diesel model. He was, however, not used to leaving the city limits and the well-stocked attendant assisted service stations to be found there. He seemed unable to grasp that although petrol might be expensive in the western Kalahari it was as often as not available but pulling over in a small village dealership in the more remote areas and asking for diesel was liable to result in a very long wait indeed.

After proudly driving his gleaming new truck out of the showroom, Kurt visited a bush supplier he knew well and loaded up with an array of hunting requisites, not to mention enough camping equipment to kit out a medium sized bush camp. From there he waited patiently until after dark and then went to an address he had been given in downtown

Pretoria. There he met the members of the group who would act as his support team including Alfred Bronkhurst. Details were discussed and he was given an address for a safe house in Gaborone where the team would hole up about three weeks in advance of the next most likely shipment date. His rifles were taken from him and he was assured that these and the weapons which the support team would use would be over the border well in advance of the deadline. All that was required of him was to make contact as soon as the Stallion made its move and they would be ready. He did not ask how they were going to get a considerable arsenal over the border into Botswana, but he was aware that some of their number had probably operated in similar punitive missions in the early days when the ANC had been in exile in several of the anti-apartheid front line states and as such had been regarded as legitimate targets. He was not at all dismayed by the apparent ruthlessness and efficiency of those who were soon to become his comrades in arms.

Upon returning to Botswana, Kurt took his Pajero to the safe house and was duly met by Alfred, who had been sent ahead to liaise with him. The truck was hidden in the garage to the rear of the house, far away from prying eyes at the mine: it was a touch on the splendid side for a humble tractor driver. After collecting some cash from his newly opened account in Gaborone he was driven out to the airport by Alfred and headed back to Jwaneng in his old bakkie. Then the waiting began, a process which he anticipated would last a further two months. Kurt did not find it too difficult despite his inner tension. He undertook his duties diligently and at the same time enjoyed the mine's varied social life. He was already fairly fit but knowing the physical demands of his plans, he took up jogging and made greater use of the gymnasium. During that time, the small Honda station wagon which was parked alongside the Stallion made a trip away from the mine. Kurt saw it go but elected not to follow it, having decided to concentrate on the Stallion. If he had pursued it, he would have seen it go straight to the Botswana Defence Force barracks in Mogoditshane. Twenty-four hours later a large blue box was loaded on board a Johannesburg flight and later transferred to a British Airways 747 flight bound for London. Another consignment of diamonds had been shipped safely and surreptitiously away from the mine.

* * * * *

After several weeks of preparation Kurt was confident that if his plan failed it would not be for lack of planning. He knew his support team was in place in Gaborone and that all their vehicles and weapons were over the border. He had met Alfred a couple of times at the planned ambush spot and while they could not be certain whether they would succeed, they had agreed the plan of action. Kurt had agonised about every detail yet had become almost calm about the whole enterprise and it was in this frame of mind that he found himself a few weeks later strolling home after parking up his tractor for the day. Unusually, he was not even thinking about the great gamble he was about to embark upon. It was late in the afternoon and he had been delayed by a few minutes. He was in the process of crossing the centre of the main compound, when, as he turned the corner towards the Jacaranda tree lined avenue which led towards Tom's place, he suddenly caught sight of the white Stallion trundling quietly out of the vehicle maintenance shop towards the main admin building. Without hesitation the door opened and it disappeared inside. It was early, there was no doubt about it. The team in Gaborone had only been in place for a week and Kurt had anticipated that there would be a wait of at least two more weeks. As he watched the Stallion disappear into the bowels of the admin block he reflected on the fact that there had been talk in recent days in the social club that the mother lode had been struck and that the mine had surpassed all previous production records. The local staff who were employed to sort the diamonds were convinced that there had been a find which had surpassed all others, a diamond to diminish all those which had been previously found in any of the mines elsewhere in South Africa or Europe. If such a discovery had been made it would be imperative for management to get it off-site as soon as possible. The international diamond market was robust at the moment and prices were high, especially for top of the range examples. However beautiful a diamond was to look at, it was utterly worthless in the southern Kalahari Desert. There had been in the past, and no doubt would be in the future, travellers who, as they breathed their last under a scorching sky, would gladly give a king's ransom for the merest sip of a cool glass of water. For the wealthy, shadowy individuals who controlled the mine, satisfaction would come, not from possession of the most magnificent specimen, but from seeing the price it would fetch at auction in Amsterdam. None of these thoughts were important to Kurt at that moment. It did not matter to him how good the gems were; they would be worth a fortune to both himself and the Rhodesia Homeland Army.

Almost on autopilot Kurt started the ball rolling. He popped into the bar, ordered a beer and challenged one of the guys at the bar to a quick game of pool. Whilst the balls were being racked, he made a brief call to Alfred at the safe house in Gaborone and set things in motion. Having surrendered the table after a lucky win, he headed back to Tom's place and announced he was going to spend the night in town. From Kurt's point of view his excuse for leaving the house for the night had the advantage that if the Stallion did not make a move the following morning, he would be able to return to the mine with nothing more to worry about than a ticking off from his manager for turning up late. Such events were not common but the management were aware that the hot-blooded young men they employed could not be kept cooped up without the occasional indiscretion and accepted these things happened from time to time. Kurt had been careful to act out this charade on a couple of occasions before so that it would not raise suspicion this time. He was confident enough that his record of diligence and hard work would be enough to ensure that no action would be taken against him. In reality he did not care that he might face censure from his line manager. What he was concerned about however was that, in the event of a non show by the Stallion tomorrow, he would still be in place to have another stab at it in three months time. Three hours later he was safely tucked up at the safe house in Gaborone with his comrades in arms. Whilst he and Alfred went over the finer points of the plan the rest of the gang laboriously oiled and checked the weapons. As the men drifted off to sleep, Kurt found he was too tense for deep sleep. He kept watch and catnapped fitfully through the small hours. Across town, at the Swedish Volunteers Hostel, Rusty McKenna slept off the effects of his journey from London and an evening of over indulgence in the bars of Gaborone, and his friend Mats busied himself preparing their vehicles for the long and arduous journey west.

* * * * *

The sun was burning down fiercely from the southern Kalahari sky, when, at eight o'clock precisely, a Toyota Stallion pick-up truck was waved through the imposing gates by the security guard. Life was in full swing at the Jwaneng Diamond Mine in the south-eastern corner of Botswana and it was business as usual. A pristine white Toyota Land Cruiser followed the smaller bakkie at a discreet distance and both vehicles turned east towards Gaborone. These were not the first to leave the mine that day but like all such routine departures they attracted no interest from those making their way on to site to take their part in the working day.

* * * * *

Seven kilometres to the east, Kurt Viljoen had been in position since sunrise. He had not been idle since his meeting with the Council of the Rhodesia Homeland Army several months earlier in Pretoria. All he needed was an element of good fortune. The site he had chosen for the ambush was a spot between two low hills where a dry river bed awaited the flash floods that would come with the rare seasonal rains that fell sporadically but with extravagant force on this part of the southern

Kalahari. The road builders had constructed a low slung bridge which went unnoticed as speeding travellers flashed by. Its squat concrete parapet and narrow carriageway was sufficient for Kurt's purpose. His immaculate Mitsubishi Pajero stood to the side of the bridge. Fixed to the winch cable was the corpse of a donkey. From the numerous occasions he had passed this way before, Kurt had known it would not be long before a donkey, left by its owner to fend for itself for a while, would pass along. The luckless animal had been despatched with a single shot and had then been unceremoniously dragged to the side of the bridge awaiting the arrival of the Toyota Stallion. The intention was to wait for confirmation from his backup team, located just to the west of the main entrance of the Jwaneng mine, that the Stallion was on the move. Kurt would partially block the narrow bridge with the dead donkey so the convoy would have to slow down in order to negotiate the obstruction. There was no reason why the presence of a dead donkey in the road should raise any suspicion. It was well known to those who frequented this part of the desert that donkeys were inclined to sleep on the tarmac strip during the cool of the night and they were often victims of an unwary early morning driver.

Kurt had just received the message that the Stallion and its escorts were on the move. A single Land Cruiser led the way, to act as an early warning in the event of trouble. The second Cruiser was tucked in just behind the Stallion. Kurt needed to act fast. His quarry was only a minute or two away over the brow of the hill. He moved the donkey into position. It would be possible for a driver to pass by after slowing to assess the situation without having to stop completely. Kurt was banking on the leading Land Cruiser passing by, to be dealt with by his forward support team, who were in hiding over the brow of the nearest hill. He gunned his powerful V12 engine up the dry river bed and out of sight behind the low hill on the southern side of the river. He was in position with his rifle at his shoulder a full minute before the first Land Cruiser approached from the direction of the mine. He heard its engine note decrease as the driver spotted the obstacle.

As the Toyota crept up to the side of the donkey the driver realised there was room to pass. Kurt watched as the driver inched the Cruiser past, moved up a gear and began to pick up speed in the direction of Molepolole. As the Stallion came into view from the west it slowed on the approach to the bridge but did not stop. Kurt saw a flash of headlights from the Stallion to show those ahead that the situation was under control. He shifted his gaze and saw the leading Cruiser increase speed. From the direction of the mine the trailing protective Land Cruiser suddenly swung into view. To its rear, and approaching at speed, was Kurt's backup team which had acted as lookouts at the mine entrance in a Mitsubishi Station Wagon. Kurt's focus was on those ahead. The Stallion crossed the bridge and the driver accelerated. It was not moving at any great speed and Kurt was confident his aim would be true. He waited for another five seconds in the hope that a further delay would put the leading Cruiser sufficiently far ahead not to be immediately aware of the attack that was taking place. The road in front crept its way through a series of low hills and if its occupants were looking out for potential dangers ahead of them it might be a while before they realised that the Stallion was not following at a discreet distance. He opened fire. The Stallion's front windscreen shattered. As the vehicle stopped, Kurt could see a body slumped over the steering wheel. The passenger, realising what was happening, reached for a concealed weapon. Two further shots from Kurt in quick succession soon extinguished the potential danger. Before Kurt revealed himself he looked up to ensure that the trailing Land Cruiser was no longer a threat. A few seconds earlier the backup team's Mitsubishi had slid past the Land Cruiser at considerable speed. Drivers from the mine would probably expect at least one such vehicle travelling at high speed on every occasion that they used the road but not the semi-automatic machine pistol which had been brandished through the passenger side window as the two speeding motors drew level. The ensuing fusillade was enough to take out the driver's side tyre and the driver himself. In that moment two tons of swiftly moving Land Cruiser and its occupants were no longer in control. As the remaining front tyre exploded the heavy vehicle lurched violently to the right and smashed into the side of the Mitsubishi, just in front of the rear axle. The Mitsubishi was pushed broadside across the front of the Cruiser. With the two vehicles locked in this position the driver had little chance of bringing it back under control and it swerved violently to the left, lurching down the hard shoulder. It careered straight towards the stump of a tree. The speeding Mitsubishi hit it dead centre still travelling at over a hundred kilometres an hour. The stump bent backwards under the impact from the bullbars. The front end of the motor drove itself down into the dirt as the rear of the vehicle launched itself skywards. It appeared to stand as if immobile in this unlikely position for a moment or two. It then proceeded to flip end over end at least half a dozen times before it finally came to rest. As it did so, vital bits of machinery were catapulted in different directions. The doors exploded outwards. The back seat passengers shot out of the gap where the rear doors should have been, during the height of one of the flips. The driver and the front seat passenger made their exit via the front window. Their heads made contact with the front windscreen a spilt second before it would have burst open from the force of the impact. Meanwhile the Land Cruiser – its front offside tyre in shreds – skidded sideways, hitting the slope of the hard shoulder on the opposite side of the road. Travelling at high speed it flung itself into a series of sickening sideways rolls that took it into the roadside bush. It continued rolling for some distance, destroying the heavy duty chain link cattle fence and leaving a deep scar in the acacia scrub. When it came to a halt, the occupants remained inside the battered misshapen shell but were rag doll in appearance and none showed the slightest motion. Kurt watched all this with a look of absurd horror. The two vehicles had come to rest some distance from him and a quick appraisal of the situation showed him that the security guys in the Land Cruiser were definitely out of the game. Kurt gunned his Pajero up the dry river bed and parked it by the Stallion. Suddenly he heard a volley of gunfire from cover a couple of hundred metres from where he stood. As he looked up he saw that the leading Land Cruiser had returned and that his forward lookout team had opened fire on it. There was no hope of escaping the broadside which they laid down. One of the rounds of semi-automatic fire struck the returning vehicle's fuel tank. A huge explosion ensued and the wrecked vehicle ploughed its way into the roadside bush. It was even less likely that there would be any survivors. Kurt maintained his steely cool during this extraordinary series of events. He and his colleagues had gained more than a distinct advantage. With his rifle slung over his arm he trudged methodically over to the Stallion. Just as he reached it the Isuzu double cab driven by his forward support team ground its way from its hiding place towards the tarmac strip.

'Man oh man, what about those security guys. We hit them hard and fast,' Alfred shouted as he jumped out in a high state of excitement.

'Sure you did, but that's not the half of it, did you see the other two go off the road. That was something I won't forget for a while. I've checked them out. No one is going to be getting up and about.'

'Shame about our boys. Some of them had been about a bit.'

'Yeah, well, they were paid handsomely and they knew what they were getting themselves into. I'm more interested in what we're going to find inside this little truck.'

Kurt and Alfred turned towards the rear doors of the Stallion. Just then the sound of an engine travelling at high speed made them hesitate and look up in an easterly direction.

* * * * *

At first light that same morning Rusty McKenna and Mats Tingstad set off from Gaborone en route to Hukuntsi in the remote south-eastern corner of the Kalahari Desert. After refuelling in Molepolole, Mats took the lead and, as he saw his friend's Toyota 4x4 hilux twin cab disappear over the brow of the first hill, Rusty settled back to listen to the quiet but reliable purr of the traditionally aspirated four cylinder petrol engine. The Kalahari Ferrari, as she had been affectionately nicknamed by Rusty years before, was an old fashioned no nonsense set of wheels which was simple enough to fix without the skills of a formula one standard mechanic.

Up ahead Mats had already forgotten about Rusty. Now that he had secured his friend for the Hukuntsi project and had seen him once again after a relatively long gap he was reassured that he was the same old reliable chap who had got him out of a few scrapes in the past. He was confident Rusty would thrive living out in the wilderness that was the southern Kalahari. His mind turned instead to the myriad of problems that were a day-to-day part of running the Training Centre and which he would need to tackle the moment he returned. Mats was passionate about the need to bring a wide variety of skills to the desert people and numerous schemes flashed through his mind as he drove. There were buildings to construct, courses to organise, teachers to train and, most importantly, students to convince and cajole. It was not every desert dweller who wanted to shake off lethargy and get things moving. The miles came and went as he steered past dawdling donkeys and overtook the occasional slower moving bakkie. Approaching the run-in to Jwaneng his thoughts were on other matters far away in Hukuntsi as he changed down the gears and came to a smooth stop to assess the chaotic scene that confronted him. It was only as he applied the hand brake and stepped out, that he became aware of the carnage that was in front of him. There appeared to have been a catastrophic accident involving at least three vehicles. One of them was still burning fiercely and there were bodies lying in the dirt close to two of them. He was relieved to see another vehicle – which was not badly damaged – and, standing behind it, two people who did not appear to have been injured. He began walking towards them.

* * * * *

As Mats strode the few yards towards the Stallion, Kurt realised there was no going back. In that instant Mats' fate was sealed. He was less than ten metres away when Kurt stepped out from behind the Stallion and fired. A single shot was all that was needed to bring Mats' life to an end. Kurt watched in detached fascination as the lone bullet pierced his victim's chest. He sank down onto his knees and then collapsed onto his face where he was enveloped by a pool of ruby red blood. The rest of the support team could not help but watch as the life blood drained from this innocent man who had chanced upon them. The fact that all eyes were transfixed on the scene immediately in front of them inadvertently saved the life of another, who at that moment appeared over the brow of the hill from the east at a more leisurely speed. He was instantly aware of the accident a couple of hundred metres in front of him as he cruised over the rise with the engine whispering. His eyes took in the horrific scene ahead. Rusty saw, with total clarity, as a distant figure casually stepped out from the side of the parked delivery truck. He saw the flash from the muzzle of a gun and the awful bloody hole appear from the centre of his friend's back. Rusty felt his stomach contract. He was not familiar with violence but it took him only a millisecond to realise that Mats was dead and that he too was in danger. He shoved the gear stick into second at the same time as he swung the steering wheel viciously to the left and hit the brakes hard. As he straightened up onto the opposite carriageway he engaged first and hit the accelerator, looking back frantically in the rear view mirror.

'Alfred, take your boys and get after that Land Rover. He's got nowhere to go. You'll soon catch him up. You know what to do then,' exclaimed Kurt.

'Sure thing, man,' Alfred replied as he raced towards the Isuzu.

'When that's done, get back over the border and vanish,' Kurt shouted after them. 'Tell Peter and Frederick back in Pretoria that I'll be heading back the way we agreed. Good luck.'

Kurt turned back to the Stallion. A macabre peace descended. Despite all the unexpected twists and turns he felt a sense of exhilaration. He had achieved his goal. Unless this had been one of the dummy runs, he now found himself standing alone on the fringes of the Kalahari Desert with a fortune in diamonds at his fingertips. Provided Alfred could catch up with the old Land Rover the only living witnesses to the crime were a car full of men who were as committed to keeping it as secret as Kurt was. They were already speeding off in the opposite direction with no definitive information about where he was heading. Even if they were caught and questioned there was little they could reveal. Kurt had witnessed many scenes of bloodshed and it did not unduly affect him. He turned his attention to the rear doors of the Stallion which he duly prised open. Sure enough, sitting squarely in the middle of the rear cab was a single strong box, similar in size to that of a large suitcase. It was not fixed in position in any way, but was merely placed on a section of rubber matting. A single well-aimed bullet neatly removed the strong hasp which secured the lid of the box. With his heart pounding, Kurt lifted the heavy lined lid and removed a single piece of grey velvet to reveal a number of small felt bags. With each bag was a piece of paper on which was written a series of symbols listing the size and value of the contents. There was no doubt he had hit the jackpot. Although Kurt was completely unaware of it he had, in fact, been doubly lucky. It had been the mine administration's original intention that the trip would be one where there was no consignment present. However a rich vein had recently been uncovered and the management team had decided to transport the discoveries as quickly as possible. It was agreed that on this occasion the Stallion would carry the diamonds. As a consequence, nestling further down inside the strong box were a handful of gems which were considerably more valuable than the others. The bulk of the shipment now in Kurt's possession would be sufficient to finance the Rhodesia Homeland Army for years to come but, unbeknownst to Kurt, there were also five individual diamonds which had astounded all of the senior personnel at the mine who had been fortunate enough to view them. Each one of the five supreme examples that Kurt now had in his possession was in excess of 500 carats!

Kurt darted over to his Pajero and reversed up to the Stallion. It was an easy enough job for him to push the strong box across the gap between the two vehicles and into the space he had left at the back of the Pajero. He arranged a sleeping bag to conceal the top of the box hoping that it would be sufficient to escape the attention of a traffic cop. While he was reluctant to engage in further violence, Kurt was keen to protect his prize and kept both of his rifles within reach of his right hand. They were placed in the hidden gap behind the driver's seat just in front of the main bulkhead cross member. He had already practised reaching his right arm over his left shoulder and into the space behind, and was confident that if it came to it, he would be able to present the weapon against any unsuspecting opponent before they had chance to react.

Less then ten minutes after he had been left alone in the desert Kurt was at the steering wheel of the Pajero, racing westwards towards the point where he would strike off to the north. So as to avoid the risk of driving straight past the main gates of the Jwaneng mine, he intended to leave the tarmac strip at a point where a track headed off north in the direction of Seletse pan. There were many such pans in the southern desert, of which this, several miles in diameter, was the largest. Filled with a shallow slick of brackish water in the rainy season they were frequented by dwindling numbers of animals that lived in this part of the desert. Kurt had visited the spot with friends from the mine for a day trip and considered himself lucky to have sighted a small herd of springbok, a family of zebra and a solitary Gemsbok. Once in the past a lucky group had come upon a pride of the fabled Kalahari lions, stalking a kill. These almost mythical creatures with their black manes were known to populate the area but were a rare sight indeed.

After reaching this large pan, Kurt would be in uncharted territory as he progressed up the southern and western sides of the desert. It would be a relatively easy task using his GPS to find the dry bed of the Naledi River and follow it to the east-west sand road which lay to his north. Given efficient map reading, and a dose of good luck, he should strike it just to the east of Takatokwane. This road had once been the main route across the southern edge of the desert before the tar had reached Jwaneng and was still used by the hardier drivers heading from Gaborone to Ghanzi and the west. For fear of an untimely chance encounter Kurt did not wish to remain on it for any length of time. After crossing it he would use his GPS to guide him to the southern edge of Khutse Game Reserve to the north-west. This was the smaller of the central Kalahari reserves and was the more easily accessible from the east. A rough sand track followed the perimeter fence and Kurt planned to track the fence line up the western side of the reserve. This fence ran up to the southern edge of the much larger Central Kalahari Game Reserve which spanned the core of the desert. Until recently this had been off-limits to all but those with a hunting permit and had been considered to be the stomping ground of the nomadic Kalahari bushmen. Although these tough, resourceful desert dwellers were now coming into contact with so-called more developed communities and their ways were beginning to change, there were still a number out there who were known to be loyal to their traditional hunter-gatherer lifestyle.

Kurt did not intend to enter the central desert immediately. This was a featureless and desolate area and very dangerous to any but the most experienced, even with a GPS system. There were few tracks and those which did exist would alter their course seasonally at the whim of the migrating herds. There was also a significant risk of becoming irretrievably bogged down in the soft sand when the track suddenly petered out in front. This reserve was also fenced and Kurt had decided that he would follow this in a westerly and then a northerly direction until he reached Deception Valley. This had once held a large seasonal water course and remained a major landmark, with high sandstone bluffs to either side of the river bed. Tracking it to the north-east would be relatively easy and would eventually lead Kurt through the desert into the neck of land between the Okavango Delta to the north-west and the central pans to the south. The track through Deception Valley was relatively well-used and he would be unlikely to become dug in. If he encountered any travellers his presence in such a vehicle would not be considered untoward on this particular route. As soon as he reached the small isolated community of Rakops on the extreme northern edge of the desert he would decide which route he would take to the north-east in order to reach the Zimbabwean border.

* * * * *

As Kurt raced to the north-west, his mind still in disarray with the after effects of the ambush and the strangely enjoyable sensation that came with the realisation that he had taken a life, things were not looking very good for Rusty as he headed in the opposite direction in the Kalahari Ferrari. Rusty was unsure what had happened, but knew beyond a shadow of a doubt that it was all over for Mats and that those who were in pursuit of him were not about to take part in a reasonable exchange of views. As he manfully tried to coax a few extra miles an hour out of the willing but struggling Land Rover it did flash through his mind that it was rumoured that the perpetrators of the burgeoning crime spree were supposed to be the local blacks. It was seared into his brain already that the person who had been on the working end of the hunting rifle had been white however, as were the characters who were pursuing him. What he did know was that if he did not act they would soon catch him up and the outcome would be swift. He was unarmed and it was pretty obvious that his pursuers were not. The road back in the direction of Molepolole wound its way over and through a range of small hills. On two occasions in the last couple of minutes, as he motored along a short straight stretch he spotted the Isuzu in his rear view mirror. He did his best to rack his brains to think of any possible landmarks he might have passed when he had driven the same length of road earlier that day. Just then he saw in the bush up ahead the beaten up but unmistakable shape of an old American Chrysler station wagon under the shade of a large acacia tree. Beyond it three sweating black figures were enthusiastically attacking a Mopane tree with bush axes. As he passed it he remembered that he had seen the same vehicle turning off the road when he had come in the opposite direction. A moment later he came to the place where he had seen it leave the road, and sure enough the metal gate in the cattle fence had been left ajar by the woodcutting team, knowing that they would be passing that way later in the day with their full load. It was his only chance. To stay on the tar would be madness and he would be overtaken in a few short minutes. Better to let the Kalahari Ferrari make a fight of it in terrain she knew best.

He hit the brakes hard and swung off onto the sand track at the side of the road just as the Isuzu launched itself over the hill behind him, a few hundred metres away. For a moment he found that the sand track doubled back parallel to the road in the direction he had just come from, on the opposite side of the wire fence. As he ground his way along, the Isuzu came within fifty metres of him. For a moment, he had a clear view of his adversaries and the array of weaponry. They passed so close that the person in the front passenger seat moved his rifle as if to try a chance shot. Shortly afterwards they too slowed and the Isuzu, like the Land Rover turned off to the left and began to make chase relentlessly along the winding sand track. Up ahead, Rusty was less apprehensive now he was no longer on the tar. On this sort of surface the Kalahari Ferrari had certain advantages which he could put to good use. The track was quite narrow but if he was fortunate it would be regularly used by vehicles making their way to distant cattle posts. As such it was likely to continue for some considerable distance. If he was unlucky it might just be a short stretch used by the woodcutters and would come to an end in a thicket of acacia. The surface under his wheels was fairly soft sand but was not too clinging for the Kalahari Ferrari to deal with. Rusty eased the gearstick up into third and gunned the motor. At that speed the heavy vehicle flew over the sand but was still sufficiently in contact with it not to be in too much danger of slewing or skidding. Rusty knew the terrain could change at any moment. He might hit very soft sand, in which case he would grind to an untimely halt.

As Rusty settled into a steady rhythm he surveyed his surroundings. The track was meandering through a seemingly unending expanse of acacia scrub. The ground was level and despite the fact that the trees had been heavily grazed by herds of goats and cut for firewood he could only see about fifty metres ahead. It was a seemingly featureless and continuous expanse of woodland, the like of which covered many square kilometres of the desert fringes. He kept one eye on what was happening behind, through the door mounted rear view mirrors. The Isuzu – equally adept at dealing with this relatively undemanding landscape – was gaining on him fast. It was only the narrowness of the track and the number of short, sharp bends which prevented Rusty's pursuers from getting a clear shot at him. With its four wheel drive and central differential lock the Land Rover was the perfect vehicle for tight bends and Rusty lost little speed as he swept through them. He knew that the ungainly Isuzu would be fishtailing through the corners and the driver would need to ease back on the speed in order to best negotiate them. When the occasional straight stretch materialised it was a different story. The Kalahari Ferrari had no real speed in comparison to the Isuzu, which soon began to loom up behind.

Without warning the acacia scrub suddenly stopped and Rusty found himself in an open expanse of cropped grass and low scrub, which seemed to stretch into the middle distance, beyond which was a low range of hills. The track headed off directly towards the lower slopes of the hills. This was his only chance of escape. The Isuzu was far quicker on the straight and this change was not immediately welcome for Rusty. If he left the track and took off into the bush he might be able to outrun his pursuers over the rougher terrain, but he decided to stay with the track. It soon became clear why the vegetation here was different. The subsoil had altered from the soft sand through which he had been driving. Here it was much more compacted and heavy. Rusty immediately felt himself having to respond to how the Land Rover was handling. It was common on tracks of harder sand such as this for the surface to rise up into a series of steep, narrowly spaced ruts, which were hell to drive over. If he were to drop down into second gear and cut the revs, the Land Rover would still rock and roll from side to side.

It made for an uncomfortable ride and felt as if everything was being shaken to bits. The other alternative was to change up a gear and to try and fly over the surface of the ruts using more power. As soon as he hit the ruts Rusty decided on the latter and, after a few hundred metres, he found that the most efficient way of covering ground over this changed material was to run at high revs in second gear. It was here that the Kalahari Ferrari came into her own. The ninety-three inch span between the front and rear axles that was unique to Land Rover, coupled with the heavy duty combination of coil spring and shock absorber that formed her revolutionary MacPherson suspension system proved the perfect combination for this particular height and length of rut. The plucky little motor seemed to fly over the surface with little discomfort and, more importantly, with no loss of traction. Rusty found he could ease her up into third gear, apply more power and race along in relative comfort. The Isuzu was making heavy going of it and was losing ground very quickly. The driver was struggling to maintain his speed and the Isuzu was lurching wildly and rocking up and down as it made its laboured progress. The problem was that the bed of the vehicle was considerably longer than the Land Rover and was not well-adapted to dealing with ruts of this sort. In addition, the designers of the Isuzu had elected not to use the newer coil-spring suspension system that was on the Land Rover and had continued with the more traditional leaf springs for both front and rear axles. Every rut the vehicle passed over resulted in it bouncing up and down in an extremely uncomfortable and dangerous manner. In order not to risk rolling, the driver had no alternative but to take his foot off the gas and let the truck ease itself over the ground at considerably reduced speed. Any attempt at raising the speed even a mere ten kilometres an hour would lead to an accident.

Rusty knew that if he could reach the hills in front without mishap then he might have a chance and was in the process of deciding how he was going to use the hills to his advantage and shake them off when things changed dramatically. He found himself confronted by a dry river bed, crossing the track and effectively blocking his path. Recent flow had scoured the sides of the cut and a quick appraisal of the situation revealed it had torn away the sloping access ways which had been used by previous vehicles. The delay had already cost him a couple of minutes and he could hear the heavy Isuzu making its laboured approach behind him. He pushed the differential lock into position and chose first gear in low range. The best place to try to make a crossing was at the spot which had been used previously. Most of the slope maintained a healthy angle of a terrifying forty-five degrees. It was only at the base that there was a near vertical drop and that was probably less than a metre in height. Rusty eased over the edge without slipping the clutch and felt all four wheels bite as he made the drop. At the base there was a heavy impact and a hefty thud as the front axle and bumper drove into the soft sand beneath. The four wheel drive and the sheer weight of the vehicle forced her onwards and outwards. Rusty changed up into second gear low range sharply and hit the gas pedal as forcibly as he could. He knew how important it was to maintain the momentum that had been gained in the fall. To stop dead in this stuff would mean a lengthy period of digging and propping on a high lift jack.

For a moment the heavy sand took hold and he felt the heavy vehicle beginning to bog down. Just before all movement was lost, Rusty eased off the gas slightly and perhaps because this had the effect of stopping one or more of the drive wheels from spinning, he felt them bite once again and the Kalahari Ferrari began to gather speed over the sand. Although it did not gain much pace it was this small amount of forward momentum which came to his aid when he reached the other side. If anything the situation was even worse here. The slope appeared to be in excess of forty-five degrees right up to the top. At the base there was a slightly ridged area of sand where the river had eddied and he headed for this to mount the incline. As he hit the main part of the bank, Rusty forced the gearstick into first and applied full throttle. There was nothing to do but hang on to the steering wheel with a firm grip and hope. As the Kalahari Ferrari gained height Rusty got a giddy sensation as though he was about to topple over backwards. The view of the sky through the front windscreen would have unnerved many drivers. Despite the steepness of the slope and the angle of attack the Land Rover still drove on. Sheer weight at the rear was probably forcing the rear drive wheels to keep on turning. Without hesitation he crested the rise and with a crushing bump the vehicle once again fell back into a normal driving angle.

Rusty decided to stop for an instant to clear his thoughts. He was sweating profusely and his heart beat was at an all time high. Suddenly Rusty's attention was drawn to the Isuzu slewing to a stop on the opposite side of the channel as the glint of a rifle barrel caught the African sunshine. A few seconds later Rusty was out of sight and within a short distance of the range of hills. Alfred, at the wheel of the Izuzu, without a moment's hesitation plunged down the bank and into the dry river bed beneath. The four wheel drive took hold and the truck negotiated the soft sand without much difficulty. As the front wheels rose up the steeply sloping incline, the long wheelbase of the vehicle proved to be its downfall again. As the front end rode up the bank, the length of the vehicle caused the rear bumper and differential to drop down into the sand, causing so much drag that the rear wheels lost traction and began to spin. Although the front pair of drive wheels continued to try and force them onwards they simply did not have enough power on their own to maintain forward momentum and they ground to a halt. Alfred reversed backwards the way he had come and using full power once again attempted to climb the bank. Defeated for a second time, he swung sideways and started to look for another suitable escape point further downstream. Twice more he found possible spots but twice more the outcome was the same. Eventually the inevitable happened and the heavy Isuzu became bogged down in a patch of soft sand. Having dug themselves out, the team quickly came to the decision that even if they made the crossing there was no way they would catch up with the Land Rover. A few minutes later they were back on the tarred road and several hours later, as the sun was beginning to dip down over the desert horizon, they were once again back in the relative safety of South

Africa. They reported in as soon as they had passed through the tedium of Customs and Immigration Control. Their weapons – carefully packed – were buried in a cache on the Botswana side of the border. All in all it was fairly pleasing to be able to confirm that they had succeeded in their part of the mission and that Kurt was heading off into the Kalahari as had been agreed, with the diamonds in his possession. They did not give Rusty a second thought.

* * * * *

When Rusty and the Kalahari Ferrari reached the base of the hills he discovered the track ended abruptly at an abandoned cattle post. On either side lay impenetrable bush and the lower slopes of the hillside were beyond even the adaptable tracking skills of the Land Rover. He spent a minute or two filling a rucksack with some water, fruit and enough provisions to last for a few days. The hill was deceptively large, perhaps rising to a height of 250 metres above the surrounding bush. The slopes were strewn with large metamorphic boulders which occasionally outcropped in clusters to form spectacular ledges which dominated the rest of the hillside. Between these rock formations the ground cover was varied and relatively verdant. Rusty planned to gain as much height as he could before his pursuers caught up with him and to use a high vantage point from which to observe and to keep one step ahead. Less than ten minutes after hiding the Land Rover as well he could, behind a dilapidated cattle post building, he was at least a hundred and fifty metres up the hill and was looking out over the plain in front of him.

Down below he could see back to the dry river bed in the middle distance. There he could see the Isuzu make one last ditch effort to ascend the bank on his side. He watched as it made its futile attempt before finally climbing the far bank and retracing its path in the direction of the tarred road. As it left, its passage was marked by a long trail of dust kicked up by its speeding wheels. Above him a troop of baboons whooped and called out. Higher still, and unbeknownst to both them and to Rusty, a solitary leopard eyed the scene below. The confusion that the presence of the unexpected human had brought upon the troop might give him a better than usual chance that day of dining on his most favourite prey.

Able to relax at last, Rusty lay back on a rock, soaked up the glorious early afternoon African sunshine and took stock of the situation, while enjoying the succulent delights of a South African orange. Until that quiet moment Rusty had hardly had a chance to reflect on what had happened to him. He found himself alone in a desolate spot having witnessed a scene of the utmost brutality from which, through a combination of little more than luck and good fortune, he had only just escaped with his life. With a jolt he suddenly realised that his return to Botswana and his reunion with Mats had been less then twenty-four hours previously.

* * * * *

As the dust cloud left by the Isuzu drifted back to the desert floor far below him Rusty was suddenly filled with a powerful combination of bewilderment, frustration and sheer bloody-minded anger. For the first time he was able to comprehend the ugly way in which Mats had been gunned down and what his death would mean to the small community to which his friend had dedicated so many years of his life. As for what he should do, Rusty was, for the moment, unsure, but he knew he had an obligation to avenge the brutal murder of his friend. Rusty decided it was safe to return to the main road. It occurred to him that the logical course of action would be to go back to the scene of the ambush to see if anything further had happened there. It was inevitable that other travellers would have reached the spot since he had made his hasty departure. He felt sure that if he returned he would find someone in authority to speak to and to whom he could report what he had witnessed. Failing that there would be police and security people at the Jwaneng Diamond Mine, which lay a little further to the west. He descended the steep-sided hill and clambered aboard his trusty Land Rover. Not long afterwards he found himself once again easing his way over the gentle rise that immediately preceded the ambush site. Acrid smoke rose from the burnt-out vehicle. The other trucks remained where they had come to rest after rolling into the bush. At the centre of it all the Stallion was still parked in the left hand carriageway. Several other large trucks were parked in a disorderly manner around those he had seen earlier. There were people everywhere. The vehicles bore the logo of the Jwaneng Diamond Mine and the majority of the scurrying individuals were dressed in the uniform of mine security. He came to a stop behind a Land Rover Discovery loaded down with camping gear just as the occupants were ordered to turn off onto the hard shoulder and to bypass the scene without stopping. Rusty drew up next to the official.

'Good morning sir. Sorry for the delay. We've had a bit of an accident here. If you drive onto the sand you should be able to get past and continue on your way.'

'Thanks. I should explain that I was here earlier and saw everything that happened,' Rusty said. 'Is there someone here I could talk to?'

'Everything is in hand sir. We would strongly encourage you to head on your way. You must have a long journey to complete today. We wouldn't want to inconvenience you.'

'Look, man, I don't want to interfere but I witnessed the whole thing,' Rusty started to explain. 'I don't believe this was just a simple accident. I heard gunfire . . .'

'Sir, with all due respect, we are professionals,' the armed guard said, severely. 'We don't need your assistance. Please move along.'

Realising he was achieving nothing, Rusty gave the official a curt nod, engaged first gear low range and followed the diversion. It was easy to navigate but Rusty drove by slowly casting his eyes across to the bridge as he did so. To the left he could see a team of medics hurriedly placing the deceased into canvas body bags and loading them into the back of a large flat bed truck. A number of people milled about, with walkie-talkies and cameras, poring over the Stallion. A couple of guys in blue boiler suits were preparing to hitch it up to the rear bumper of a Toyota recovery truck. The Stallion was the focus of the investigation and the mine's security staff were extremely worried. Rusty's attention was suddenly diverted to a vehicle drawn up at the side of the road fifty metres away under the shade of a tree. The white livery, wide blue stripe and distinctive gold emblem of the Botswana Police Force were clearly visible. As Rusty drew alongside the pristine Toyota Cressida saloon he could see the driver was wearing the resplendent uniform of a Police Inspector. Despite the searing afternoon heat the white dress shirt was gleaming and the tie was knotted neatly in position. Rusty finally rolled to a halt. The officer was wide awake. A pair of dark brown eyes were trained on the activity on the road and nothing at all, not even the merest detail, was being overlooked. For a moment everything was peaceful. Then slowly the window opened.

'*Dumela Ra*,' a gravelly voice said from within. 'Thank you for not obstructing my view. Quite a lot seems to be happening and I don't wish to miss any of the entertainment.'

The Inspector paused and gave Rusty a wry look and smiled.

'I haven't seen that little Land Rover in many a long year. It's wonderful to see her on the road again. You must have friends in high places.'

Rusty was completely unprepared for this recognition of the Kalahari Ferrari. Then it came to him. In a flash, Rusty realised that the relaxed and confidently smiling Inspector in front of him was the man he had encountered many times in years gone by. And in this moment of crisis he was reassured beyond belief that it was the same man now.

'This old Land Rover and I go way back,' Rusty explained grinning. 'And not only that, I've seen your signature on the bottom of a few speeding tickets in my time. I seem to remember Sekoma being a favourite lair of yours.'

Laughter came from within the car. All of a sudden the same brawny arm that Rusty knew of old was thrust out from within the Cressida and he found himself receiving the traditional Motswana handshake.

'Yes, come to think of it, I remember you too. Always heading out into the desert with some pretty girl in tow. I sure do recall how jealous I felt when you had one of our Motswana beauties sitting next to you. It gave me great satisfaction to slow you down when you were out on one of your jaunts.'

'I can assure you, Inspector, I always had the last laugh,' Rusty replied. 'While you were still stuck at the side of some dusty road I was out there under the stars having the time of my life.'

'I have no doubt of that. But where has it got us both? Here we are once again together in the desert. You're alone and I'm sitting here faced with the biggest screw-up of my career.'

'That's why I pulled over. Those security guys wouldn't give me the time of day so I thought you might be interested. I was here about three hours ago when all of this was going down.'

'Is that so?' the Inspector replied. He paused for a moment and then continued. 'Why don't you park that clapped out Land Rover under the shade of this tree and come and join me. They still seem to be pretty busy over there and I don't want to miss any of it while passing the time of day with tourists like yourself. We can chat while we watch.'

Minutes later Rusty was seated in the pristine air-conditioned cab of the brand new police car.

'Allow me to introduce myself. Inspector Thabo Setshedi of the Botswana Police Force. I'm their only representative in this part of the desert. I am based in Jwaneng, for my sins, where these characters are from.'

'Pleased to meet you,' Rusty said shaking his hand. 'Rusty McKenna. I've just arrived from England and am about to settle in Hukuntsi for a while. Or at least I was until a good man was murdered in front of me.'

The Inspector did not appear particularly surprised at what Rusty said.

'Now that, *mona*, is very peculiar. When a passing tourer dropped in at my station this morning with the news about this little episode I headed out here straight away with my blue light flashing. When I got here this circus was already in full swing. And do you know what, the top man told me that they'd had a little local difficulty and that one of their number had had an argument with a donkey. This apparently caused an accident in which two of their vehicles went off the road. He said that three of their people were dead but assured me that they could clear up the mess and respectfully asked me to stay out of the way. He certainly did not mention that a crime had occurred but it does not surprise me.'

'What do you mean?' Rusty asked.

'There is some bad blood between us,' Inspector Setshedi began to explain. 'Traditionally there has always been a police presence at Jwaneng to cover the southern and eastern approaches to the desert. When the mine was built it established its own internal security force to deal with any problems that might arise. I'm perfectly happy with this arrangement. I can see it makes sense for the mine to be responsible for its own difficulties. The complication comes with incidents like this, away from the mine premises itself. Road accidents are a perennial headache, as are thefts of equipment, not to mention attempted thefts of the diamonds themselves.'

'Where do they hire their security staff from?' Rusty asked.

'They bring them in which creates another set of problems. Fights between locals and mine staff at the bars in town are commonplace. It's become the norm for the site's security men to take over the policing of such incidents when mine workers are involved. It's inevitable that this creates tensions among my local lads. Personally, I am appalled at how leniently they handle the staff. Not once has anyone from the mine been placed in police custody or appeared before the local magistrates to face charges.'

He paused and sighed. His frustration was obvious.

'Is that why you observe at incidents such as this?'

'Yes although my presence is deeply resented. It's been made abundantly clear that if I attempt to intervene then my career will be in jeopardy. The mine owners have friends in high places. They intimidated my predecessor for years. They'd be quite happy if my officers restricted themselves to catching the odd speeding tourist, such as yourself, and spend the rest of the day sleeping in the shade.'

Rusty listened thoughtfully to what the Inspector was describing. As he did so he could see the mine security personnel preparing to winch one of the damaged vehicles onto a low loader.

'So you won't be able to conduct your own tests on the cars or the bodies?'

'No,' Setshedi agreed. 'And I'm certain that numerous deaths have been caused already among the local people and their livestock by mine personnel driving recklessly after far too many beers and brandies. If I can at least monitor the number of accidents I might be able to reduce this particular scourge. So this is how you find me. Sitting here twiddling my thumbs in this swanky piece of Japanese machinery because some jumped-up South African security chief wants me to keep my distance.'

He sat silently for a moment reflecting upon the chaos in front of him. Suddenly he became quite animated.

'I should be down there,' he said nodding in the direction of the bridge. 'It drives me mad to sit here like a spectator especially now I know this is a major crime scene.'

After a sudden intake of breath as if to calm himself he continued.

'I tell you what, why don't you explain exactly what you saw today, and between us we'll try to work out what the hell is going on here.'

As Rusty talked, work continued in front of them. The vehicles which had rolled off the carriageway were cleared of bodies but were otherwise left in situ for the moment. The Stallion was finally hitched up to the back of a Land Cruiser.

'We set off for Hukuntsi and had driven without any difficulty for about ninety klicks,' Rusty continued, pausing briefly as he thought about his friend. 'My mate Mats was ahead and as I came up over the hill I could see he'd stopped to help. That's his motor over there,' Rusty said as both vehicles were positioned on a low loader. 'There was also a white Mitsubishi Pajero but I can't see it anywhere.'

'Wait a minute. Let me get this straight. You say you were chased by an Isuzu double cab but there was also a Pajero parked alongside the Stallion? You're sure? There is no Pajero here now, and it wasn't here when I arrived.'

'Yes, I'm positive,' Rusty replied emphatically. 'I won't forget what I saw this morning in a hurry. There was a brand new Pajero sitting in the middle of it all as I approached.'

'So now I have two missing vehicles,' Setshedi said thoughtfully. 'And furthermore the ones that are here cause me a problem. The Stallion and the two busted Cruisers are from the mine, and the twin cab was driven by your friend Mats, but I have my doubts about the Mitsubishi. It isn't an official mine vehicle. I suppose it could belong to one of the mine workers but if that's the case I would have seen it before. What intrigues me is that those guys out there are heaping up difficulties for themselves. There is only so much they can achieve by keeping matters to themselves. They must know they have a murder victim on their hands. Sooner or later they will have to admit that at least one of the vehicles isn't theirs. Quite how they will explain the gunshot wounds, God alone knows. Once they have examined the bodies, they will have to come clean. Given I am sitting right here, and they have told me that this was just a simple case of an accident with a donkey, they must realise that it could call into question their right to have jurisdiction over incidents such as this one.'

'What are you getting at?' Rusty asked.

'I am convinced they're trying to cover something up, and that the Stallion and the Pajero are at the centre of it. The question is why. They have been taking photos of the back cab of the Stallion but it's empty. Is something missing? And, if it's just a straightforward case of machinery theft, why did the thieves need to kill your friend and pursue you? I did wonder at first if the payroll had been stolen but that doesn't make sense either. Salaries are paid directly into the bank in Jwaneng. Added to which the Stallion was heading away from the mine. That only leaves one thing,' Inspector Setshedi said quietly.

'I'm sorry sir, but you've lost me. What do you think was in the Stallion?'

'I think they were secretly transporting diamonds and now the shipment is missing. It explains everything. If they have lost some diamonds, especially a priceless shipment, then they won't want DeBeers to get wind of it nor will they want the international markets to discover the loss. A large consignment of gem quality diamonds dumped on the world market all at once would undermine the price and disrupt the delicate balance between the key players. They will do their best to keep it under wraps for as long as they can. Deceiving a slow-witted policeman like me would be the least of their worries.'

Both men fell silent.

Right,' Inspector Setshedi suddenly said, 'if they are going to play that game, let's see whether we can stir things up a bit. We need to find out where the Isuzu and Pajero have gone. There aren't too many routes out of this spot after all.'

He picked up the handset of the police CB radio set, pressed a few buttons and started to speak rapidly in Setswana.

Rusty listened in a state of feverish anticipation. As soon as the conversation drew to a close the Inspector pressed yet more buttons and a new voice emerged from the depths of the radio. Another animated discussion followed. After several minutes he replaced the handset and looked at Rusty.

'Well, I've just spoken to both the veterinary officer at the Kubung road block and the Customs officials at Ramotswa. An Isuzu fitting the description you've given me passed through the vet fence at four o'clock this afternoon and crossed into South Africa without difficulty. So that accounts for one of our troublemakers. Your pursuers seem to have given up the chase for the time being. The Pajero took off in a different direction. If it went towards Gabarone we don't have much chance of putting a tail on it. There are no vet fences in that direction so no one will log it. If they've holed up in the bush or have headed west we might be lucky. It's surprising how little goes unnoticed in the desert and I know some characters who keep their eyes and ears wide open. Let's go and see if they can help us. Follow me up the road,' he instructed Rusty as he turned the ignition. 'We're not going any distance so I won't leave you and that old bucket too far behind.'

With a wry smile Rusty strode back to the Land Rover and was soon following in the Inspector's wake. As they headed westwards, Rusty reflected on what Inspector Setshedi had said. It was highly unlikely that anyone who had been involved in the fracas earlier in the day would be holed up in the desert. Despite its expanse, the presence of a strange vehicle would not go unnoticed and would be the subject of local gossip if it stopped for any length of time in an unlikely spot.

* * * * *

After speeding to the west for several minutes a collection of dusty, round thatched rondavels came into view in the middle distance. Inspector Setshedi took his foot off the gas and came to a stop in front of the hut nearest to the road. Rusty pulled over beside him. Loud music was blaring from a battery powered ghetto blaster. Several poorly dressed old men were sitting languorously in the shade, scooping traditional maize beer from a large communal clay pot and drinking it out of gourds. The men chatted while a brightly dressed woman stirred a pot of maize porridge for the evening meal. A couple of young children in tattered t-shirts played at her feet and fought with the hens over the food scraps in the clean orange sand. The woman cooked over a wood fire, using a three legged pot and behind a low wind break fashioned out of wooden off-cuts and rusty oil cans. Behind the rondavels, and further from the road, a sturdy corral penned in a dozen or so long-horned cattle who dozed fitfully in the baking sunshine. They swished their tails to keep the flies and tics which plagued them at bay. Several teenage boys sat on the wooden fence watching over the beasts and passing the time of day whittling slingshots from twigs. In the shade of another hut girls plaited each other's hair and giggled at the unexpected arrival of a muscular white man.

'*Dumelang Borra, Lo Kae,*' said the Inspector as he stepped from the cool interior of the car into the late afternoon heat.

From each of them he received the correct response and in some cases an elaborate handshake. There was a gentle rapport between the Inspector and the older men. One of their number immediately went into the nearest hut and returned with a chair. It was a measure of the esteem in which the policeman was held that such a fine chair – a *Kgotla* chair – had been produced from the interior of the hut. Rusty, as an honoured foreign guest, was also given a place to sit amongst the men. Smiling to himself he thought it best not to dwell upon how the roughly hewn stump he was sitting on reflected his status.

Before their discussion began the beer pot was passed around. Inspector Setshedi drank long and deep and then passed the pot to Rusty. Some of the men smirked at this gesture for it was well known that the *lekgowa* who frequented these parts shunned the traditional beer of the African, preferring the cooler taste of the Pilsner lagers from South Africa. Rusty had forgotten nothing from his previous visits to Botswana and he too drank deep and long, to the surprise of the assembled group. Their amusement at this unexpected turn of events was evident and they laughed uproariously as Rusty wiped away the dregs from his upper lip, and passed the pot to the man on his right. As he did so Rusty saw the Inspector smile and give him a quick nod. Formalities over, the discussion began but the transition into Setswana left Rusty floundering. The group of elderly men may have appeared to have been quietly getting on with their own lives but they were acutely aware of what had been happening on the highway. It was obvious from the lengthy explanations and wild gesticulations that they had much to say about the comings and goings of the day and little had escaped them. There was laughter at what some had to say but the Inspector was listening intently to each man's observations, sometimes countering with a question when something intrigued him. When the conversation came to an end the Inspector once again drank from the beer pot.

'Well these old boys have had a pretty lively few hours by all accounts,' he said. 'They spotted the small convoy with the Stallion in the middle of it, but it did not overly excite them because it's a regular occurrence, every few months or so. So much for the mine's much-vaunted security system! What got them going was the arrival of an anxious South African tourist from the east a bit later who said there'd been an accident and asked where he should report it. He's the one who turned up soon afterwards at my station. Later they saw the big contingent from the mine with me in close pursuit.'

The Inspector then paused as if reflecting on what had been said, before pressing on.

'They reported other comings and goings that I'm already familiar with, but the big news is that just before the tourist pulled over, a white Pajero flew past at speed heading west. One of the men said that the vehicle was travelling so fast he heard the engine note long before it came into view. He also said that a few minutes after it passed the sound altered again as if the driver had changed gear or speed. He could be mistaken, of course, and the others just laughed at him, but sound travels a long way out here and the old man does spend his days listening to the noises made by passing motors.'

The Inspector leaned into the cab of his Cressida, picked up the radio handset and spoke rapidly in Setswana.

'Okay that was the vet fence this side of Jwaneng. They've had the same procession of vehicles through their gate today, with one important exception. I'll give you just one sweet guess which one that was!'

'So our little Pajero has gone astray, right?'

'That's it brother. Why don't you and I go a-looking? And do you want to know something else? I have a pretty good idea where he's sneaked off to. Before we set off though I will have to ask a favour of you.'

Rusty was puzzled.

'Much as it pains me to admit it, I am afraid that we will have to leave this useless heap of Japanese junk here. We'll have to investigate some serious sand roads. Can I hitch a ride with you?' he asked, smiling wryly.

'Yeah, of course, no problem,' Rusty agreed, laughing, 'but let's have no more derogatory comments about the old girl from now on.'

'Okay, okay. I know when I'm beat,' the Inspector said laughing and shook his head, throwing his arms up as if in surrender. 'Let's get going. Maybe next year those bastards in Gabarone will issue me with a Land Cruiser. How they expect me to run a police force in the Kalahari without a 4x4 I'll never know.'

Inspector Setshedi turned back to the seated group of men and bade them farewell.

'*Go Siame Borra, Sala Sentle.*'

'*Eh, heh Ndata, Tsamaya Sentle.*'

* * * * *

'Keep heading west,' the Inspector instructed as they clambered into the Land Rover.

As they cruised along, Rusty glanced sideways and could see from his bemused expression that Setshedi appeared to be enjoying the smooth ride in the simple high-sided cab although he was not a little frustrated at being a passenger.

'Pull over there,' the Inspector said after a couple of klicks, pointing to a spot several hundred metres ahead.

As they approached Rusty could see a carpet of low grasses and thorn bushes bisected by a narrow track, just visible as two wheels ruts snaking their way into the middle distance. Inspector Setshedi hopped out as soon as the Land Rover came to a halt and spent a minute or two walking a few metres away from the main road, all the while carefully inspecting the soft sand in the ruts.

'No. No luck here,' he explained jumping back in. 'This track hasn't been used by anything bigger than a jackal or a Kori bustard for a few days. Still there are a couple of other places where we might hit the jackpot. Let's go.'

They continued heading in a westerly direction. Two more small tracks were reached and inspected. Both were clean of tyre tracks. That was not, however, the case when they reached the third one.

'Hey, look over there.' Rusty shouted pointing to a set of tracks neatly indented into the surface of the clean wind-smoothed sand.

Jumping down from the truck to take a closer look the two men discovered that the tracks of a small antelope, probably a duiker, had been crossed by the marks of tyre treads.

'A vehicle must have passed through here recently,' Rusty said looking around.

'Yes, you're right. It was pretty windy down this way last night. If these tracks were from yesterday, or earlier in the week, then they would be less marked than they are now,' Inspector Setshedi agreed. 'Look, you can see every part of the tread pattern. If I'm not mistaken they are good quality, top of the range sand tyres. I don't suppose you saw enough detail to recognise what type of tyres the Pajero had, did you?'

'No, I didn't. I had one or two rather pressing things on my mind at the time.'

'These would certainly be the type that would be fitted to a model of that specification, similar to the one you described. Anyway we will know for certain if we head further on. There's only one more track where our friend could have gone between here and the vet fence. Let's just check to make sure that he hasn't headed off somewhere else.'

Ten minutes later the two of them were sitting at the side of the road, next to the track where they could see the tread marks in the sand. As they drank a couple of cokes from Rusty's cool box, the Inspector spoke.

'I'm certain we're tracking the hijacker and I'm certain he's got the Jwaneng shipment. It must be quite a haul. It's an audacious attack. Who needs that many diamonds?'

'Do you think the mine will admit the loss?' Rusty asked.

'Not a chance. They'll be trying to trace the diamonds before they come close to admitting what's happened. That's why we've got to find this Pajero. There's no time to lose. If we wait for backup he'll be hours ahead of us. We need to start thinking like him. He's got the advantage. He must have been planning this for months. Is he working alone? Where's he heading? Is he due to meet someone or is he going to pull a switch and vanish with the goods? Where has he picked up his supplies from? Has he switched identities?'

'Look, to the north we've got the original sand road that spans the southern side of the desert,' Rusty said pointing to the map. 'He could have turned either east or west.'

'Yes, you're right. If he goes west he's heading into the wide open spaces of Namibia. If he heads east he can make for South Africa, assuming he can cross the borders without being detected. So we're dealing with someone who knows the terrain and isn't afraid to use it to his advantage. Taking the sand road to the north would be a logical choice for someone heading towards the Khutse Game Reserve or the central Kalahari from the south.'

Setshedi paused for a moment and studied the map intently.

'There's a track that follows the western side of the game park which would lead to the northern part of the country. It's poorly policed, and from there, it's an easy run into Namibia, Angola or Zambia. If I were in his shoes that's the way I'd go,' Setshedi continued, stabbing at the map. 'He must know that all hell has broken loose at the border crossings into South Africa, and he's clever enough to avoid detection in that way. If he heads north he has the benefit of a few days for things to calm down and then miles of open border from which to choose a plum spot to cross.'

'If we don't pick up his track soon, we won't have the slightest chance of finding him,' Rusty observed. 'He'll get away with both the diamonds and several murders. I'm not going to let that happen. I suggest we head straight on up the track, pronto. We've got food and water for a few days and we'll either catch up with him or will have lost him long before we run out of supplies. The Land Rover's tanks are fully loaded. We can probably get somewhere in the region of nine hundred kilometres before we need to fill up again. If we go right now and drive through the night we might get on his tail.'

'That, my friend, is a fine idea,' replied the Inspector. 'We know he's travelling alone. If we hit lucky he'll be feeling the effects of a long hot day and may bed down somewhere for a few hours. He probably doesn't suspect anyone will be following him. If we share the driving and are fortunate with our choice of route we might just surprise him at dawn.'

'Okay partner,' Rusty said. 'I'll take the first shift at the wheel. You can watch how she handles and take over later on when I've had enough. Let's get to it!'

A couple of minutes later the Kalahari Ferrari was once again heading into her adopted home. The track was composed of reasonably firm brown sand, shaped into long, evenly-spaced wave like undulations. As they bumped northwards the golden disc of the sun dipped over the western horizon and for a few minutes the southern Kalahari sky was filled with a deep crimson glow reflected off the dome of the heavens. Minutes later dusk descended and Rusty switched on the Land Rover's headlights. In the bright beam it was easy to pick out the white ribbon of the track and even the heavy tread marks left by the vehicle they were pursuing.

'Did you say you were from England?' Inspector Setshedi asked.

'Yes, that's right. Liverpool. I grew up there,' Rusty explained. 'But then I moved up to Aberdeen and got work on an oil rig in the North Sea.'

'Quite a contrast to the experiences you've had here.'

'Absolutely,' Rusty laughed. 'It was brutal, physical work but we were well paid and we partied hard when we were off the rigs.'

'Do you miss that life?'

'No! I used to escape into the Cairngorms at the first opportunity and go walking. Scotland's wild and beautiful and the people are fiercely independent.'

'Why did you leave?'

Rusty was silent for a moment as if unsure what to say but then spoke quietly.

'We used to come and go to the rig by helicopter. Our platform was about fifty kilometres out into the North Sea, east of Aberdeen. It was always a rough journey with freakish winds. As we flew we just looked down at the sea . . .'

For a second Rusty hesitated but then went on.

'On my last trip the gearbox in the rear rotor failed. When that happens you are going nowhere but down. We were not far from the rig but I was in the water for fifteen minutes. The rescue boat pulled me out easily but I bashed my head when we hit the water and, as if that wasn't bad enough, I nearly froze to death as well.'

Almost as an afterthought Rusty blurted out.

'Of course I was the lucky one. I managed to get out. I was the only survivor. It was days before they recovered the helicopter and the seventeen bodies. I didn't know the crew but the rest of the guys were off my shift. I lost all my mates . . .'

There was a short silence and then the Inspector spoke.

'What a desperate story and what a waste of life. I have seen some terrible things on these roads with people travelling far too fast and causing great damage to themselves and others, but you have been through a grim ordeal.'

As he spoke he reached across and touched the younger man on his shoulder in a gesture of great compassion. It was then Rusty's turn to speak again.

'To be honest, as I recovered, I mourned for my friends and it just seemed wrong to go back to the rig. I thought long and hard about my life and it all seemed utterly futile. I realised fate had given me a second chance and decided to take a different path. I suppose it's that decision which has brought me out here into the desert. Quite a contrast to the North Sea on a freezing day in February.'

For a while the two men journeyed on in silence as darkness

enveloped them and the Milky Way emerged over the distant horizon into the night sky. The scene ahead of and above them could hardly have been more beautiful.

As Rusty gently nursed the Kalahari Ferrari along the desert track his mind was in overdrive. The events of the past day had been traumatic and as if that was not enough the policeman's patient enquiries about his background had brought other painful memories to the fore. As if to compensate his mind drifted back to his family and the comforts of his home.

The perceptive policeman sensed the vulnerability of the younger man and left him to his thoughts.

* * * * *

Rusty's early life had been spent in Liverpool. He and his family lived in a comfortable three bedroomed Edwardian terraced house in Bootle with a view down the length of the street to the bustling River Mersey beyond, with New Brighton visible on the opposite shore. He was one of six children of a happy marriage between an Irish woman, whose parents had come across the water soon after the 1916 Easter uprising, and of a Liverpudlian father through and through. In those days his dad had worked as a foreman on the crushing plant of the massive Tate and Lyle sugar refinery that had dominated the waterfront immediately adjacent to the impressive twin towers where the famous Liver Birds stood as if ready to swoop down over the grey waters of the river beneath them.

Life had been good. His father brought home a good wage packet every Thursday, the family enjoyed each others' company, taking occasional trips to the northerly resort of Southport where hilarious afternoons were spent on the beach, at the funfair and in piloting 'phut-phut' motorboats under the elegant wooden bridges that spanned the marine lake. His dad had faithfully taken him and his two brothers to stand behind the goal at the famous Spion Kop end of Anfield, the home of Liverpool Football Club for each Saturday afternoon home game. With Graham Souness in the centre of the midfield and the elegant Kenny Dalgleish and the wily Ian Rush up front, the team had been something to support, constantly doing battle and more often than not emerging victorious from epic encounters with the hated enemies from Old Trafford and in particular the stylish, Cockney teams of Arsenal and Spurs. That Liverpool team had been renowned for its tenacity and there were many occasions when a game had been won after soaking up much pressure and then breaking the hearts of the opposition with a goal in the dying seconds.

On Sunday afternoons the family stayed together. The girls would return from Mass and Mum would prepare a huge Sunday roast for all eight of them. As they all washed up together the teenagers took great delight in listening to Pick of the Pops on Radio 1 and revelling in the number of chart hits that still originated from Merseyside. These had been good times and had burnt into Rusty a fierce sense of pride in the toughness and honesty of his birth place.

Rusty had not shown any particular aptitude at school and was frequently to be found messing about in Stanley Park or mud-larking on the Mersey foreshore. He was lucky that the mates that he had knocked around with had been no worse than scallywags and, although his education had suffered considerably, he had done little worse than simply fritter his time away. The best that could be said of him was that he had become streetwise and was able to handle himself in the argy-bargy that frequently erupted in some of the dodgier areas of Bootle. He had not, however, involved himself in the sort of petty theft and vandalism that many of the other kids did and which had ultimately doomed them to a vicious circle of approved school, poverty, unemployment and, in some cases, prison.

The blow had come in the economic recession that had hit Liverpool in the early 1990's and which had put his dad out of work just at the time of life when he would be unable to find another job. It was into this declining industrial spiral that Rusty was pitched when he finally left Linacre Lane Secondary School with absolutely nothing to show for it. The one thing Rusty had going for him was his street toughness and for a couple of years he was able to get by with odd jobs unloading lorries at the Marsh Lane Fruit Market, as a deckhand on one of the Mersey ferries and for one happy summer as a redcoat at the funfair in Southport, where he had spent many happy days as a kid. The limitations of this life began to show and the pressures slowly built on Rusty when the supply of short term jobs began to dwindle. Soon he, his dad and his brothers were all unable to find worthwhile long-term employment and had all become lunchtime and evening habitués in the Steam Packet public house on Scotland Road. It was here one early autumnal evening over a pint of Higson's best bitter that his eyes idly scanned a piece on the BBC Six O'Clock News. What was being discussed was the fact that oil production on the North Sea oil fields had finally reached full capacity and that as a result Aberdeen Airport currently had more air traffic movements daily than any other airport in the world. On the large television screen above him Rusty saw a seemingly never ending stream of Bristow helicopters disgorging medium sized groups of tough looking young men dressed in navy blue survival suits. What Rusty noticed was that many of them were of much the same cut as himself, but what hit him in particular was that their faces to a man showed that they were animated by the great enterprise they were participating in. Rusty looked around the pub and the contrast with the already flushed faces of his father and brothers and the other regulars could not have been more marked. Although the television report had made no mention of possible job opportunities Rusty decided to investigate. That night, after briefly mentioning his plan to his Mum and Dad and packing his old army and navy rucksack, he slept soundly. The following morning he was up early and within a few minutes had thumbed a lift onto the East Lancashire road. By mid-afternoon he was north of Glasgow and the following morning was dropped off, disorientated and tired, in the heart of the Granite City.

His decision to take his chance in the boomtown that was Aberdeen had proved to be the pivotal decision in Rusty's life. It only took him a couple of hours asking around in the city centre pubs to ascertain that there were numerous recruitment agencies who were looking for tough, determined characters like himself. By the end of the week he was sweeping eastward over the uninviting waters of the North Sea in the belly of one of the very helicopters he had seen on the television only a few days earlier. Within a month he was fully integrated into, and accepted by, the gritty team who had the arduous task of working at the drilling head itself.

Rusty was one of the gangers who manhandled the drill sections into place and attached the massive hydraulic drill head from the gantry above. There was nothing intrinsically difficult about this repetitive work but it required strength and teamwork and injuries were commonplace. Despite these drawbacks and the grueling twelve-hour shifts that the company required the teams to work, Rusty found he was up to the rigours of the job and particularly enjoyed the camaraderie.

His life settled into a not unpleasant routine of hard physical work interspersed with wild episodes of relaxation in Aberdeen and trips to the mountains of Northern Scotland. In Aberdeen he knocked around with the lads he worked with, competing against them in fearsome drinking bouts and chasing after the women who were attracted to these hard individuals. When he tired of this lifestyle he took himself off for lengthy periods in the Cairngorms. The skiing in winter was superb and in the spring and summer the rivers were amongst the best in the world for white water rafting and canoeing and the lakes provided excellent windsurfing. Whatever the season, there was always a ready supply of fit, lithesome young girls leading the same easy going lifestyle as himself and who were more than willing to share the pleasures of the bed with his easy laugh and his well-muscled body.

For two rip roaring years he carried on in this way, earning large sums of ready cash, none of which he managed to save. He probably would have continued in this undemanding fashion until the Scottish oil bubble had burst had it not been for the fateful winter afternoon when he had been pitched into the ice-cold water of the North Sea only to survive and to be given the opportunity to reassess the direction in which his life was heading.

* * * * *

Rusty's thoughts were abruptly cut short as suddenly in front of them the track that they were following reached the main east-west sand road which runs under the southern fringe of the Kalahari. The tyre marks of the vehicle that they were pursuing turned neatly to the west and it did not appear that there had been any further traffic that evening. The Inspector spoke once again.

'We're in luck. You might get a couple of vehicles through here in daylight every hour, but most sensible travellers will pull over for the night on such a difficult road as this.'

He looked across to Rusty.

'Are you tired? Do you think you can keep going?' the Inspector asked.

'Don't worry about me. I'm fine. We don't have time to relax,' Rusty replied resolutely as they pressed on with their pursuit.

'If this character doesn't turn to the north soon we're going to have to chase him into Namibia,' Setshedi observed dryly, breaking the silence.

'Inspector, look over there,' Rusty cried out, leaning forward eagerly across the wheel.

Sure enough just before they reached the desert outpost of Takatokwane the tyre tracks crossed over the right hand carriageway and continued on up another track heading off in a north-westerly direction. It seemed now that they were about to be led into the central Kalahari itself or perhaps, via the interconnecting tracks that led up the side of the game reserves, to the northern part of Botswana.

'Let's take a break,' Inspector Setshedi suggested.

Rusty turned onto the new track and stopped. He had been driving for several hours and didn't realise how exhausted he was. He jumped down stiffly from the Land Rover and stretched. It was well past midnight but at this time of year, in the early part of the summer rainy season, it was pleasantly warm under the shimmering Kalahari night sky even at this late hour. Rusty pulled out some bread, cheese and tomatoes from his cool box and heated some water over a gas burner. The two men talked as they fortified themselves with sandwiches and scalding hot coffee.

'I am sorry to have made you recall your accident. It must have been hell to have gone through that and to have lost your friends.'

Rusty was quiet for some time as he stared upwards at the swirling mass of the milky way.

'Yes it was tough – very tough – for a while. But I was lucky enough to find this place soon after. When I recovered I wanted to try something different and when I saw the job advert from Skillshare Africa looking for oilmen to work in the desert it was too good to resist. The first time that I drove out here was a trip to Khutse Game Reserve with some new friends from Gaborone. I knew immediately it was what I was looking for.'

'Yes, like you, I can appreciate the beauty of this place, although for us Batswana we also have memories of the tough times. The rains failed for several years when I was a child and many people lost everything. It's not always an easy place to live.'

'No it's not,' replied Rusty in a hesitant voice. 'I first met my friend Mats on that trip to Khutse. Look at me now. Out here in the desert chasing his killer.'

There was a long poignant silence. As if to break the sombre mood, the Inspector spoke suddenly.

'At least tonight we are lucky. There's been no rain. A heavy downpour would have been catastrophic for us. Maybe the desert gods will be on our side tomorrow.'

He then lay back on the soft sand and gazed at the clear night sky. He did not know it but he could not have been more wrong.

* * * * *

Just at the south-western corner of Khutse Game Reserve and about eighty kilometres north-west of where Rusty and the Inspector had stopped to rest, Kurt Viljoen slept deeply in the back of his Pajero. He was accustomed to sleeping in the bush so this was no particular test for him, despite being alone in the middle of the vast wilderness. Shortly after the sun had set, he had decided that he could afford a period of relaxation and had reassured himself that it would be better if he took the opportunity to rest and to replenish his reserves. He had kept a good check in his mirrors as he had made his stealthy progress north but had seen nothing. Admittedly, if he had spotted anybody, it probably would have meant that the game was up anyway. Each time he had come to one of the rare places in the desert where there was a rise in the land which provided a vantage point, he had pulled up and clambered on to the roof of his Pajero. On each occasion, he had carefully scanned the horizon to the rear and, thankfully, had seen nothing to fear immediately to the south-east. After reassuring himself once again that he was alone, the exhausting day had finally taken its toll on him and he had looked for a suitable spot to spend the night. The landscape he was passing through was southern Kalahari grassland and was relatively flat but in a few places there would be a dry river bed with an outcropping of calcrete boulders. Kurt had encountered one such place where he could hide the vehicle but still have a good view of the approaches to both the north-west and to the south-east. After a few minutes spent carefully concealing the Pajero in a thicket of camelthorn he convinced himself that he was in a secure enough location to observe what was happening in either direction. If he was lucky it might also provide enough cover for him to lay low and let any travellers simply pass him by. Before falling asleep he prepared himself a decent meal from the copious quantities of tinned and dried food that he had packed away in Johannesburg into two large tin chests. Cautious about how far light might travel across this clear landscape he had cooked inside using a small gas stove.

He had even relished a single cool beer from out of his well-stocked refrigerator. As he drank Kurt looked up at the glorious night sky. The Southern Cross glimmered brightly above and down below the track behind him was empty and unlit. All appeared perfect and Kurt was content. After packing away his food and cooking utensils in case he had to make a swift departure he rearranged his equipment in the back of the truck so that it formed an even raised platform. He rolled out a cushioned camping mattress. Once he was inside his top of the range goose down sleeping bag he soon found that the exquisite comfort eased his anxieties and sleep came easily.

* * * * *

As the silver disc of the moon advanced towards the horizon, Rusty and Inspector Setshedi headed off in pursuit of their quarry. They found that the sand became more fine-grained and, as a consequence, softer as they moved northwards and the terrain was much more difficult. Both men were becoming tired and they had to stop for a break on a couple of occasions. Their progress was not made easier when they became badly bogged down in a particularly nasty patch of sand and had to use the high lift jack and sand ladders to release the Land Rover from its clawing embrace. Still they remained resolute and continued their implacable chase. Later on, much closer to dawn, they pulled over and changed positions. As the first light of the new day crept over the eastern horizon the Inspector was back at the wheel. The thin dawn light began to strengthen and as it did so the cluster of rocks concealing their quarry's hiding place emerged out of the bush ahead of them. In response to the slight incline in front of the rocks the Kalahari Ferrari began to labour a little in the sand and the Inspector double de-clutched as he changed down from third to second gear.

* * * * *

84

Kurt awoke immediately. He could hear the unmistakable sound of a heavy vehicle labouring uphill through sand and changing down through the gearbox in the process. It was only a moment before he was lying in readiness along the upper side of a large flat slab of rock which was partially concealed by a similar, but larger, block which overlooked it and cast a deep shadow over his chosen spot. Kurt was confident he would not be visible to the occupants of the approaching vehicle. His efficient and well-oiled South African hunting rifle was nestled contentedly in the crook of his arm. He had already decided that he would allow any tourist traffic to pass by but if he was faced with either a government vehicle, or one from the mine, then he would do all he could to ensure that further pursuit would be halted. As the approaching vehicle came into view Kurt was not certain that what he was seeing was believable. He had fully expected to see a small convoy of powerful police vehicles making the arduous passage up the sandy slope. He was realistic enough to know that the authorities would have worked out that his chosen route was one of the more likely possibilities available to him and would therefore have sent a patrol this way, as well as perhaps along several of the other tracks that criss-crossed the southern Kalahari. If the government was serious about running him to ground then it would not have required too much initiative and organisation to have put together an efficient web of chasing vehicles. The fact that he was now faced with the same curious, battered, old-fashioned short wheelbase Land Rover left him dumbfounded. He had given clear and specific orders to his backup team that they should deal with the problem and it seemed absurd that the vehicle should appear in front of him in this inaccessible spot. It was either him or the guy at the wheel of the old vehicle which had just crested the low rise and was now less than a hundred metres away from where he lay in wait. He shouldered the rifle and squeezed the trigger. The windscreen shattered into smithereens. The Land Rover lurched violently to the left towards a small group of medium-sized boulders. It had just crested the rise and was beginning to accelerate away. Because of this momentum, when its front offside drive wheel hit the boulders the whole vehicle leapt into the air and twisted sideways. As it did so the passenger side door burst open. The Land Rover continued to move at considerable speed as it rolled over on to its right-hand side with a crashing thud. Its trajectory slewed at an acute angle away from the boulders in the direction of a steep bank which led down to the dry river bed which skirted the base of the outcropping rocks where Kurt was concealed. In a flurry of dust the doomed vehicle shot over the top edge of the river bank and plummeted onto the compact sand beneath. The drop down the steeply sloping bank was probably less than ten metres but it proved to be an effective method of bringing the old truck to an immediate stop. Kurt watched as the front of the sturdy vehicle crumpled, warped and lost its distinctive box-like shape. As the dust settled Kurt could see the body of the driver slumped over the steering wheel. In that instant he was almost certain that he was looking at the face of a person of indigenous African stock. Before he had a chance to register this thought fully there was the sudden whoosh of an explosion as the reserve tank released its contents over the hot, still sparking engine. A few seconds later the one hundred litres held in the roof top Jerry cans added their fuel to the flames. The fierce petrol-fuelled blaze took hold of the vehicle and its contents and a huge column of thick oily black smoke provided the most spectacular of funeral pyres. If there were others in the vicinity, regardless of whether or not they were part of the chase, they could not fail to see the smoke and would be sure to come and investigate. In a flash Kurt leapt from his niche to inspect at close quarters the burning remains of the Land Rover. He moved cautiously in case there was anyone lying in wait for him with a cocked gun. When he was as close as he could get to the raging inferno he could see the driver was no longer a threat. His body had already been almost entirely consumed by the intense heat. Kurt completed a cursory examination of the blazing vehicle and then scrambled up the river bank. Cautiously he followed the haphazard marks left by the side of the Land Rover where it had careered sideways through the scrub. He went as far as the point where it had initially hit the boulders after his well-aimed bullet had struck home. He checked to the left and to the right but could see nothing in the dense thorny undergrowth which led him to believe that there was anything in there which he needed to investigate. With one last look back down the track to the south-east from which any further threat to him was sure to come he ran back to his Pajero, turned the ignition and continued his escape to the north-west.

* * * * *

It all happened so quickly that there was no chance for Rusty to register shock or any other kind of emotion.

'There's no power in this blasted English relic of yours!' the Inspector said as they laboured up the shallow sandy incline. 'Who'd have thought I'd have missed my Japanese roadster eh?'

'Hey, treat my old motor with some respect!' Rusty laughed.

In the passenger seat Rusty was half turned towards the Inspector as he spoke. In that instant the single, well-aimed bullet struck the policeman in the throat and in the course of its devastating passage through his body severed the artery that pumped the precious life blood to his brain. The Land Rover immediately veered off the road. The impact buckled the bulkhead and the passenger side door burst open. Rusty was thrust against the door as the vehicle began its uncontrolled roll to the right as it twisted through the air. He fell to earth through the open doorway and into the centre of a small patch of sand nestled in a hollow between the group of boulders that the Kalahari Ferrari had just struck. As he was forced down into the surface of the sand at speed his upper body arched viciously and just before he came to rest the back of his head hit a small boulder. He lay utterly motionless. He was still lying in the same position a couple of minutes later when Kurt passed within ten metres of where Rusty had fallen. As Kurt gazed to the south-east, Rusty's eyes came into focus giving him a perfect view of his adversary. Rusty had not attempted to move nor would his body have allowed him to do so had he tried. As his opponent moved away in the direction of his Pajero, Rusty lost consciousness again.

The remainder of the long hot day was torture for Rusty. He spent the day alternating between periods of intense pain which blocked out rational thought to periods of discomfort when the agony periodically subsided and allowed his thought processes to partially function. His thoughts were delirious, irrational and disconnected. Bizarre memories of his early life and family flashed across his mind in a constantly changing kaleidoscope of nightmarish images. His extreme discomfiture was increased as a result of the superficial injuries he had received when he had crashed into the unyielding earth. His face and arms had been badly grazed by the sharp grains of sand. The wounds were minor but nonetheless very attractive to hordes of small desert flies which, as if by magic, became aware of his presence almost from the minute he had landed. They plagued him incessantly. Although Rusty was thankfully unaware of it in his semi-confused state, the flies that fed upon his body were but the first in a series of scavengers which would gradually over the course of the day become aware that a wounded and sick individual was being offered up to them by the desert. If he was to stand any chance of surviving their potential attacks it was essential that Rusty regain his senses sufficiently to make some form of rudimentary defence. Unfortunately for Rusty the intense bruising was unlikely to subside until such time as he received water, nourishment and medical help. In his current predicament none of these seemed likely to be forthcoming and throughout the blistering heat of the afternoon he lay prone. The sun parched his body and his store of vital body fluids rapidly dwindled. As he drifted in and out of consciousness the only constant factor was the searing pain that thudded away at the back of his skull.

* * * * *

Twenty odd kilometres to the west of where Rusty lay stricken, a small group of Kalahari San bushmen broke their simple camp on the western lip of the small salt pan. When they had awoken that morning a column of smoke had been visible in the eastern sky. They were curious about what had caused it and agreed that they should go and investigate. They had been intending to move in that direction in a day or two so it was not inconvenient to start now. Toma had been the one who had been reluctant to move, arguing that whatever it was that was burning would still be there the following day. He had more than one motivation for not wanting to strike the camp. On a superficial level he was still feeling the effects of the feasting the night before. Two days previously he and his younger brother Koto had scored a rare success. They had successfully stalked a young male gemsbok and killed it. Toma and Koto were brothers and joint leaders of a small band of Kalahari San bushmen who still tried to live their traditional lifestyle as nomadic hunter gatherers. They were increasingly feeling the impact of the encroaching herds of cattle owned by both the local Batswana tribes and also the more recently arrived white farmers. The cattle required huge tracts of land. This was bad enough in itself but in addition they had to be protected from foot and mouth disease. This meant that the desert was becoming increasingly zoned with substantial fences to keep the cattle and the indigenous animals apart. Traditional migratory routes were blocked. This had a devastating effect not only on the animals but also on the bushmen who hunted them. If the game was not there, it prevented these tough and resourceful people from preserving their age old hunting ways. Toma had tried adapting to the new ways, working on the cattle ranches as a herdsman and a tractor driver when the rains had failed but he had consistently found that it was a better life to risk the vagaries of the desert than accept the exploitation and degradation which was a constant companion in his relationships with those with whom he shared the desert.

The San Bushmen, traditionally nomadic in habit, had few belongings, even shunning an association with domesticated animals. A cornerstone of their life was that the land and its bounties were shared in common and in equal amounts. Alcoholism was a persistent problem among the bushmen who resorted to the attractions of the bottle when they could no longer cope with the distress that came as an evil part of the great changes that they were having to face. Toma and his brother were leaving their camp at about the time two days earlier that Rusty had been landing at Gaborone airport. At dawn that morning an observant member of the group spotted a trio of Gemsbok on the other side of the salt pan. Their pale fawn coats with the characteristic black marks on the back, flanks, throat and face immediately marked them out as the animal which the bushmen most coveted and most revered. Their majestic sweeping horns rising upwards and proud with a slight backward curve, indicated that it was a young bachelor group, biding their time, quietly ranging across the desert before it was their turn to go into battle to secure a mate and a place in the survival of their species. The two young men picked up their hunting equipment and tracked the animals efficiently and resolutely throughout the long day. As the hot sun rose high in the sky they settled into a steady rhythm, Toma in front dictating the pace and direction and Koto at the rear, constantly chatting with his brother in the characteristic clicking sound that is the unique and incomprehensible trademark of these ancient Kalahari dwellers. They maintained an apparently effortless pace throughout the day which always kept them undetected but within contact of the wandering animals. It was more than luck when, at sunset, they were close enough to try a shot with their bows and arrows. Both scored at least one direct hit into the side of the unfortunate animal that they had selected. The bows Toma and Koto were using were delicate constructions made from the slender branch of the raisin bush, bound for strength and grip with sinew. The critical part, the bowstring, was made from the tightly twisted sinew from the long back muscles of an eland they had killed the year before. This gave their slender weapons considerable power and grace. Toma and Koto used the scrub at the edge of the pan to maintain their cover but the timing of their final thrust was perfect, just before sunset.

As soon as the two young hunters saw their arrows strike home they relaxed, knowing that they had done all that they could for the moment.

Their only concern was that it should be them who would reach the carcass first. There were many scavengers and other predators out there who, if they were the first to lay claim to the meat, would be impossible to chase away. The two men were lucky that they had wounded the gemsbok on a night when the moon was almost full and the sky was cloudless. As they followed the tracks into the brightly lit night the desert was bathed in a clear milky light and the stars shone. As they walked silently they caught the occasional glimpse of a black backed jackal dogging their steps and once passed over the labyrinthine burrow system of a family of Springhaas.

Less than two hours after they had successfully attacked the beast they finally caught up with it. In the pain and confusion caused by the poisoned arrows it had lain down in a small hollow close to a thicket of undergrowth. It was not yet dead and tried pathetically to rise as they approached. The dying beast was however too far gone to protect itself and Toma swiftly cut its throat. As its life blood ebbed away into the clean desert sand its large brown frightened eyes gradually dimmed and the twitching stopped.

As the animal lay dying the two men collected sufficient brushwood to make a fire for the remainder of the night. There was no prospect of a cold night at this time of year but they knew that they would be joined by others as the night progressed and needed the fire to keep them at bay. Sure enough it wasn't long before a lone hyena heralded its arrival with a series of chilling whooping barks. Occasionally it would come close enough for them to see its heavy body with the characteristic dark brown spots. This powerful grinning animal made an imposing sight in the half light and would have disconcerted lesser men.

Just before dawn, having rested sufficiently, Koto left the temporary camp and made off in the direction of his family at a steady loping run. It was not long before he was shaking them awake to report the news of the kill. The bushmen had no means of keeping meat fresh in the harsh environment in which they lived and their pragmatic, effective and hugely enjoyable response to such an event was to feast and gorge themselves until their bounty was consumed. Their sense of anticipation was infectious and the camp was soon alive to the sound of their distinctive speech. Shortly after Koto had reached the camp, four of their number set off with a skip in their stride to assist Toma in bringing home the carcass. When they arrived they found that daylight had diminished the bravado of the hyena, which had retreated to the shade of a nearby bush from where it would occasionally howl. As soon as the other young men arrived the carcass was immediately cut into quarters. The men then cheerfully slung the sides of meat over their shoulders and began to make their steady way back to their family.

As the young hunters approached their home camp the children were the first to spot them making their way across the pan. They came scampering out in a flurry to be the first to see the treasured animal. The older women contained their enthusiasm but nonetheless began chanting when the meat was thrown down at their feet. Toma and Koto were deemed to be the owners of the meat since they had caught it and it fell to them to prepare the fire into which the meat was placed for consumption later in the day. For them this was a simple process. A small fire was already alight in the centre of the camp. This was increased in size by the addition of several large branches from a nearby fallen tree. The fire was left to burn until the flames had died down and all that remained was a dull orange glow. The meat was then placed on the flames and then covered over with more embers until the pieces could not be seen. As the children played around the camp, most of the older people spent the day quietly at the fireside, talking and singing while they tried to convince Toma and Koto that the meat was ready and that the fire should be broken open so they could start feasting.

Late in the afternoon Koto relented and broke open the fire. The delicious aroma of roasted meat soon pervaded the whole camp and there was an air of anticipation as Koto cut off a sizeable chunk and devoured it. In order to gently pay back his family for the chiding that he had endured during the afternoon it was some time before he finally declared that the meat was done to perfection. Koto also took some of it to his younger sister Khangdu's children. By midnight the whole group were utterly content and deeply asleep. As the sun rose over the eastern horizon the following morning the children were the first to wake and gazed in wonder and dread at the huge column of smoke that seemed to rise up in the distance, partially blotting out the morning sunshine. It seemed that they were experiencing many new things in a few short days.

* * * * *

The toddlers watched the smoke for a minute or two and then crept quietly to where their mother slept comfortably. It took them more than a few minutes to prise her from her dreams. When she was fully awake she was as perplexed as they were as to what the smoke might mean. She gently nudged several of the older tribe members awake including Koto and Toma. A lengthy discussion took place concerning what would be an appropriate course of action for them to take. Toma's greatest fear by far was the fact that whatever caused the fire and smoke would almost certainly bring them into contact with either the white or black-skinned travellers who they had been doing their best to avoid. Others argued that if there was a burnt out vehicle at the scene, as seemed likely, then there might be pickings for them. The others were insistent that they should take a look and in the end it was perhaps inevitable that their natural curiosity should get the better of them. Toma had argued that it would be better to wait until the next day when the fire would have died out but it was decided that a small group would go on ahead to see what had happened. They estimated that it was a three to four hour walk and if they kept up a reasonable pace they should arrive shortly before sunset. At about mid afternoon they set out, led by Khangdu and Kangao, one of the senior and wiser men of the group.

* * * * *

Rusty lay helplessly in the dangerous rays of the sun. His injuries sent out painful signals to warn his brain that if action was not taken soon all would be lost. He was not capable of anything that could be described as rational thought and a sick inner feeling began to grow as the afternoon progressed. Subliminally he was aware that he was badly injured and was in a place of great danger. As a consequence of this the disjointed thoughts passing through his brain gave him no solace from the nightmare, as images of the dangers of the desert began to flash across his consciousness. Once or twice his body twitched in response to a sound or shadow of movement which might represent danger. It was his body's inability to respond to these pressing signals which led to the hideous thoughts which now enveloped him. If he had been capable of conscious thought his surroundings would have given little cause for hope. Other than his own solitary presence and the marks left by the careering Land Rover, all was normal in the empty desert and there was no sign of humanity that might be able to offer him assistance. As he lay still, the afternoon thermals began to provide perfect lift and he was finally spotted by a lone vulture. It was soon joined by others. Gradually the large birds became bolder and began to circle lower and lower, carefully inspecting his inert form as they did so. His occasional muscular spasms made them cautious and kept him alive throughout the afternoon. It was only as the light began to fade that the first of them glided in at low level and settled on the largest tree in the immediate vicinity, from where it scrutinised him carefully with its distinctive death mask. Soon, like aircraft on a holding pattern coming in to land at a busy airport, others began to settle in the upper branches of the nearby trees As the day cooled, Rusty's injuries, the pain and the dire lack of water and the consequent dehydration got the better of him and he fell into a stupor. Soon afterwards he came to his senses momentarily as a shadow passed over his face and his brain registered the unpleasant sound of the beating of many wings. Although he fought against what, even in his befuddled state, he realised was the inevitable end his body would not come to his assistance and he still

94

could not move. Suddenly he became aware of a presence hovering over him cautiously.

* * * * *

As the afternoon turned to evening Kangao and Khangdu led their small band in the direction of where they had seen the smoke. It had died away and was no longer a beacon for them to follow. They knew this part of the desert well, however, and were unerring in their choice of direction. It was evident that the smoke signal of the morning had been coming from a series of low hills. As one of the few vantage points in the immediate vicinity it was a spot that they recognised and had made camp at on many occasions in their past wanderings. The first thing they noticed was that tracks belonging to two separate vehicles could be seen in the smooth sand on the southernmost track heading up the side of the low hill. As they followed these tracks up the rise they became aware that several of the larger trees to the left were filled with a congregation of the large ungainly birds which were a sign of death in the desert. Although they were well used to vultures and knew what they were likely to find, the sight unsettled them all and they fell silent as they trudged upwards through the sand. When they crested the top of the rise they saw that the tracks of one of the vehicles suddenly slewed and then ceased immediately, to be replaced by a series of irregular ruts and pits, the like of which they had not seen before. Kangao and the other members of the group followed the marks over the hill and down the steep slope towards the top edge of the dry river bed on the other side.

Khangdu was aware of the presence of the birds and was concerned as to what that might mean. They were situated just off to the left of the place where the vehicles' routes suddenly diverted off the track, less than forty or fifty metres away. She turned off into the undergrowth in the direction of the ominously populated trees. The vultures, became unsettled and bobbed their necks and flexed their wings in apparent warning and aggravation. As Khangdu pressed on, disregarding their malevolent glares, she saw that others were on the ground and were about to approach a small group of medium-sized boulders which she had not seen previously. As she moved forward silently they began to back away. Suddenly as one, in a great explosion of sound which shattered the still of the evening, they beat their wings and rose to the safety of the upper branches of the surrounding trees. Only then did Khangdu notice that, huddled in the centre of the group of rocks, was a human being. She approached, dreading that all that she might find would be a corpse with its eyes and organs pecked out. A moment later she reached the inert form, and as she stood over it, she inadvertently blocked out the thin light which the moon cast over the scene.

Rusty momentarily came to his senses. As soon as Khangdu saw that the stricken person below her was still alive she lifted her cloak which she had over her shoulder and which covered the length of her body. She then took out one of the three ostrich eggs in which she carried a supply of water. As soon as she had released the shell from the leather pouch she knelt down over the collapsed figure and eased the egg to his parched lips. She knew that patience would be required and at first just ensured that a small amount of the precious liquid entered his mouth. As he lay there slowly breathing but without showing any other signs of life she sat at his side passively. After a few minutes she became aware of the others approaching from the river bed. She heard them shouting loudly and saw they were throwing pebbles at the vultures. The birds at last relented and accepted that this was not to be their day. As one they flew away noisily to tree-top level.

Kangao and the others, like Khangdu, were quiet and cautious in the way that they approached when they realised what was happening. The younger members of the family stayed in the background as Kangao pressed her for information. She explained the injured man was alive but was in need of water. Kangao was reassured and immediately made the decision that they would camp there for the night so that they could care for the stranger. The younger people went off in search of suitable wood for the campfire, while Kangao set about the task of preparing the base of the fire. Khangdu continued to watch over Rusty and the others took out some pieces of meat which they had brought with them and were soon relaxing around the hearth after their lengthy walk. The others described the burnt-out vehicle that they had found less than a hundred metres away. Although it had been almost entirely gutted by the great fire they had seen that morning there had been no mistaking the remains of the ravaged body that was within it. As the others gradually drifted off to sleep, Kangao and Khangdu assessed the strange situation in which they now found themselves. They were not used to being responsible for people from outside their group. This sudden alteration in fortunes and reversal of roles unsettled them greatly. For the moment, however, they agreed that they would do all that they could to help the stranger to come to his senses and return to health. Kangao was particularly worried that the white man might die while in their care and that they might be found responsible for his death. He was relieved therefore when Khangdu stated firmly that she would watch over him for the night and that he should get some rest. Nursing a white man was not something that he particularly wished to add to his rich store of life experiences and he sat reflectively smoking for a while on the other side of the fire from her before falling asleep. Khangdu remained alert throughout the night and, every now and again, would release a few more droplets of cool water into her charge's partially open mouth. Rusty's condition changed little during the course of the night, breathing strongly in an apparently deep sleep. There were no clouds in the Kalahari night sky and the stars above shone down upon her. The Milky Way cut a giant swathe above her in the heavens. For some reason the sky was active that night and she gazed in awe as several spectacular shooting stars hurtled silently above.

* * * * *

At dawn, Rusty's condition was unchanged although his eyes had flickered open once or twice to stare at the young woman unseeingly. He did not appear to have worsened. Khangdu knew a little about healing but was unsure as to what was wrong with the man. If he had been suffering from simple dehydration the amount of water he had consumed during the night should have been sufficient to restore him to health. Yet he still lay in a coma in front of her. She began to examine the man carefully, checking for broken bones or signs of bruising and swelling. It was only when she carefully lifted his head and softly probed the back of his cranium with her sensitive fingers that she realised that the area at the back of his skull hidden by the thick mop of wavy brown hair was swollen. The man flinched sharply in his stupor. She had not seen many injuries like this but she knew of people who had suffered blows to the head when out hunting or falling from rocks. It seemed to her that if he was to have any chance of survival then it would be up to the elderly healer, Samgo, to perform his rituals. He would arrive with the others later in the morning. For the moment, Khangdu decided that she needed to replenish her supply of water so, leaving the patient in the care of one of the younger women, she left the camp.

Khangdu carried her three ostrich eggshells, as well as a long, thin, hollow stick about a yard in length. She used this for collecting water. She was aware of the proximity of the dry river bed and knew she might have to resort to finding water there if she was unable to locate another source. She would go to a low spot where the water had swirled and scoured out some of the sediment during the brief period that the river had flowed after the last downpour and firmly push her hollow stick down as far as it would go. If water was present within the range of the stick then she would be able to suck it up into her mouth, from where she would transfer it to the eggshells. This was a laborious and unreliable way of obtaining water, so for the moment she decided to hunt around the immediate vicinity in the hope of finding a tree which might be hollow at its core. When the rain came in the desert it would not fall for long but it would invariably be heavy. When that happened there was a strong possibility that it would collect in considerable quantities inside such trees, where it would remain until it evaporated in the heat. Sure enough, after scouting around in the scrub for few minutes, Khangdu found a small tree with a single trunk which grew to about shoulder height where it split into four separate slender branches. At the point where the branches divided there was a deep hollow spot within which there was a small reservoir of water. After a few minutes sucking through her sipping stick she filled all three eggshells and made her way back to the camp.

When she reached the camp she found that the others had already constructed a small hut. Khangdu put her eggshells inside to keep them cool and saw that the others had already collected a few tubers and melons. Khangdu went to see how the injured man was progressing and, finding him unchanged, she settled down in the sand and, not having rested at all the night before, fell asleep. She remained that way until just before noon, when the other dozen or so remaining members of the group arrived, quietly, in single file from the west. Everyone was pleased to see one another again but the new arrivals stood in respectful silence when they saw the sad prone figure of the white man. Khangdu was awakened by the increased activity in the camp and it was not long before she was in deep discussion with the senior members of the group. She explained to them and in particular to the medicine man that she had discovered the man was unhurt, apart from the deep swelling at the back of his head. They surmised that he had been thrown from the vehicle when it had hit the rocks and struck his head on landing. Samgo, the medicine man was the first to speak. Given his age and his success on many previous occasions in restoring sick people to health he was held in great esteem and his words were treated seriously. He concluded that in view of the swelling to the victim's head it was clear that a spirit of the dead had taken over the man's consciousness and was waiting to take him to meet his maker. Whilst the spirit prepared him for this journey to the afterlife he would remain asleep. Only if a healer acted promptly would there be any chance of wrestling with the spirit and restoring the man to health. He was certain that all his healing powers would be called upon and he would need to use his most powerful weapon, the healing dance. What concerned him however was that the victim was not one of them. He did not feel confident that he would be able to reach into the man's mind as easily as he could with someone that he knew well and this would reduce his chances of successfully destroying the spirit. He concluded by saying that he would make the attempt at healing that evening but felt there was every likelihood that he would fail. The healer had been placed in a very difficult situation as a result of this incident. From his great experience of dealing with sickness and injury he knew that damage such as this was almost always fatal. He was aware, however, that in order to maintain his status within the group he would have to make an attempt to cure the man. He had mentioned the fact that the victim was an outsider in order to prepare them all for what he inwardly conceded was likely to be an unsuccessful outcome. He was also clever enough to realise that if he saved this white man his position would be greatly enhanced not only within this small band but with others throughout the region.

Toma had much to say during this debate. He knew it was their duty to report this accident as soon as possible. Despite his inner fears that they would be questioned at length about their part in the whole incident he believed that someone should leave the camp and report what they had found. He agreed reluctantly that it should be he who would go. He insisted that a couple of the others should join him to provide moral support. They had met others earlier in the year who had told them that the government had established a small settlement to the north-west on the edge of a pan at a spot next to the large fence which ringed Khutse Game Reserve. It was about a day's hard trek for fit, young individuals and they decided to go immediately. This would mean that they would be fresh the following day and would be able to divide the long march into two separate legs. They were hopeful that they would return with assistance in the splendid comfort of a government Land Cruiser or heavy truck. As soon as they had collected water and provisions the three of them moved off at a swift pace in a north-westerly direction.

* * * * *

There was a hybrid community of Batswana, bushmen and some of mixed-race living in a series of impoverished villages clustered around the south-western corner of Khutse Game Reserve. They made their living from tending a few goats and sheep and precious little else. Their lives were very tough in this extremely marginal environment and sickness, drought and famine were endemic. The new settlement had been placed where a number of tracks met the fence at the south-western corner of the game reserve. A compound had been created within which a small cluster of rudimentary tin-roofed mud brick huts had been erected. Electricity was a far-off dream but the centre piece was a new borehole operated by a diesel pump. It was hoped that the existence of a reliable supply of water would make the area less vulnerable and it might even be secure enough for the locals to bring in the more water-dependent cattle which would make them better off and less dependent on government support. In the long term villages like this one would solve the problems of the rural dwellers and at the same time save the government revenue. It was a long way yet from achieving that lofty ambition. Several staff were required to run the village not least to keep the pump operating. A trained mechanic was needed and diesel had to be hauled by heavy Toyota truck from the depot on the tarred road to the south every other week. It was this delivery which provided the main link with the outside world. As a result of the presence of this lifeline, one enterprising Motswana had brought in a few items of tinned and packaged goods and now successfully managed a tiny shop. The few locals who had any money could now get hold of maize meal, corned beef, beans and perhaps incongruously, so far from the sea, tins of sardines. These were considered to be a particularly up-market luxury and were priced accordingly. The shop owner had thought about

101

bringing in beer and other cheap alcohol but this plan had been well and truly quashed by the District Commissioner who was well aware of the problems that could be created by the heady mixture of heat, unemployment and brandy. As well as the pump house and the shop there were also plans to open a school. The ambition was that education would greatly assist the younger people to escape the poverty trap that had for so long been a part of their upbringing. Foundations for a new primary school had been laid and it would open the following year if the builders kept to schedule. It was not easy to monitor progress this far out in the desert and there were many occasions when the project had been hampered by the total lack of materials. When the village had been planned there had been much discussion as to which should be constructed first, the school or the clinic. There was so much poverty and malnutrition that everyone was liable to be laid low by the simplest of viruses. These often spread dramatically through the close-knit communities and the mortality rate was high. Away from the remote areas Botswana had a creditable track record in the provision of medical treatment for all its people and was one of the few countries in Africa where there was an efficiently run health service available to all in the major villages. After much consideration, the organising committee – back at the Ministry of the Interior in the capital city – decided that the clinic would be built first. As a direct result of that decision as well as the solid building in which the diesel pump chugged away steadily during the hours of daylight the other substantial building so far built inside the perimeter of the compound housed the clinic. Like the pump this was already in operation and as the sun grew high in the sky over the desert that summer day a long, haphazard line of people had formed under the veranda. No one was seriously ill that day. There were several children with ear infections which required treatment with antibiotics, mothers with newly-born children and an elderly man with an undiagnosed disease. Inside the nurse was going about her daily routine. It was to this clinic that Toma and his friends were inexorably making their way. Without their efforts Rusty would die that day. Without the presence of the clinic their efforts on his behalf would have been futile. The clinic was a simple two-roomed affair set under a well-constructed insulated tin roof in front of which was a spacious veranda area where several long benches were laid out in the shade. Built from materials brought in from Gaborone, the walls – painted in a clean, cream colour – were neat and well-laid. The external doors and windows were made from strong steel strips and tin sheeting which unlike wood would resist the rampaging termites. They had been painted in the pale blue that was the main colour of Botswana's national flag.

Just inside the main gate at the front of the compound a sturdy flagpole had been constructed. The intention was that as this was the most important building at the new settlement the flag should be run up on a daily basis and proudly displayed. The left-hand room served as the store. The medical supplies were placed in neat racks of tin shelving down each wall and in the back of the room in the deepest shade a large fridge stored additional medicines. The right-hand room was the consulting room – equipped with a simple desk, a couple of chairs and a high couch – where the nurse met her patients in private.

As the morning progressed, Polinah Mabina worked with her customary efficiency and cheerfulness. The patients waited outside the consulting room on the wooden benches under the veranda. Even those who were not ill would stop to enjoy the relative coolness afforded by the shade and pass the time of day with their friends. Polinah was twenty-eight years old and this was her first posting since graduating as a registered nurse. During her childhood and adolescence in Mochudi it had always been her ambition to work as a nurse and she had worked hard, first at Isang primary school and afterwards at Linchwe II junior secondary. Few of her compatriots had been trained in the medical profession and she was determined that she would be one of the first. During the long years of study as a junior nurse at the Princess Marina Teaching Hospital in Gaborone she had less opportunity for sporting activities than when at school, but despite this she maintained her fitness and had developed into an attractive and enthusiastic young Motswana.

Although Polinah was genuinely unaware of it, thinking only of herself as young and healthy it was not just her attractive frame that was to her advantage. She also had a beautiful face. It was rounded, with perfectly flawless light brown skin, a small nose and with a sensuous mouth and large brown eyes. Perhaps however its most important feature was the big broad smile that always seemed to be there when she greeted people. Certainly there had been many a young doctor who had been crestfallen when his advances had been met with her standard rebuff. Polinah's graduation had coincided with the decision to create new clinics in the remote regions of the country. She had immediately signed up for the Remote Areas Programme when the initiative had been explained to them by a representative from the Ministry of Health at a long afternoon seminar the year before. When the time came there was little surprise when a candidate of her obvious calibre was selected to participate in running the Khutse Clinic. She had been in post for six months but already she felt confident that she could deal with the workload and the problems which the desert people brought to her. She found the administration a burden but accepted that it was part of the job. What she enjoyed was her contact with the patients. She found that she could deal with all of the varied people, whatever their background, who came to the clinic and was beginning to realise that they had accepted her. An odd situation had begun to develop over the last month or so, in that the health of the locals would apparently deteriorate when Polinah was running the clinic. Because of the remoteness of the posting it had been agreed that two nurses would share the load, working alternately on site for four week periods. During the four weeks layover in Gaborone each of them was expected to report back to a committee about the general progress of the project, undertake further study at the hospital and then have a couple of weeks leave. It had become evident that the clinic was vastly busier when Polinah was in charge, despite the fact that she was the more junior of the two nurses. It was not that the other woman was not good at her job or that people were more ill when Polinah was there, it was just that her colleague did not have her rapport and people simply stayed away. Some no doubt just let their illnesses fester, whilst others took their chances with the traditional healers, both Batswana and Bushmen. There was no doubt that Polinah was a gifted person and in the years to come had the ability to develop into an extremely able and dedicated nurse.

* * * * *

Kurt Viljoen's path had crossed that of Polinah's twenty-four hours earlier. As soon as he had brought the Kalahari Ferrari and its driver to a very effective journey's end he had headed away from the inferno in a north-westerly direction. He knew that in order not to become hopelessly lost it was imperative to locate the southern perimeter of Khutse Game Reserve with its strong chain link fence and external track. From where he had left the burning shell of the Land Rover, the tracks that led to the reserve were notoriously unreliable. They were rarely used by motor vehicles but were constantly crossed by herds of migrating animals. Because of this they tended to weave about and split into several smaller branches only to join up again subsequently. Without his GPS he would have found it difficult to navigate this hostile terrain alone. He hit the fence that delineated the game reserve at a spot less than a kilometre east of where it turned to the north. Realising where he was, and satisfied with himself for having negotiated his way through an area where he might easily have become lost, he pulled over for a cold beer and a simple snack.

Once refreshed Kurt hopped up on to the roof of the Pajero and looked in all directions but could see no sign of life other than a solitary secretary bird which was feeding on the edge of a small pan. Little did he know that he was within a kilometre of a small settlement which would register his appearance. Despite the thoroughness of his preparatory work, circumstances had overtaken him. As he reached the south-western corner of the game reserve he slowed down in order to negotiate the ninety degree bend in the track as it turned to the north. Ahead of him he expected a featureless drag alongside the fence. At first he would have to track to the north until he reached the southern perimeter of the Central Kalahari Game Reserve. After that he would continue to follow the fence, at first to the west and then once again to the north until he reached Deception Valley. In all, a mind numbing three hundred kilometres. At the point where the track turned to the north the tree cover was relatively thick and the land also undulated slightly. Kurt found that the track right in front of him was straddled by a substantial metal gate, beyond which was a medium-sized compound and a number of recently erected buildings. According to his research this area of the desert should have been devoid of anything other than a few huts which would have been easy for him to bypass should he have felt it necessary. What he was looking at was a fairly substantial settlement. Indeed the light blue and cream paint that was evident everywhere was a clear indicator that the government were involved somewhere along the line. As he lurched to a standstill he panicked briefly, fearing that he might have stumbled upon a military encampment. Initially he thought about reversing and trying to find a way around the fenced area unnoticed, until he suddenly became aware of a small hut to the left of the gate from which a wizened and dishevelled old Motswana emerged and who had already fixed him with a beady stare. Kurt decided that to turn tail and head off into the bush would be suspicious so he decided to face up to this unexpected turn of events.

* * * * *

Rapula Matshome was seventy-two years old but, despite his age, was exceedingly glad that he had this job and was quietly very good at it. All government compounds experienced problems with loss of materials, especially during the construction phase. After a long day hauling building supplies across the desert many a driver would simply off-load and head back to civilisation without making sure that the consignment had been received by the appropriate person. The locals had grown wise to the inefficiency of the system and many essential items ended up refurbishing distant cattle posts rather than ensuring that the project was completed on time. An enterprising official in Gaborone had effectively put an end to this practice by ensuring that a gateman should be appointed at all such institutions whose responsibilities were to check all incoming and departing vehicles, to see that the documentation was in order and that the goods had been delivered to the correct department or member of staff. When recruitment took place for the new settlement at Khutse it proved difficult to find anyone with the appropriate credentials and experience who was prepared to do a mundane job at such a remote location. Rapula was local, however, having been born only a few kilometres away at an out of the way cattle post to which he had returned on retirement to see out his days. He had spent the bulk of his working life on the gate of a busy depot of the Ministry of Home Affairs in Gaborone West and when a friend had told him they were recruiting for the new settlement he immediately volunteered his services. No one else applied for the post he had been appointed to and, despite his age, he had been at the gate since the day when the first fence posts had been inserted into the ground. The task was well-suited to an alert older man, who would not grow impatient and who would adapt to the periods of stultifying inactivity. By nature Rapula was a taciturn man but he had the eyes of a hawk and he was certain that if there was any pilfering from this compound it was not going to leave through his gate.

* * * * *

Ra Matshome plodded out in the direction of the gate in response to the sound of Kurt's Pajero. As for Kurt, he was less then impressed with this shuffling old black man and as Rapula reached the gate, and realising that he was not in the presence of the military, he wound down his window and let rip.

'Come on, you old fool, hurry up, I don't have all day to sit here while you wake yourself up. Get this damn gate open.'

It would have been prudent for Kurt to have ignored the instincts of his Rhodesian upbringing and been more courteous to the elderly Motswana. The Batswana as a people had never accepted the yoke of the British Colonial powers and an older man such as Rapula was only prepared to accept such treatment when working in the mines in South Africa. It made his blood boil to have to listen to such verbal abuse on home soil and he reacted accordingly. He took his own time to reach the gate and open it. As he did so Kurt once again spoke.

'I'm heading north up the west side of the reserve and I was not expecting to come across this dump. Which way do I head to get back on the track?'

Rapula took a moment or two to reply. Scratching his scalp through his beret, he readjusted his leather belt which was beginning to chafe his scrawny midriff.

'You just go straight through the compound sir, to the left of the clinic and pass the staff houses behind. You will find the gate beyond them.'

Rapula had swung the gate open to a sufficient width for Kurt to pass through. He was just about to gun the motor when the gateman added.

'Of course, it's locked, is that one. We don't get much through traffic. If you just park up in front I'll follow with the key. The keys are kept in the office. I'll have to go there and sign for it. Shouldn't take more than a minute or two though if the secretary is at her desk.'

Kurt gave the little man a withering look but was now regretting his earlier outburst. He had been brought up in a community of two races and had much experience of working with the black labourers on his father's farm. He knew of old that a sharp tongue would not be met head on but would be dealt with in more subtle but, nonetheless, devastating ways. It was with a heavy heart that Kurt engaged first gear and quietly drove the large truck across the sandy compound in the direction the old man had indicated. Sure enough as he looked in his wing mirrors he could see that the recalcitrant man was dawdling as he closed the gate and had even taken the opportunity to urinate through the chain link fence. As Kurt reached the other gate he could see that it was secured with a large padlock and sturdy chain. He could also see in his mirrors that Rapula was heading off slowly towards a featureless hut in the middle of the compound. Kurt knew that there was no point in creating any further fuss and waited silently in his comfortable vehicle. As he did so he idly gazed to his right where behind the clinic he could see two simple huts providing staff accommodation. At the rear of one and in the direct glare of the sunshine some enterprising individual had planted a row of tomato plants. Kurt had already registered this incongruous spectacle when he saw Rapula heading his way across the central part of the compound with a large keyring in his hand.

'I am so sorry, sir, but I will try not to hold you up too much longer,' the old man said as he drew level. 'There are so many things to keep safe and we have so many keys. It will only take a minute or so to find the right one.'

With that the old man proceeded to laboriously make his way through the keyring. As Kurt watched him he was going about it in a thoroughly unsystematic manner, not bothering to go round the ring in order, simply selecting a key at random. Suddenly the padlock snapped apart and the gate swung open so that he could pass through. Kurt decided to show his good side and rather than race immediately away he wound down his window and thanked the gateman profusely. Rapula was not greatly impressed with this display of appreciation and spat noisily in the dirt. Kurt breathed a sigh of relief, and, as he engaged the engine, his attention was drawn to where a young Motswana woman now stood with her back to him, removing clothing from a washing line. As she stood there the bright sun shone through her dress and he caught a brief, breathtaking glimpse of her slender figure. The young woman turned and, as she placed the garments over her arm, caught his eye and smiled.

Back in his hut Rapula took his clipboard down from the hook on the wall where he kept it and started to write down the registration and details of the vehicle. It was only as he started to fill in the register that he realised that it was not his duty to record the passing tourers. Only a tally of official vehicles and those which delivered supplies was required. He thought about tearing out the page with the entry that he had just started but then decided to simply score a line through what he had just written with his pencil. Without further ado he put the clipboard back on its hook where it swung aimlessly for a few seconds. Over in the far corner of the hut Rapula made himself as comfortable as he possibly could on his canvas cot and, before long, was fast asleep.

* * * * *

All was peaceful and still at the settlement. The sun was high in the sky and most people had sought the sanctuary of shade. Polinah sat in her living room reading a medical textbook. For a moment or two she wondered about the solitary traveller who had passed through. Such visitors were rare and she was curious. She had felt very uncomfortable when he had looked at her and she hoped he would not travel through the village again.

Kurt tracked remorselessly onwards, following the perimeter fence along the sandy track. There were few potholes and it was firm and smooth to drive on. He changed up into fourth gear and kept up a steady fifty kilometres an hour. He hoped that, after a good layover in some out of the way spot, he would reach Deception Valley within twenty-four hours. He was still uncertain about the nature and strength of those who might be pursuing him, but the fact that all he had seen so far was the old-fashioned Land Rover left him strangely relieved. He was reassured that there had been no official presence at the small settlement through which he had passed. He now began to think ahead and he believed for the first time that he would be able to merge in with the many other touring off-roaders that were such a feature of the northern part of Botswana. As every kilometre slid by he was confident that he would be able to reach the unmanned border crossing at Pandamatenga. He had not yet decided which road he would then take but the most sensible option was to go through the Okavango Delta and the Moremi and Chobe Game Reserves.

* * * * *

Samgo, the medicine man, spent the day preparing himself for the ordeal to come over the coming evening and night. He sent his two sons off into the bush to collect enough firewood to ensure that two fires could be kept blazing through what would be a long night. One fire was for the group to sit round, the other would be set aside for his purposes. Throughout the afternoon, Khangdu continued to care for the young white man. He would take water and occasionally his eyes would flicker but his condition remained unchanged. Samgo checked on him from time to time. He had an extensive knowledge of the plants that grew in the southern part of the Kalahari and often used their healing properties. He would have to call upon his innermost powers to drive away the unwanted spirit. In essence he perceived it as a contest of wills between himself and the unseen being and genuinely believed he had the power to be victorious. He ate the last of the meat in mid-afternoon and then appeared to doze under the shade of a nearby tree. In reality he was preparing himself mentally by using a form of meditation which he had developed and practised regularly.

As the afternoon turned into early evening the tension could be felt and the women sitting around the smaller fire began to chant quietly and methodically. As the healer meditated, his two sons prepared their father by winding his dance rattles around his lower legs and ankles. As darkness descended on the small encampment the women sang loudly and with more insistence. As if signalled by this increase in the noise and the tempo of the music, Samgo suddenly burst into life, leaping forward and swaying his body in front of the fire which had been left for him.

Dressed only in a small loincloth and his ankle rattles he cut an imposing and mysterious figure as the firelight flickered across his light brown skin. In his right hand he held an implement which could only be described as a fly whisk. It was about eighteen inches long and was made out of the tale of a wildebeest attached to a short decorated wooden handle. At first his demeanour was relaxed and he undulated his body from side to side in a series of sweeping movements without moving from the spot at which he was standing. As he did so the rattles chattered in unison at his feet and he beat out the rhythm by swishing the fly whisk backwards and forwards across his body. After some time the darkness deepened and the nature of the performance became more animated. The women now sang more loudly and the others clapped their hands together to create a hypnotic beat. Samgo gradually increased the pace of his dance and his body movement changed from rhythmic swaying to a motion which matched the more insistent beat. He began to stamp both his feet into the ground together, at the same time bending forward at the hips and shaking his outstretched arms at right angles to the line of his body. While he did this the beat built up to a loud enthralling crescendo. At the peak of the sound, Samgo fell to the ground at Rusty's head and pressed his hands onto his body, even occasionally his head. As he was doing this he moaned quietly and swayed in time to the now softly chanting women. After a few minutes massaging the prone form of the sick man he leapt to his feet and continued the insistent dance. As soon as he returned to the glowing fire he proceeded to dance more energetically than before. Still with his arms akimbo and with his body bent at the waist he began to encircle the fire with a series of powerful alternating movements. First of all he moved around it a number of times by swiftly pounding forwards with both feet moving together, only to quickly follow this with a series of steps in which his left leg was held straight beneath him and supported him whilst he thumped the ground with his right foot at an unbelievable speed. As soon as those watching his dance became accustomed to him moving in this way he would swap so that it was his right foot which appeared stationary whilst his left now pounded the ground. After continuing in this way for several frenetic minutes he repeated the whole process so that the circles that he drew around the fire were now in the opposite direction to those that he had just completed. The firelight lit up his sweating body and the concentration on his face. Whilst Samgo was pounding the sand in this way the scene gradually became all the more theatrical as a fierce storm built up in the distance. A couple of kilometres away heavy rain was falling from a huge bank of leaden clouds which blotted out the moon and the stars. In addition to the sheer weight of rain, huge quantities of electrical energy were being transferred from sky to ground and at the same time from cloud to cloud. This natural virtuoso performance created two very different effects. As the energy discharged into the ground strikingly powerful bolts of forked lightning lit up the night sky for what seemed like several seconds. When that happened the small encampment was illuminated with a harsh glare. Sometimes these bolts came in quick succession and Samgo seemed to be leaping disjointedly from spot to spot as if by magic, such was the intensity of the darkness between the bolts. The desert downpour was so close to where this scene was being enacted that the dramatic thunderclaps which were a by product of the lightning appeared to come at virtually the same instant as the tremendous displays of light. As Samgo danced, nature appeared to offer him an orchestrated sound and light show of magnificent proportions and he reacted accordingly, shaking and jerking his body in a performance which was beyond even his wildest dreams. As the thunder and lightning rolled across the heavens he fell deeply into a trance and was truly on a different plain from those who were observing his dramatic movements. Time and time again when the crashing sounds from the skies seemed to reach a peak he would throw himself to the ground at Rusty's side and press his hands onto his body, at the same time wailing and shrieking loudly. The sounds he made were often lost as another almighty thunderclap beat down upon him. There were periods when the heavens appeared to tire of this awesome display but even then they offered a still magnificent backdrop as electrical energy was passed from cloud to cloud without coming to ground. When this happened the effect was different but still spectacular. The relative energy level between two clouds was less than from cloud to ground and therefore, instead of producing powerful forked lightning and thunder, the display was more muted. Energy passed across the heavens largely without sound and far less brightly. Each of the large energy laden clouds would spasmodically light up and glimmer and flicker internally for several minutes before gradually fading, only then to be superseded by their neighbour. This mesmerising display was repeated in steady succession across the sky from west to east and then back again repeatedly. Occasionally there would be sufficient discharge of energy for thunder to be generated and then this would manifest itself as a long low rumble which might go on for what seemed like a minute or two. The whole effect was more spectacular than the powerful and immediate show which was generated by the forked lightning. The low energy light produced by the sheet lightning was however plenty enough to give Samgo the opportunity to exhibit his skills under the backdrop of spectacular lighting effects and as the night lengthened he continued to gyrate and pound his way around the fire which his sons kept glowing for him. As he did this his pounding feet eventually beat a perfectly circular track in the sand. When his dancing was at its most energetic his lower body was often entirely hidden to those watching by the dust which his momentum had caused to be thrown up into the agitated air. It was perhaps no coincidence that Samgo exhausted himself at about the same time that the storm faded out and as the blackness of the night began to be replaced by the first glimmerings of dawn over the eastern horizon he threw himself to the ground for the last time. On this occasion his trance was replaced by fatigue brought on by physical exhaustion and he fell into a deep sleep. It remained to be seen if his efforts had driven the spirit from Rusty's damaged body and if a recovery would be observed at daybreak.

* * * * *

When the sun began to rise it was Khangdu who was the first to wake and check on the condition of the invalid. She walked quietly and calmly over to him. As she approached she could see there was no change. He lay in the same position and his breathing had the same steady metronomic quality of someone in profound sleep. She was sad for the man and for Samgo who had never before put so much vitality into the healing dance. She knew he would feel that his failure had let everyone down and would reflect on the whole group. Khangdu did all that she could for her patient, and found he was still prepared to take water. At least, she reflected to herself, his condition was not worsening. As the morning drew on others woke and approached her with queries as to the patient's condition. On being told that there was little change they all sat around the camp fire in a sad and sombre mood. Only Samgo slumbered on, still fast asleep in his exhaustion, as yet still blissfully unaware that his rigours of the night before had proved utterly fruitless. It remained unspoken but it was now known that if help did not come soon from the government settlement then all would be lost.

* * * * *

Later that morning Polinah's clinic was as busy as ever. She had several young mothers in the consulting room and was endeavouring to explain the benefits of breastfeeding their small babies. They had all enjoyed the occasional handouts of powdered milk which sometimes reached this distant outpost. Malnutrition was not uncommon at this remote spot and the milk was a vital supplement. The women were ill-prepared to receive the news that in future the milk ration would only be handed out under carefully monitored conditions and only to those who, due to malnourishment, were unable to breast feed. It took all of Polinah's gentle powers of persuasion but she felt she was beginning to succeed. As she chatted amiably to the women she noticed that some of them were looking carefully at the colourful posters that she had recently put up. These attempted to explain using pictures rather than words the benefits of a good balanced diet. She realised they would have a limited effect but at least it was a start. The women weighed their babies under the watchful guidance of two young assistants while Polinah began to plan her campaign to tackle the problem of Aids which was as much a problem in the desert as it was elsewhere in the country. The neighbouring communities were notoriously casual in their relationships and swapped partners frequently. As a result, sexually transmitted diseases were extremely common. Polinah smiled ruefully as she recalled the embarrassed glances and laughter that she had received when she had tried to hand out condoms during her last get together with the young mothers. As each child was weighed and its examination was completed each was given a string of beads that was firmly attached around its waist so that the mother could just get a couple of fingers inside them. The mother was then advised that if the beads should become loose then it was important that she should return to the clinic immediately. When they became tight then it would also be time to come back and have the beads changed. Polinah found that this strategy worked very well with these illiterate people and her careful records showed that the number of mothers who failed to return for successive visits was beginning to diminish. As she hustled the happy throng out of the consulting room so she could begin to tend to the short line of sick and injured who were waiting patiently under the veranda she noticed Rapula bustling towards her from the main gate.

Two large Toyota lorries had shown up in quick succession with building materials for the school and it had been his duty to check the contents of each against the inventory. One of the lorries had already left and he had checked to see if it was empty. The other truck had had to wait until the labourers had unloaded the first and its driver had decided that he would join the others for lunch before making the long journey back to Gaborone. He was currently resting in the shade of his cab while two of the female labourers prepared lunch in a large cast iron pot under the shade of a tree on one side of the compound. One was chopping cabbage to make coleslaw whilst the other was laboriously stirring maize porridge.

Rapula was making his way towards Polinah's clinic because he had just had visitors at his hut. Shortly after the first truck had departed and he was once again relaxing inside he heard the main gate swing open and realised that there were a number of individuals hovering uncertainly at his door. When he had taken the trouble to go out and find out what it was all about he had been unnerved by the presence of three young bushmen who he did not recognise from the settlement. Rapula did not react well to his rest period being interrupted. As soon as he saw the trio he tried to chase them away from the compound. Toma was well used to being treated this way by many Batswana and he was particularly determined after his long trek that his journey should not be in vain. He immediately recognised what he knew to be a clinic when he came through the gate and so, despite the fact that Rapula did not speak his language and his own command of Setswana, although good, was heavily accented, he pressed on and insisted that he wanted to speak to a doctor. After protesting for some time that there was no doctor at the settlement, Rapula accepted that the young men with their stubborn leader would not leave and decided to go and speak to the nurse about them. Rapula did not want these light-fingered bushmen wandering around the compound while he was away from his post so he told them to go back outside the gate whilst he went to speak to the nurse. He asked one of the labourers to keep an eye on them while he did so. So it was that Toma and his two young friends waited patiently by the gate in the heat of the day whilst the Motswana gateman headed off towards the cluster of buildings in the centre of the compound. When he got there he politely addressed Polinah, whom he admired for the efficient way in which she conducted herself despite her tender years. As Polinah came to her door in response to his arrival Rapula spoke.

'Sister, there are three Bushmen at the gate who are talking a lot of nonsense about needing to see a doctor. I have told them we have no doctor here but they are persistent and will not go away. Shall I chase them away or will you talk to them?'

Polinah listened patiently to this outburst from the normally reticent gateman. She liked him but regretted his old-fashioned attitude towards the Bushmen and decided to reply forthrightly.

'Ra Matshome, I have told you before that those people are as entitled as you and I to use this clinic. You should not keep them waiting at the gate. It is because of them that this village was built in the first place and because of them that you have this nice job which gives you so much good money in your old age. Bring them to me at once.'

Rapula knew the young woman was soft-hearted towards the bushmen and wanted to chastise her for her foolish views. Instead he decided to hold his tongue and took a different tack.

'Sister, I am responsible for looking after the compound. If we let them in then I am sure that they will soon start stealing things if we do not watch them carefully. One of them seems to be in charge. I will bring him to you and keep my eye on the other two.'

'Yes Rapula,' replied Polinah. 'I will speak to him and find out what the problem is.'

Polinah was intrigued by this turn of events. To date the clinic had been used exclusively by the local Batswana and some of the bushmen communities living a sedentary lifestyle in the immediate vicinity. This was the first time that any of the small bands who she knew to be in the desert had come to the compound and she was fascinated to know what it was that had brought them to her. As she watched the man cross the compound she looked at his traditional leather cloak and loin cloth. He had a bow slung across his shoulder and carried a quiver of small arrows. She waved Rapula away and led the newcomer into her consulting room where she offered him water which he took gratefully. She could not speak his tongue and upon greeting him was relieved to ascertain how well he spoke Setswana. After allowing him a moment or so to enjoy the cool water she asked him what she could do for him. The story which he blurted out took her by surprise. She had expected that one of their elders had become ill beyond the skills of their own healer or that a woman was having difficulty giving birth. These were the sorts of problems for which she felt that she had been sent to this out of the way place to help with. She wanted to help the poor desert dwellers. If she had wanted to assist the rich white men who criss-crossed the desert in their powerful vehicles then she could easily have taken a well paid position at the new private hospital in Gaborone. This she had not done and now one such man of that type had found his way to her doorstep and got himself into difficulties this far out in the desert. At first she wondered if the accident victim was the same sharp-eyed young man who had passed through the day before, but after quizzing the bushman further she realised the injured man was somewhere to the south. She could not work out from the basic description of the symptoms what the accident victim was suffering from, but the fact that he had been unconscious for some time set alarm bells ringing in her head. She had been told that the injured party was being cared for more than a day's walk away. A vehicle had not been assigned to the project, as the intention behind the clinic was that it would become a magnet for the surrounding people and that they should find their way to it. Still, as luck would have it this day there might be something that she could do. As she looked out of the window she saw the driver dozing happily in the shade. Despite the fact that her brief was to care for the rural dwellers she had sworn an oath to care for all and decided that she would take this one chance to try and save the life of this luckless traveller. Leaving the young bushman with a long cool glass of water from the refrigerator she stepped outside into the bright sunshine to have a word with the resting driver.

* * * * *

As Polinah approached, the driver was suddenly alert and all eyes. It was unusual for the nurses at these out of the way places to fraternise with the drivers. When sent to places such as this the nurses were specifically warned to be careful of involvement and relationships. A one-night stand with a passing driver might not be too damaging but there was many a project that had been destroyed because two members of staff had a fling and could not get on with one another afterwards. The advice from the authorities was to be safe rather than sorry. Polinah had taken this instruction to heart. The driver was therefore extremely surprised as Polinah approached but was inwardly very appreciative of her as she moved towards him.

'I am sorry, Ra, but we have not met before and I do not know your name. I am Nurse Polinah Mabina and I have something to ask of you.'

'I am Victor Moroka. I can assure you, sister, that I will do whatever I can to assist you,' he replied swiftly.

'We have been told of an accident twenty or thirty kilometres from here. Someone has been seriously injured. Normally we would not be able to help in such a situation since we have no truck but as you are here, maybe it would be possible to go and see if we can assist.'

'I am supposed to return to Gabs tonight. If I stay I will not be able to get back and I have no facilities for sleeping in the desert.'

'I'm sure we can make a bed up here for you for the night and I will give you a note to take back with you so that you do not get into trouble back at the Ministry. I will take full responsibility for delaying you.'

Polinah was not at all certain that she had such authority but she was learning that there was no one else around to take such decisions and she was finding that she had quite a liking for making such judgements.

The driver immediately concurred that if that was the case then he would be happy to assist, as soon as he had eaten his lunch.

Polinah was about to argue that they should go instantly but then realised that she had no idea what to take with her and it would take a while to get a mobile medical emergency kit organised. So, she left the driver to his lunch and headed back to the clinic. Victor had a double motivation for staying. He would take the opportunity of the enforced stopover to try and push his luck with the gorgeous nurse. He had not had much success with nurses in the past, but who knows . . . he thought to himself. On top of that, although he had not told her, he would receive an overnight allowance of fifty pula for being away from home for the night and that would enhance his low salary quite dramatically. Although he was not going to admit it to anyone he would be content to stay at the settlement for several nights if he could get the opportunity. Financial and other possible rewards, he mused, were very attractive indeed.

* * * * *

Shortly afterwards, the driver – fortified with maize porridge and sugary tea – and Polinah, with her medical bag, lumbered over to the main gate in the big truck where Toma and his two friends were waiting patiently. The two younger men had never travelled in one of these large open lorries before and were more than happy to hop aboard the rear open flat bed from where they could survey the scenery and enjoy the ride. Toma was ordered to travel in the cab with Polinah and the driver. The driver was crestfallen when Polinah insisted that the Bushman should sit in the middle of the seat. She said it was so that he could best direct Victor as to the best route. Polinah had journeyed in such vehicles before and was only too aware of how a driver's hands could wander in search of the gear shift. She was crushed between the window and the little bushman, but was perfectly confident that she had nothing to fear from this earnest man. As soon as they cleared the gate and Rapula closed it behind them, Toma directed them to the track on the left. Once they had negotiated the tight bend at the corner of the game reserve he pointed them to a track which took them off in a south-easterly direction. Polinah had never been out this way before and soon started to enjoy the ride. When she travelled to and from Gaborone they normally used a better route which took them further to the west before joining the main east-west desert highway to the south. She found the truck's height gave a breathtaking panoramic view of the desert all about her which she was not accustomed to seeing. There had been sporadic thunderstorms and downpours in several locations in the vicinity in recent weeks and as they passed through she saw that everything was in bloom: the desert grass stood tall and green, upward of a metre in height. Once or twice a duiker would dart across their path or she would see a lone jackal in the distance. Other than that the desert appeared beautiful but empty. Although the landscape was lush it was also apparently featureless and Polinah had no idea how the Bushmen were able to navigate their way through the unchanging scenery with such certainty. Whenever they came to a place where there was a choice of tracks Toma would move one of his hands this way or that. They came to a spot where the rough track forked into two and he elected to take the track to the left but as soon as they went that way there was a hullabaloo from the back of the truck, quickly followed by a series of sharp thuds on the roof of the cab. Victor instantly pulled over and they clambered out to see what was going on.

When Polinah alighted from the truck she was astonished to see that the two younger bushmen had mounted the anti-roll bar which went over the top of the driver's cab and were enjoying the view from that slightly dangerous vantage point. They were totally unaware of the potential danger of their position and were adamant that Toma had taken the wrong track. There followed a lengthy discussion in the soft clicking sound which was their language. The two younger men were so strongly in agreement that Toma was forced to concede he had made an error and shortly afterwards they were all aboard once again and Victor was reversing the truck back down the track to the junction where they now took the other fork. After several minutes looking rather apprehensive Toma suddenly saw something which convinced him that he had been in error and he visibly relaxed and nodded to the driver that all was well. After a lengthy period of driving through the unchanging landscape which the bushmen navigated without further mishap, a low ridge appeared over the horizon which Toma pointed to animatedly.

* * * * *

As the afternoon drew into early evening Khangdu became less optimistic about her patient's recovery. There was no single symptom to explain her concerns but it was obvious the man's health was declining. The bruising at the base of the back of his head had not receded. If anything it was a little more accentuated and if touched the patient would flinch sharply. His breathing had became shallower. Khangdu gave him water every few minutes but other than quietly massaging his forehead and crooning to him as a mother would to a sick child, she was lost for anything positive that she could do. The older people sat around the fire chatting quietly and smoking and even the youngsters, normally so exuberant, were affected by the distress of the others and were all huddled together playing a game of counters in the sand. The sun slid westward and as the afternoon began to cool the gloomy atmosphere was deepening. Suddenly Guikwa, a young boy of four who was known to have excellent hearing stood bolt upright and looked to the north. He could not say what it was but it was clear from his reaction that something was out that way. He did not speak but the others became aware that his reaction was an early indication of the fact that something was approaching their camp. Koto was particularly concerned that Toma should return that afternoon and was immediately alert when he saw the young boy turn his head to the north. Sure enough, after less than a minute or two, Koto picked up the sound of a heavy truck, which he was sure could only mean that his brother had been successful and was returning with assistance. As soon as he was absolutely certain that what he was hearing was a truck, he darted to where Khangdu was leaning over her charge. Koto could see that the patient was by now very weak.

* * * * *

Polinah could see that the bushman was indicating that the low ridge was the place that they should head for, but even from her high vantage point she could not see anything other than the waving grasses and the slight rise in the ground. Both she and Victor remained alert as they approached. The track offered them no choices and as their guide was happy that they were on the right course they continued. When they were within a hundred metres of the beginning of the low ridge it became evident that there was a dry river bed running in front of them at a tangent to the direction in which they were travelling. Just when Polinah was becoming concerned that they might have to negotiate this awkward obstruction with the heavy lorry she saw a wisp of smoke from amongst a tree covered and rock strewn glade on this side of the river bed. She was immediately reassured that they would not have to cross this obstacle and perhaps, more importantly, that they were not on a wild goose chase. Victor slowed down as Toma pointed out a gap in the grass and scrub cover through which they could pass. They saw the encampment in front of them. By now the group had constructed several huts in a rough circle at the centre of which a fire was smouldering. Polinah saw children running towards them and beyond she could see others had become aware of their arrival. Victor parked just clear of the edge of the sandy area. As soon as the truck came to a stop there was pandemonium. The two young men jumped down and started shouting and swaggering around. They felt their station in life had been much improved by their role in this affair and by their chauffeur driven trip through the desert. Victor was slightly nervous at finding himself in the unaccustomed surroundings of the primitive camp and elected to stay with his truck. Polinah climbed down with her medical bag. Toma – who was looking suitably pleased with himself, as well he might given the success of his mission – followed.

It was a rare sight for a temporary bushman camp to be visited by a large government owned Toyota truck. Polinah was unsure what to do at first and was bemused at the greeting she received. With her white nurse's uniform and its blue belt denoting her station as Sister she had to admit to herself that she must have cut an incongruous figure out here in the desert. Certainly, the people she found herself among were

124

awed by her presence and stood in a silent arc a few metres away from her. The older bushwomen studied her minutely whilst some of the youngsters giggled nervously at the presence of this statuesque black woman. Toma took charge and led Polinah over to the shady spot where Khangdu was waiting with the still prone figure of the white man. As soon as Polinah saw the young woman huddled down over the invalid, her professionalism took over and she leant down on the opposite side of the man. She greeted Khangdu and introduced herself. She could see that the man had been well cared for, so before she undertook her own examination she allowed the other woman to show, with a mixture of simple Setswana and a number of deft hand movements, what she considered the problem to be. Polinah then carried out her own swift examination. There were no broken bones or damage to the abdomen or chest. The man's injuries were restricted to the back of his head where there were signs of swelling. Polinah knew that there was the possibility that he might have suffered a fractured skull and that his internal injuries might be very severe. If that were the case then there was little that she would be able to do for him here. He would die before he reached the hospital in Molepolole, which was a long day's drive away on some of the worst tracks in the world and enough to kill even the toughest of patients, especially one with internal head injuries.

If, however, the damage was limited to internal bruising alone then she did have drugs that she could administer which might give him a chance. She was certainly aware that the steady supply of water that he had been given had kept him alive long enough for her to reach him. She gave Khangdu one of her wide smiles in recognition of her understanding of how well the other woman had persevered with her patient. Polinah knew the man's body, after two whole days without food, would be depleted in vital vitamins and nutrients. She had brought with her a mobile drip feed. This was little more than a saline and sugar rich solution within a sealed plastic bag with a length of tube at the end of which was an intravenous needle. As she looked for a vein she showed Khangdu what she intended and gave her a length of bandage so that she could suspend the bag from the low bush which was offering them shade. After less than a couple of minutes, she was ready to release the contents into Rusty's left arm. If he were to die it would not be through lack of nutrients and minerals. Ideally his head needed to be x-rayed in order to see how bad the damage was. If his skull was fractured and there were severe internal injuries, these would be found in an autopsy for he would die as a result of the journey. If he was suffering nothing more than internal bruising then the best thing for him would be to have that bruising treated. If his brain was bruised it would swell and cause the symptoms from which he was now suffering. She needed to reduce the swelling as soon as possible. What the young nurse was unsure of was if using the drugs available to her would be the wrong course of action if he was suffering from a fractured skull and other severe injuries. It was the type of decision which was not normally required of a nurse. Polinah had enough common sense, however, to know it was her only option. If she headed straight back to the clinic or the nearest hospital the patient would die. If she stayed here with him and did nothing then he would also die. She opened the insulated box of medication which she had taken from the clinic fridge and selected the one that she judged would best help her patient. All she had to do was remove the sterile wrapper, shake the syringe a few times and then administer the dose. As the afternoon was fast progressing, Polinah decided to let nature take its course overnight. The following morning she would transport the invalid to the clinic. He might die on the way. If he did then it would not be through lack of care. As Polinah tidied up after herself her conscience was clear that she had done all that could be done for him. Polinah explained her intentions to Khangdu who made a space available so that she could sleep alongside the injured man.

When Victor was told what was happening he shrugged his shoulders and announced that he would make up a bed for himself in the back of the truck. He had achieved one goal at least. He would get his overnight allowance. As it was now late afternoon he decided to go and take a look at the burnt-out wreck. Polinah had persuaded him that as a driver he was better equipped to assess what was to be found there. He headed off towards the dry river bed with several of the young bushmen as his guides. After half an hour or so looking at the vehicle and its tracks, he concluded that the driver had fallen asleep and hit the rocks. It was this that had caused the roll which had resulted in one death and another life to hang in the balance. After seeing what was left of the incinerated body of the driver he headed back to his own truck to collect his spade. He returned to the Land Rover, buried the remains and marked the spot with bits of the wreckage. He did this to prevent scavengers from digging the body up and so that they could be relocated in the future. By the time he had finished, the sun had set and he bedded down for the night in the back of his Toyota with a heavy heart.

As Victor drifted off into a troubled sleep, Polinah settled herself for a vigil at her patient's side. The first thing she did was open the small bum bag which Khangdu had given to her as she arrived, explaining that it had been around the man's waist but she had taken it off to make him more comfortable. Inside was a traveller's paraphernalia: cash, credit cards, traveller's cheques as well as a couple of dog-eared letters, the stub of an airline ticket and a packet of condoms. Nestled in amongst these was what she was hoping to find, the well-made booklet that was his passport. The first thing that she saw was the unmistakable claret colour and the Royal insignia which marked him out as British. When she flicked it open she found herself gazing at a quizzical looking but bright and attractive face hidden beneath a mop of soft curls. The contrast between the photograph and the gaunt figure who lay in front of her could not have been more striking and she had to look carefully to see if it was indeed the same person. There was no doubt that his ordeal in the desert had taken a dreadful toll on him.

'Well then, Rusty McKenna', she whispered to herself, 'let's hope I can make you as handsome as you were when this photograph was taken.'

* * * * *

Polinah rested as darkness descended and the camp became silent. At first little happened and she herself drifted off into a fitful slumber. At some point later, much deeper into the night, she was woken by the injured man. She was uncertain what state he was now in. He was not fully conscious but equally he was no longer dead to the world. As the night progressed he proceeded to toss and turn this way and that in a state of delirium and partial wakefulness. He began to blurt out uncoordinated and disconnected ramblings which made no sense to her as she listened. He was becoming more lucid. Whether or not it was her care that had caused this change she did not know. However painful if was for him now, it did seem at least to be a positive development. As the night progressed it became evident that although not wholly conscious, he was referring to the accident and other recent events that were uppermost in his mind. He mumbled names, places and violent events which meant nothing to her, but which she did her best to commit to memory, as she felt that what was coming to the forefront of his mind might be of tremendous importance for him in his later recovery. Amidst the babble he mentioned a Mitsubishi Pajero twice in the same breath as he recalled the image of a sharp-faced white man standing over him. It was this latter recollection which caused him great distress and Polinah was glad when his mind raced onto other matters. She could not help but be aware of the juxtaposition between what was in Rusty's mind and the rare visit by such a vehicle driven by a lone white man to her settlement only the day before. After listening to his disjointed utterances for more than an hour she was relieved when he became silent once again and she was able to doze until dawn. She was thoroughly confused by what she had heard but felt that some of it at least made partial sense.

* * * * *

The first thing Rusty became aware of was a blinding headache, not unlike a powerful hangover, in tandem with a searing pain across his forehead, which seemed to be the result of a bright light shining directly in his face. All in all not a very pleasant way to resurface, but one which at least confirmed, through the fog that was his recent memory, that he was not dead. As his eyes blinked open in response to the light he realised that he was looking directly into the yellow disk of the sun climbing into the sky. He immediately twisted his head in the other direction to escape its effects and as he did so he was met with a sight which triggered another, altogether different, response. As he turned his head he found himself staring into a pair of deep and friendly chestnut-coloured eyes, set in a perfectly round and very sexy, light brown face.

'Good morning. How are you feeling today Rusty? You're looking better.'

Languorously, the woman sat up and stretched across him to check that the contents of the saline drip had been fully released into his body. As she did so he inadvertently caught a glimpse of her elegant upper body through the thin fabric of her white blouse. This garment had become slightly dishevelled during the course of the night spent sleeping under the desert sky and the top two buttons were undone. Polinah's firm round breasts came into Rusty's range of view in a way which left very little to the imagination. Polinah – oblivious to the effect she was having on the invalid – busied herself checking that he was recovering as well as he appeared to be. The sight of the attractive nurse was indeed having a galvanising effect on his recovery but there was a downside to this. Recent events suddenly surged back into his memory in a way that left him deeply distressed. He recalled the shattering windscreen of the Land Rover and the vivid spurt of blood from the Inspector's neck. As he did so, and although he knew what the response would be, he blurted out:

'Where is the Inspector? Is he okay?'

Polinah had been expecting his question and responded as kindly as she could.

'Was he the driver of the Land Rover you were travelling in? I am

129

afraid that you were both in a bad accident and when we got here, you were the only one still alive.'

She knew of no other way to tell him the news and it was indeed the way of her people to be direct and matter of fact on such occasions. Sickness and swift, violent death were no strangers to the people who chose to live in this beautiful, but inhospitable, part of the world.

Rusty did not at first appear to take in the news.

'How long have I been like this? Unconscious I mean.'

'You were found by a family of bushmen. As far as we can piece things together, they saw smoke two days ago. We think you were thrown from the vehicle before it crashed over the edge of a dry river bed and exploded. You hit these rocks and were still out cold later in the day when they found you. Despite their best efforts you stubbornly refused to wake until I filled you up with a concoction of my own.'

As Polinah told Rusty about the sequence of events that had befallen him he became visibly angry.

'God damn it. First Mats, then Thabo. And the bastard who killed them is now two days ahead. He has got clean away. There is nothing anyone can do about it now.'

'Rusty, we thought you had been in an accident. Are you telling me that there is something more to all this? You were mumbling in your sleep which concerned me.'

'Yes, yes, this wasn't an accident. Someone shot my friend Mats and then murdered Inspector Setshedi. I saw them both killed. The murderer was driving a white Pajero and the Inspector and I were trying to track him. Looks like he made a pretty good job of us instead.'

'Rusty, last night when you were delirious you talked about a tall thin man standing over you and it seemed to frighten you. Could he be a part of all this?'

As the nurse spoke the image of the man who had cast a shadow as he stood over him soon after the crash, with his hunting rifle in his hand, came back to Rusty in a flash. For the first time Rusty linked him to the man whom he had seen shoot Mats, an event which now seemed such a long time ago.

'Yeah, that's the guy that shot Mats. Still he's long gone now. Let's forget it.'

Polinah was now certain that the man who had come through the settlement the day before was the same shadowy person who had attacked her patient. Rusty's description of the figure that he had seen shortly before his brain succumbed to its injuries, matched her own observations entirely, even to the extent of the sinister aura about him. She could see however that her patient was almost weeping in his anger and frustration and she tried to soothe him.

'Rusty. Leave it for now and try to rest. You need to concentrate on your recovery. As soon as we get packed up here, I'll take you back to my clinic. When you are a little better we can talk more about all of this. You will need to go to see a doctor, to get a clean bill of health. Looking at you now though, I am convinced that your major problem was bruising and internal swelling. You should make a swift recovery now.'

Rusty was in no mood to argue with either her gentle demands or her diagnosis. He already felt stronger and he was having no difficulty thinking clearly. He lay back in the sand and tried to make sense of the chaos that had overwhelmed him and those close to him in a matter of days. Two days ago he had been on his way to a new job and was looking forward to the new challenge. Now he was lying injured in the desert and, given that Mats was dead, probably out of a job as well. He could not think where he would go from here. Perhaps the first thing would be to get back to civilisation, ensure that there was no lasting damage and then report the confused recent events. He drifted back to sleep. After about an hour he was gently nudged awake by Polinah who was ready to take him back to the clinic.

'Rusty, we need to go. When you are feeling stronger, my driver and some of the others will lift you onto a bed we have made in the back of the truck. Don't argue please. You might be able to walk, but I would prefer it if you didn't tax yourself until after you have rested a bit more.'

Rusty accepted her logic and nodded. Polinah drew his attention to Khangdu who had been busying herself assisting them to get Rusty ready for the journey.

'Rusty, you will never fully understand how much you owe your life to this girl. She looked after you for nearly two days. Without her and her supply of water I don't think you would have survived.'

Rusty looked at the girl who smiled back at him shyly. He suddenly felt embarrassed and was unsure how to respond.

'Please thank her for me, and ask her if there is anything that I can do to repay the debt I owe her.'

Polinah spoke quietly to the young woman who replied at length with much giggling.

'You will never believe this but she says you were a very easy patient and that she is very glad that you are improving. If it is no trouble she would like to keep the little bag that you had tied around your waist. She says she could put it to good use.'

The simplicity of her request was almost laughable and Rusty happily agreed. Polinah removed his things for safe keeping and the little green canvas bag was duly handed over. A few minutes later Rusty was loaded aboard the big truck, to the satisfaction of both Polinah and Victor. As they drew away into the desert, Rusty caught a glimpse of Khangdu proudly wearing the bag around her bare hips. She would treasure both the bag and the memories attached to it, until it was too threadbare to be of any further use.

* * * * *

Later, as the sun was setting, Polinah bedded Rusty down on the cot in the clinic. She made up a bed for herself out on the veranda. She could see from his demeanour that he was recovering although he was still immensely tired. She felt in her bones that he would sleep deeply after his recent ordeal and now she was certain that he had no major traumas to contend with, she did not think it would be long before such a fit man would be restored to health. She elected to stay close by though, just in case he should have another nightmare. Rusty slept deeply that night but was awake and alert before she was the following morning. Victor had wandered over when he had seen that Rusty was up and about and wished him luck with his recovery. Rusty in turn thanked him for his part in the rescue. Shortly afterwards he watched the heavy truck lumber out of the camp to make an early start on its long haul back to Gaborone. When Polinah awoke she found Rusty testing out his legs after days of enforced inactivity. Although he was light-headed with the effort there was no major problem and he was soon tucking into a healthy breakfast of porridge with lots of sugar and plenty of tea. This was the first proper food he had had for three days and its impact was immediate. There was no doubt now he would make a full recovery.

'Good morning, my Florence Nightingale of the desert,' Rusty said laughing as Polinah joined him on the veranda for a bite to eat. 'It seems I am in debt to you and those bushmen out there and I was not even polite enough yesterday to ask your name.'

'No need to apologise. I am Polinah Mabina. I am a nurse from Mochudi but at the moment I am one of two who run this little institution.'

'Well, Polinah, I'm very pleased to meet you. I love the Kalahari but I would not want to end my life here, at least not just yet and I have no doubt that without you, I would be dead. A lot has happened to me over the last few days and as you are the nearest thing to a government official I feel it is my duty to inform you of it all.'

Polinah listened intently as Rusty recounted the extraordinary events that had taken place.

'And so, you see,' he concluded, 'I am very pleased to still be alive but I just don't see how I can keep up the chase. The man must be well gone by now and I am not even sure of his identity.'

Polinah spoke but chose her words carefully.

'Rusty, on the morning that the bushmen saw the smoke we had a visitor here a couple of hours later. A white man in a brand new Pajero.

I am sure he is the same man you have described. I got a good look at him and I am sure I could identify him again.'

'I'm sure we both could. It's just that we don't know anything about him, not even his vehicle registration. There will be hundreds of white Pajeros on the bush roads in the Delta and in Chobe and the other parks. It would be like looking for a needle in a haystack.'

Polinah had been very moved by the stark story that Rusty had told. The anger and grief had been evident in his narration and she wanted to do everything in her power to bring the criminal to justice. Still, she had to concede that Rusty was right and that the man would be impossible to find in the vastness that lay to the north. Suddenly she became quite animated and almost shouted.

'Rusty, I've had an idea. Come with me.'

She darted across the compound at great haste and headed to the small hut at the entrance. She disappeared inside quickly, much to the consternation of her patients who were gathering for the morning clinic and who were accustomed to seeing the young woman behave more sedately. Rusty had not been able to match her speed through the soft sand. As he dawdled he caught sight of her shapely legs and thighs as she raced away ahead of him. He had not noticed her legs before and there was no doubting in his mind that she was utterly gorgeous. Her face was beautiful and her figure was tremendous. As he cautiously entered the hut Polinah was chattering excitedly to a bemused old man.

'Rapula. I need your help. Did you write down the details of that Pajero which came through two days ago and which left by the gate to the north?'

'That swine, I'm glad we don't get his like every day,' the elderly man replied humourlessly. 'He treated me like they used to in the old days. I won't be pushed around by the likes of him.'

With that he left the hut and spat noisily over by the perimeter fence. When he returned he appeared to have calmed down but announced to a crestfallen Polinah.

'I am sorry Miss, only the official vehicles are supposed to be logged.

This is not a veterinary fence so there are no orders to write down the private ones. Or at least that is what I was told when I started work. I hope that I have not done wrong.'

'No, no, Rapula, you have done your job correctly. I was unsure of the rules. I am sorry to have disturbed you.'

'*Go Siame,* that's okay, sister. I am expecting a Land Cruiser from Maun sometime today. Have you forgotten that Nurse Segobye is coming to take over from you. You've done your stint for now.'

With the excitement of the last few days Polinah had forgotten that she was to be relieved but even that piece of good news did not serve to improve her spirits. She had been under the impression that details of all vehicles were recorded and it was a blow to learn that this was not, in fact, the case. With a look of apology to Rusty she left the hut and headed soberly back across the compound. Rusty could see the hurt in her eyes and was about to say something to try and cheer her up when there was a loud bellow from behind them. As Rusty turned he saw the old gateman was standing at the threshold of his hut waving an old clipboard vigorously in front of him.

'Sister Mabina. I just remembered that when that bastard drove through the other day I started to fill in the log book by mistake. I only got as far as his registration number and I nearly threw it away. But in the end I didn't . . .'

As he was speaking Rusty and Polinah ran back towards him. Polinah took the clipboard from him and the old man pointed to a neatly written entry that had been struck out in pencil but which was still legible. He had not filled in any other details, just the registration number. There it was in black and white: TBT 446GP.

'I didn't get any further, Sister, before I realised my mistake but that was definitely him all right. Nasty little vermin from South Africa. That is a Gauteng registration.'

Polinah's face was transformed by their good fortune.

'Rusty, this changes everything. It means there is a chance he can be traced. You might be able to get on his tail again.'

'Okay, okay, you're probably right. We might be able to, but don't forget he is still miles ahead of us. Having his number plate doesn't mean we'll find him. Let's give it some thought.'

The two of them headed back to the main part of the compound. Polinah needed to start her morning clinic. The veranda area was busier than usual. A number of the village folk had come over that way to see the sick white man who the nurse had brought in from the desert. Life had definitely got livelier in these parts since she had turned up. Some were all for change but others would have been happier if things had stayed the way they always had been. One way or another there was certainly plenty to gossip about that sunny morning and there was a lively hubbub about the place. One enterprising woman had even brought a basket of hot, doughy fat cakes with her and was doing a roaring trade. There was no doubting that the settlement was beginning to become a proper community. As Polinah held her clinic, the rest of the village chatted about Rusty, occasionally glancing towards him where he sat on a bench under a shade tree. He meanwhile was doing some serious thinking about this latest discovery. At the midway break in her morning clinic Polinah came over and sat with Rusty, who by now had decided what was his next course of action should be.

'I'm sure the mine will have reported Mats' death but we are the only ones who know what really happened to Inspector Setshedi. We need to report everything to the authorities as soon as we can. The fact that we know the registration number means we should act fast. The quicker the police get the facts the better their chance will be of catching the guy who did this.'

'You've picked the right day to want to get on the move,' Polinah explained. 'The Land Cruiser which brings Sister Segobye will be heading back to Maun at first light so you will be there by evening if you return with them. I would suggest rest for the remainder of today. It's a long haul to Maun and I have travelled with the driver before and I can assure you he doesn't hang about.'

Rusty was pleased with the news that he would be on his way

tomorrow but was also secretly relieved that he did not have to depart immediately, partly because he felt exhausted and partly because he was loathe to leave this stunning nurse. Polinah turned back towards him from the entrance to the clinic where she was going to complete her duties.

'By the way, you will have to put up with me for a little while longer. When Sister Segobye arrives from her home village I have to take the roundabout route back to Gabs. I will be heading for Maun tomorrow as well.'

As Rusty rested for the remainder of the day on the veranda in front of the clinic, those who saw him were reassured that the apparent grin on his face was a positive sign that he was well on the way to recovery.

* * * * *

For a man travelling with a fortune in diamonds secreted away in the back of his truck, Kurt Viljoen was now considerably more relaxed than he had been three days earlier when he had chanced upon the small settlement in the desert. Since then there had been no untoward incidents. He had breezed up the west side of the Central Game Reserve without meeting a single soul. The track that hugged the fence had been firm and smooth. When he reached the easterly turn off towards Deception Valley and the village of Rakops to the north-east it was clear where he was and he hardly had need of his global positioning device. He parked up for the night off the track and out of sight. He slept well – no vehicles came out of the dark night – and awoke refreshed. He tracked to the north-east, along the twisting path which followed the dry river bed, and quietly enjoyed the stark beauty of the desert scenery as he snaked his way along the meandering trail. Towards mid-afternoon he chanced upon a quartet of beaten up but powerful and well-maintained 4x4s which were parked under a large Baobab tree. Two were registered in Botswana and two were from Cape Town. His initial reaction was to give them a cheery wave and drive by, but as soon as they saw him a large ruddy-faced man with a protruding stomach lumbered out onto the path and forced him to stop. For one awful moment he thought it was some sort of a hold-up but then he realised that most of the group sitting around a fire on comfortable folding camping chairs and waving jovially were drunk and were in the midst of preparing a barbecue. He could not avoid the large man's forceful advances so he pulled over. He was immediately thrown a cold can of Castle and asked why he was out in the desert alone. He made a joke about getting away from a nagging wife. This they took in great humour, saying that they did not get on with their wives either and were on their trip for much the same reason. This was definitely a trip for the boys. It turned out that they were all cousins. There were nine of them in all. Four were from farms in the Gauteng Province in South Africa and five were from Ghanzi. They had prospered well from beef and every other year went on a three-week hunting trip together in either the Central Kalahari Game Reserve or the remote Etosha reserve in Namibia. In the true spirit of Boer hospitality, even though he was a stranger, Kurt was invited to stay and share their meal. Although his initial instinct was to decline, it was late in the day and it might appear suspicious if he pressed on. He quickly changed his mind and parked up on the edge of their camp. As he joined the campfire gathering, Kurt could see they were well-equipped for a boisterous, boozy time. The hunting was just an excuse to be out in the desert. The delicious meat from the carcass of the springbok would make an excellent meal. All four trucks were kitted out with gas freezers and one of them had been given over entirely to the transportation of the alcohol. It was stacked high with cases of Castle and Amstel and more than a few crates of strong brandy. Their preferred method of drinking was to pour the beer quickly down their necks and then to follow this with a shot of brandy. This concoction was downed with great regularity as the evening progressed. Some of the group had been in the South African military during apartheid and as they became more inebriated they told hair-raising stories of excesses that had taken place. As well as swapping embellished stories of their own bravery they bemoaned not only their own government but also that of President Khama in Botswana. Despite having lived under their black leaders for more than a decade, they still had not come to terms with the drastic changes which had occurred in Southern Africa and had nothing positive to say about the black people they lived alongside. They regarded them as lazy, stupid and fit for nothing other than poorly paid farm labourers. As they were all farm owners there was perhaps a perverted logic in their twisted reasoning, from their point of view. As the evening progressed they lapsed into melancholic singing. All of the melodies were traditional Boer ballads and told of the great trek and their struggles with the British, whom they detested and the Zulus, whose fighting prowess they secretly admired. Kurt knew the songs and had no problem with their sentiments but inwardly he derided these men for their weakness, their excesses and their lack of resolve. It was not the likes of them who would bring down the black governments and their strutting, arrogant leaders but tougher more resourceful people like himself. As they whinged about the changes that Nelson Mandela had brought which they perceived were ruining a once proud land, Kurt itched to tell them of his outlandish stunt and the future impact it would have. He kept his counsel however. While the drinking continued, Kurt kept pace with their consumption of beer but he avoided the brandy chasers, which would have given him a thick head and made him ill-prepared to remain alert so he could continue his journey in the morning. In the event the party petered out into drunken snoring shortly after midnight and Kurt made his way back to his bed in the back of the Pajero.

When he awoke at daybreak only one of the revellers had stirred. His eyes were bloodshot and he was nursing a fearsome hangover as he morosely prepared a pot of coffee on the campfire. Kurt wished him well for the rest of the hunting expedition, told him to pass on his regards to the others when they arose and was very quickly on his way. A couple of hours after leaving behind the sleeping huntsmen he came to the park rangers' camp and he knew he would soon be leaving the Central

Kalahari Game Reserve. As he passed through the gate he was hailed by a fresh faced individual driving a zebra striped Land Rover. For a moment his heart raced but he held his nerve and opened the electric window. It transpired the young man was an American student who was doing a two year stint in the Peace Corps. His research area was the African wild dog and he was keen to find out if Kurt had spotted any. He went on to explain at some length that they usually travelled in packs of a dozen or so and were unmistakable, being rangy in appearance with a blotchy black, yellow and white coat. He explained how they normally hunted small antelope but had recently, not surprisingly, adopted domesticated cattle as their staple food. The earnest American detailed how this had made them the most endangered carnivore in Africa and therefore the subject of deserved scrutiny. Kurt had not seen these opportunistic dogs and as he drove away was convinced that the puffed up little academic was so self-obsessed that there was little chance he would take much notice of travellers passing through his patch. Kurt did not envy the locally recruited park rangers who no doubt had to put up with this character at their campfire night after night.

Shortly after leaving the rangers' post Kurt came to the gate which demarcated the northern limit of the game reserve. As he passed through he saw the Telecommunications microwave tower in the distance which meant that Rakops was not far away. As he continued he saw the tin and thatched roofs of the village and proceeded cautiously. Rakops was a dusty out of the way spot sitting at a key juncture on the main road which ran to the south of the large salt pans that dominated the central north-eastern sector of Botswana. Originally the track had been a more direct route between Maun and Gaborone via Serowe for those with a tough off-roader than that which lay to the north of the pans via Nata. The northern route had been tarred recently, however, and was now much swifter so the bulk of the traffic went that way. The trickle of vehicles which had once come through Rakops had all but dried up. Kurt was hopeful that the remote nature of the place would be to his advantage. He had already decided to take a very circuitous route in order to reach his father's old farm in Zimbabwe. He hoped he would be swallowed up by the sheer size of the bush and the relatively high number of similar vehicles that criss-crossed the northern parks. He could not however ignore places like Rakops and Maun if he was going to follow that route. On the westerly route, Maun was the only potential bottleneck of major proportions. As he drove into Rakops, Kurt was inwardly calm and had two plans of action prepared. From his point of view the ideal would be to refuel and then head north to the newly tarred road between Francistown and Maun. There he would turn west and head for Maun itself where he intended to stock up with additional provisions and head off into the Moremi Game Reserve. There he would dawdle through the beautiful park for several days and mingle with the other tourists. If he was challenged in Rakops he would, if at all possible, use the speed of his V12 turbo-charged engine to make an escape and then cut off to the east, crossing the Boteti River and out into the middle of Makgadikgadi pan. In the immense space of this ancient, dry ocean bed he hoped he would be able to shake off any pursuers. He had plenty of speed and could cross just about any terrain. In addition, there were places in the pans where there were raised beaches and other terraced areas which might, at a pinch, provide cover. They would give him a chance of survival but it was an option he hoped he would not have to use.

As he turned off the track and onto the main drag through the village he felt tenser than he had for a couple of days. Still, there was no sign of a security presence, police or a road block. As he pulled onto the Caltex station at the side of the road he found the attendant fast asleep. That did not seem to be the most likely of scenarios if there was a security alert. The Batswana might like to take the opportunity to sleep when the daytime sun was at its highest but they were also extremely curious and did not like to miss out if there was any excitement going on. The pump attendant filled the Pajero's tanks and since he had bought so much fuel, Kurt was told he was entitled to two scratch cards. The company had recently introduced these as a promotional stunt to try and damage their main competitor, Shell, whose station in Rakops was about a hundred metres away on the other side of the road. Caltex had invested so much money in the scratch card campaign that Kurt won ten pula on each card. The attendant was pleased with his customer's luck and was sent into a delighted apoplexy when Kurt presented him with a five pula tip after he cleaned the windscreen. As Kurt headed out of the dusty village in a northerly direction he saw nothing to attract his attention or which made him uneasy. After around five kilometres he passed a recently erected compound which was full of heavy earth-moving equipment where a number of pre-fabricated huts were being erected. A couple of klicks further on, his suspicion that the road builders were preparing to tar this stretch was confirmed when he came upon a team of Korean surveyors setting up a base line and checking levels. They had with them a gang of Motswana assistants who were holding the surveying targets. In the heat of the day it was not the most pleasant job in the world. They were used to passing off-roaders and they all gave Kurt a cheery wave as he passed them by, despite the fact that the dust cloud which he was kicking up would make it difficult for them to see anything for the next few minutes and was probably doing untold damage to the interior of their expensive theodolite.

As Kurt progressed to the north, the road came close to the Boteti River which lay on his right hand side. This was completely dry but it was fringed in places with palm trees, a legacy of the day when elephants had trekked this far south and brought the seeds down from the Okavango Delta. Beyond the trees Kurt caught the occasional glimpse of the grey expanse that was the vast pan that lay to the east. As he headed towards Maun the scenery began to change. The road passed through land which was kept fertile by the river and had been heavily settled as a consequence. As he headed on through a succession of small villages he saw herds of healthy cattle at the roadside or dozing in large communal *kraals*. A number of strategically placed veterinary fences had been built in recent years which prevented the movement of the migrating herds and thus protected the cattle from disease. As a result he saw no game. Strangely enough the one animal which seemed to be able to get around, or perhaps over, the fences was the ostrich. He saw increasing numbers of these extraordinary birds as he continued his journey. Sometimes he would see a large male resplendent with his black plumage in close formation with a pair of grey females. On other occasions he would see a small family group – male, female and young – moving in convoy together. They had a habit of following the low fence which was designed to keep the cattle and donkeys off the road and would veer away if Kurt slowed to try to get a better look. They were his only companions as he journeyed to the north to join the Francistown road. He made this connection only a couple of hours after leaving Rakops. As he approached the tarred strip he found that the tar had been continued down the track that he had just come up for a distance of perhaps fifty metres. This was presumably in preparation for when it, too, would be tarred. At the junction itself there were impressive signs giving the distance to Maun to the west and Nata and Francistown to the east. Despite the fact that he could not see a settlement in any direction, there was a bus stop. Predictably enough there was a group of young men, perhaps students or soldiers, slumbering in the heat under the rudimentary shelter. When they saw that Kurt was turning to the west two of them leapt up and flagged him down urgently with vigorous up and down movements of their right arms, coupled with anguished looks on their faces. Kurt – in no mood to have company – accelerated. One of the would-be hitch-hikers shook his fist at the rapidly moving Pajero and kicked at a loose stone angrily.

The tarred strip between Nata and Maun had been the final link in the chain which had joined the northern and southern ends of this large country. As such it had been well-constructed and was a joy to use compared with many other roads. For the first time since returning from South Africa several weeks earlier Kurt found himself able to press the pedal to the floor and enjoy the power the vehicle provided. There was no chance he would be overtaken as he drove the one hundred and sixty kilometres between the road junction and Maun. He could see clear ahead and decelerated well in advance of any approaching village just in case there was a speed cop tucked away in the trees at the side of the road. Otherwise he gave the fantastic motor its head, sat back in comfort and luxury and enjoyed the sensation as he coasted by at speeds of in excess of one hundred and eighty kilometres an hour.

Shortly before he reached the point where he thought that it prudent to slow down for the approach to Maun Kurt decided to overtake a dilapidated bakkie. At precisely the instant that he crossed over to the opposite carriageway to pass, the bakkie suddenly made as if to turn to the right, across his intended path. If it had, there would have been an immediate and spectacular impact as Kurt drew level. Fortunately some sixth sense told the driver, belatedly, to check his mirrors and at the very last moment he saw the Pajero looming up at an unimaginable speed. The bakkie swerved to the left and a collision was avoided. As Kurt shot by there was an instant surge of adrenaline which make him light-headed and giddy. As he tried to calm himself he realised he had been foolish in the extreme and had almost jeopardised his mission. He vowed silently to himself that in the future he would not let such weakness affect him again.

A few minutes later he found himself on the approach to the outer suburbs of Maun. This once sleepy, out of the way, village had, in recent years, become the administrative centre of Ngamiland and was also the base of operations for a number of safari companies who plied their trade in the Okavango Delta and the Chobe Game Reserve. Many of them ran luxurious trips through the parks and over the border into Zimbabwe to see the Victoria Falls. Some no doubt would be using the same tracks Kurt intended to follow in the next few days. As a result Maun airport was as busy as any in this part of Africa. Commuter flights would bring the wealthy tourists from Johannesburg and they would then be ferried, by light aircraft, to their cosseted camps in the bush. Not many days would go by without some famous celebrity being spotted decamping to one of the small planes for the ultimate 'get away from it all' vacation. This influx of wealth, together with the newly created tarmac strip from the south, had caused Maun to flourish at a fantastic rate. This had allowed a whole new calibre of tourist to find their way to this remote spot. The middle classes of South Africa and visitors from Gaborone were now able to travel in their family saloons. In response to this a new breed of less expensive lodges and camps had sprung up. In the old days there had been no choice but to stay at the famous Riley's Hotel in the centre of town. The advent of the new road also meant that fresh provisions could be brought in by road rather than by air. Now it was available to all and as a result a number of supermarkets had sprung up. There were many in the old community who resented this change to the town. Previously the riches of the wilderness on their doorstep had been for their exclusive use.

As Kurt cruised slowly up the main street there was no doubt that the place still had the look of a frontier town. Trucks and off-roaders were re-fuelling and stocking up on provisions for trips into the bush. Souvenir shops were everywhere, especially around the airport, enabling those who did not have the time or inclination to visit the villages to buy traditional carvings or basketry. This hubbub was perfect cover for Kurt. He pulled into the car park in front of the recently opened Woolworth's store in the middle of a long line of similar vehicles and instantly felt anonymous. He had soon restocked his food chest and his cool box. After leaving the superstore the only thing left for Kurt to do was once again refuel the Pajero. He did this at Riley's Garage and also had the coolant water checked. He was then shown to a tap at the side of the building where he filled his water containers. He then crossed over the Thamalakane River and headed north-east, passing the airport and a line of safari camps on either side of the road. These soon petered out and he began to pass a number of roadside villages. These differed from their counterparts to the south in that each of them was protected by a high reed fence. This was done not just because that particular extremely functional commodity was readily available in the delta swamps but because it could be a necessity. Heading north out of Maun was back into big game country and there was a real risk that unattended cattle would be picked off by lion or other predators. He did not slow down until he reached Shorobe. Here he was surprised when the tarred strip suddenly ran out and he once again had to adapt to more testing driving conditions. The sand in the delta region was much finer than elsewhere in Botswana and at first he found his heavy vehicle overly sluggish as he fought his way through the clawing sand. He soon adapted, changing down a gear and increasing the revs and made it through with relative ease. The sophisticated suspension system under him made an easy ride of it. After an hour or so driving through the sand he stopped under a magnificent Marula tree and looked at the guidebook he had bought in South Africa. If he was going to lie low for a few days then there was no earthly reason why he should not enjoy himself. He had already decided he was going to spend a few days in the Moremi Game Reserve. He planned to make the campsite at Third Bridge his base for that time. Having made this resolution and refreshed himself he continued. Soon afterwards he arrived at the fork in the road. He took the lesser, left-hand branch and after a few kilometres arrived at the park gate. The main track headed due north towards the Chobe reserve, Kasane and the Zimbabwean border. Kurt would rejoin that route after waiting up in Moremi for a while. After he had filled in the gatekeeper's book with his name, nationality, registration and make of vehicle, he paid the fees for a four-day stay and headed on into the thick acacia woodland that was the predominant ground cover in the southern part of the park.

* * * * *

Lexi, the government driver who had arrived with Nurse Segobye the previous evening, was keen to get on his way and to take advantage of the cooler part of the day for at least some of the journey. When she emerged from her house Polinah had a small bag. She wore a colourful woollen jumper and a pair of blue jeans which hugged her slim figure. It turned out there would be four of them making the journey, since the pump engineer was travelling to Maun to submit his periodic report.

As Lexi pulled in front of the clinic, the engineer was already aboard, in the front passenger seat, chatting to his friend. Rusty and Polinah clambered into the capacious rear seats whereupon the nurse dumped her bag down in the central section of the seat between the two of them. Just as they were about to depart, Sister Segobye appeared to wish them a safe journey and to wish Rusty a speedy recovery. She waved as they were escorted through the gate by the ever vigilant Rapula.

As they settled into the rhythm of the first part of the journey Lexi took a subsidiary track that led in a south-westerly direction towards the old main road across the southern part of the desert. After a short while they reached Tswaane pan, one of the biggest in this area measuring more than two kilometres in diameter. Up until then the track had been bumpy and very windy but as they reached the pan it diverted onto the smooth and compact silt at the pan edge and Lexi was able to increase his speed. He was confident driving in such conditions and they raced around its perimeter at a giddy speed. As they did so Rusty looked over his shoulder. The front of the government vehicle was still pristine white but the rear wheels were kicking up an immense cloud of fine grained grey particles which boiled in the turbulent air in their wake. The dust was beginning to coat the rear end, where the spare wheel and jerry can were located.

There were a few small settlements which hugged the fringes of the pan which they flashed through without acknowledging the waves of the small children who gathered to watch them pass. At the south-western end of the pan they took a track which was straighter and wider than others. It was typical of the sand roads in this part of the desert. The driver, using all his skill and experience maintained speed over the powdery sand. To lose speed on such a surface was to risk sinking and he maintained the momentum with apparent ease. As he did this, he and the engineer chatted away like the old friends that they were. Polinah seemed lost in her thoughts. Rusty passed the time by watching the scenery unfold through the window.

Most of this part of the desert seemed to be relentlessly arid. The grass cover was minimal and non existent in places and the occasional acacia tree that he spotted looked stunted and parched. The predominant ground cover was a mix of brown sand and white calcrete nodules. There was also a considerable number of small and medium sized pans. Despite the apparent lack of settlement at each of these there would always be a small herd of cattle dozing in what little available shade there was and occasionally a herd boy would wave his stick at them enthusiastically. After an hour passing through this terrain Rusty saw a microwave tower looming up ahead and shortly afterwards they rolled into Motokwe. Reaching this point meant they were now once again on the old cross desert road between Letlhakeng and Kang. They pulled over in front of the Post Office where the driver and engineer were well known. After greetings were exchanged, the jovial post-mistress produced tea and fat cakes and the four of them settled down for a welcome break.

Once they left Motokwe, on the main east-west highway, driving conditions were very different but no more pleasant. Local materials had been bulldozed into position to make a vast cambered carriageway on either side of which were wide, shallow ditches. Earth moving equipment and heavy graders had been used to produce the makings of a decent surface, at some point in the recent past but wear and tear coupled with heavy rainfall had broken up the smooth surface and it had reformed into small compacted ruts. Potholes and small loose boulders were also an occasional problem. The overall effect made for an uncomfortable ride and one which required considerable skill from the driver. The main difficulty was that traction was lost as they drove over every rut. This caused the rear end to fishtail violently. You could slow down to a speed at which traction was not lost or you could accelerate out of a potential skid and proceed on your way at breakneck sped. Predictably Lexi selected the latter option. He evidently felt it was his duty to get his passengers to Maun as quickly as possibly, or kill them in the process. His driving technique also had the advantage that potholes were eaten up under them without apparently hindering progress. As they drove the sun rose in the clear blue sky and they were fortunate that the air conditioning was switched on and working efficiently. As the monotonous journey continued Polinah succumbed to drowsiness and lolled sideways against the door. Each time they hit a pothole she was jerked awake by the impact only to immediately fall back into fitful slumber. Observing her discomfort Rusty slipped the bag that she had placed on the seat between them onto the floor at his feet and gently reached over her shoulder and pulled her to him. As he did this she stiffened immediately and opened her eyes for a moment in alarm. When she realised what he was doing she at first appeared to be about to move away, but then accepted his gesture and nestled into the crook of his arm and fell into a comfortable sleep. As he became used to the warmth of her body against his, Rusty realised he was experiencing a tingling sensation where she was touching him. It was thoroughly enjoyable and the long leg of the journey as far as Ghanzi passed far too quickly. At Ghanzi Lexi announced that if they were to reach Maun that night there would be no time for a break. On this occasion all that Rusty saw of Ghanzi was the inside of a government compound on the outskirts of the town, where the driver pulled in to refuel. As he was driving a BX registered official vehicle there was no need for money to change hands and the long range tanks were soon full again, giving them more than enough to reach their destination. Lexi was able to change up into fifth gear and they rocketed onwards through the long afternoon. As the Land Cruiser progressed towards its destination in the north, the surface deteriorated and made the ride less comfortable. One downside to this change in their circumstances was that the resulting pitching and rolling startled Polinah, who awoke with a quizzical look on her face. Smiling she slowly moved back to her side of the seat. By now it was Rusty's turn to feel the effects of the journey and he began to drift in and out of a daydream in which recent events were once again jumbled up in his head and brought to the fore in a disorganised and unpleasant manner. After a while he was jerked into wakefulness by his own thoughts and he was immediately grateful to Polinah who pointed out some low rounded hills to the east.

'Rusty look over there. Those are the Tsao Hills. I have a cousin who has a cattle post near there. We should be in Maun in a couple of hours.'

The Land Cruiser began to cool as the sun sank in the western sky. Reaching a T-junction they joined a tarred road. They had come to the highway which started out at Maun in the east, from where it dipped down under the Delta to Toteng where they now found themselves. At Toteng they could head south in the direction from which they had just come or head west and north in the direction of what was called the panhandle. This road skirted the western side of the myriad of streams and swamps that made up the Okavango Delta until it reached a point where the flood plain formed a long straight stretch where the Okavango River found its way into Botswana. The road had been tarred recently because there was a border crossing there – much used by tourists and commercial vehicles alike – coming from Namibia and Zambia. As they headed east to Maun, Rusty was brought back to the present by the sound of Polinah's voice.

'We will soon be there, now we're back on the tar. My uncle and his family will be pleased I am bringing a guest with me. They are very proud of their home and like to welcome visitors.'

Rusty had been expecting to say his goodbyes to Polinah when they reached the town so he was pleasantly surprised to hear this. Nonetheless, instinctively, he allowed his British reticence to get the better of him.

'You have done so much for me already, Polinah. I can't impose on your family as well. I'm sure I can find a lodge or a hotel where they will have room for me.'

'Don't be silly, Rusty. My aunt and uncle would be mortified if I did not bring you. Anyway you forget you are my patient. I have not discharged you from my care yet and I will not do so until you have fully recovered,' she said with a mischievous grin.

Rusty chuckled. He was perfectly happy to stay with this gorgeous creature for as long as possible, so he made no further comment on her invitation.

As they travelled north-east towards the town, the delta and its supply of water began to make its presence felt in the landscape. The sand at the side of the tarmac strip was fresher and whiter than the compacted stuff in the desert and was able to support a strong and more diverse flora. The scrub acacias and the parched grasslands had been replaced by flourishing stands of large trees, through which the tarred highway had been cut. As they progressed they passed many cattle *kraals* and small villages. These increased in number as they approached Maun until it became apparent from the sheer volume of tin roofed and thatched houses at the side of the road that they had reached the burgeoning town. Once again there was a sea of humanity all around as people made their way from their jobs in the town centre to their homes in the suburbs. Lexi had made this trip with Polinah before and, after negotiating a variety of side roads, they reached a dusty lane to the side of which were a number of fenced compounds.

* * * * *

As soon as Rusty and Polinah stepped down from the truck they were surrounded by a gaggle of children who pulled at Polinah's hands as they shouted out their hellos enthusiastically. Watching Rusty follow Polinah through the gate, shyness overwhelmed some of them and they retreated to the corner of the yard. At the sight of the children, Polinah explained to him that her uncle, Mothusi, her father's older brother, had moved here many years ago to work after he had married his wife, Lebitso, who was from Maun. They had moved onto her family's property where they still lived, with his wife's brother and his family and their very elderly grandparents. Rusty realised from the sea of smiling faces now before him that he would never remember everyone's names. He picked up Polinah's bag and entered the outer gate in the fence taking the well-trodden route through the outer compound in Polinah's wake and reached the inner rectangular compound which measured about ten metres across. This was surrounded by a low mud brick wall about a metre in height through which there was a small opening on each side. On three sides of this compound Rusty could see that houses were positioned, facing inwards. He saw that all three were traditional in design topped with a richly coloured yellow thatch. Two of them were large circular rondavels. The third house was different from the others. It was rectangular in shape with a long, low thatched veranda formed out of a continuation of the roof, which fell to within six feet of the ground. This veranda faced into the centre of the compound. Under it he could see an old man and an old woman resting in the deep shade on a low wooden bench. What set these houses apart from those which had been built recently in this developing town was that, not only were they constructed using locally available materials, but they had been simply and traditionally decorated. In each case the lower half of the house was dusty red whilst the upper part was a buff sandy colour. At the join between these two colours there was a neatly constructed geometric linear pattern in white which stood out in the half light of the dusk. As Rusty's eyes adjusted to his surroundings he also saw that the surface of the inner compound was compacted and perfectly smooth and that it was decorated with an understated but well-crafted curving pattern. Along the fourth side of the inner compound there was no dwelling. In this case the wall curved outwards to enclose a medium-sized semi-circular area which was protected by roughly hewn lengths of unworked timber. The natural shape of these hardwood branches had been used to create an interlace which formed a sheltered enclosure within which a fire was glowing. Rusty knew that this was the family cooking area and as such was the heart of the home. He could see two large cast iron pots bubbling away on the fire tended by several people including a middle-aged woman and two teenage girls.

Rusty followed Polinah as she walked towards, and then stepped over, the threshold of the inner compound. As they approached she called out to announce her arrival. Recognising who had arrived they all stopped what they were doing and came to greet her. As soon as the welcomes were made the conversation slipped into Setswana and Polinah explained the presence of the strange white man. He knew enough Setswana to understand they were being told about the accident in the desert and the subsequent adventures. When Polinah had finished Mothusi stepped forwards and announced.

'Young man, you are welcome. Polinah has told us of the troubles you have endured. You must have the constitution of a lion to have survived. We are very happy to have you with us in our home until you are strong enough to travel again.'

Rusty was not surprised by this unstinting generosity.

'Thank you. If it were not for your niece, I would surely be dead. She is a great healer and you should be very proud.'

His words were greeted with acclaim and one or two of the woman applauded his generous acknowledgement.

Polinah took Rusty to one side and showed him to the rectangular rondavel. Inside he could see the white-washed interior was divided into two small rooms by a partition which reached up to head height but which still left the underside of the thatch visible. A plaid blanket was draped across the entrance to the room furthest from the door. Polinah explained that the far room was where her aunt's elderly parents slept, but that the room at the entrance was used by her cousin who was away working. He was in his mid-twenties and had a job at the Moremi Game Reserve and would not return for a few days. She went on to say that her uncle had insisted that Rusty should have his bed.

As Rusty started to settle in there was a tap on the door and two boys, smiling shyly, entered holding a large tin bath. They were followed by a succession of others carrying buckets and before long the bath was full with hot water. Polinah suggested that he borrow some of the clothes which she said ought to fit him while his own were washed. Just before leaving the room she half turned back towards him and watched him as he started to unbutton his shirt. She smiled at him in a way which he could only describe as saucy and then she quickly left.

He did not know how to cope with this alluring woman but of one thing he was certain: it was enjoyable being in her company. Twenty minutes later, Rusty – dressed in a plain white T shirt and a natty pair of denim overalls – found himself sitting in the midst of a large group adjacent to the fire in the inner compound, eating rice and corned beef with coleslaw, washed down with cold water.

Darkness descended and the only light came from the rising moon, stars and the flickering yellow flames from the fire. As soon as the meal was over a large shallow enamel bowl was produced and one of the teenage girls started washing up. Water was brought from a tap by the fence to replenish the large bucket that was warming at the side of the cooking fire. As he digested his meal, Polinah came over and, with a sparkling grin, bade him goodnight. She too took herself off in the direction of the children's houses and he realised that she had given him the bed that would normally have been hers. After thanking her aunt for the food Rusty also went off to bed. As he approached the house he saw Junior and Phenyo, the two boys who had prepared his bath, dragging it across the outer compound where they unceremoniously dumped the contents onto a healthy looking bed of spinach.

'Waste not, want not,' he thought to himself.

Polinah's grandparents had already made their way to bed so he entered the house quietly. Inside, the oil lantern cast a dull, but pleasant, yellow glow. As he settled down to sleep under a pair of heavy tartan blankets he watched the lamplight flicker on the dark wood of the intricate roof trusses and the golden underside of the thatch. After turning down the wick the darkness enveloped him and in these plain and simple surroundings he slept soundly and awoke the next morning feeling utterly refreshed.

* * * * *

Rusty found that the day was already well in progress. The tin bath he had used the night before was now placed near the fire and was filled to the brim with warm sudsy water. Polinah's aunt and one of her daughters were bent double over it, busy pummelling away at a load of clothes. On a line suspended between the corner of one of the houses and a tree at the edge of the outer compound a number of items were pegged out to dry. Rusty could see his own clothes fluttering in the warm breeze. Over on the other side of the outer compound Rusty spotted Mothusi fitting the tyre to a wheel having repaired the punctured inner tube the evening before. He was struggling manfully with a pair of long slender tyre irons in an effort to get the unyielding tyre back over the rim. Rusty was about to go over and offer assistance when Polinah called him from the hearth.

'Good morning, lazy bones. You must have slept well last night. We've all been awake for hours. Come and have some breakfast. You need to build your strength up.'

'Good morning to you too,' Rusty replied. 'I did indeed sleep well. It's the first time since the crash that I've not had a nightmare. I feel much better.'

He sat on a stool next to the low compound. Polinah handed him a tin plate filled to the brim with sugar-coated porridge. As he tucked in she poured some tea, liberally laced with sugar.

'I am sorry but I cannot offer you any milk. My uncle does not have a fridge so we do not often have fresh milk.'

'I'm used to it this way,' Rusty explained.

'Good morning, young man. I hope you slept well and are feeling better today?'

'Yes, I was very comfortable, sir and I do feel much better. All due to your excellent hospitality, I might add.'

'Good, good,' Mothusi replied. 'I am pleased you are on the mend. You certainly landed yourself in a big mess. What do you think of that house you slept in last night? I built it myself,' he explained, settling down with a cup of tea.

'I wondered if you had,' Rusty replied. 'Polinah says you're originally from Mochudi and it's certainly similar to those I saw there when I visited Phuthadikobo Museum a few years ago.'

'Oh, so you know a bit about our houses, do you? You are quite right. The locals around here would never build a house like it and my wife's parents were most indignant when I planted one right in the middle of their compound. And now look at them!' the older man chortled and gestured towards the veranda. Beneath it the old couple had already retreated from the increasing heat of the morning and were preparing themselves for a siesta on the comfortable bench.

'They spend hours in the shade of that lovely veranda, but they still won't admit that it's a damn fine design. They like me well enough but I am sure that they secretly wish that their first born daughter had not been so daft as to marry a *MoKgatla*.'

Polinah overheard this last remark and chided her uncle for his comments.

'Polinah, my lovely niece. I am only speaking in jest. They have both been very good to me and I have enjoyed my life with them. Anyway I must get on with repairing these blasted punctures. You take good care of this sorry specimen of a *Lekgowa*.'

With that he winked good-humouredly at Rusty and headed off to the other side of the yard.

'He is a good man, my uncle. They are not a wealthy family here in Maun, but he held down a good job as an instructor at the Brigade here until he retired and is now taking good care of their cattle. He has always had a peculiar sense of humour though.'

'You don't need to apologise, Polinah. I understand his humour and he has been very kind to me.' He paused and then said 'I think it's time to deal with the business of the day. Can you point me in the right direction for Maun police station?'

'I can do better than that,' Polinah replied. 'I have business of my own in town so I will take you there.'

* * * * *

A few minutes later, Rusty found himself squashed up against Polinah in the rear seat of a Combi as it made its way towards Maun. The family lived more than four kilometres from the town centre and this was the most direct route. The vehicle they were travelling in was an ancient twelve-seater Toyota minibus. When Polinah and Rusty had hopped aboard there had been two passengers sitting up front with the driver and a man in the rear section who gave them their tickets. The minibus was flagged down regularly and there were now more than twenty people occupying the twelve seats. Several of them were on their way to a market of some description and had with them cardboard boxes stuffed full of spinach, sweetcorn and even in one case, a brace of hens. Rusty found himself pressed up against the side window and, despite the distraction offered by the fact that Polinah was almost sitting on his lap, he was rapidly becoming claustrophobic. The driver, in his haste to complete this lucrative trip, would build up as much speed as he could between stops. The light van swayed alarmingly on its overtaxed suspension as they made their rapid progress. Rusty was relieved when they arrived at Riley's Hotel. He had visited Maun before and knew that the life of the town took place along this one stretch of road. The police station was further down this same street. As he looked, he could see the striped flag of Botswana, outside the modern two-storey building. While he stood there collecting his thoughts the hustle and bustle went on around him. As they started to move off together in the general direction of the police station Polinah broke the silence.

'Rusty, I have one or two things to do in town, so why don't we meet up later? Let me know if the police want me to corroborate your story.'

'Sure, that seems fine. I don't need you to hold my hand and after all you weren't part of all this until after the action had taken place.'

'There's a pool-side bar at Riley's. I'll meet you there in an hour. If you don't show up, I'll come back again an hour later. I doubt they'll keep you much longer than that!'

The two of them said an awkward goodbye. Polinah headed off in the opposite direction towards the large roundabout at the end of the main street which led to the airport and many of the other administrative buildings. A moment or two later Rusty entered the police station.

* * * * *

When Polinah arrived at the pleasantly appointed bar behind the hotel an hour later she found Rusty sitting at a table under the shade of a large umbrella, nursing a beer. He had the same angry and yet defeated look she had witnessed in the desert shortly after they had first met. As he caught sight of her approach, he gave her a rueful smile.

'Something tells me your trip to the police station has not filled you with the joys of spring.'

'Indeed not Polinah. Inspector Setshedi restored my jaded faith in the police out there in the desert but I am afraid that this lot have thoroughly pissed me off.'

'Come on then, tell me what happened, while I get a drink.'

Rusty told her his exasperating story. First of all they had kept him waiting for the best part of thirty minutes whilst an irate tourist reported the theft of all of his camping gear from the roof rack of his Land Rover. It transpired that he had spent the night in a lodge on the outskirts of town after several days in the bush. When he returned to the car park that morning everything was gone. The police had been disinterested and Rusty felt a certain sympathy for them. There was a huge local black market in stolen camping gear and anyone travelling in the district should have been aware of that and kept their kit secure. The police were used to a procession of incidents such as this and their chances of recovering any of the property were slight. Rusty managed to get past the young constable at the front desk and had delivered his report to the duty sergeant in a small unkempt office in the back of the building. He recounted everything from the moment Mats had been murdered, right up to his arrival here. The policeman had listened impassively and made no attempt to interrupt or to ask for clarification. When Rusty finished he had expected that there would be a certain amount of action but all that happened was that he was asked if he could put it in writing. The sergeant gave him a pencil and a pro forma sheet to use and left him to his own devices.

'Do you know what he said to me, Polinah, when I handed it back to him? He checked that I had signed it, stamped it and then said that he would report it through the relevant channels. When I asked him what that meant he said he would pass it on to the station commander who was currently out of town investigating a burglary at the post office in Gweta. He said he felt certain that the commander would take it up with the local police in Jwaneng. When I told him that the local police were absent, being dead and buried out in the desert, he just said that it would need to be corroborated before he could take any further action. That really made me angry!'

Rusty stopped for a moment and took a long draught of his beer before he went on.

'Then I asked him if he had any information regarding the fatal accident near the Jwaneng Mine. Once again he seemed indifferent, explaining that as it had occurred in another police district then he would have to make enquiries. And that, of course, would take time.'

As Rusty sipped from his beer he went on to explain that the Sergeant had asked him where he was staying so that he could report any findings to him. The officer knew Polinah's uncle Mothusi and where he lived and he tried to assure Rusty that everything would be done to sort it all out and that he would keep him informed of any developments and he would get back to him later in the week.

'Later this week, Polinah. If that murderous thug is out there then he'll be long gone. I could not make him understand the urgency of it all. I got the distinct impression that he thought I was a hysterical foreigner. I don't think he believed me. I'm so angry but I don't see what I can do until the senior officer returns. I don't know what to do next . . .'

Polinah spoke quietly but confidently.

'Well Rusty, I've had a more productive morning. After we separated I went to the Department of Parks and Wildlife, which is just on the edge of town, near the airport. I had this idea that if our friend in the Pajero was heading north then he might use the park trails to make his escape. I wanted to find out if records were kept of vehicles entering and leaving the parks.'

Rusty was amazed.

'As you know, my cousin Mpho works for the Parks Department in Moremi. Through him I know one or two of the guys who are based here in town. I tracked one of them down and explained that I was trying to find a friend who was known to be in Moremi Game Reserve. Mpho talks about his job and he's mentioned that they're frequently called upon to try to locate tourists and travellers who do not re-emerge when expected. More often than not they'll have got into mechanical difficulties and need assistance. Each vehicle is logged on entry and noted once it has left. The drivers are asked to give their length of stay and the gate they'll use to leave. If they don't turn up when they're expected someone will go to look for them. It's all monitored through a radio system which links the head office in Maun, the gatekeepers and the rangers. One of the Maun officials introduced me to the radio operator and he put me through to Mpho, who is manning the North Gate at the moment. He asked for the details of the vehicle and the gate we thought he'd used. He suspected my friend would have entered from the South Gate. His log book showed no one answering that description leaving via the North Gate in the past few days.'

Rusty was crestfallen. He was certain that someone would have noticed the Pajero entering the reserve.

'It was disappointing to hear but suddenly one of the other rangers joined in. It was tricky to work out what everyone was saying – there was a lot of interference on the line – but the Maun radio operator explained that the gatekeeper at the South Gate had seen the vehicle enter the park through his gate two days previously. The driver – who was travelling alone – had explained that he was planning to stay for four days and up to today there is no record of his exit.'

'Do you think he's heading for the North Gate?'

'They couldn't tell me anything else but he'll be travelling through the reserve for the next forty-eight hours. I was feeling so pleased with myself so it's quite a jolt to find you sitting here looking so glum.'

Rusty was genuinely astonished at the young woman's resourcefulness.

'If we go back and tell the Police what we now know, perhaps they will go in and pick him up,' Polinah suggested.

'That Sergeant isn't going to move a muscle unless he receives a direct order from his boss. I've got a better idea. I'm going to tail the bastard myself so we don't lose him again. Can I hire a 4x4 somewhere in Maun?'

'Rusty, are you sure you know what you're letting yourself in for? The man has already murdered at least two people and he won't hesitate to kill again. I did not nurse you back to health so that you could go out and get yourself butchered by a psychopath a few days later.'

'I know the guy's armed. I have no intention of getting involved with him. I'll just keep an eye on him from a safe distance until the authorities can get their act together. I was hoping that if I can get hold of a vehicle then I can head off and you can report to the police on my behalf. Hopefully, if they think I'm about to do something foolhardy they might send in the cavalry.'

'The receptionist might be able to help us find a vehicle,' Polinah explained. 'Let's go and ask.'

They headed up to the front desk but while the staff were helpful they could only offer a handful of saloon cars.

'Of course, there's the big car-hire outfit at the airport. Have you tried them? Here, use our phone to check whether they can help.'

* * * * *

Ten minutes later they were waiting at the front of the hotel as a brand new zebra-striped long wheelbased Land Rover Defender roared up to the front of the hotel. The driver parked it in the full glare of the sun because it was too high to fit under the canopy. A big, bald barrel of a man stepped out into the heat of the day, mopped his brow, held out his meaty hand and introduced himself.

'Hi there. Are you Miss Mabina and Mr McKenna? My name is Jake Tenkrooden from Imperial. Pleased to meet you. Let me show you round this little beauty.'

As the big red-faced South African enthused about the Land Rover, Rusty tried to hide his disappointment. He was used to the simplicity of the Kalahari Ferrari. He estimated this great hulk must be twice the weight of his old Land Rover. It had all the trimmings: the V8 engine, bull-bars, power steering, front winch, fridge, long-range tanks, air-conditioning, tool box and high lift jack. As the big man continued the list went on and on. Although this was not a motor which Rusty would ever have bought for himself he had to admit it was perfect for the situation they found themselves in. The hire company had thought of everything that could possibly be required by the independent traveller. Mr Tenkrooden assured him that they had cooking equipment, folding chairs, tables, cookers, gas bottles, lights and even sleeping bags back at the depot. He emphasised that all of these could be hired at a very reasonable extra cost. All they needed to supply for themselves would be food and drink. Once Rusty had established that his single credit card would be acceptable they shook hands on a deal and headed off to the airport's hire desk so that the formalities could be dealt with. It did not take long for them to agree on a price for the additional camping equipment that Rusty selected and that was swiftly loaded into the rear part of the Land Rover. Mr Tenkrooden added the option to take the vehicle through Immigration controls and into Zimbabwe. It would not be uncommon for tourists to make the trip through the northern parks of Botswana and to complete their journey at Victoria Falls. They had an office there and Rusty was assured that he could drop the Land Rover there if he wished. After a few short minutes he was standing in the airport car park with the keys in his hand and Polinah at his side. He also had the bit between his teeth.

'Okay, food and fuel and then I can hit the road. Hop aboard and let's head off to the shopping mall.'

'Rusty, you said that the sergeant knew my uncle. Don't you think that it would be a good idea to tell him what you are up to?'

'Sure thing Polinah, You're full of good ideas. That's an excellent thought. After we've fuelled up I'll drop you back at your uncle's and the two of you can go over to the police station together.'

'No, Rusty. I have a better idea,' Polinah replied firmly. 'Mothusi can fill in forms and wait around at the station but I'm coming with you.'

They were pulling into the supermarket car park when Polinah dropped this bombshell. Rusty almost lost control of the powered-steering and earned the wrath of a middle-aged woman who was just reversing out of the bay adjacent to the one he was driving into. Rusty had never considered the possibility that Polinah might choose to accompany him on the trip and his immediate reaction was that she should stay in Maun. He could not quite put his finger on why he felt like this. There was no doubt that he was very happy to have her around and he was being honest when he said that he was not going to challenge the armed individual who he was pursuing. Still, there was no doubting from all that had happened over the course of the last few days that the potential for danger was very real and he felt the need to protect her. As if she could read his thoughts, Polinah spoke.

'Rusty, you don't need to try and protect me. I enjoy a challenge. I won't give you any nonsense about you needing me with you in case you get ill again. You are perfectly well and no doubt can tackle this on your own. It's just that I feel involved with it all now and I want to see this evil man caught as much as you do.'

Rusty tried to resist her enthusiasm but she remained implacable, saying that if he tried to drive off without her she would simply refuse to get out of the Land Rover and he would have to eject her by force. He still felt great pain when he thought about Mats and Inspector Setshedi and he knew he would not be able to bear it if something should befall this young woman as well.

'Okay then, you can come. Just one thing though. I'm doing all the driving.'

'Fine by me. I wouldn't have a clue how to control this great beast. Let's get the shopping done and get going.'

In less than an hour they were parked outside the family compound on the edge of town, having got food, fuel, extra clothes for Rusty and cash from the bank. Polinah insisted that this was her part of the deal and she had withdrawn her maximum limit from the cash machine. As they sat by the hearth drinking a cup of hot tea, Mothusi listened carefully as they explained what was required of him and what he should tell the police. He readily agreed to help, but Rusty was not sure if he had taken it all in, because throughout the conversation he kept looking in awe towards the big Land Rover.

'Just look at that wonderful machine. What I would give to have one of those at the cattle post. Such a fine motor.'

Rusty had tried to dent his enthusiasm by reminding him of its thirst for fuel but he would not be deflected and in the end Rusty had to make a promise that one day he would come back and give the man an opportunity to drive such a machine. A few minutes later, Rusty drove off, with Polinah at his side, leaving the family waving madly in their wake.

* * * * *

As they crossed the river and headed north on the tarred road out of town, Rusty was silent. As soon as Mats had contacted him he had promised himself that he would make an early return to the Okavango. He had been there half a dozen times on his previous visits to Botswana and had grown to love the place. Many of the other temporary contract workers would take the opportunity of their time in Southern Africa to travel widely, taking the garden route to Cape Town or perhaps crossing the continent from west to east, bathing in the Atlantic and the Indian Oceans on the same holiday. Rusty had taken a conscious decision not to spend his spare time travelling throughout several countries but had always stayed within Botswana, apart from a single trip over the border to Zimbabwe to see Victoria Falls, and to make a canoeing trip down the Zambezi. In the course of his travels along the sand roads of this predominantly desert country he had constantly been drawn back to the Okavango Delta and to Moremi Game Reserve in particular. The forested glades, the open grasslands, the reed beds and the shimmering water holes were a consistent joy to him. As they drove off the tar at Shorobe he remembered his previous visits with great affection but could not forget the very different circumstances of this trip. As he looked across to his left and looked at Polinah he tried to push any dark thoughts to the back of his mind and instead concentrate on the pleasures of the journey. After all, he thought to himself, there were few people in the world who would give up a chance to make the trip that they were embarking on, whatever the circumstances.

As he ran through sand for the first time in the new vehicle Rusty found he needed to concentrate on his driving. The big machine handled differently to the Kalahari Ferrari. It was carrying so much weight it felt as if it was riding the uneven surface like a boat on a choppy sea. In contrast to this the power steering meant that the handling was much lighter than the older Land Rover. Mastering the weight of the machine with these sensitive controls was an art which took him more than a few minutes to acquire. As he accomplished this there were a few alarming moments as they lurched and fishtailed violently through the occasional sweeping curve or over a large pothole. Polinah held on to the handhold above the passenger window, but despite the look of slight apprehension on her face, she had thrown her lot in with him and therefore had no choice but to trust him. By the time they reached the fork in the road and had taken the left branch to the park's South Gate, Rusty was in command of the truck and they started to relax in each other's company.

Shortly before the turn-off they had been ushered through a veterinary fence by a cheerful attendant and were now truly in big game country. At first the trackside vegetation was largely featureless acacia scrub, but as they navigated their way along the left-hand fork the track grew more twisty and curvy and the ground cover became much more varied. The area was predominantly flat, with the occasional boulder outcropping, and the bulk of the land they passed through changed to open grassland with many thick stands of thorn bushes. Occasionally this would give way to large glades of huge trees of several different species. It was this change to varied tree species which indicated that the delta was now beginning to influence the landscape. After an hour or so of travelling in silence Polinah suddenly let out a loud and excited squeal.

'Rusty, slow down. Look at those thorn bushes to the left. What are they? They look like goats.'

As they slowed down Rusty could see a small bachelor herd of twenty or thirty impala, browsing in the late afternoon sunshine. They watched as the graceful reddish brown bodies of the delicate looking animals, with their long legs and the narrow black and white stripes on their rumps, ambled past.

'They're impala. You can see the differences between the adult and juvenile males.'

Suddenly something spooked the animals and they darted from the safety of their cover, leaping and bounding in several different directions, the large horns of the adult males flashing in the sunlight. Rusty had forgotten how graceful they were in flight.

'Look how high they leap. I have never seen anything so beautiful. When I first caught sight of them I thought they were goats. And now I have seen my first Okavango impala.'

Rusty had forgotten that visiting the game parks was primarily a pastime for tourists and ex-pats and remembered Polinah was going to experience the beauties of the delta for the first time. He felt a brief twinge of jealousy that this would be a new experience for her, but then he realised that on this trip one of the joys for him would not necessarily be watching the animals for himself, but watching Polinah watch the animals. Her shining face was aglow with delight as she tracked the long-legged antelope as they zigzagged their way into the middle distance. Shortly before achieving the cover of the next glade of trees they all stopped as one and looked back in the direction of the Land Rover, their brown eyes watchful and their big pointed ears cocked forwards towards them. Before getting under way again, Rusty let Polinah watch the impala for a while as they moved away into the trees.

'If we stop for every group of impala we're not going to make much progress you know,' Rusty warned her.

As they covered the next few kilometres they came upon many of the same antelope, bachelor herds and family groups alike. The animals had grown accustomed to vehicles and it was only on rare occasions that they would leap away into cover as the Land Rover passed them.

Polinah and Rusty wound their way towards the park gate but as they rounded a tight bend the track in front of them dipped down without warning into a slight incline which led to an adjacent dry river channel. The width diminished and the tree cover increased to form a large canopy under which they passed. Rusty had been relaxing at the wheel, enjoying the scenery and Polinah's evident enjoyment of it. All of a sudden all hell broke loose. Rusty was immediately on autopilot, seemingly unaware of his surroundings yet responding very directly to them. He swung the wheel hard over to try and avoid the large immobile object in their path and as he did, it lurched upright towards him and screeched defiantly. The bellow that it let rip seemed to shake the ground under them. It was all over in a matter of seconds. Rusty had succeeded in preventing the Land Rover from rolling or going into an uncontrollable skid and had done just enough to avoid the obstacle. It had turned in his direction and had rushed down the left-hand side of the Land Rover. It had come so close that it bent the passenger's wing mirror. It was now standing its ground about forty metres away from where they had come to a standstill. Rusty felt his heart beat begin to slow but he knew the danger was not yet over. He did, however, for the first time, have a clear view in his rear view mirror and felt that he was in some sort of command of the situation.

'My God, Rusty, what on earth was that monster? We almost hit it head on.'

'That, Polinah, was a very large old bull elephant spending a quiet afternoon in the shade of the trees, right in the middle of our little track. And somehow I don't think he is very happy with us. Have a look through the back window.'

'God, he's huge. Look at those massive tusks.'

It was not the elephant's size which was Rusty's immediate concern however. It was his ears. These were standing out at right angles to his head and Rusty had to admit that he made a very fine sight indeed. He just wished he was seeing it all from a considerably greater distance then he in fact was. Rusty was fully aware of the speed an animal like this could muster over a short distance. He decided it would be imprudent to race away in a cloud of dust. He was not sure he had the acceleration to succeed at such close quarters. Instead he kept the engine ticking over at a gentle idle, then pressed the clutch pedal to the floor and engaged first gear. If the elephant should decide to charge then he would at least be able to try and affect a getaway as quickly as he could. It was little tricks like this which could make the difference between survival or disaster out here in the bush.

The next two or three minutes were crucial. The powerful animal swished its ears backwards and forwards and pawed the heavy earth with its large plate-like feet. All the while it peered at them malevolently through its incongruously small and sinister-looking eyes. All of a sudden the elephant swung its great head and trunk to one side and with a tremendous screeching blundered off noisily into the undergrowth at the side of the track. Rusty's decision to face the animal out had proved to be the correct strategy. As peace once again descended they could hear it careering wildly through the trees, flattening everything that stood in its path.

'Well at least it's just a few trees that fine old bull is destroying and not us and this Land Rover,' he laughed, trying to relieve the tension of the moment, but he knew they had been lucky. His lapse in concentration had almost been the cause of a major calamity.

'Are you all right?' he asked.

'Wow that was exhilarating,' Polinah exclaimed. 'I won't forget him in a hurry.'

'I was too busy watching the tracks and looking out for elephant dung,' Rusty said. 'We were unlucky to have encountered him like that.'

'All these amazing things around us and we haven't reached the park yet.'

'We'll be there soon. There's a campsite at the South Gate. I think we should hole up there for the night,' Rusty suggested. 'We've had enough excitement for one day and anyway we need to get the hang of how to put up this silly rooftop tent.'

After another hour of cautious, uneventful driving they were cruising along a lengthy straight stretch when Rusty saw the thatched entrance to the park. As they drew up two rangers came out and casually greeted them.

'It is good to see you Polinah Mabina. How is your uncle Mothusi and his lovely wife Lebitso?'

'They are both well, thank you. This is Rusty McKenna. My cousin has probably told you that we're trying to catch up with a friend of ours who entered the reserve via the South Gate.'

'Yes, but we've not heard of any sightings of the Pajero yet. We know your friend has not left the park yet. You should be able to catch up with him.'

'I know all the likely spots where he might make camp for the night,' Rusty assured them.

'We'll get your registration. Do you know how long you'll be staying in the park? Which gate will you leave by?'

Once the formalities were complete and the park fees paid, the gate in front of the Land Rover was lifted so they could pass under it.

'Thank you for all your help,' Polinah said as she waved goodbye.

'Enjoy your stay in the reserve. We hope you'll find your friend.'

As he drove through, Rusty noticed the rangers' accommodation on the right hand side of the track. A number of neatly constructed simple rondavels – painted green to blend in with the surroundings – stood in two rows. They drove quietly past this small encampment and then the public camp site came into view on the left. Two medium-sized areas had been cleared between which a small ablution block was discreetly positioned. Dotted around the cleared sandy area were a number of concrete hearths where a fire could be constructed and to one side was a handy pile of firewood. Tucked away in the far corner of the site were two blue and white Toyota twin cabs bearing Namibian registration plates. Three tents were arranged in a semi-circle beyond the two trucks. A collection of folding chairs and tables were positioned close to one of the hearths. Someone was cooking over a wood fire and two others were returning from the ablution block with wet hair and towels thrown casually over their shoulders. They waved to Rusty and Polinah as they pulled up on the opposite side and climbed down from the Land Rover to stretch their legs after the eventful journey.

'You know, I have never camped out in the bush before,' Polinah said. 'I hope I won't be frightened.'

'There is no need for you to be apprehensive, but I suppose if you have never camped before you will not be able to help me set up our camp.'

'Rusty, I might not have stayed in one of these fancy tents before but I have been to my father's cattle post on many occasions,' she retorted sharply. 'Don't you worry about whether I can pull my weight. You get the tent sorted out and I will get cooking.'

With that, Polinah strode purposefully to the back of the Land Rover, opened the rear doors and set about unloading tables, chairs and cooking equipment. Polinah proved to be more skilled in the completion of her task than Rusty. No instruction manual had been supplied with the tent and although it was pretty simple in theory, in practice it involved scrambling around on the roofrack to ensure that all the various struts were locked into place. After several minutes of thought and ingenuity he had it all in place and as he stepped back from his handiwork he had to admit that it did look impressive. To the nervous bush camper it provided protection from snakes and scorpions and could also form a viewing platform should any large, dangerous game encroach into the camp. As he turned to look at Polinah he saw the fire was lit and a single pot was bubbling away merrily. She was just about to set out a small area of wire mesh over the fire which she had raked flat so that just the red embers were showing.

'I thought we could barbecue those chicken pieces and have them with coleslaw and a potato salad. We can eat out of tins when we have used the fresh stuff,' she explained as she handed him a glass of white wine. 'Bon appetit.'

The smooth Cape chardonnay was perfectly chilled and as Rusty enjoyed his first taste, he reflected on how much a camping fridge enhanced the pleasure of a trip into the bush. After a long day sweating behind the hot steering wheel, either travelling at speed on the tar or after watching game in the heat of the day, there was nothing better than a long cool drink as the sun set and dinner cooked over an aromatic wood fire.

'And good health to you too. Do you want to have a look at our accommodation for the night?'

Polinah clambered excitedly up the aluminium ladder mounted over the front bumper leading up to a small door which afforded entry to the large compartment. She pushed the mosquito screen aside. After a moment or two she re-emerged.

'It's lovely but there is only one room. Where are you going to sleep?'

Rusty was genuinely taken aback. The inside of the canvas chamber was probably more than two metres square, enough space for at least three people to sleep comfortably. It had usually been the case, or at least it had been in Rusty's experience, that when travelling in the bush, the niceties of social etiquette would be dropped and that buddies would be prepared to accept loss of privacy. One look at Polinah's stern expression told him that was not to be the case on this occasion and so he blurted out a reply.

'There's plenty of room in the back of the Land Rover. That's where I'll sleep.'

'That's good,' said Polinah, as she climbed down the ladder. She picked up her wine glass and smiled mischievously.

An hour or so later, after a tasty meal, Rusty unrolled a couple of camping mattresses while Polinah washed up and packed up the cooking equipment. As night descended over the almost deserted camp they drank a small night-cap of Amarula and listened to the sounds of others nearby enjoying some after dinner banter. Rusty could just make out the glow of the fire on the underside of the trees near where they were parked. As soon as Polinah had finished her drink she bade Rusty goodnight and climbed to her bed on the roof. A few minutes later he clambered into his makeshift cot in the back of the Land Rover.

As Rusty lay pondering about another eventful day he heard the unmistakable sound of a hyena whooping and cackling in the nearby trees. Polinah made no comment about this spine tingling noise so he assumed she was already fast asleep. Rusty was himself deep in slumber soon afterwards and passed a relatively untroubled night, which was mercifully free of nightmares. At one point he was awakened by the sounds of an animal in close proximity to the Land Rover, coupled with scuffling noises and what sounded like metal scraping against earth. He had been so deeply asleep that as soon as it ceased he instantly succumbed to his drowsiness once again.

* * * * *

As soon as Rusty awoke he realised he had overslept. The sun was high in the sky and the Land Rover was growing uncomfortably warm. As he sat up he looked out of the window half expecting to see Polinah emerging from one of the showers or, if he was lucky, preparing breakfast over the rekindled fire but there was no sign of her. He felt a momentary pang of anxiety and, slipping on a t-shirt and a pair of shorts, hopped out of bed to look for her.

As soon as he was outside he heard her voice.

'Rusty, I am so glad you are awake. I have been too frightened to get down from here since I saw that big animal come right up to us during the night. I could see it through the mosquito net.'

Once she had described it to him he was certain that it had been a hyena and he could spot the tell-tale signs that the camp had had an uninvited guest in the night. The area where they had cooked their chicken was covered in tracks and the metal rubbish bin a few metres away had been tipped over and its contents were strewn everywhere.

'I am sorry Polinah, I've forgotten my bush skills. I should have told you to put the chicken bones on the fire last night when you cleared up. Did you put them in the bin?'

'Yes. Why?'

'Every bush campsite has its semi-tame hyenas which make a dreadful nuisance of themselves to the unwary traveller,' he explained. Rusty had experienced problems with vervet monkeys and baboons breaking into food boxes in the past. 'From now on we'll burn all the food debris. We won't have problems with scavengers in the future if we do.'

Reassured, Polinah finally came down from the roof top and went off to have a shower while Rusty prepared a nourishing breakfast of boiled eggs, bread and slices of mango and set the coffee on. For a while they enjoyed the solitude of the camp. The Namibians had long since departed for an early morning game drive and it was unlikely that any new arrivals would turn up until later that day. Their only companions were a few nervous-looking vervet monkeys who eyed them from the top of the trees and one of the rangers who was patrolling the perimeter of the camp with an old bolt action British Army issue rifle.

By mid morning Rusty and Polinah had packed up their camp and set off to explore the interior of the park. Although neither of them had mentioned the man they were pursuing he was always at the back of their minds and it was inevitable that they would soon come face to face with the person who had murdered Mats. For the time being however they enjoyed the simple pleasure of viewing the beautiful parkland.

'Look over there,' Rusty said, pointing to some of the tracks he was able to identify. 'No elephant tracks however.'

The terrain through which they were passing – comprising open grassland with camelthorn scrub interspersed with glades of large trees – was similar to the landscape they had driven through the day before. Now they were within the park proper however, they were coming very close to the area where the fingers of water from the heart of the delta itself spread out in a south- easterly direction. The Okavango Delta consisted of countless numbers of small creeks and lagoons fed by a series of larger channels which ran to either side of Chief's Island. This was the only substantial piece of permanent dry land that existed in the core of the delta. All the individual small streams flowed haphazardly towards the south-east where a natural fault line fed them into the Thamalakane River. When the rains fell in Angola the resultant flood passed through the delta and the water flowed to Maun and sometimes to the great pans to the south and east. As these small streams meandered through Moremi Game Reserve there were a few places where the track had to cross over these riverine obstacles, particularly after rain. A series of four pole bridges were constructed when the park was opened and the traveller has to pass over each one of these in order to progress from South Gate to North Gate. Soon after seeing their first major stand of reeds and a flash of open blue water on their left-hand side Rusty and Polinah came to the first of these bridges. It currently spanned a dry creek bed and, because of the unevenness of its surface, recent travellers had made their passage by driving through the bottom of the adjacent stream bed. In order to see how Polinah would react to her first experience of one of these odd structures Rusty elected to cross the bridge itself, despite the lack of water. As he did so the Land Rover rocked and rolled violently as its suspension reacted to the shape of each individual horizontal pole. This caused the young woman to shriek in mock fright. Shortly after crossing the bridge they came to a wonderful spot which Rusty remembered from his previous trips to the delta.

Let's stop for lunch,' Rusty said, as he parked under a large fig tree to avoid the glare of the midday sun.

The track they had been following ran parallel to the edge of a large lagoon. All around this body of water there were individual stands of trees set in rolling grassland. As they took in the panoramic view in front of them several things were visible. The lagoon measured several hundred metres in length and perhaps just under a hundred metres in width. Not far from where they had parked, a number of large hippos were lying partially submerged in the water but visible in the mud close to the bank. They moved very occasionally and, as they did so, their soft pink bellies came into view. There were more than twelve of them in all, including two small calves.

'I bet you haven't seen these characters before have you, Polinah?'

'They're more grotesque than I thought they would be.'

'Polinah, look over there,' Rusty said directing her gaze to where the lagoon narrowed and a slender promontory of land ran out into the main body of water which, as it petered out, turned into nothing more than a spit of mud.

Rusty could see from the hoof prints indented into the dirt that small antelope and other animals came down here to drink and forage. Right at the end of the spit was a large tree-trunk like object more than three metres in length. Rusty recognised the distinctive shape immediately and was about to point it out to Polinah when a family of warthog suddenly darted out of the bush at the edge of the forest and scampered down to the water's edge to drink. There were eight in all, two adults and six adolescents, not yet wise in the ways of the delta. As Rusty watched them crouching down on their front knees and rooting for food with their tusks, he saw one of them move out onto the spit of mud. It was foraging happily in the soft wet earth. The young warthog seemed oblivious to the hidden dangers at the water's edge and as Rusty pointed out the large immobile log like object to Polinah, the warthog wandered to within less than ten metres of it. Large crocodiles could survive for six months without feeding after a substantial kill so perhaps of all the large predators they had developed tremendous powers of patience and could wait for days for the perfect opportunity. It pounced forwards on its short, powerful legs directly at the dawdling warthog.

It also used its large tail which had remained in the water to provide forward momentum. It shot towards the unwary warthog at great speed. At the last possible instant the warthog realised the predicament it had blundered into and ducked despairingly to the left. The big croc's reactions were not quick enough and it only succeeded in hitting a glancing blow with the side of its jaw. Both animals lost their bearings in the impact but the first to respond was the warthog. Perhaps a surge of adrenaline came to its aid and it picked itself up and darted away across the mud, squealing loudly. It did not stop until it was lost from view in the forest and was soon joined by its parents and its siblings, who, although unaware of what they were running from, were prepared to accept the squealing as the danger signal that it was intended to be. The lucky warthog would no doubt think twice in the future before going out onto the same piece of unprotected ground. Rusty could see from Polinah's expression that she was torn between the excitement of seeing nature in the raw, and the sheer horror of the fact that she might have seen the small mammal torn to pieces and consumed right in front of her.

'We ought to get going.'

Just as Rusty started to remind Polinah about the real reason for their journey through the park, they were once again delayed, this time by the arrival of a small group of giraffe – four adults and an ungainly infant – which appeared out of the forest on the opposite side of the lagoon. Cautiously they made their way to the water and as they did so nibbled at the succulent upper branches of the trees that skirted the lake. Rusty loved these extraordinary animals and was relieved when they had satisfied their thirst and had moved into cover.

For the moment peace descended over the lagoon. Polinah and Rusty knew it was time to get back into the real world. Rusty engaged the motor and drifted off quietly around the southern edge of the lake in the direction of Second Bridge. As they moved the track skirted the lip of the change in environment between the permanently wet areas and the permanently dry. To their left were huge stands of reeds through which they could see the occasional glimpse of water. To the right was a seemingly endless forest of mature trees. As this was the hottest part of the day they saw little moving about, just a few impala taking advantage of the cool shade which the tree canopy afforded.

'Hey, look over there. Is that a kudu?'

'Where?'

Rusty was sure he had spotted a shy kudu in the depths of an impenetrable thicket but when he took a second look the animal melted away into deep cover as soon as it became aware of the intrusion. Rusty had not seen any horns so he suspected it might have been an adult female. It took them more than a couple of hours to make their stately progress through the park, during which they reached Second Bridge. As with the first, the channel beneath it was dry and on this occasion Rusty elected to take the lower route. It was already late in the afternoon by the time they reached the open meadowland which preceded the Third Bridge and its camp site. In all the time that they had been in the park they had seen only one other vehicle – a South African registered Land Cruiser – cruising slowly and watching out for game. They had exchanged cheerful waves and passed one another on the narrow track.

'We should check out one of the camping pitches I've used before,' Rusty suggested as they reached the Third Bridge area. 'It has a view down to the reed beds.'

The Third Bridge campsite consisted of a number of shady glades on the edge of the reed beds stretching for several hundred metres down to the bridge itself. On the other side of the creek there were several more secluded camp sites tucked in at the water's edge which could only be reached by crossing over the narrow bridge. Rusty drove past the first few camping areas and was pleased to see that his preferred spot was vacant. It was about seventy metres from the ablution block and was ringed with thick scrub and shaded by two mature Sausage trees. The trees provided excellent cover. The campsite appeared to be deserted and Rusty and Polinah would be assured of complete privacy that evening.

'What time is it?' Polinah asked.

'It's almost five. If we get our camp established we'll have time to wander out to the bridge.'

* * * * *

As they left the shade of their camp and neared the bridge it was apparent from the proximity of the resplendent clumps of reeds that they were approaching water. As they drove out into the centre of it Rusty opened his door. Looking down he could see the fresh clean water flowing briskly underneath, perhaps a metre or so in depth. He could see at a glance that it was teeming with life. Insects rested on the surface and small minnows and other fishes darted in and out of the bridge supports. Polinah leaned across him.

'It's crystal clear,' she said as she looked deep into the crisp water.

She found her eyes were drawn to the clean water flowing beneath them. They looked at it for several minutes, all the while Polinah supporting herself as she gazed through the open door by resting her hands lightly on Rusty's left thigh. He made no effort to move and for a short while enjoyed the sheer perfection of the beautiful African day. After a while Rusty slowly engaged the engine and they continued their bumpy way across the bridge. At the far end he had to slow down to pick his way gingerly on to the track beyond the bridge. The water had at a time of flood in the recent past flowed beyond the end of the bridge and had scoured a deep hollow, across which it was not possible to use speed. After engaging low ratio the big engine performed the task effortlessly, but it took all Rusty's driving skills to get through the obstacle without damaging the vehicle or causing discomfort to himself and his passenger. On the right-hand side of the track a large leadwood tree provided perfect deep shade. Lying sprawled out majestically in this cool spot were five adult lions, three females and two males in their prime. Three of them were asleep, lying on their backs with their legs spread-eagled and their full fat bellies exposed, but the others were wide awake and were playing good-naturedly with one another. Apart from a quick glance with their piercing yellow eyes neither gave the Land Rover another look. As soon as Polinah had seen the lions she gripped Rusty's arm instinctively and now after watching them for what seemed like an eternity she spoke.

'Rusty, I've always been so frightened of lions. I didn't realise they could be so beautiful.'

He did not reply. Polinah, puzzled at his silence, turned to face him. He was looking over in a different direction. His demeanour was gaunt and haggard.

She followed his gaze and saw, set back in cover on the other side of the track, a white Mitsubishi Pajero. Despite the contrast between the sharp glare of the sun and the darkened interior of the cab she recognised the same piercing eyes she had seen in the desert a few days earlier. Her fascination at seeing lions for the first time was instantly dissipated by the sheer horror that was evident in that predatory human stare.

'Rusty, that's him!' she blurted out. 'That's the man I saw at the clinic. Quick, we need to move.'

Rusty was sick to his stomach for foolishly letting his guard down and leaving them both exposed to this stark danger. It took Polinah's warning cry to kick him into action and he automatically engaged first gear and started to draw away. His inner tension got the better of him and for once he did not get the revs right as he engaged the clutch. The heavy Land Rover lurched forward in a series of bunny hops before the tyres gripped properly into the soft sand under them. The driver did not move as they passed within ten metres of the Pajero, but he watched them with malevolent intent.

* * * * *

Despite his statuesque appearance Kurt was inwardly seething. He had been aware for some time that a new vehicle had arrived and made camp on the other side of the bridge. The campsite had been abandoned by several other parties earlier in the day. They had departed in the direction of North Gate leaving him alone at the site. Shortly after they had left, the quintet of lions had cautiously crossed the bridge and immediately settled down in the shade right in front of him. The arrival of the other vehicle had not caused any alarm. He had seen it arrive and watched as it parked up in shade a couple of hundred metres away but he did not recognise it. He could see there were two occupants: a white male and a black female. He could not make out their features at such a distance and had assumed it was another rich white man having his sport in the wilderness. He had almost drifted off to sleep, such was his lack of concern, until he heard the engine start up moments ago. Then he was instantly alert to any potential danger and had watched impassively as the Land Rover had drawn up and stopped on the bridge. It was soon close enough for him to be able to recognise the attractive girl from the settlement near the Khutse Game Reserve. There was no doubt in his mind that she was one and the same. It was too much of a coincidence for her to have found herself out in this remote spot without good reason. He did not fully understand why it could be, but he was convinced she was pursuing him. He did not know who the driver was. He did not recognise him. He could see, however, that the man was in shock. Then it had been the reaction of the girl that had finally convinced him that he was no longer anonymous. She had reacted with alarm and had spoken urgently to the driver. After they had disappeared around the next bend in the track Kurt's customary control did not desert him and he did not panic. He could have cut and run but instead he decided to follow them. He was still armed and there was nothing to stop him from picking them off at his leisure should the opportunity arise. As he fired up the engine and began his pursuit, he realised that he had been wrong to dawdle in the delta but for the moment he had the advantage and the roles of the last few days had been reversed.

* * * * *

Rusty panicked. Over the course of the last couple of days and because of the sheer delight at being with Polinah he had pushed all the horrors he had witnessed to the back of his mind. The sighting of the murderer had, however, brought it all back to the surface and struck mortal terror into his heart. He was driving like an automaton, unaware of where they were heading and definitely without paying sufficient attention to his surroundings. A couple of kilometres after leaving the campsite the big Land Rover, with its engine howling, came to a point where the track swung first one way and then the other in response to the contours of the edge of a nearby lagoon. Initially Rusty reacted correctly to these sharp swerves but as he came out of the last of them he had almost completely lost his forward momentum and was in too high a gear. He did not respond quickly enough when the first thing he saw as he came out of the bend was a deep spread of soft sand spanning the track into which some earlier vehicle had become bogged down. In their efforts to dig themselves out of the predicament, previous travellers had created a series of pits and potholes under each of the four drive wheels. Rusty's heavy Land Rover ended up squarely in the middle, moving at insufficient speed to climb out of the other side. Instantaneously they ground to a halt. The engine stalled.

'Oh fucking hell! Oh fuck, oh fuck it. I've killed us both. I'll never get us out of here before he's on to us. Fuck!'

Rusty banged his fists onto the steering wheel in frustration and the expletives came long and hard. To all intents and purposes he was beaten. Polinah was not at all used to hearing a tirade of foul language but she knew instinctively it was fear that she was listening to. She quickly leant across the cab of the Land Rover, put her arms around him and hugged him. When he did not appear to respond she pressed her hands to his cheeks and looked directly into his wildly staring eyes.

'Rusty, you lovely man, I trust you. I know you can do it. If you try to get us out of here you can do it.'

With that she kissed him full and hard on the lips.

The sensation of the unexpected physical intimacy brought him

181

back to his senses and his eyes focused on hers. In that instant a bond was created between them and time seemed to stand still. As Polinah smiled warmly into his eyes, Rusty's subconscious feeling towards the young African woman turned from simple attraction to understanding and deep respect. Gripping her wrists in front of his face he returned the embrace. After a few long seconds he tore her from him.

'Thank you, Polinah, thank you. Whatever happens after this I'll never forget your strength. I lost it there for a while and you've shown me the way back.'

Rusty took a deep breath, mopped his brow with the back of his sleeve and very deliberately turned the ignition key. After a second the whine of the starter motor was replaced by the satisfying hum of the powerful engine. Its reassuring sound seemed to give Rusty renewed hope and energy. He opened up the driver's side door and looked out under the wheel arches to front and rear. There was no doubting how deeply they had ploughed into the soft sand. Still, there had been occasions in the past when Rusty had extricated himself in similar circumstances. Whether or not the stranded vehicle would release itself in such a situation seemed to be almost a lottery. He checked that the small black knob which controlled the gearbox differential lock was in the left hand engaged position and then pushed it forward in order to select low range. The gear exchanger fell into position with a dull satisfying thud under and slightly to the left of his seat. He sat still and paused for a second.

Rusty knew that this heavy vehicle was never going to move if the engine was under utilised. He very deliberately pushed the main gear stick forward into first gear but kept his foot hard down on the clutch pedal. Then he pushed the accelerator to the floor and listened intently as the engine note increased.

'Hold tight.' he shouted at Polinah.

As soon as he felt there was enough power available, but not so much that would result in a four wheel spin, he released the clutch pedal.

The surge of power was enough to push the heavy vehicle directly forwards a few centimetres, into the soft sand that enveloped it. What was needed was for at least one of the drive wheels to bite and push them up and out of the obstacle. No differential lock in the world would come to his assistance if all the wheels started spinning. The effect was certainly spectacular, for a moment or two the Land Rover seemed to buck and kick in a stationary position but then slowly began to inch its way forwards through the sand. Despite the noise that the V8 engine was making Rusty could hear the distinctive grinding sound of the big low range first gear cog as it rotated slowly in the gearbox. With its huge power potential the gear continued to push them straight through the clawing sand. With a sudden rush, true grip was achieved with at least one of the axles and they leapt out of the sand pit and hit firm ground once again. As they did, Polinah ululated in celebration, her lips vibrating at great speed and releasing a high pitched resonating note. The traditional sound of an African woman in celebration brought a powerful surge of emotion to Rusty's breast. He now pressed the brake and the clutch at the same moment and they stopped. Pushing the shift back from low to high ratio, he engaged normal drive and they took off up the track leaving a cloud of dirty sand billowing behind them in the early evening air.

'I'm not quite sure what my plan is, Polinah, but we have to assume that he will come after us. I'll get us off the main track as soon as I can.'

'Yes,' Polinah said, nodding her assent.

She held on for dear life as they bumped along the rough trail at a speed which would have earned them censure from the park authorities. As they skidded through the sand they twice more came to deeply-rutted patches, but Rusty rode them with ease. As he did so he tried to remember the geography of the park. The next few kilometres between where they were and the Fourth Bridge led them away from the swamps and through open grassland. It would be difficult to lie low and collect their thoughts in such terrain. He decided that he would go at full tilt as far as the bridge. Once over he remembered that there were a series of subsidiary tracks which headed off towards the heart of the delta itself and which circled and crossed over each other in interconnecting loops, through areas which comprised a mixture of wooded parkland and lagoons. Rusty was confident that in such country it would be difficult for any potential pursuer to find them. When they reached Fourth Bridge Rusty pounded over at great speed, startling a small family of zebra who had come down to water for their evening drink on the opposite side. There were eight of them in total and they had been noisily relishing the invigorating water before the rude interruption. As the Land Rover sped past they bolted for the cover of the trees, high kicking and twisting in mid air as they went, in a reflex attempt to fend off a non-existent lion attack. Once over the bridge Rusty and Polinah came to a small track on the left. On the assumption that their pursuer might expect them to take the first available side track, Rusty ignored it and took the third small track that they came to. After a few hundred yards of skirting the reeds on the left and the woodland on the right they suddenly shot out into a large open grassland perhaps a kilometre in length and half that in width. In the centre of this meadow was a large lagoon. Small groups of impala were grazing out in the open area and a troop of baboons was creeping towards the water's edge for a drink. Here a group of six or seven elephants were wallowing in the water and rolling in the thick mud close to the bank. Far more important from their point of view was the fact that two buff-coloured open-sided Land Rovers were drawn up in formation and a gaggle of tourists were happily clicking away with their expensive cameras. Rusty slowed down to a more sedate crawl and parked up at a discreet distance, apparently also enjoying the sight of the big animals. He was unsure what he was going to do next but he did not think they would get shot at in full view of a group of tourists. He turned the engine off and they sat in silence for several minutes and allowed the peaceful scene in front to them to calm their shattered nerves. Only too soon were they plunged into a state of tense alarm when they heard the sound of a large engine approaching from the forest to their left.

* * * * *

Rusty had his hand wrapped around the ignition key and was once again prepared for flight when the big vehicle that they could hear suddenly burst into view from under the canopy of trees. At once Rusty let out a huge sigh and the tension visibly went from him.

'It's okay Polinah, it's an overlander lorry. Normally I'd be pissed off to have this lovely spot disturbed by these crazies but as far as I am concerned, the more the merrier today!'

What Rusty and Polinah were now looking at was a large Mercedes lorry, painted bright red with the words 'Freedom Finders' emblazoned in big yellow letters down each side. Behind the covered cab the back of the lorry was equipped with a striped red and white awning which was rolled up at the sides. As the big rig approached them they could see that the rear flat bed had been fitted out with several rows of comfortable looking canvas seats. A dishevelled collection of young people lounged in a variety of bizarre clothes. The giant lorry pulled up with a squeal from its air brakes. While the sun-bronzed and sweaty back-packers looked down at them, a tall swarthy character with a cropped head and a large floppy moustache bounced down from the driver's seat and came over to the Land Rover.

'Hi, my friends, I'm sorry to trouble you but we're on our way down from Kasane and we're looking for Third Bridge campsite. We are supposed to be staying there tonight. Have you any idea where it is? They are getting mutinous in the back and they definitely need a shower.'

With that the big man looked up to his travelling companions who were whistling and cat-calling at him from above. As he introduced himself as Didier Beauchamp in heavily accented French it turned out that he was part-owner of a Safari company which ran trips from Marseilles, along the length of Africa, eventually ending up at the Cape. This lot were into the twelfth week of their trip and Rusty could see that, for some of them, it had become more of an ordeal than an

185

adventure. While Rusty gave the avuncular Frenchman clear directions to the campsite he could not fail to notice the admiring glances directed at Polinah. When Didier was finally satisfied that he would not get lost he bowed to her theatrically and then once again jumped into his driver's seat with a friendly wave. As the truck drifted away from them Rusty turned to Polinah.

'Those guys certainly add colour, but they never seem to understand the rules. They've really disturbed the elephants,' he said nodding over to the animals who were silently retreating into the cover of the woods.

As they watched, another vehicle appeared out of a track at the far right end of the lagoon.

'Rusty, he's on to us again. I am sure that's the Pajero,' Polinah whispered.

* * * * *

The distinctive white livery of the new truck was now becoming all too familiar. The track it appeared on took it on to the far side of the lake, from where it had a long anti-clockwise circuit to follow before it would reach where the two of them were parked. The nearest it would get to them while still across the water was about five hundred metres. Rusty did not know much about rifles but he was confident that they were safe until that distance was halved, at the very least. In addition he believed that the presence of the other vehicles would deter trouble. As this thought was crossing his mind he heard the distinctive sound of the two Land Rovers firing up their engines and he watched impassively as they moved away. As the Pajero began its leisurely promenade around the far side of the lagoon, which would eventually bring it right to them, Rusty had already decided what they needed to do.

'Polinah, I'm sorry if this turns into a bit of a merry go round but the safest place for us is the Third Bridge campsite. It looks like it's going to be fairly lively there tonight.'

They moved away along the edge of the lake in the same anti-clockwise direction as the vehicle that was following him. As the Pajero reached the far end of the lagoon, about a kilometre away, Rusty and Polinah disappeared into woodland and up the very track from which the murderer had emerged five minutes before.

* * * * *

Kurt had left the campsite only a couple of minutes after Rusty and Polinah. He had delayed for a moment to regain his equilibrium and to double-check that both his rifles were in position and readily available behind his seat. He did not move off at the same breakneck, reckless speed as Rusty had and it was not long before he was trailing well behind them. When he reached the series of bends that had led to Rusty's downfall he saw the dust had not yet settled in the wake of his target, but he too almost fell into the same trap. He kept the momentum going and as soon as he was past the series of soft sandy spots he was once again in pursuit and had gained some ground. Thereafter, their speed was roughly equal and, because of the twisting nature of the track and the amount of tree and scrub cover to either side, Kurt did not catch sight of the fleeing Land Rover.

He had explored much of this part of the park over the course of the last two days and was beginning to understand its layout. Like Rusty, Kurt crossed over Fourth Bridge and as he reached the spot where the first track diverged to the left he slowed down and paused. There were numerous tyre marks heading off every which way, but the sand was so soft it was impossible to determine which was the most recent. Thinking that he would have elected to take the first available option in order to go to ground he immediately turned left up a minor track. He was heading up a long finger of land which ran out into the delta heartland. After a couple of kilometres he found himself at the water's edge and was forced to retrace his steps.

Having once again rejoined the main track, he took the second track on the left. This led him unerringly on a more circuitous route to the open space where the afternoon's action was taking place. After twenty minutes or so he emerged out of the cover of the woodland into the sunshine and saw the three vehicles parked on the other side of the lagoon. The zebra striped Land Rover was the one he had spotted earlier in the day. He was relieved to have them in his sights again. He relaxed and cruised slowly around the lake as if watching out for game, while he assessed his options. The idea of taking a shot at them was out of the question. He could not guarantee from this range he would inflict anything other than superficial damage to the outside of the other vehicle. As for the occupants they were completely safe unless he could get considerably closer. He also knew that the two other buff-coloured Land Rovers were from one of the game lodges and that they would be equipped with radios which could be used to inform the authorities that there was gunfire in the park. It was out of the question, even for Kurt, to consider murdering all of them and then making his getaway under the cover of darkness.

Kurt had just seen the family of elephant disappear into the woodland, but he arrived a minute or so after the overlander had departed the scene and was oblivious to its presence. As Kurt moved around the opposite side of the lake he immediately became aware of the sound of the engines of the two buff-coloured Land Rovers being started up and soon afterwards saw them move away, leaving the zebra-striped vehicle isolated. He heard the note of their engine starting up and saw them depart up the very same track he had used only moments before. Given the direction in which they had left and with dusk rapidly approaching, he was convinced that it was their intention to return to Third Bridge for the night. He would have preferred to have settled the issue in his favour out here in the bush but he was not unduly concerned. He now knew the area well and believed he could get closer to them under the cover of darkness. He did not follow immediately, having decided to use the dusk as his ally. After half an hour or so he headed back to Third Bridge at a steady pace, watching the game as he drove.

* * * * *

As Rusty rounded the last bend in the track and approached Third Bridge he almost laughed out loud at the spectacle that confronted them. The first thing he could see was that the lions were no longer lying under the shade tree where they had observed them earlier in the afternoon. Passing over the bridge he suddenly saw two of them. They had also crossed over and were lying on a grassy hillock about a hundred metres from the campsite. Although Rusty was unaware of it one was the dominant male and the other was a female in season. They had consummated their dalliance of the afternoon and the male was now sleeping off the effects of his exertions. The female was however alert and was sitting bolt upright looking towards the campsite. She was swishing her tail and her demeanour conveyed anger and irritation. The object of her annoyance was a group of about twelve people who were watching her from the safety of the compound which surrounded the ablution block.

The camp was completely transformed from the desolate spot they had left in such inauspicious circumstances a few hours earlier and it was this change which had nearly brought Rusty to a state of laughter. In the foreground, occupying the space that led down to the bridge, were three Land Cruisers, belonging to a single, small, but expensive Safari company. They had set out a semi-circle of khaki coloured tents at the centre of which was a fireplace and an open-sided mess tent. Within this, two smartly-attired black attendants had set up a long trestle table and were now laying out pristine white tablecloths, cutlery and wine glasses. Two others were preparing food at a small table adjacent to the fire. Judging from where they were standing it was their clients who were watching the lions with such evident enthusiasm.

On the other side of the ablution block and filling up the space between it and where Polinah and Rusty had made their camp, was the Freedom Finders lorry. Several people were unloading kit and others were in the middle of erecting a number of small-domed tents. In the grand traditions of the company these were all a tasteful shade of lilac. The layout of this camp was unstructured. Their tents were popping up at random spots under shade trees. Two at least had been positioned close to Rusty and Polinah's space. Rusty saw two large wooden doors in the rear section of the lorry had been opened to reveal a very neat and well-organised mobile kitchen and was impressed by this clever example of Gallic ingenuity. As with the previous camp, two of the travellers were setting about preparing the evening meal. That was not all. In the unkempt ground at the far end of the campsite were two more vehicles.

In the gloom Rusty could not see them clearly but they appeared to be independent travellers carrying Botswana plates. Rusty suddenly recalled that Mats had mentioned that his arrival from England had coincided with the President's weekend. This meant a four-day break from work. It occurred to Rusty that the two groups on the fringe of the camp were probably from the wealthy middle-classes of places like Francistown or Gaborone, who were well-equipped and well-used to taking advantage of this remote and beautiful spot when the opportunity arose. They had already laid out their camp fires and had suspended gas lanterns in the trees in preparation for the evening's celebrations. As Rusty and Polinah drove sedately through the camp to reach their pitch he suddenly noticed yet more vehicles parked out in the bush a few hundred metres from the campsite. He could see several people who were keenly observing something from the safety of their roof racks. As he and Polinah crossed the open ground he noticed the spoor which indicated that a large herd of grazers had passed through recently. As they arrived at the scene they could see where the other three lions had disappeared to. They were huddled together in front of the two Land Cruisers, feasting on a buffalo carcass. Polinah seemed unnerved by the spectacle and asked if they could go back to the camp. As Rusty started up the engine and turned to go, the single female lifted her head from her feasting. She had torn off a large chunk of flesh and this was hanging from her teeth. Her flanks and face were stained bright with blood. What Rusty noticed, however, were her eyes, which glistened with blood lust. Cameras flashed in the half-light but the beasts took no notice.

Back at the camp, Rusty quickly erected the tent and was just thinking about preparing dinner when he was surprised by the sound of a woman's voice, speaking in heavily accented French.

'Bonsoir, Je suis Silvia.'

The woman hesitated but then plucked up courage and continued.

'You were kind enough to direct us here this afternoon when we were very lost alone, so as soon as we have seen you arrive here, we are all agreeing that you should eat us with dinner. Would you wish?'

Rusty wondered if Polinah had had enough for one day and was just about to turn down the kind invitation when she replied.

'Thank you. That would be lovely. We'll come over as soon as we have showered and refreshed ourselves.'

'Bon, we will look forward to accepting you. We will be eating you in about one hour.'

With that inadvertently delivered threat of cannibalism, the French girl headed back towards the lorry and Polinah decided to grab a shower. Rusty was slightly concerned for her safety. Having collected some clean clothes and their toiletries the two made their way together through the camp. When they reached the ablution block Rusty saw immediately that any fears about danger were unfounded. There was complete safety in numbers. The group who had been watching the lions were now sitting in canvas-backed bush chairs facing down towards the bridge, and cool drinks were being served in tall glasses. Behind the ablution block several of the overlanders were taking advantage of the simple facilities and were merrily hand washing a huge collection of clothes. Inside the men's section, Didier, the leader of the French group was shaving his dark stubble, being careful not to inflict any damage on his impressive moustache. As soon as Rusty had taken his shower and changed he waited outside until Polinah emerged from the other end of the block.

'Rusty, you've brought me all the way out here into the wilderness, and I still have to queue for the shower, just like back at the nurses' home in Gabs.'

Rusty did not reply. He had nothing to say. All he could do was look at her like a foolish schoolboy. After showering she had changed from her bush clothes into a simple white dress. He was unsure what made the overall effect so stunning. Perhaps it was the contrast of the dress against her perfect brown skin, perhaps it was the fact that she had still been slightly wet when she had put it on and it was now hugging her slim figure. He could not quite say, but he knew his pulse was racing and he was completely tongue-tied. She moved towards him where, standing directly in front of him, she came up to his shoulder. She then looked up at him and smiled one of her brilliant smiles. Taking his right hand in her left she said simply.

'Come on, let's eat. I have a hunger.'

With that she led him across the campsite towards where the French group had laid out their trestle tables. As Polinah and Rusty diffidently entered the lamp-lit scene all the faces turned towards them and there was a moment of silence. If they had but known it they would have realised that the whole group was admiring this beautiful and well-matched couple who were joining them for the evening. Dinner was delicious and the company was entertaining. For once it seemed that the normal rules of camp etiquette had been abandoned for the night. The group camped down at the bridge clearly had a great story teller among their number and there was much laughter and merriment from their direction. As for the independent travellers on the fringe of the camp, they had a sound system playing softly in the background and the rowdiness elsewhere clearly did not concern them. The French group numbered about sixteen in all and they were ranged along one vast trestle table. Rusty and Polinah were declared guests of honour. Rusty was seated at one end of the table with Didier and Polinah at the other, next to Silvia. Rusty noticed with amusement that most of the French men gravitated to the other end of the table as soon as seating arrangements had been set. Rusty experienced more than a twinge of jealousy.

Dinner consisted of a succulent stew made from what he was assured was warthog marinated in red wine. This was served with rice and an excellent bean salad. It was accompanied by rough but palatable South African wine and rounded off with fruit. The French were pleased with the wine which they considered to be a huge bargain and the best that they had sampled on their trip to date. The food was superb and served with customary French panache. The conversation centred on stories and exploits of African travels. Rusty was a good storyteller and had much to say about his previous visit to Botswana. As for the others, they had had a number of thrills and spills as they made their way across the Sahara and through Central Africa.

As the night descended, life beyond the camp made itself heard. In the middle distance the silence was spilt asunder by the sound of a male lion roaring in rage. This was repeated several times during the course of the next half hour or so and was interspersed with the sounds of hyena whooping and barking. These two noises increased in intensity as time passed. The three lions would have to make a fight of it if they were to keep the carcass for themselves. There was the distinct possibility that several hyenas acting in concert would be able to drive away a small group of lions. As the sounds of conflict continued, Rusty saw one of the Land Cruisers from the next camp head off that way with its headlights blazing. Even from a distance of a few hundred metres the indistinct forms of several hyenas could be seen ducking and diving in among the more powerful lions. There was no doubting that the sounds added an extra element of excitement to the evening's entertainment.

After the meal the French travellers began to disperse for the night. Some went to their tents to sleep off the effects of their long journey while others cleared up after the meal. Rusty joined Polinah and a few others left at the end of the table. A bottle of cognac was produced from somewhere by Didier and the conviviality continued. Later on another sound pierced the night. This time it comprised a series of low but persistent guttural rumbles and grunts. The French group were unsure as to what the sound was. None of them had heard such a noise before, even Didier, who had travelled throughout Southern Africa on many previous occasions. Rusty however knew, and he told them. The two lions down by the bridge had recovered their strength and were once again coupling noisily. Rusty knew from previous experience that it was a sound they would hear long into the dark African night. Several of the group were keen to see if it was possible to witness such an event and, after some deliberation, a small patrol headed off in the direction where the sound was coming from, armed with a powerful torch. Polinah declined the invitation and stayed behind chatting to several of the French women who were intrigued to meet a young Motswana. Silvia had worked as a nurse for *Médicins Sans Frontières* in Rwanda and so the two of them had shared experiences. As Rusty and the others walked down cautiously towards the bridge they soon realised that it was going to be a problem to see anything at that distance and they were in agreement that it would be foolhardy in the extreme to approach any closer. As they were turning to leave, one of the Frenchmen called out that he had caught sight of something moving off to the left on the other side of the river. The person who was carrying the torch turned it that way. Caught in the full glare of the beam was a Mitsubishi Pajero station wagon in the process of executing a three-point turn at the other end of the bridge. As it was lit up broadside the features of the driver were distinctly visible. He instantly span the wheels and roared away into the night. Rusty knew immediately who it was and was disconcerted to think that they had been under observation and was relieved that their adversary had disappeared. As they trooped back to the dining-table one of the Frenchmen commented on the strangeness of the incident but as it meant nothing to them the others did not pick up on the point. As he walked back to their camp, Rusty resolved not to tell Polinah that the Pajero had driven off at speed once it had been spotted. He was concerned that the tension of the day might affect her and disturb her sleep.

* * * * *

Kurt pulled into the shady place on the north side of the bridge where he had made his camp for the last few days. In the main camp on the other side of the bridge several gas lights shone brightly down from the trees where they had been suspended and he could see at least three fires blazing. Around each, shadowy figures were stirring pots and turning meat. Directly in front of the bridge several people were sitting in a tight group drinking from tall glasses and enjoying the evening warmth. For a moment or so Kurt just sat there in open-mouthed astonishment. During the earlier part of the week there had never been more than two other groups in the camp, in addition to himself. Now he was confronted with a great throng. As he watched, his earlier rage completely left him. All he felt was a numbness combined with bitter disappointment. He had subconsciously prepared himself for the kill but he knew that that was now out of the question. The use of a high velocity hunting rifle within the close confines of the camp would only attract unwelcome attention to himself. Whether he decided to go over the bridge and park in the vicinity of the others or whether he attempted to get close on foot, there was no avoiding the fact that he could not use his weapon without creating uproar. He had never killed in any other manner than with his gun and now was not an appropriate time to experiment. Although he had decided on the course of action he was going to take, he sat for an hour watching the evening unfold on the opposite bank. At one point he thought he saw the two people he sought coming out of the showers but he could not be sure in the half-light and it seemed that he was mistaken as they were soon swallowed up in the ranks of the party travelling in the garishly painted overlander truck.

The hubbub and the gaiety on the other side of the bridge was in stark contrast to Kurt's isolation in his Pajero, brooding in the darkness. Within a few minutes of returning to the campsite and seeing the busy scene in front of him he decided to distance himself again from his pursuers. Although it was strictly against park rules, he resolved to make the sixty kilometre trip to the North Gate entrance during the night and be ready to leave the park as soon as it opened at seven thirty

195

the next morning. He knew there would be dangers on the tracks at night, especially from elephants and giraffe which were prone to being spooked by the headlights. He was confident though that if he drove carefully and slowly he would arrive unscathed. Before he made his departure he did have one final trick up his sleeve. Going to the rear of the Pajero he reached into the tool-kit and took out a large adjustable spanner. Under the cover of the dark he walked down to the bridge. He hopped down into the large crater in front of the bridge which Rusty had negotiated so gingerly earlier in the day and ducked down under the span. Two minutes later he re-emerged, satisfied that his handiwork would cause the maximum disruption. Back at the Pajero he stowed the spanner in the tool box and, without hesitation, started up the engine and engaged reverse gear. As he swung round he was suddenly dazzled and surprised by a bright light shining directly at him. He gunned the engine and slipped away into the night. After a few minutes he realised he was not being pursued and headed off towards the North Gate. Less than two hours later he had completed his journey. As he arrived he drove up cautiously to the edge of the camp where there were a number of small fires glowing. These were, however, no more than embers and it appeared that those camping out here had already bedded down for the night. Parking some distance away, he turned off his engine and hopped into the back of the truck where he slept fitfully for a few hours. He awoke at first light and quickly traversed the lengthy pole bridge which signalled that he was about to leave Moremi Game Reserve. For a few minutes he was forced to sit and wait as the sun rose and lit up another splendid African day. On the dot of half past seven, one of the park rangers emerged from a house away to the right and, still half asleep, completed Kurt's exit formalities.

A few minutes later, Kurt was once again heading north on the main dirt road which led from Maun to Kasane. He knew that within another hundred kilometres or so the track would reach Chobe National Park and, if he was aiming to go north, he had no choice but to take that route. Once again his details would be logged at the gate post. As he was driving, his mind raced and it dawned on him that perhaps that was how he had been tracked down in Moremi. He also knew that his sabotage of the bridge was merely a delaying tactic and that he would have to take action to ensure that he was not followed into Chobe and beyond.

* * * * *

When Rusty and the others returned they discovered that most of the group at the table were ready for bed, especially when they heard it was difficult to get a clear view of the two lions. Rusty noticed that Polinah had disappeared. One of the Frenchmen who had remained behind at the table with Didier laughed.

'You lucky guy. That desirable creature has already taken herself off to your bed. She says she is tired and needs sleep. I think you should join her quick!'

Rusty laughed off the well-meant comment and as he thanked them for the excellent meal and said goodnight he reflected ruefully that he would be sleeping alone inside the big Land Rover. When he reached the vehicle he thought about telling Polinah about what he had seen back at the bridge, but all appeared quiet. Thinking she would have fallen asleep after such an eventful day he opened up the rear door quietly, slipped off his shirt, ready to hop into his makeshift bed. As he was about to loosen his belt he noticed that his sleeping bag was missing. Puzzled, he stepped backwards. Perhaps he had drunk too much wine and his mind was playing tricks on him. A second look confirmed it was gone. Ever so faintly he heard a familiar voice from the front end of the roof rack.

'So, someone has stolen your bed, Englishman. I suppose you will be asking to join me up here then.'

Rusty walked around to the front of the Land Rover and looked up. In the moonlight he could see that the door to the tent was ajar and Polinah was gazing down at him. In the milky light he could clearly see her shining face and her bare, light brown shoulders.

'If you want, you can.'

By the time he had clambered into the small enclosure Polinah had retreated coyly under the bedding. She had zipped the two sleeping bags together to form one large bed. There was no mistaking the luscious smile that played on her lips and the look of invitation in her eyes. As he sat down at her side and eased off his chinos he found that he was already aroused and smiled at her in embarrassment. He was also nervous, more nervous than he could remember for a long time when he had been in similar situation with a desirable woman. He knew what troubled him. What was happening to him now meant much more to him than his previous casual affairs under the African stars. Like a fool he was concerned that he would hurt her or he would in some way fail to satisfy her. Despite his experience he was sure that this was to be a new sensation for her and he felt the heavy weight of responsibility. As soon as she saw he was naked, she threw aside the sleeping bag. There was no question as to the invitation in her languid movement. As the bedding was thrust aside, her long slim body and her full breasts were visible to him in the dim light for a fleeting moment. The next second he lay at her side and felt her warmth as she nestled against him. He was unsure of himself and for a quiet moment they lay side-by-side, barely touching. Then he felt her move against him and she began to nuzzle his neck and cheek with her gentle lips. If Rusty had been nervous of the significance of the moment, Polinah was apparently not. Over the course of the next hour she took control, seeming to know how and where to move to give them both pleasure and satisfaction. Rusty was swept along by her vigour and her freshness. She explored his body with complete frankness and prompted him to do the same. She led him through passages of gentle intimacy and quietness to moments of urgency and desire when the perspiration glistened on her breasts as she moved above him, looking down at him with her big brown eyes sparkling. After a while they lay still, not touching and not speaking. Throughout their lovemaking they had not spoken. Their actions, in particular Polinah's uncanny ability to bring him to a high state of almost painful pleasure, had transcended the need for words. The only sounds made had been the quiet murmurs she had uttered in the release of pleasure. As they lay silently Rusty was unsure what to say. He felt warm, satisfied and fulfilled but was unsure how to communicate with her. He lay there lamely. In the same easy way she had taken charge of their lovemaking, so she did as they lay at rest. It was Polinah who broke the poignant silence.

'Rusty, I have just one small request,' she said in a quiet whisper.

Thinking that he had in some way hurt or angered her he asked,

'Of course, anything, what it is?'

'Again please,' she stated simply and giggled.

Rusty leant across and over her and this time took the lead. For a long while they were swept along in a powerful surge of passion. Any fears that he might not be able to satisfy her were quickly dispelled. He found he could control his own arousal until she lay softly moaning beneath him. They were uncaring of the sounds they were making and any disturbance they might be causing to the others quietly sleeping in close proximity to them. If they had been at all concerned about this, they had no need. The calm of the delta was shattered by the sounds made by the two powerful lions by the bridge as they too filled the sky with the sound of their own abandon.

When they had tired of their lovemaking, Rusty and Polinah lay in each other's arms and this time, they talked. The first thing he told her was of his last sighting of the Pajero on the edge of the camp and its sudden disappearance. They then discussed what they should do and argued amicably over a plan of campaign for the next day. Long after that, when they should by rights have been sleeping, they continued to chat contentedly to one another, sharing dreams, stories about family, friends and their childhoods. They talked long into the night. Finally, they came together once more, this time quietly, affectionately and easily and before long were both fast asleep in a tangled heap. When dawn broke, the lions could be seen lying beside each other in the long grass. Back at the camp Rusty came gently awake from a deep and satisfying slumber to find Polinah lying languorously against him. As he gazed at her striking beauty and counted his blessings, she slowly roused herself. For a moment she looked confused, then she kissed him in a matter of fact way and jumped out from under the covers.

'Come on you lazy man. We have work to do today.'

With that she unzipped the tent flap and climbed out, still entirely unclothed. Rusty was left to ponder the sight of her shapely figure as she lowered herself down the ladder. By the time he had reached the bottom of the ladder he found that she had already dressed in shorts and T shirt and was setting about dismantling the tent. Five minutes later, largely at her insistence and due to her efficiency, they had broken camp and were quietly making their way past the other, still peaceful, tents and once again began to cross the pole bridge. Polinah was determined that no more time should be lost in their hunt for the killer.

As they reached the other side of the bridge, Rusty prepared to negotiate the awkward pothole in front of it but just as the weight of the front end of the Land Rover passed over the main bridge abutment there was an almighty crack. At first nothing happened, then the left-hand side of the wooden span collapsed under them. They pitched forwards slowly, to the left, and ended up lying at a drunken angle, with the Land Rover's front wing fully submerged in the shallow water to the side. If the drop had been greater and nearer the centre of the bridge, they would have fallen onto their side into relatively deep water. Rusty's first reaction was one of terror. He half expected to hear the crack of a bullet shattering their windscreen. He hurriedly scanned the bush directly ahead. The Pajero was not parked where it had been the previous day. Having established that they were in no immediate danger his next concern was for Polinah who had hit her forehead on the windscreen and seemed dazed. As Rusty leaned across towards her, she recovered her equilibrium and he satisfied himself that she would be all right. He climbed out of the driver's door and jumped down into the water to inspect the undercarriage. He could not see any damage. As he stood on the bank, taking stock of what had in the space of a second or two turned into a disaster, he heard a shout from the direction of the camp and saw one or two people hurriedly pulling on clothes and running down towards them.

* * * * *

If the scene at Third Bridge the previous evening had been extraordinary, the morning's was even more so. The night before had seen much activity and bustle, but each group had kept to themselves but now there was a sense of community and shared resolve. As Rusty and Polinah prepared to leave, the sun was already just emerging over the eastern horizon and it would not have been much longer before the camp would be busy with the sounds of the travellers starting their new day. The unexplained loud crack as the bridge support collapsed, followed by the loud splash as Rusty and Polinah became immersed in the water, had been sufficiently out of the ordinary to alert everyone to the fact that something unexpected had taken place.

Within a minute or two of emerging from the water Rusty found himself surrounded by an excited and animated gaggle of people, who all had their own opinions about the accident and held firm opinions about how to recover the vehicle. At first it was chaotic. Silvia could see Polinah was distressed.

'Polinah, come with me and I'll look you over,' she said gently, leading the young woman away from the Land Rover.

'I don't know what happened. One minute we were driving along and the next we were in the water,' Polinah began to explain.

'The bridge looks as if it has given way. The men will be able to winch your Land Rover out of the water. Sit down here. I'll be back in a moment.'

Polinah could hear a series of animated discussions back at the bridge. She hadn't been able to talk to Rusty before Silvia had whisked her away. She wondered if he was hurt as well.

The kindly French nurse was armed with a bag full of equipment. As Silvia chatted away and Polinah tried to keep up, the nurse checked to see if there were any injuries and reassured herself that her charge was not suffering from concussion.

The imposing man in charge of the group who had camped close to the bridge introduced himself as Marius, a South African national and part owner of the safari company. Like many of his compatriots he bristled with energy. His group had been due to head off through the northern parks of Botswana and then on into Zimbabwe so they could visit Victoria Falls. Until the obstacle had been removed and the bridge repaired their plans would have to be put on hold.

'Anyone who gets hungry just head over to our camp site. We'll have hot food available all morning,' Marius explained as he hurried across to get his staff organised. It wasn't long before coffee was brewing and a large cast iron pot of porridge was bubbling over a wood fire. The cook had also made a big pile of pancakes, liberally covered with sugar and lemon juice. These proved popular with the workers as the morning progressed and the cook was kept busy at his griddle.

The French tourists were full of ideas about how to raise the stricken Land Rover and approached the challenge in a methodical manner. Having travelled many thousands of kilometres along some of the most inhospitable roads in the continent this was not the worst incident they had encountered.

'It'll only take a couple of hours to right it. We'll go and get our equipment.' stated Didier, as if there was nothing out of the ordinary in attempting to rebuild the bridge.

Minutes later Didier and his willing helpers returned carrying sand ladders, three high lift jacks, some spades and several hydraulic bottle jacks.

'Hey Rusty, this is Gaston and Pascal. They have been travelling with me since Marseille. We have been through a few scrapes together along the route.'

Gaston smiled at Rusty as he man-handled the jack and quipped:

'You, Monsieur are a lucky man, to be travelling with such a woman. Elle est mignon.'

After last night Rusty was not about to disagree!

Their plan was to construct a solid base in the stream bed directly under the front axle using several wooden blocks and the sturdy sand ladders which would give them sufficient support to lift it back into a roughly horizontal position using their selection of jacks.

'Then we can make a start on repairing the bridge,' explained Didier. We need to backfill the large crater. That's probably weakened and undermined the whole structure.'

Pascal and Didier jumped down into the water. Suddenly those up on the bank began to shout and holler as they spotted a large crocodile in amongst the reeds less then fifty metres away. The two Frenchmen scrambled out of the river bed and Rusty's blood ran cold as he recalled how he had jumped down into the water without thinking only a few minutes earlier in order to check if the vehicle was damaged. He had had a lucky escape.

After about an hour or so Polinah returned – looking considerably less shaken – with a tray of drinks. As she passed around the refreshments and was told enthusiastically how work was progressing Rusty watched as the Frenchmen good-naturedly crowded around her. There was no doubting they had taken her to their hearts. As they vied for her attention she looked up over their shoulders towards Rusty as he stood by the bridge. She knew instantly that he was watching the way they were responding to her and, without anyone else noticing, winked at him impishly. His heart swelled with pride at the sight of her.

Less than two hours later, the gang of French men had succeeded in constructing a firm platform which would support their high lift jacks.

'Right, Pascal, can you go and collect those jacks? We're going to fix three of them along this front section on the left hand side. Then we can lever the old girl on to an even plane.'

They took each jack in turn, placing an extra length of hollow bar over the fulcrum arm to add more leverage. With each haul on the lever there was another resonant click as the thick steel pin slotted into place one more level up the notched main leg of the substantial jack. Little by little the Land Rover was inched upwards.

'Hey, Gaston, can you get down into the water and check that the base isn't being pushed down into the soft stuff in the bed of the river?' Didier paused for a moment and wiped the sweat from his brow.

After some time they were satisfied they had achieved sufficient lift and then very cautiously inserted two heavy duty bottle jacks under the main bridge support itself. This was still lying downwards out of alignment but after their efforts with the high lift jacks was no longer supporting the weight of the Land Rover. As such it was fairly easy for them to use the hydraulic power of the bottle jacks to slowly force the bridge back up into an approximately horizontal position. Once it was again as high as the underside of the Land Rover they jammed it into position with some more large chunks of hardwood which they had cut for the purpose. Once they were satisfied that the bridge superstructure was not going to slip back down, they put their backs into the jacks which were supporting the vehicle. Slowly but surely both the Land Rover and the bridge were brought back to an even keel and preparations were made to repair the bridge.

While the French team were mulling over the best way to proceed they were joined by an elderly man who had been hovering on the edge of the scene rather diffidently for some time.

'That's a great job chaps. Do you need any more help?'

'They've made light work of it haven't they?' Rusty said.

'Allow me to introduce myself. My name's Frank. I'm American but I've spent most of my life here working on any number of engineering projects. My wife's a Motswana and now I've retired we've settled at Maun. What's caused the bridge to collapse then? Do you think anybody would mind if I took a closer look?'

Frank had worked on pole bridges such as this during his working life so he knew that they were a happy mixture of old and new technology. Traditionally they had been built entirely out of locally available materials so they could be repaired and maintained without having to wait and to pay for external expertise. The technique used to construct them was to drive a number of large timbers vertically into the ground until a firm deposit was located which would support them in an upright position. A simple framework of horizontal poles was then placed along the line of these uprights. It was upon these main horizontal timbers that the individual poles were placed that vehicles drove over. The original method of construction had been to use locally made rope to lash the whole edifice together but it was prone to wear and tear and in recent years the main method of support in use were long steel bolts driven horizontally through the main uprights. Once bolted up tight, these formed a solid construction which was more reliable.

'Sure thing, feel free to check it out,' Rusty replied.

Frank carefully examined the bridge supports to see if he could ascertain why it had collapsed. He could see the large crater in front of the bridge and was in agreement that it could easily have undermined its front edge. After only a few moments he called out from underneath and a few of the group gathered round to see what he was pointing out.

'As you can see the large steel bolt which supported the wooden upright at the left hand end of the bridge has been badly bent out of shape. This has probably been caused by it being next to this large pothole. Continual passage of heavy vehicles over the bridge has put direct strain onto the bolt, rather than the timber it was intended to support.'

He pointed this out to Rusty and Didier, who crouched down next to him as he bent to show them what he meant.

'What mystifies me,' Frank continued, 'is that the nut which should have been firmly fixed to the bolt is absent. I am fairly certain that if it was not there when you drove this hefty Land Rover on to the bridge just now, then its weight would have forced the bolt out of position and would had been the cause of this mess.'

Frank was puzzled.

'I've worked on bridges like this before and never known a situation where one of these bolts became loose by itself. Normally they are so rusted into position that it's often necessary to cut through them with a large hacksaw when effecting a repair or replacing timbers.'

As far as the French party was concerned, although his views were very interesting, it was all academic. The damage was done. All they wanted to do was to put the bridge back into some sort of decent shape so it could be used again.

Both Rusty and Polinah however had been among the group who had listened to the engineer. He had spoken with authority and there was no doubt in Rusty's mind that what he was saying was correct. He looked over at Polinah as Frank delivered his final judgement on the cause of the collapse. They both knew this had not been an accident. There seemed no point in instigating an unnecessary furore so they both remained silent on the matter. Less than an hour later and well within their own self-imposed three hour time limit, the exuberant French team announced that it would be possible for Rusty to drive slowly off the far side of the bridge. They had replaced their jacks with a number of large blocks of roughly-cut hard wood and had also been able to reposition the bent bolt back within the hole from which it had become displaced. They had not been able to locate the missing nut and did not have a replacement with the correct thread. Despite this minor worry they seemed confident that they had done enough to carry out a temporary repair. As Rusty eased gingerly into the cab, he was bombarded with advice. There was a consensus of opinion that caution was of the essence. Rusty started up the engine and paused for a moment to see if the vibrations caused by the powerful motor would precipitate another disastrous collapse. The amateur engineers had probably put in far more support than was required. Rusty engaged first gear and, with minimum revolutions of the big engine, bumped the Land Rover forwards over the round poles.

Didier looked relaxed enough but exclaimed.

'*Allez mais lentement, mon Ami!*'

As he fell down the far side of each pole with a dull thwack Rusty was convinced that once again he was going to be pitched earthwards. In reality he had little to fear and it was only a matter of a few seconds before, in the midst of a ragged cheer from either side, he reached the far bank. Sinking slightly into the soft material which had been used to refill the large crater was the only moment that gave him the least sense of concern. Feeling relieved now he was across the bridge he turned off the engine and jumped down. There was a great deal of hand-shaking and back-slapping among all concerned as one of the French group produced a bottle of sweet sparkling wine. This was passed around and each took it in turn to take a celebratory swig from the open bottle. Rusty and Polinah felt rather guilty about leaving their new friends behind. The French did not have to worry about crossing the damaged bridge with their heavy truck as they were heading away from it, towards South Gate and Maun. It seemed that the trickiest decision lay with the three vehicle safari. Although they did not have anything heavier than Rusty's Land Rover there was always the possibility that the bridge might not last out the passage of three trucks, one after another. They decided that they would make their decision over a leisurely lunch. Everyone agreed that Rusty and Polinah should get on their way. It was felt that it was essential that the damage to the bridge should be reported to the Park Authorities forthwith and all concurred that Rusty and Polinah were the obvious candidates to carry out this task. Amidst a heartfelt, tearful and very French adieu they parted.

'À bientôt, Polinah,' Silvia shouted, as she blew them both a kiss.

A few minutes later Rusty once again negotiated the sand in which he had been stuck only the evening before, on this occasion with considerably more success. Rusty knew they had two choices of route in order to get to North Gate. They could elect to cut to the north-east, skirting the wetlands that formed the main body of the delta fringes or they could turn due east into the thick Mopane forest. Here there was a more direct but less interesting track which also led to the gate. He decided to get to the gate as quickly as possible, so they could report that the bridge was damaged and find out if the Pajero had left the park. Rusty and Polinah were sure he had, but there was always the nagging possibility that the murderer was lying ahead of them in wait somewhere in the park. It was with a certain amount of tension that they rounded every blind bend, knowing that there was always the possibility that they might encounter another rogue elephant, or more sinisterly a lone gunman lying in wait. Ninety minutes later after perhaps the easiest and least interesting journey they had made so far during their time in Moremi they drove into the space adjacent to the North Gate campsite. Moments later they were across the pole bridge and parked in the thatched shaded area in front of the rangers post and the gate. Several of the staff were sitting in the deep shade playing cards. One of them was Polinah's cousin Mpho and he recognised her as soon as she stepped out of the Land Rover. Again there was a great deal of handshaking and exchanges of greetings, followed by a quick-fire discussion in Setswana. It appeared that the young men at the gate were more comfortable speaking in their mother tongue, allowing Polinah to act as Rusty's interpreter. After a few minutes Polinah suddenly looked ashen and put her hand to her mouth. She then spoke to Rusty.

'Mpho is very apologetic because it appears our "friend" left the park very early this morning when he was off duty. The ranger who was manning the gate was half asleep and is mortified because he forgot that he was supposed to tell him that someone was looking out for him in the park.'

Rusty could see why Polinah looked so concerned.

'Thank God for the fact that your cousin is a late sleeper. God alone knows what the man's reaction would have been if he had been told that. It doesn't bear thinking about.' He paused and then suddenly said, 'I don't suppose they know which way he went, do they?'

It was clear as they gestured that the Pajero had headed north towards Chobe. After the exit formalities had been concluded and the damage to the pole bridge had been reported, Rusty pulled out of Moremi Game Reserve. They passed through the small settlement at the gate without a second glance and once again headed out on the main dirt road to the north.

* * * * *

Kurt was deep in thought. In his left hand he unthinkingly held the large steel nut he had removed from the bridge back at the campsite and was nervously rolling it between his fingers. As he had made his escape to the north the following morning he had been pleased that his handiwork would gain him some time. It was only later that the realisation that he would once again be logged at the entrance to the next park began to concern him. He could either make a stand, in the certain knowledge that those following him would come the same way. When they did he knew he would be able to deal with them. From what he could tell of the man travelling with the striking African girl, he did not seem to have much fight in him. This was a tempting option but events in Moremi Reserve had already shown that perhaps the best course of action would be just to get as far in front as he possibly could as quickly as he could. The Zimbabwean border and his father's old farm were no longer distant dreams but a mere two days' drive away. He had left the lush meadows of the River Khwai behind him. This river flowed out of the Okavango delta and formed the northern boundary of Moremi Game Reserve before it turned to the south and fed into the Thamalakane river. Kurt had moved into land which drains to the north and eventually he would reach the Mababe depression and Savuti marsh – low lying areas which formed a vast open grassland. To the north the Savuti River feeds into the Linyati swamps on the banks of the Chobe River. The magnificent blue ribbon of water – Botswana's only permanent watercourse – flows beyond the border of the country and is soon swallowed up by the mighty Zambezi. It was a singularly inappropriate landscape in which to hide or from which to mount an ambush. It was flat and open with only the occasional stands of stunted acacia to provide the meanness of cover. None of it would provide an adequate spot in which to conceal his large vehicle. He was aware that the further he moved out onto the Mababe depression this difficulty would become more accentuated. While he was wrestling with this problem he became aware of the beginnings of the Magwikhwe sand ridge on his left hand side. The track that Kurt was using crossed the ridge at a low point, to which the beginnings of the Savuti River can be traced in times of flood. Although only a maximum of about ten metres in height the sand ridge is a significant feature in comparison with the flatness of the surrounding plains and it gave Kurt ideas. After the track passes over the east side of the ridge and before it begins to move off towards the heart of the open grasslands, for a while it skirts its base. Kurt quickly realised that he would be able to hide his vehicle behind it with ease and still provide himself with a magnificent vantage point from which to view the southern approach. As he was already tired from the after effects of his busy night he decided that he would take a break at this appropriate spot. He could not decide however for how long it would be sensible to stay. Nonetheless he started to look out for a suitable place to call a halt. Shortly afterwards a small track ran off to the west which had been used by other vehicles in the recent past. He followed, knowing that his tracks would not look out of the ordinary among the others.

A few minutes later he had parked the Pajero on the western side of the ridge. A moment later he had found a shady vantage point at the southern tip of the sand ridge just to the east of the point where the Khwai River flowed from the south. He now sat impassively looking back to the beautiful country beyond, still squeezing the big steel nut in the palm of his hand, his body and mind filled with tension and conflict. His rifles were at his side. Looking back down the track and knowing that his cover was absolute, he was certain that he could deliver a killing shot at any pursuer without endangering himself. As the morning turned into afternoon he waited patiently in the shade. At one point the stillness was shattered by the sound of a large government registered truck labouring its way down to Maun from the north. Other than that there was no sign of human activity. In contrast, out on the plains, there were signs of life everywhere. In the far distance, large birds were circling in stacks to a great height and Kurt surmised that they were vultures awaiting their turn at a kill. Judging from the herds that he could see in the middle distance it was clear that he was sitting on the edge of a huge wilderness, perfect for predators who preferred to hunt in the open. Leopard and cheetah would be out there, slinking through the low cover awaiting their chance to streak out and make a kill. This type of country would also be magnificent hunting territory for lion, who although less fleet of foot than the leopard would hunt as a team and bring down their quarry using cunning and stealth instead of raw speed. As Kurt looked out over the plains he tried to fill his time by estimating the number of animals that he could see spread out in front of him. There appeared to be a great many zebra and wildebeest quietly grazing in the hot sun. These animals always seemed to be found together, perhaps finding strength in their collective numbers. Kurt had heard tell of huge herds of such beasts in their tens of thousands in the northern parts of Botswana. He was now looking at a large number of individual groups. Some of these were no more than extended family clans and others seemed to number several hundred in strength. If they should all come together in one great agglomeration they would indeed make a spectacular sight. There had been rains in recent weeks so the animals were able to graze across the full expanse of the open plains, feasting on the rich nutrients in the fortified grass. It would only be later, when the rains eased off and the sun baked the earth and scorched the grass, that food would become scarce. Then the animals would form a single herd and would move off elsewhere as one, in search of sustenance. As Kurt continued to remain patient but still undecided as to whether to stay or to move on, he noticed a distant change in the pattern of the weather. The stultifying and still heat of the morning air was gradually replaced by a cool breeze heavy with moisture. Looking far to the south he saw that the clear blue sky was rapidly being replaced by steepling thunderheads beyond which at the level of the horizon was the thick black line of a storm front. As he watched it seemed to be moving relentlessly towards him. A very severe storm was in the offing. He knew very well that if he stayed where he was in the path of a powerful tropical storm it could be a long time before he would be able to move again. The sand roads would become utterly impassable until the water drained off them and the mud once again would support the weight of a vehicle. There were some fine grained black sands in this vicinity which, if they became wet, would form into a thick, oozy mire out of which escape was impossible without assistance. In addition many of the dry river channels would flow once again. If there were a heavy downpour it was possible that they would run for some considerable time, during which crossing them could prove not only difficult but potentially dangerous. If the glowering threat of the impending storm were not enough to persuade Kurt that he should take flight, the next thing that he saw to the south convinced him that it was indeed time to move on. As he looked out at the huge clouds in front of the storm and saw the bolts of lightning striking the earth in the distance it became clear that a group of animals had become disturbed by the powerful display of nature. Unknown to Kurt, as he had been waiting on the sand ridge, a breeding herd of elephant had been slowly following the course of the Khwai river, moving northwards on the western side of the ridge. As the storm approached and the intensity of the thunder increased, they altered course and began to move off around the southern extremity of the ridge, at an angle away from where the eye of the storm was heading. Their chosen route took them across the track that Kurt was watching so carefully. At first all he saw was half a dozen young adults moving out to the edge of the plain. In fact they were scouting ahead of the main group in order to ensure that it was safe for them to cross the track on to the open plain. He noticed how two of their number took up position on the track itself, effectively blocking it in both directions. The others moved on ahead in a steady rolling gait. It was only then that the main body of the herd appeared from round the end of the sand ridge, where Kurt had been unable to see them. He had seen elephant before, but never in these quantities. The procession spilled out on to the plain in an apparently never ending column. They composed perhaps the largest matriarchal herd that was to be found anywhere in the Chobe and Okavango district and they were on the move. Among their number were old and wise females who led them and decided when they would move, how far they would travel, for how long and in which direction. It was they who would dictate when they would stand their ground for a few days, stripping the trees of foliage. When that happened a whole area could be laid waste, from which it could take many years to recover. As well as the older females, younger females with offspring were present in countless numbers. Some already had calves, others were carefully cajoling their diminutive newly born into making their first lengthy trek. Others were still heavy with the weight of their two year pregnancy. Kurt estimated the size of the herd to be about five hundred altogether, perhaps more. It was certainly an amazing sight but after gazing at them in awe for several long minutes he could see they were drifting northwards in his general direction. As they did so the track became thick with them. If he stayed where he was he would be enveloped by them until such time as they decided to cross the ridge or veer off out into the plain. He stowed his rifles behind his seat, fired the engine and raced away to the north.

He would only stop in order to rest. He had plenty of fuel and he intended to get to Zimbabwe as quickly as possible. Shortly after setting off from the sand ridge and leaving the storm front behind him he reached the southern entrance to the Chobe National Park. His vehicle details were logged and once through the gate he flashed across the depression and arrived at the Savuti River crossing by early evening. There was a rangers' post and campsite here and he was advised to remain, since night was approaching. The campsite was some distance from the rangers' accommodation and, to his relief, he found it was deserted. It had been ransacked some years previously by a small gang of delinquent bull elephants who had knocked everything down in their search for water. They knew if an underground pipe was feeding an ablution block and during a drought, would dig down relentlessly with their tusks to uncover the precious liquid. Given the pressure of numbers of the huge animals in the area the camp had become increasingly vandalised. In response the government had built an ingenious ablution block defended with a large rampart that was a barrier to even the most determined elephant. Kurt had a fitful night's sleep. At the crack of dawn he was awake and alert and soon lurching north along the sand track that led to the forest skirting the Chobe River. This track was the worst he had encountered in Botswana: in places it passed through patches of fine powdery sand which were extensive but impossible to bypass. At these points the tracks effectively ceased to exist. Drivers simply ploughed their own furrow through the potential trap. This had resulted over the years in a corridor of disturbed ground up to a hundred metres in width. Everywhere there were potholes where others had come to grief and it took a lot of skill for Kurt to maintain momentum. To drive into a large pothole could mean an instant halt and possibly broken shock absorbers or worse. Kurt was adept at choosing the right set of ruts to follow and he made his way through the sinking sand without mishap. After leaving the worst behind, his mind was now set, and, driving at moderate speed but with care, he reached the derelict Serondella camp on the Chobe River at the north-eastern end of the park by mid-afternoon. The long drive had been without incident and he still felt fresh and alert. Less than half an hour later he had been checked out of the park at the Kasane Gate and was cruising slowly down the dusty main street that led through the village itself. This was a more cosmopolitan settlement than those through which he had passed in recent days. It was strung out along the southern bank of the Chobe River and a number of lodges had been built there over the years. These served the wealthy tourists and the overlanders who followed this well-worn trail. The village itself was of significance for the local people because it represented an important international cross road. Within Botswana there was a tarred road which led due south skirting the Zimbabwean border towards Nata and ultimately to Francistown and Gaborone. The unmanned crossing point which Kurt was still considering as one possible route into Zimbabwe lay about a hundred and sixty kilometres down this road. There were two other possible options for the traveller at Kasane. The Chobe River was crossed by a ferry which led into Zambia and all points to the north, as well as the Caprivi strip and Namibia to the west. To the east there was also a much used border crossing into Zimbabwe. As well as local people, this was frequented by those making the trip between Maun and Victoria Falls. Kurt could elect to travel south to the unmanned border crossing at Pandamatenga and from there make a break for his father's old place. His other option was to cross here in Kasane and hire a new vehicle in Victoria Falls. He was concerned his Pajero was becoming a liability and if he went south to the unmanned crossing it meant more driving through Botswana in a vehicle in which he felt vulnerable. It also meant that he would not be able to find a new set of wheels once over the border. He knew Victoria Falls well and the myriad of tracks from there leading south through Hwange Game Reserve. This was the safer option if the border post here at Kasane did not prove to be a threat. He drove through Kasane, ignoring the turn-off towards Nata and continuing on until he reached the car park adjacent to the Customs and Immigration building on the Botswana side of the border. He drew up discreetly on the edge of the parking area in the middle of a line of vehicles. There was no evidence of additional security, which might signal a possible alert. A steady stream of young, sturdy Zimbabwean women, carrying goods to trade in Botswana, were making the crossing. They travelled on foot and were subjected to a thorough search by the irritated customs officials, whose task it was to extract customs dues from them. In addition, several heavy goods vehicles were parked up while their inventories were checked. What interested Kurt, however, was the fate of those like himself who were on the off-roader circuit to and from Victoria Falls. He watched for at least an hour, during which time several such vehicles arrived from each direction with their tell-tale loads of camping equipment and spare jerry cans. They were registered in South Africa, Namibia and Botswana and there was even one overlander truck from the United Kingdom.

The occupants of these vehicles entered the immigration hall, filled in the appropriate documentation and emerged with a small slip of paper showing that they had been pronounced fit to cross the border. This declared the number of people authorised to be in the vehicle and was dutifully handed over to the man at the gate. If a search was to take place, or if a vehicle was to be impounded, it was here the swoop would be made.

As far as Kurt could see, all was quiet. The gateman was slumped on a bench and appeared to be asleep. After watching a succession of 4x4s make the passage, Kurt was reassured when a Pajero, almost identical to his, bearing plates from Durban, passed through without a flicker of interest from any of the border post officials. He felt certain that if the international agencies were hunting him, he would have seen some sign of it here. Taking his courage and conviction in his hands he locked the Pajero and entered the relative coolness of the Immigration hall. Despite his hatred of the Mugabe regime he was still a citizen of Zimbabwe, although for the purposes of this trip he was using falsified documents. The presence at such a crossing point of a South African national was not at all out of the ordinary. There would be many business men who would make the journey between Kasane and Victoria Falls on a regular basis. The only time he felt anxious was when he was asked about the nature of his trip. When he explained to the bored-looking official that he lived in Johannesburg and had been making a tour of the game parks with friends who had flown home ahead of him, his story was accepted without demur. All the paperwork was filled in quickly and efficiently, including the hard-backed notebook on the front desk in which every driver was obliged to enter the registration and mileage of his vehicle. This was intended in some way to deter fraudulent importation of motor vehicles within the Southern African region, but Kurt could not envisage how this shabby volume could in any way be used to entrap a determined smuggler. Kurt left the immigration building and a few moments later drew adjacent to the gate which signalled that he was about to leave Botswana. Although he felt certain that the official would notice his pounding heart there was absolutely no sign of an alarm or security alert. The gateman hardly gave him a second look as he took the slip of paper and raised the bar. Kurt engaged the motor and quietly entered no man's land. The tarred road led down a slope and then crossed a low bridge over a dry river bed which was the border itself. He then climbed out of the valley on the other side and approached the car park in front of the corresponding Customs and Immigration complex on the Zimbabwean side. As he entered this old fashioned building Kurt was more confident than he had been on the opposite side. He was sure that if he were to be challenged it would have been by the Botswana authorities. The Zimbabwean officials were politeness itself to a citizen of a country with whom since the elections they were more than proud to be associated. Without any delay, the officials, had they but known it, gave him permission to enter the country of his birth. At the gate the official did not even bother to look at his papers and the bar was raised before he had even reached it. Feeling light-headed with relief he entered Zimbabwe. As Kurt drove past a line of traders making their way home to Victoria Falls and having ignored their frantic requests for a lift, he found himself cruising along the well maintained tree lined avenue that covered the hundred kilometres between the border and the Falls themselves.

It had taken over an hour to complete the immigration formalities and it was now moving rapidly into the latter part of the afternoon. Kurt was feeling the effects of his long day and resolved to spend the night at Victoria Falls. As he drove he could not help but feel a surge of emotion to be once again in his home country. Despite all that had happened there, and perhaps because of it, he still felt patriotic towards the land itself and hoped for the day when he might be able to live there again. He hoped passionately that the scheme in which he was engaged would directly contribute to make this dream a reality. As he drove he thought of the wars, the upheavals and the deaths that had happened in recent years. If he had used this very road less than two decades previously there was every chance that he would not have reached journey's end.

The bandits who had operated in the beautiful forests to either side were notorious for their efficiency and their bloodthirstiness. Despite the events that had taken place here, Kurt could still see with pride the influence of the previous government's good practice all around him. The road was securely fenced off from the bush and there was little sign that wildlife or domesticated animals could stray on to the road with ease. This was in marked contrast to the situation in Botswana where they were a constant menace to speeding traffic. The other thing he noticed was the sheer cleanliness of the place. During the wars, and the years of isolation under sanctions imposed on the regime of Ian Smith, the local communities had become used to self-sufficiency. There was no free passage of goods and it had been impossible for them to obtain goods and foreign exchange from abroad. They had learnt to make and grow things for themselves and to recycle everything. This attitude was still very much to the fore in the Zimbabwe of today as it began to return to the world community. The most obvious manifestation of this was that there was no litter. Everything from bottles, tin cans and even plastic bags were collected and made use of. In Botswana, where the diamonds had brought such instant wealth, the reverse was the case. Everything became disposable and was cast aside into the sand after use. Over the years these two conflicting lifestyles had led to the road sides of the two counties giving a very different impression to the passing traveller. Kurt could even remember a situation years before, when, as a result of the shortage of glass, the only way you could buy a beer was to bring back a bottle and exchange it for a full one. It was an enforced policy but one with which environmentally friendly pressure groups would have found no fault.

Just over an hour after entering Zimbabwe, Kurt reached the major road intersection which joined the main road from Bulawayo. At the junction he turned left in the direction of the town and a few minutes later was rewarded with his first view down the valley through which the River Zambezi flowed. The Falls were not visible nor were they at their most impressive at this time of year, but nonetheless, there was a great plume of spray hanging over the town. As he drove down the long incline towards the gorge he saw several shimmering rainbows come and go as the suns rays refracted through the water droplets. Above them a helicopter circled lazily and a micro-light aircraft buzzed, as tourists enjoyed their fabulous aerial view of this most spectacular of the earth's natural wonders.

Kurt drove quietly into the neatly laid out municipality. On the outskirts of town he went round a well-manicured roundabout, resplendent with colourful flowers. Two black gardeners in clean green overalls were planting seedlings. A sprinkler ensured the young plants would not go thirsty. Kurt had seen the Falls on many occasions in the past and had no romantic notions about visiting them now. His sole intention was to disappear as quickly as possible. He also needed to track down a new set of wheels. He drove almost all the way down the main street through the centre of town but at the last moment took the left-hand turn which led him away from the Falls and towards the newly built Elephant Hills Hotel on the edge of the town, overlooking the Zambezi. As Kurt looked at the new hotel for the first time and saw its ugly facade he wondered if it had been built with defence in mind. It had all the style and panache of a military blockhouse. Perhaps those who had invested their money in it were taking fewer chances than those who had owned the place in the past and who had seen it obliterated in a mortar barrage. Kurt's destination was to be far less impressive than the Elephant Hills Hotel. Just before reaching the edge of town he turned into a narrow tree lined avenue which led into a rather run down suburb. This was not an area which was much frequented by the tourists but was more the sort of place where the lower middle class inhabitants of the town made their homes. The much more basic but vastly more lively black township was away to the east on the other side of the main road. As a young man Kurt had once stayed at a small Asian owned guest house at the far end of this short street. When he pulled up outside the remembered building he noticed that it was still in business, although clearly not doing desperately well. When he knocked at the door it was opened by a middle-aged Indian woman in a colourful sari who was very glad to welcome a new customer. A few minutes later, without having to show any identification and using his assumed name, he had checked in for a couple of nights and been shown to his clean, spacious and simple room. Returning to the Pajero, and after scouring the sunlit street, Kurt took the pouches containing the diamonds from the strong box and placed them in a canvas hold-all from which he had removed his clothes. After ensuring that the internal battery was fully charged, he also took the satellite phone. Having stashed these important items, he took the unimpressive looking bag into his room and hid it under the bed. Locking the door he left. He drove back into town and parked the Pajero at the back of the Spray View Hotel. There were several other vehicles there, so it did not look out of place. Kurt was not worried about it being found. He had no intention of retrieving it. Strolling down the long slope into town his first port of call was the Avis car hire desk. He arrived just before it was closing and the receptionist was happy to book him a Suzuki jeep for eight the following morning. The sporty little two seat off-roader was very popular with young tourists who came to this part of Africa by train and wanted a quick look at the wildlife. These lightweight and easily managed little runabouts were perfect for this, and there were several parked on the forecourt. Kurt told the young woman that he wanted to take a nostalgic trip into the Hwange Game Reserve and that he would be away for two or three days. This park was the main destination for tourists hiring vehicles in Victoria Falls so his plans did not raise any eyebrows. Kurt had once again used his fake documents to book the vehicle and, as he walked away from the office, he wondered how long it would take the company to locate their vehicle right out in the bush parked at the end of his father's old landing strip. Satisfied that things were once again going his way, Kurt dropped into the spacious back bar at the Ilana Lodge Hotel. As he enjoyed a cool bottle of Zambezi, an excited and expectant group gradually filled the place. They had rafted the river earlier in the day and were still animated by the experience. As they settled down for an enjoyable evening at the bar the large overhead screen suddenly burst into life and the slick film made by the Shearwater rafting company started its nightly screening. This company had been the first to commercialise rafting trips on this river. As the large rafts floated by, they had video cameramen on both the banks and in canoes. They shot plenty of footage of the many escapades in the rapids and then had these back in the studio shortly after lunch. By evening they had spliced together the major events of the day into a very professional looking film and added a lively soundtrack. As Kurt listened, the familiar strains of Queen singing 'We are the Champions' belted out of the large speakers. The audience sang along merrily and laughed loudly at the line, 'this was no pleasure cruise.' There were few participants who, once they had seen themselves starring out there on the foaming white water, could resist the temptation to shell out the fifty dollars that the company charged for a single copy. There was no doubt that the directors of Shearwater had put together an excellent package and there was no doubt also that they were making fantastic profits. The Zambezi rapids were the most spectacular to be found anywhere on planet Earth and those who piloted the ungainly rubber dinghies came from the elite of the world's white water rafting aficionados. Kurt sat quietly at the back of the throng and watched the antics both on and off screen in mild amusement. He had to admit that when he had run the river on a number of occasions as a teenager he too had found the whole experience thoroughly stimulating. In those days no one had thought to turn it all into a business. Then the rapids had been the domain of the sons of the wealthy white landed class who could afford the equipment and who had come together from all over the country for an annual pilgrimage. Somewhere among his few treasured possessions Kurt still had a small silver cup which he had won as a member of a team of young farmers who one year had completed the course in the fastest time. He still remembered the event with pride. It was from these small beginnings that the burgeoning industry had been born. As the film ended the evening began to get more rowdy and exuberant. There was no doubt that these predominantly young and happy tourists would party long into the night. Kurt had made plans to be away as soon as the car hire company opened its doors in the morning, so finishing his beer, he quietly left the bar unnoticed. A few minutes later he had completed the short walk back to his lodgings and was soon fast asleep, secure in the knowledge that he could not be traced.

* * * * *

After leaving the park Rusty had at first been cautious of a possible ambush and had tried to avoid a situation in which they might be confronted without being aware that there was the possibility of a trap. He had crept around the first few bends in the track at a snail's pace, following the course of the Khwai River. Although the stream was a mere trickle, it could on occasions flood to several hundred metres in width. As a result, there was a strip about of fifty metres in which there were no mature trees. This area was rich in grasses and clumps of short reeds. There was nothing to provide cover for a large vehicle. The stream itself meandered its way along, in places widening out into medium sized pools. As they were able to relax, it was the abundant wildlife that became uppermost in their minds. Although Rusty did not let his guard drop he gradually began to enjoy the trip once again. He could also see that Polinah, although she was wide eyed and alert to the track ahead, was also clearly enjoying the game viewing. Once again impala and zebra were plentiful in small groups and, in the water, families of hippo were to be seen wallowing in every pool. Once or twice they were able to stop very close to a basking crocodile. At first the reptiles would remain still as statues in the hope that they would not be spotted, but as soon as the Land Rover came to a complete standstill, they would splash irritably into the water. On each occasion that they were able to view one of the impressive reptiles in close up, Polinah would hug her arms around herself in genuine fear of the gaping jaws and the razor like massed ranks of teeth. Although she was fascinated by all that she was seeing, she still had a Motswana's innate and very sensible fear of the violent death that any of these extraordinary creatures could swiftly administer to the unwary. The close escape of the warthog was still uppermost in her mind. As the small stream began to peter out into stretches of dry mud between isolated pools and ultimately disappearing altogether, the surrounding scenery also changed. Just before they left the effects of the river behind they were rewarded with one final sight which Rusty knew was very rare indeed. Scampering along the track in front of them, making their way from one pool to the next was a female otter with her family. There were seven or eight of them in all and they moved in one fluid line which rippled ribbon like as they ran. The small animals were however aware of the huge contraption as it loomed up behind them and skipped into cover at the first possible opportunity. After that the pleasant parkland became less wooded and gradually opened out into a grassy plain stretching away into the middle distance. They could see large herds in the distance and for the moment were able to enjoy the sheer grandeur of it in the full knowledge that an attack was not a likely possibility. For a while they sped along a well-maintained track and began to see more clearly the large number of wildebeest and zebra spread out in front of them. At one point they came too fast around a wide sweeping curve in the track and surprised a medium sized group of zebra numbering several hundred in strength. The animals were too close to feel confident in standing their ground and they bolted away to the left of the Land Rover in a great mass. The sight of their fat striped bodies moving in one great wave made a fantastic image. For a fleeting second Rusty considered the awesome sights that the nineteenth century hunters must have witnessed when they had seen the same animals in great multitudes. He could not imagine why anyone should wish to shoot and kill such beautiful creatures. As the animals dashed away into the distance they left behind a curtain of dust kicked up by their retreating hooves. Shortly after they had passed this imposing scene Rusty became aware of the change in the weather and could see the storm clouds gathering in the rear view mirror. He said nothing to Polinah but he knew that if the rains fell heavily it would become impossible to travel and they would have to pull over and sit it out. Although he maintained his silence he became slightly more tense during the next few kilometres as he saw the storm increasing in strength and volume behind them. It was not long before the whole of his rear view mirror was filled with black clouds and he could both see and hear the distant bolts of lightning and the thunderclaps. It was perhaps because he had half an eye on what was happening behind them that he did not become aware of the elephants until it was too late and he was in among them. As he was travelling north out on to the edge of the open plain he had not noticed the changes in the terrain on his immediate left hand side. He was on a course that would coincide with the sand ridge that formed the western edge of the Mababe depression and which was the cause of the Khwai river deflecting to the south towards him. The fact that the river turned in that direction resulted in a finger of slightly better irrigated land running out over the plain. The slight increase in the volume of moisture in the soil resulted in the presence of a thin strip of mature woodland encroaching on the plain. The track had been positioned in such a way that it just skirted the edge of that woodland. It was this spot that they were fast approaching. As soon as Rusty completed the sharp bend in the track and found the woodland on his left hand side he also became aware that elephants were spilling out of it and on to the track in quite large numbers. Although he could see them up ahead strung out on the track, he had no idea at first how big the herd was or how much potential trouble he had got them into. He pulled up as soon as he sighted the beasts and quickly became aware that not only was the track in front of him already blocked with their heavy bodies, but that many more were emerging from the woodland behind him. In fact the huge column of elephants had been approaching the track through the wood at an oblique angle to it. As a result the whole herd appeared in the space of a few minutes. It was Rusty's misfortune that he had inadvertently arrived in the very heart of it. Rusty knew enough about these immensely powerful animals to be aware that in the position that he and Polinah now found themselves, they had little choice other than to remain completely still. To move off in the midst of such a large group would almost certainly result in a charge from one or more directions. He also knew straight away from the presence of very young animals that this was a breeding herd. As such it was likely to be extremely nervous and possibly show hostility towards a vehicle in the middle of its ranks. He could see that the Land Rover was already the object of attention of one or two of the beasts, as they loomed out of the woods close by. He had a good clear view all around him and thankfully, for the moment, it did not appear that any of the elephants were unduly troubled by their presence. He left the engine running slowly at minimum revs and was grateful that it made only a slight whisper. As before, when he had been confronted by the old bull, he kept his foot hard down on the clutch pedal and with the gear stick shoved firmly into first. For five minutes or so the animals lumbered out of the woods in increasing numbers until it was literally impossible to see anything other than their bodies all around them. Rusty realised that for the first time in his life he had stumbled into one of the few remaining great African breeding herds and he was awe struck. He knew his life was now in nature's hands and that there was absolutely nothing he could do about it. For a while he had quite forgotten about Polinah and so he reached out and held her to him. She was clearly not viewing the fantastic action all around in quite the same positive light as was Rusty and she had shrunk down into her seat to try and give herself some sense of security, however false it may have been.

'Polinah,' he whispered, 'You may not thank me for saying this right now, but very few people have been lucky enough to have seen a sight like this at such close quarters.'

'And lived to tell the tale,' she replied with what was intended to be a smile but looked more like a grimace.

Polinah was to say the least very scared and was not in the mood for polite conversation. Rusty held her hand in his in an effort to give her some of the confidence that he felt. He had great respect for the intelligence of elephants and he was hopeful that they would realise that the Land Rover was not a threat to them and would quietly by-pass it. For a while that appeared to be the case. A procession of the great animals brushed along the side of the Land Rover, pushing back the mirrors and as they did some stopped to investigate them carefully with their trunks. None of them, however, made any threatening display. At one point one of them stopped and dipped his large head down towards the ground. For several minutes he peered inquisitively into the interior of the vehicle with his beady eye. It seemed to be looking directly at Polinah who sat stock still, quietly whimpering. When it finally chose to move on again she started to sob softly. Rusty knew that there was nothing he could do. His only choice was to stay where he was and only try to make a run for it if they seemed to be the object of attack. Suddenly, a young frisky elephant stopped right alongside them and decided to investigate the side of the Land Rover by prodding it with its tusks. After a while it shoved one of them into the drivers side front wheel arch. For a stomach churning moment it appeared as if it was about lift them, perhaps even toss them right over. Rusty was sure that it would be able to do just that, if it decided to try. He was within an instant of hitting the gas and trying to make a break when it put them down again, apparently satisfied that they were of no interest. It moved off and was soon swallowed up in the great huddle of slowly moving grey bodies. The long procession continued on past them until eventually the numbers began to thin out. Rusty found himself breathing more easily and began to hope that they might escape from this episode unscathed. It was at this point that they ran into the worst of the trouble. At the rear of the long column were the young adults whose duty it was to protect the back of the herd if they were attacked from behind. Once the main group had gone by, they abandoned their positions in the woods where they had been blocking several narrow paths and only then became aware of the presence of the Land Rover. There were still forty or fifty of the main herd including several newly born within close proximity of the vehicle. The young guardians were aware of their duties and immediately began to show interest in the vehicle, trumpeting wildly and pawing the ground with their front feet. They flapped their ears backwards and forwards in irritation and made as if to charge. One of them lowered his head and ran full tilt towards the Land Rover. He began his run from at least a hundred metres away so Rusty had time to judge if it was a bluff. At about fifty metres distance it stopped in a cloud of dust and proceeded to trumpet loudly in evident anger. Rusty's heart was pounding wildly but he was glad that he had trusted his judgement. He did not dare look down at Polinah who was staring, wild-eyed, out of the window in a state of abject fear. Although the animal had been bluffing, the noise that it was now making affected several of the others who now turned towards the Land Rover and joined in the challenge. For the first time Rusty really began to fear for their lives and began to look for a clear escape route. As soon as one opened up in front of him it was immediately filled by the irritated animals as they moved about at random. Just when he had reached the point when Rusty knew that there was little he could do which would influence the outcome of this nightmare, he noticed that the bright afternoon sky had blackened and the light had all but been extinguished. The storm was upon them. A huge bolt of lightning lit up the sky all around them for what seemed like several seconds and then hit the ground less than a few hundred metres away. It was followed by a clap of thunder which shook the earth and deafened them. Polinah screamed. Silence was no longer a necessary part of their survival. Hell broke loose all around them. After the opening salvo the storm proceeded to throw several more bolts of lightning into the ground close by. Ear-splitting thunder inexorably followed. At the same time the wind came in a rush and the heavens opened. Vast quantities of water were hurled to the earth in great stair rods, hitting the ground with such velocity that it bounced up again to the height of several centimetres. In what seemed like an instant the sand was transformed into a lake and the track into a raging torrent. The effect on the poor elephants was as spectacular as it was on the occupants of the Land Rover. They were frightened out of their wits and careered off in all sorts of different directions. Some ran back into the trees bellowing loudly as they went, others ran out on the open plains to try to join the main herd which had already passed that way. The storm had such a devastating effect on them that they split into several groups, some in the trees and some out on the plain where they did not stop running until they had escaped the path of the storm. It would be several confused days before they were able to recover from its effects and once again regroup. Those that had been in close proximity to the Land Rover and had been becoming angered by its presence were instantly diverted by the storm but were nonetheless still a threat. In their haste to escape the thunder and the lightning they ran this way and that, uncaring of their own safety and of that of others. In the chaos of the next few minutes two of them hit the Land Rover glancing blows, but feeling the heavy mass of the vehicle veered away without doing too much damage either to themselves or to it. Two or three minutes after the first lightning strike they had all disappeared from view, leaving Rusty and Polinah physically unscathed but psychologically battered inside the cab, listening to the rain beating a heavy tattoo on the roof as it still fell in torrents. They both watched in fascination as the scene around them was transformed. They did not speak at all for a while. If they had tried they would have found that they would have been unable to hear each other, so deafening was the sound of the rain. Perhaps only half an hour later the downpour ceased as quickly as it had begun. The heavy clouds rolled away and once again the wooded glade was lit by the late afternoon sun. For the moment there was no point in getting out of the vehicle unless they wanted to wallow around in oozing mud. The ground quickly began to drain however and after only a few minutes the track was no longer a torrent. For the first time in a long while Polinah spoke.

'Rusty, I was very frightened just now. Have you any idea how close we were to being hurt?'

Rusty had to think hard before he replied.

'Polinah, I was at fault and should have been aware of the fact that

228

there were elephants in the woods. I do not seem to have a very good track record with them at the moment. Even so, I am sure that they recognise when you are not threatening them. I am certain that we did the best thing by not moving at first, when there were so many of them around us. Perhaps we might have had to make a run for it right at the end there, if the storm had not intervened.'

'I suppose I am learning that if you come out here into the wilderness you have to accept that there will always be some danger. Perhaps that is what makes it all so exciting.'

Polinah seemed to relax visibly and asked Rusty what their next move would be.

'Well, the storm has passed and I don't think there'll be another like it here for a while. Its strength has been spent. We won't be able to move for some time. The tracks will be awash and all the channels will be dangerous to cross.'

After some discussion they agreed, given the lateness of the hour, to make camp here for the night and assess the situation in the morning. They knew that losing time like this would make it harder to keep track of the Pajero. As before in the desert there was a sense of failure. They could not now realistically envisage a situation in which they could pick up the scent.

As they sat in the cab, idly chatting about the storm, the water all around them slipped away into the spaces between the particles of sand and in a surprisingly short space of time there were islands of dry ground amid the pools. As soon as there were enough of these dry spots, they both hopped out from the Land Rover and busied themselves making a camp. Polinah opened up the tent on the roof and made the bed. She also took out the camping tables and chairs and Rusty took the axe and went in search of firewood. Normally this would be an easy task but all the brushwood and the smaller branches were soaked and would be impossible to ignite. After some time he found a fallen leadwood tree and set about one of its medium-sized limbs with a vengeance. He chopped enough to provide sufficient fuel to get the fire going. Later, when it was alight it would be possible to throw damp wood on it. Leadwood burnt slowly and with tremendous heat and would not be extinguished by the addition of wet wood. The fire alight, they together prepared a simple meal of pasta and tinned meatballs and opened a bottle of wine. As night descended on their damp island the firelight flickered off the canopy of trees around them. As Rusty gazed through the smoke at the young African woman he reflected on his luck. Despite the fact that the chase was over, he knew there would be very few who would not swap with him this moment out in the bush.

Rusty had forgotten how the rain transformed everything in Africa. As soon as the water percolated down into the ground there was a sense of life being reborn. You could almost feel the trees sucking up the water and invigorating themselves and the smaller plants and grasses preparing themselves for regeneration. It was the strong aroma of damp earth and leaf mould –at the same time fragrant and pungent – that brought back the memories. There was no mistaking it. Anyone who had ever experienced the after effects of an African storm would never forget it.

By the time they had digested their meal and tidied the camp it was already dark. Rusty and Polinah climbed the ladder to their rooftop den and slowly undressed one another. As if in contrast to the tension and the anxiety of the last few hours they made love more slowly and more tenderly than they had done previously. As they did they never took their eyes away from one another in the pale light. The pleasure was exquisite as they moved together as one. Afterwards, when they were lying wrapped around one another, Rusty became aware of strange, loud noises all around them.

'Rusty, I know what that sound is. Those are frogs. There must be thousands of them. What can they be doing?'

Rusty laughed as he explained to her that the banks and the beds of all of the dry watercourses in the desert would be home to a surprising number of frogs of several different species which could dig down to the permanently damp ground below. He told her that when the rains came they would take their chance to come out and breed.

'Yes, but that does not explain the noise.'

'That, my lovely, is the male of the species. They each make a different sound to attract a mate of their own kind. And they can be very vociferous about it. They only get a few days a year to have their fun.'

Hearing this Polinah drew herself deliciously alongside Rusty and began to massage his flat stomach with her delicate hand. The effect on him was instantaneous.

'And I want my share of fun too', she said, as he pulled her to him.

* * * * *

Polinah and Rusty were awake at sun up the next morning. After a short patrol up and down the track, Rusty pronounced it fit to drive on, as long as they were careful to avoid any flooded potholes and that they would have to assess every river bed that they came to on its own merits. After breakfast they were once again on their way northwards. The sand to either side of them was a deeper hue than normal, because of the moisture it contained and Polinah was quick to comment that the conditions seemed to make the driving easier and more comfortable as long as the softer spots were avoided. She was perfectly correct. The ground had dried out sufficiently to support the heavy Land Rover but the presence of the moisture lessened the effect of the corrugations in the surface of the track so that the ride was smoother. In addition, the wheels did not kick up the huge clouds of dust which could make driving unpleasant. As they progressed the sun rose high in the clear, blue sky, the conditions of yesterday long since forgotten, and the ground around them began to steam as the heat increased. Up ahead the damp air shimmered. There were fewer animals than of late. The deluge had been extensive and they had been able to disperse widely as there was groundwater available everywhere. They still saw animals but they tended to be further away from the track. At one point they both thought they saw the distinctive silhouettes of elephant on the far horizon, but the distant air was shimmering too much for them to be certain. An hour after breaking camp they came to the entrance into the Chobe National Park. The gateman was friendly and commented on the heavy rains which had passed through his camp the night before. He concurred that they had been very wise to interrupt their journey for the duration of the storm. Whilst he took their details Polinah looked across the counter and her pulse raced as she observed the entry, only two above their own, which indicated that they were still following the right route.

The recorded time showed that the Pajero had entered the park just after two o'clock the previous afternoon. As they drove across the rapidly drying Mabebe depression in the direction of the Savuti River crossing, Kurt was pounding his way through the sand to the north of the river on his way to Kasane and the Zimbabwean border. For the remainder of the day, Rusty settled into the rhythm of the journey, enjoying the magnificence of the plain but still with his mind on their quest. When they reached the Savuti Gate just before lunch they saw a second entry which signalled this time that the Pajero had been there the evening before.

Rusty casually asked if the campsite was occupied and was told that a vehicle had spent the night there but had departed at first light. Bearing in mind that they were perhaps only a few hours behind the vehicle they were pursuing they both became tense and were vigilant in scanning the countryside in front of them. The open country all around them meant that they would not be in any real danger. When they reached the thick woodland that fringed the Chobe River the situation was rather different. There were many places in which their adversary could lie in wait. Rusty knew there was a risk of ambush in this type of environment but he was also aware that the main track split into several smaller ones which wound their way through the thickets. This was a popular area for viewing game for tourists from Kasane and so there were a great number of individual tracks. Remembering something of the park's layout, Rusty struck off north and soon located the Linyati swamps that fringed the river itself. As they dropped down into the flood plain they had a magnificent view out across the marshes towards the north and Lake Liambezi in the distance. Not only was the scenery as spectacular as any in the country but the winding track that followed the course of the river to the east ran right out into the centre of the plain itself. The views unimpeded and magnificent, there was no chance of an unwanted encounter. As they headed east they caught sight of a herd of buffalo in the rich grassland close to the river. There were several thousand of the heavy beasts, some drowsing in the sunshine and others lazily grazing out in the open. For the moment there did not appear to be any threat to them although Rusty was aware that the open plains were the favourite hunting ground of several prides of lion. It was common knowledge that if you only had a little time to game view in Botswana and wanted to see lion that this was the place to come. After a richly enjoyable and leisurely drive along the river valley they reached Serondella campsite towards the end of the long day as the sun sank low over the river to the west. Rusty pointed out to Polinah the Chobe Game Lodge on a platform raised up above the river. It is perhaps the most famous place to stay in Botswana and had a deserved reputation for excellence and exclusivity. Rusty told Polinah that Elizabeth Taylor and Richard Burton had enjoyed their second honeymoon there, but she did not seem impressed by this singularly redundant piece of information. Shortly after passing the entrance to the lodge they chanced upon a sight which utterly bewitched Polinah and which restored her faith in the intelligence and tenderness of elephants. Strung out in the centre of the river was a family of these giant creatures quietly swimming across to the Botswana bank from the far side. They made a fantastic sight out on the placidly moving water as the dying sun cast gold, scarlet and crimson beams down on the reflective surface from the wide open heavens above. They swam in formation, trunk to tail and right in the middle was a new born. It had its trunk twisted around its mothers tail and was being gently prodded from behind by another. Rusty stopped the Land Rover close to the bank and they watched in silent reverence until the elephants pulled themselves up the steep bank some distance

233

upstream. As the baby elephant scrambled for a foothold in the soft earth it was unceremoniously shoved upwards from behind by the trunk of its minder. Their lengthy bathe had cleaned all the dust from their skin and for the first time Polinah could see the true battleship grey coloration of their tough hides. As the sun finally sank over the river and the colourful light show was extinguished, they made a break for the gate to ensure that they reached it before it was closed for the night. They were not the only ones that had been watching the magnificent sunset and when they arrived they found a small queue waiting to complete the exit formalities. While they waited their turn they were easily able to make a quick appraisal of the register.

The Pajero had passed through only five hours ago. Rusty knew Kasane well and, because of his nervousness about the whereabouts of the murderer, decided that they should stop there and then. He had been driving over rough terrain for twelve long hours and he was absolutely dog tired. Immediately outside the gate to the park was the entrance to the Chobe Safari Lodge. He went in through the gate which led to the camp site and quickly scouted around to see if there was any sign of the Pajero. There were just two Overlander trucks and several assorted off-roaders. He tucked the Land Rover into a parking bay around the back of the hotel and led Polinah into the reception. He decided they would be safer inside the hotel rather than on top of the Land Rover or in one of the thatched chalets in the garden. He was in luck. The rooms inside the hotel were the most expensive accommodation available and were often the last to be fully booked. He was able to acquire one with a view down to the river. Having done that he was also assured that they would be able to eat in their room. After taking a drink at the bar Rusty and Polinah ordered a meal from room service and retreated to the safety of their room. Once they had eaten, the two of them were so exhausted after the long day that they quickly showered together and flopped down on to their king-sized bed. A couple of minutes later they were both fast asleep under the spacious mosquito net.

* * * * *

As Rusty and Polinah were enjoying their leisurely drive along the southern bank of the Chobe river that afternoon the slow bureaucratic process of the Botswana police force finally clicked into place and started to make progress. The Chief Inspector of Police at the Maun station was an efficient, thorough man and as soon as he returned from his trip to Gweta he read through the reports on his desk, all of which mentioned the Pajero. He had the lengthy report from Rusty as well as a much shorter one from Victor the truck driver, outlining his part in the eventful trip to Khutse. He had even taken the opportunity to interview Polinah's uncle, Mothusi. As soon as he had digested the details and tried to make as much sense of it as he could, he telexed the police stations at Kang, Ghanzi, Hukuntsi and Jwaneng. The reports which filtered back from those stations over the next day or two served to flesh out the bones of the story as he already understood it. Two things were evident. There had been a serious accident close to the mine in Jwaneng which had resulted in several deaths and Inspector Setshedi was missing. He had no doubt that the two facts were linked. He also received a report that a Swedish national had failed to report back to the Technical College in Hukuntsi from a trip to Gaborone. It seemed self evident that he had been a victim of the road accident near Jwaneng. That accident remained difficult to resolve, as the official report stated that the mine authorities were cautious in the information that they were prepared to release. They had indicated, however, that all the victims of the accident had been their own personnel. He had gradually come to the conclusion that even though he was not yet able to corroborate what Rusty had stated had been the role played by the driver of the Pajero, it was imperative that he find the vehicle and its driver. He had been about to circulate its description throughout the country when two more events took place which were crucial. Throughout the investigation he had been hopeful that Inspector Setshedi would emerge unscathed from the desert. When a report came in that his car had been found under a layer of dust at an out of the way cattle post he began to realise that the situation was extremely serious. That opinion was reinforced when he received a call from one of the Senior Officers at Police Headquarters in Gaborone. The officer was either unable or unwilling to give him any details but informed him that there had been a serious security incident near the mine which had resulted in death by gunshots and that the President himself had ordered the police and the other security services of the country to do their utmost to resolve the situation. Although he could get no further details about the nature of the incident, the Pajero was once again mentioned. It appeared that an independent inquiry had been made, presumably by the mine security people and that a white Pajero had been seen on the Molepolole to Jwaneng road on the morning of the accident and had then disappeared for a while only to resurface at the fence near Rakops at the other end of the desert. The senior officer was keen to emphasise that it was imperative that any vehicle answering that description should be intercepted so that the driver could be questioned. He went on to say that the Pajero was now thought to be in the northern part of the country and that armed force could be used to stop it. The officer implied, guardedly, that they were concerned with recovering whatever were the contents of the vehicle. If the driver were to be damaged in the process that was not necessarily a major concern. As he listened to this extraordinary story the policeman now knew that he had no reason to doubt what Rusty had reported. He was also certain that Inspector Setshedi had indeed been shot to death out there in the desert. His final official act that afternoon was to send out a telex to all police stations, airports and border posts throughout the country giving the details of the white Pajero and stating that it was an issue of the greatest national importance that the driver of this vehicle and its contents should be apprehended. The instruction stated that the man was thought to be armed and dangerous and that force could be used to apprehend him. The Inspector was also keen to interview Rusty, so he also gave out the details of the hired Land Rover provided by Polinah's uncle but he stressed that the occupants had not committed any crime and were not to be harmed.

* * * * *

The room in which Rusty and Polinah were staying had French windows which opened out onto a small veranda overlooking the river. Rusty ordered breakfast and they spent an enjoyable hour discussing what their next move should be as they gazed out at the wonderful scenery. The opposite bank was lower than the side of the river on which the hotel had been built and as a consequence periodically flooded. All they could see in every direction across the Chobe River were dense reed beds growing at the water's edge. In the middle distance was a wooden tower which Rusty knew was a BDF post overlooking the Zambian border. In places there were small openings in the reeds where animals came down to drink and at one or two of these they could see that crocodile had taken up station for a possible attack. As they had lain huddled together after awakening at first light, they had heard the characteristic grunt of a hippo from across the open water. Shortly after that the serenity of the morning was shattered as a powerful BDF motor cruiser raced by in mid-stream, sporting a large machine gun mounted amidships. It hove to under the lookout tower. The BDF liked to let the Zambian Military know who was boss in this neck of the woods and the gunship was a manifestation of that. It also deterred poachers who came over from the northern border. Most of Botswana's famous Chobe rhinoceros had sadly met their deaths at the hands of these ruthless characters and as a result the remaining population had been moved far to the south to the Khama sanctuary near Serowe, hundreds of kilometres from any insecure international boundaries.

As they enjoyed a hearty traditional English breakfast of bacon, eggs, toast and fresh coffee Polinah and Rusty watched a pair of reed cormorants preening themselves on the bank below. Rusty showed Polinah the map which showed the options that were open to the driver of the Pajero. They were both aware that if he had crossed over into Zambia they had a very difficult chase on their hands if they wanted to stay with him. Equally if he had turned south in Kasane down the long tarred road towards Nata he could soon hide in the bush. They did not feel that such a route was a likely option. Neither of them was aware of the unmanned border crossing at Pandamatenga and it seemed ludicrous for the fugitive to head back in the direction of the scene of his crime. Rusty was convinced that the most probable route was into Zimbabwe, although he knew that if the Pajero had crossed over yesterday, which seemed likely, then it could already have covered some considerable distance in several possible directions both on and off the tarred roads. Polinah pointed out, that as with the game parks and the vet fences, there would be a log registering every vehicle which made the crossing. It seemed sensible therefore that the nearby border crossing into Zimbabwe should be their first port of call. After checking out of the hotel and paying the bill with Rusty's overstretched credit card, they pointed the Land Rover in the direction of the Kasangula border crossing, a few short kilometres away through the village of Kasane itself. As they pulled up in the line of parked vehicles waiting to make the crossing it did not look as if things had yet hotted up for the day. Several Customs Officials were lounging about outside in the shade chatting and joking. One of them however had a clipboard in his hand and as Rusty and Polinah went into the building he strolled across the car park towards their vehicle. As soon as they were inside, Rusty and Polinah picked up their immigration forms and began the laborious process of completing the details required in order to exit the country. There were only one or two others ahead of them in the queue so they were hopeful that they would soon reach the desk so that they could peruse the entries in the log book for the earlier part of the morning and the latter part of the previous day. Rusty was still filling in his form when the same officer now strode purposefully into the front office. He stared at Rusty and Polinah momentarily and then lifted the hatch in the desk which led to the rear part of the office. He then tapped on the door which led into the glass cubicle beyond. Rusty briefly noticed the scurrying officer but took little heed and did not look up from his deliberations with the tedious customs form when the senior officer behind the glass screen rose from his desk and peered inquisitively into the front lobby where Rusty and Polinah were standing. As the two of them handed their passports and forms to the official on duty, for the first time Rusty noticed the senior officer. He had now come to stand behind his junior and was scrutinising their two passports over his shoulder. Satisfied with what he saw, he spoke, politely but with firmness and authority in his voice.

'Good morning Mr McKenna. Good morning Miss Mabina. I am pleased to meet you. Perhaps you would be good enough to come into my office? I have a couple of questions for you.'

With that the flap into the rear of the customs hall was opened and they were politely escorted into the inner sanctum. Once introductions had been made, the senior official was quick to come to the point. He told them that he had received notification by telex overnight to look out for two vehicles, their own and a white Pajero. He also reassured them that they had nothing to be alarmed about. They were required simply to corroborate the information that Rusty had previously given in Maun. He made it abundantly clear that he had been told that the driver of the Pajero was known to be armed and was considered to be extremely dangerous. Having said that, it was perfectly evident that he was exceedingly disappointed to have to report that when one of his officers had checked the file for yesterday's exits, he had found that the Pajero had gone through this very crossing late the previous afternoon. That piece of news did not particularly amaze Rusty and Polinah who looked at each other as they heard that their suppositions had indeed proved to be correct. The officer then went on to explain that he had instantly telephoned the source of the alert, the Chief Inspector of Police in Maun. That officer had told him to anticipate the arrival of their Land Rover and had fully explained the circumstances of the affair down the telephone line. He concluded by saying.

'It did not take us long to agree that the proper place for you two right now is over the border as promptly as it can be arranged. You are the only witnesses who can positively identify this cop killer.'

Rusty inwardly digested this flood of information while the Immigration Officer went on to explain that the Zimbabwean authorities had been contacted. As it was clear that the suspect was now under their jurisdiction they had extended the hand of friendship and co-operation. It had already been confirmed that the Pajero had not been spotted on the long roads travelling in the direction of Bulawayo, nor had it crossed over into Zambia. Everyone was therefore of the opinion that it was probably still somewhere in the Victoria Falls vicinity. The whole town had been ringed with road blocks since just before eight that morning. It was considered impossible that the Pajero would be able to escape the net in such a small place, even if the driver tried to use some of the lesser tracks that led in and out of the town.

'We have been in contact with our colleagues over the border and we are assured that you will be given instant access into Zimbabwe. The necessary formalities will be completed after this unfortunate incident has been concluded. You are to be escorted by the Zimbabwean police to their headquarters in Victoria Falls. I understand that you are to be asked to give a formal identification when the murderer is apprehended.'

Rusty was not convinced that this unfolding drama would have the simple conclusion that the Immigration official anticipated. Still he could see no reason to question his optimism and instead thanked him warmly for his assistance and efficiency. Polinah added her own appreciation in Setswana.

The atmosphere was upbeat as they were ushered out of the office and into the car park. As they reached the Land Rover and climbed aboard, the senior officer sent them on their way with the news that a Zimbabwean police officer would be waiting at the border to escort them into Victoria Falls. As they drove through no man's land Rusty thought back to previous enjoyable visits to the quaint town ahead of them with the preposterous natural display on its doorstep and reflected how different the outcome of this particular visit might be. True to the assurance given to him by the Motswana official, when they reached the other side they were swiftly waved towards the gate by several excited looking officials. As they approached, the barrier was raised and they saw a silver grey BMW swinging out in front of them. The roof mounted lights and the large crest attested to its official status. The driver did not waste time with words. He flashed his lights and instantly took off in the direction of the town. Rusty had to push the heavy Land Rover to its limit in order to keep pace with the gutsy saloon car. Back at the border post both the officials and those waiting their turn to make the crossing were agog at what they had witnessed. It was not often that anyone was whisked through and spared the tedium of the customs and immigration procedures. As they raced along the well-maintained road into town the flashing yellow lights and the whoop of the siren spoilt the otherwise tranquil scene. As they passed the lines of roadside traders with their displays of wood, stone carving and basketry, word quickly got about that something was afoot. Travellers coming out of town had spoken of road blocks and unprecedented searches. No one could remember such excitement since the end of the troubles and there was a degree of anxiety in the air, in addition to the rumours and the gossip. As they approached the outskirts of town Rusty spotted the well-constructed road block and could see that all vehicles leaving town were being stopped and carefully, if politely, inspected. The two officers undertaking this duty were dressed in the traditional garb of the British mounted police, with immaculate long leather knee length boots and a large pistol holstered at the waist. They both looked as if they knew their business. Parked just off the road, partially concealed by trees, Rusty could see two fast saloon cars similar to the one he was following, at the side of which were more officers – two armed with machine pistols – watching the scene intently. It would not be easy for anyone to run this gauntlet.

As they began the descent into the flood plain of the Zambezi, Rusty pointed out the plume of spray above the Falls. He promised

Polinah that he would take her to see the Falls as soon as he possibly could. All about them the townspeople were going about their daily routine and above the Falls the helicopters buzzed. For most people it was just another ordinary day in Africa, if there was such a thing. Just before they reached the town centre the police driver turned off to the right and pulled up in front of a large complex of buildings sporting the Zimbabwean flag and the insignia of the police force. It appeared that this was a very busy place indeed this fine sunny morning. There were men milling about everywhere and cars and trucks constantly coming and going in and out of the car park. Just as they pulled up, a large figure emerged from the main entrance and ran down the concrete steps leading to the parking area. Other officials stopped and saluted, clearly surprised to see their chief in such a hurry. The driver escorting Rusty and Polinah came over from his own car and opened the door to the Land Rover just as the man arrived at top speed.

'Good morning. Good morning to both of you. My officer radioed ahead to say that you were arriving. I am Inspector Moloi of the Zimbabwean Police Force. There has been a development since you left the border post. Might I suggest you leave your Land Rover here and come with me in the police car? Speed is of the essence.'

Rusty and Polinah soon adapted to the pace at which things were developing and complied instantly. Once inside the car, introductions were made as they sped into the centre of town with lights flashing and siren blaring. Inspector Moloi explained that the Pajero had been located a few minutes previously. It only took a couple of minutes to drive from the Police headquarters to the Spray View Hotel and as they drove to the rear of the low building Rusty saw that an area had been cordoned off, and enclosed within was the distinctive shape of the elusive Pajero. Two police cars were at the scene and their officers marshalled a modest group of civilians outside the taped barrier. As soon as Rusty, Polinah and the senior officer approached, the tape was lifted and they were able to inspect the Pajero at their leisure.

'Is this the one you have been following?' the Inspector asked.

'Yes. Yes it is. I'm sure of it.' Rusty replied.

'It's definitely the same one,' Polinah agreed.

As they walked up to and peered inside the big truck the scene of crimes officer, who had been investigating inside, reported to his boss.

'There's a considerable amount of camping equipment inside but we have not found anything to identify the owner. I'm concerned about a large empty blue container in the rear. I think the driver has abandoned the vehicle and he's not planning to return.'

As Rusty and Polinah went around to the back door of the vehicle to examine the box, their eyes met. Something had indeed been inside the blue container and there was no doubt that it was no longer there. As they looked inside the back of the truck the Inspector spoke.

'Do you know anything about this box? The Botswana police told us to try to apprehend a police murderer. They did not give us any further details. If the person who owns this vehicle has indeed killed a policeman then it is my first duty to bring him to justice.'

Rusty considered telling the policeman about their suspicions regarding the diamonds and hesitated briefly.

'No, like you, we're unsure of the facts. All I know is that my friend was killed near Jwaneng at what appeared to be the scene of a multiple road accident and that when we attempted to chase the person responsible, Inspector Setshedi also met his untimely death. Other than that I know very little.'

Rusty felt a twinge of guilt about not mentioning the possible theft but was not sure that his unconfirmed suspicion was material to the present task of finding the driver. Rusty made his way to the front of the Pajero and looked into the cab.

'There are two rifles hidden behind the driver's seat. Don't touch them. They're going to be examined by forensics. They could be the murder weapons,' exclaimed a junior officer.

'It seems to me that our friend knows the Pajero has become a liability and has decided to lie low in town until he finds a new set of wheels,' Inspector Moloi observed. 'I will ensure that my officers check any reports of stolen vehicles and meanwhile we will go round all the hire companies, hotels and guest houses to see if they have seen anyone answering his description.'

He barked out a series of orders in quick succession to his subordinates and then took Rusty and Polinah to one side.

'We would like you to remain here so that you can identify this character. I have arranged rooms for you at the Victoria Falls Hotel. I think you will enjoy the place.

Rusty was overwhelmed by this generous offer but before he could say anything the smiling officer continued.

'Perhaps once you have settled in you could go for a stroll through town. Who knows, our friend might make a mistake and show himself. Do not approach him however. Just report back as quickly as you can. I would not wish to see you in danger as long as you remain on my patch.'

In more than a slight daze Rusty allowed himself to be driven away from the rear of the Spray View Hotel. He and Polinah were taken directly to the Victoria Falls Hotel and upon arrival were told that their own vehicle would be collected from the police station and that their luggage would be taken up to their rooms. As they pulled up outside the elegant Edwardian facade with its glass canopy Polinah's eyes widened in amazement. The door to the police car was opened by a large and jovial bellhop, dressed in a red coat, who greeted them enthusiastically. The hotel had been informed of the importance of their visit by the police and in what seemed like a moment they were whisked through the cool black and white tiled reception hall. Two adjoining rooms had been set aside for them in the most exclusive area of the hotel. The room that they opted to use was spacious with two large windows which looked out on to the restaurant terrace and the gardens beyond. The terrace was filled with comfortable armchairs and small tables and was busy with guests enjoying lunch and scurrying waiters bringing the excellent food to the tables of the lucky few. The gardens were manicured and resplendent with green shrubs and vividly coloured flowers. On either side water cascaded from two fountains into ornamental ponds thick with flowering lilies. The stone floor and the pristine white walls gave an overall effect in which it was a delight to eat. The view across the rolling gardens into the middle distance was breathtaking. The Falls themselves were out of sight but the hotel had been positioned in such a way that guests had a panorama down the first part of the gorge before the river twisted away to the south-east. There was an unrestricted view down this narrow chasm and away at the bottom the swirling white water, filled with energy from its descent, dashed against the rocks. The solid curve of the bridge spanning the gorge formed the border crossing into Zambia, and was clearly visible in the middle distance, with the aptly named 'boiling pot' just beyond it. Rainbows shimmered and glinted as the sunlight played on the spray. Having observed all of this in silence, Polinah turned back towards the interior of the room. It was plainly furnished with a couple of armchairs, a dressing table and a double bed covered with a patterned bedspread. Two doors led off from either side of the bed, one to a bathroom and the other into a large closet. On the bedside table was a tray of chilled drinks and some crisp fruits. The atmosphere was soothing and cool. Just then their luggage arrived.

'You sort out the luggage, Rusty. I want to freshen up a bit,' Polinah said, rummaging in her bag.

When she emerged a few minutes later, Rusty was lounging in an armchair eating an apple. She had changed out of her jeans and T shirt. His breathing became shallow and restricted as she walked toward him wearing a short silk robe which was loosely fastened about her waist, opened wide at the neck and barely covered her thighs. She moved slowly, her feet bare, and, reaching him, placed her hands on his shoulders. As she raised her arms the smooth fabric of the robe became slightly stretched and the loose knot at her waist came undone. It opened to reveal her body to him. Turning away from him she dropped the robe and slid, cat-like, into bed.

'Come and join me, Rusty. I am sure that policeman did not intend for us to go and parade about in the heat of the day. There will be time for that later.'

Rusty joined her in the large and comfortable bed and, sensing her mood, allowed her to control him and take possession of his body, so urgent was her embrace. As she moved rhythmically above him, whispering softly, he looked up to the ceiling, where the large wooden fan stirred the warm air and cooled their hot bodies.

* * * * *

Much later, as the heat of the day lessened, the two of them sat in the lounge overlooking the terrace and were served tea and scones by a young waiter. Polinah knew a few words of Shona and the young man could also understand Setswana. While the food was served a ribald conversation took place between the pair of them which Rusty suspected was at his expense. Both Polinah and the waiter laughed at what had been said. When the waiter had moved on Rusty asked her what the conversation had been about.

'Oh we Africans you know, we are very perceptive. That boy, he could tell that we are lovers and he wanted to say that he was pleased how happy we both looked.'

'Well he has a point. I feel wonderful and I hope that you do too.'

Polinah smiled shyly and for an instant he was reminded of how young she was.

'Polinah, it's cooler now. Shall we go and see the Falls?' Rusty suggested when they'd finished eating.

Polinah was eager to see them and as the afternoon turned into early evening they set out on foot to make the short journey down to the river. Wary of what Inspector Moloi had said, they took a more circuitous route which led them through town before crossing the railway track which stood between them and the Falls themselves. After passing the entrance to the Makasa Sun Hotel, Rusty pointed Polinah to the right and they set off along the tree-lined avenue towards the water. At the entrance to the park, and having seen the plume of spray hanging in the air ahead of them, Rusty paid the entrance fee and hired two

246

brightly-coloured capes. The two of them wandered through the simple museum before following the track through the verdant canopy, which was much thicker here because the spray had created a mini equatorial forest. What Rusty remembered from his previous visits was the sound. It reminded him of several Jumbo jets coming into land, right in front of you. All of a sudden they emerged at the river's edge. The Zimbabwean Parks authority had built a modest thorn fence – about half a metre high – at the drop. This did not give the right impression at all because as their eyes suddenly adjusted to the blinding spray Polinah discovered she was standing on the opposite side to the fault over which the river was throwing itself. The chasm was not particularly wide and the water disappeared into the void at her feet. In that instant she realised the only thing protecting her from the maelstrom was the flimsy fence. The river was vast. This was not a piddling little stream, but one of Africa's great rivers plummeting into a chasm before you, millions and millions of gallons a second. Polinah took a step back, then she took ten steps back. Only then did she fully understand what she was seeing. She knew this, her first ever view of Victoria Falls in almighty flooding flight, was a vision that would remain with her for the rest of her days. She burst into tears at the sight of it, so overcome was she by the power and immensity of what she was witnessing. Rusty had led her to the spot at which he had first seen the Falls and he had not been surprised by its perpetual demonstration of raw energy nor had he been disappointed in her reaction to it. They were standing on the western side of the Falls known as the Devil's Cataract and it was here that the bulk of the water tumbled out into the void below. Rusty and Polinah moved to where the Livingstone statue was situated, above the first cascade down into the Devil's Cataract. Polinah drank in her fill of the amazing sight and then Rusty led her to the east. Nearly a kilometre in length, a path followed the southern edge of the chasm and, as they moved on, it provided continually changing views and vantage points. They passed Main Falls, Horseshoe Falls, Rainbow Falls and the Eastern Cataract. Sometimes the sun and the wind combined to blow back the spray and, for a few seconds, they suddenly saw a long length of it all at once. There was even a place where they were able to climb down the rock face and look up at it falling towards them. As they stared up at the tumbling water in silent wonder they clutched each other in a tight embrace and kissed in the glistening spray.

After witnessing such power and beauty the rest of the day passed as if in a glow. They walked back slowly to the hotel and arrived in time for cocktails. After that they enjoyed a wonderful al fresco meal, as the cool air from the river washed over them and the traditional dancers performed for them. As Rusty watched the lithe young bodies move rhythmically in unison to the beat he could not help but make a comparison with his graceful companion.

Shortly after the dance ended they retired to their room and Rusty took her in his arms. As the sound of the river racing through the gorge pounded away in the distance and filled the room with its thunder they made love with passion and urgency. Much later their perfect day ended as they lay entwined together, blissfully asleep.

* * * * *

Kurt was awake as soon as the sun began to rise over the town. Apart from the sound of a few early risers setting off for work all appeared to be calm. He headed off to pick up his Suzuki just before eight o'clock and arrived at the rental office as the security grilles were being removed. The night guard greeted him politely as the door swung open but he was distracted by a couple of police trucks driving by on the main street. Their presence did nothing more than make Kurt a touch anxious for a moment or two. It was a passing sensation and he was soon busy completing the car hire agreement using his illicit papers. The girl was friendly and helpful, offering him a cup of coffee and keen to despatch her first customer of the day with speed and courtesy. It was only a matter of minutes before Kurt was being shown the simple controls that operated the lightweight off-roader. Once she was satisfied that he was sure of what he was about, the young woman gave him the keys to the Suzuki. Soon afterwards he parked the nippy little motor in the cul-de-sac adjacent to where he was staying and returned to his room. As he left the proprietor appeared in the hall. He had told her that he was staying for another night and wished her a pleasant day telling her that he was off on a pre-arranged fishing trip up the Zambezi and that he would be back after dark. Five minutes later he had stashed what he needed in the small compartment behind the driver's seat and was heading out of town up the steep slope towards the main road to Bulawayo and the Kasane border crossing. He was confident that he was starting out on the last leg of the trip that would take him to his family's farm and an air trip to safety.

Shortly after negotiating the floral roundabout at the top of the hill he was brought to an abrupt halt by a line of parked vehicles in the road. He could see at least a dozen ahead of him. Several drivers were chatting to one another. Up ahead a lone white man in a Land Cruiser stood by as his vehicle was searched by two tough-looking policeman. For the first time for several days Kurt was instantly on full alert and immediately doubled back the way that he had come. Kurt knew Victoria Falls well and was familiar with the back routes out of town which would circumvent the road blocks.

An hour later he was once again back in the middle of town, having tried all the other possibilities. Despite the fact that the more minor tracks were nothing like as busy as the main road they were all blocked and there was no way through. He had even driven over to the border crossing into Zambia. The sleepy place was much more officiously controlled than was customary and the same level of security existed there. In order to collect his thoughts and consider his options Kurt drove into the car park opposite the entrance to the Victoria Falls National Park. Having parked the Suzuki in deep shade, he reclined his seat and lay back so that he was hidden. He felt confident that a commonly seen vehicle such as this one would not raise comment. It was while he was pondering his future, listening to the thunder of the

Falls nearby, that an event occurred which meant that there was now no chance for him to escape by car. If he had but known, it only became an event of significance because of a fatal lack of resolve and error of judgement on his part at a crucial moment. The Pajero had been found at the rear of the Spray View Hotel. Up until that moment, if Kurt had stayed long enough to observe the roadblock clearly, he would soon have become aware that all vehicles were being stopped and searched but it was only the Mitsubishi Pajeros which were thoroughly scrutinised. There had been a good chance that if he had maintained his place in the queue in the well-known Suzuki he might have run the gauntlet without coming under close inspection. All that had now changed as soon as the police radio had informed all those involved in the manhunt that it was now possible for the fugitive to be travelling in any vehicle. From that moment on every vehicle leaving Victoria Falls that day was to be thoroughly and efficiently checked. The delays to both locals and tourists alike were horrendous but it was effectively accomplished and there was now no chance Kurt would escape via that route.

As the morning wore on, and the town descended into chaos, Kurt realised that he would not be able to escape by car, or at least not one which had originated in Victoria Falls. A number of ideas flashed through his mind. He considered trying to charter one of the tourist light aircraft but decided against it: the authorities would already have thought of it. He considered hijacking one as it was making a routine trip over the Falls, but rejected this as it required a degree of recklessness which was not yet called for. His mind drifted back to events of the evening before and he resolved upon a course of action. He realised it was dangerous and might not succeed and that it would leave him without a vehicle for the final leg of his journey. He was sure that it would give him the decisive edge of surprise, which would be to his advantage. He was also familiar with the land that lay between Victoria Falls and his father's farm and he could think of several out of the way places where he might be able to steal some form of transport. Having made up his mind he acted with characteristic swiftness. He drove away from the busy car park and dumped the Suzuki in a quiet cul-de-sac several blocks away from the guest house where he had been staying. Taking the stuff from behind the two seats he cautiously made his way back there. On the way he stopped at an ironmonger's store and bought a couple of items which he thought would be essential if his plan for tomorrow was to succeed. As he returned to his room he saw the Indian landlady eyeing him cautiously from her living room. He explained to her that the fish had not been biting and that he and his friends had decided to stop for the day and to try again the following morning. He tried his best to relax for the remainder of the day, considering how tense he was. He did not intend to leave the room until early the next morning unless it was imperative to do so.

Having made his plans there was nothing further that he could do to help his own cause and to go out around town would do little more than increase his chances of being captured. That was a possibility that he could not contemplate, despite the setback that he had suffered during the course of this unpleasant day.

The afternoon sunlight filtered through the curtains as Kurt dozed fitfully but somewhere deep within him was an element that was alert. If there had been any untoward activity about the house he would surely have awoken and have been at the ready. He was now weaponless. The only option in any circumstance, was flight.

* * * * *

Rusty and Polinah awoke early. They lay quietly in each other's arms as the sun rose and banished the shadows from the room. In the distance the noise of the river persisted reassuringly. With the exception of waiting for a call from Inspector Moloi, they had no firm plans so they did not hurry to start their day. Rusty arranged for breakfast to be sent up to their room. Polinah showered and Rusty lounged in bed, aimlessly channel swapping. When breakfast arrived they sat at the window and enjoyed their excellent food, each other's company and the unmatched beauty of the view beyond. As they watched the first of the aircraft circling the gorge above the spray, Rusty asked Polinah if she fancied a flight. She seemed mildly interested in a helicopter trip, but was thoroughly terrified when she saw the tiny microlight plane buzzing just above the spray. Rusty was quite taken with the seaplane which he saw for the first time as it approached the Falls at tree-top level. It was a small biplane with large floats underneath and he could see as it came almost overhead that the pilot and his passenger were in an open cockpit, no doubt not only enjoying the spectacular view but also the purity of the early morning African air, as they cut through it at speed. It was by all accounts quite a ride and Rusty was seriously considering it.

Suddenly a group of about a hundred people emerged from the Makasa Sun Hotel's garden sporting canoe paddles, orange life preservers and crash helmets. As soon as they came out from behind the cover of the bushes Polinah asked Rusty what they were doing in such numbers so early in the day. Rusty instantly remembered the exhilarating trip that he had taken down the gorge when he had rafted the Zambezi with Shearwater several years before.

'They're going to spend the day on the river, Polinah. Why don't we have a go tomorrow if the Inspector doesn't need us?'

'Rusty, I'm a Motswana, and we're not used to water. When there is a lot of it about, we stay indoors. If that is your suggestion for tomorrow, that's exactly what I intend to do with my day. You can go on your own if you really want to . . .'

Suddenly Polinah stopped talking and stood up from her seat and stared anxiously out of the big picture window. She was peering intently. Rusty looked in the direction of her gaze but couldn't see anything untoward.

'Polinah, what is it? What have you seen? It's just a group of people going rafting for the day.'

'Rusty, look at that guy towards the back of the group. He's wearing pale blue shorts and a red T-shirt and he's got a black baseball cap pulled down over his forehead. He's just behind that tall blonde couple.'

Rusty scanned the slowly-moving crocodile of tourists and quickly located the pair Polinah had described. Then he saw the lone figure walking unobtrusively in step behind them. He was carrying a substantial canvas bag slung over his left shoulder. Like Polinah, despite the shade that the baseball cap cast over the top half of the face, Rusty was sure of the man's identity. At that instant the group reached the end of the garden and started to drop down towards the gorge below. As they did it was no longer possible for them to be seen from the hotel window.

'My God, Polinah it's him! You're a marvel. I would never have noticed him from this distance. The bastard's going to try and make a break for it downstream in the rafts. There's no time to lose.'

'I'll get down to the gorge,' he called as he started to get dressed, 'and see if I can intercept him or at least see where he gets to. Contact the police and tell them what we've seen and where I am.'

With that he quickly turned to the door and opened it. Just before leaving he darted back towards her and kissed her.

'We'll get the bastard this time!'

A few seconds later Polinah saw him running across the lawn. It had all happened so quickly there had been no time for Polinah to react. Only now as she saw his chunky figure drop out of view into the gorge did she respond. Leaning forward on the window sill and pressing her forehead against the crystal clear glass she mouthed the words.

'Please Rusty, please don't go and get yourself killed. Not now.'

* * * * *

After spending a relatively peaceful night Kurt Viljoen got up at first light and began to prepare for the day. He had bought a tough canvas bag, drawn at the neck with a stout cord within which he had stashed most of the diamonds in a pillowcase tightly sewn together with a fishing line. The weight of the contents sent a surge of excitement through him. He packed his satellite phone in a large plastic bag and taped it as securely as he could. He then placed a second bag over the first and secured it with more tape. He was well aware of the power of the water should he have the misfortune to be pitched into the river. He was confident that the canvas bag could be firmly fixed to a raft and would not break free. As for the satellite phone he hoped that it would remain waterproof but was not entirely sure that it would. The phone would not work if it got wet and although he had contingency plans the phone gave him an edge and an element of security which he felt was essential. Having made the decision to lash the bag containing most of the diamonds to the boat, Kurt had one final trick up his sleeve. Although he was confident that the bag of diamonds would remain with the raft he was not sure that he would be able to. If the raft should flip over and he should go for a swim then it was a certainty that the raft would right itself and due to its exceptional buoyancy soon get well ahead of him in the current. There was no guarantee he would be able to catch up with it. During his examination of the diamonds, although no expert, he established that there was a modest number which were exceptional in size and quality. He placed this small collection and his false documents in a tough plastic bag which he then put into a stout bum bag. He concealed this firmly around his waist. As soon as he was ready, he made his way into town alongside the procession of early morning workers. Reaching the road junction at the centre of town he turned left towards the Makasa Sun Hotel. It was still too early for any tourists to be about so he made himself comfortable on a garden bench discreetly hidden from view by several substantial shrubs. Ensconced there he waited for the day to begin in earnest. Shortly afterwards a black gardener opened up a small wooden hut and started to unwind a large plastic hose pipe. After attaching this to a stand pipe he began to water the whole garden. Once or twice he glanced over at Kurt but he did enquire as to why anyone should be relaxing in the garden so early in the day. He made his circuit of the shrubs so as to not disturb the occupant of the bench. A little later two athletic-looking young men, one black and one white, arrived and opened a set of double doors which led into the rear of the hotel. From there they emerged with two wooden trestle tables and several folding chairs. They positioned these in the courtyard on the edge of the garden. They then placed a tea urn on one of the tables and laid out a number of plastic cups and two plates of sweet biscuits. They were also armed with an impressive array of paperwork and two large black tin boxes which they placed next to the wall behind the tables. Soon afterwards others arrived and the atmosphere started to become businesslike. The Shearwater Rafting Company had set up its temporary office and was ready for its daily influx of clients. They started to arrive in twos and threes from about eight o'clock onwards. The atmosphere was convivial and friendly but there was a considerable amount of tension within the group. Kurt kept out of sight. He knew that – with the formalities completed – the whole group would be led through the Victoria Falls Hotel's garden to the small patch of bare ground for the safety briefing. Several staff members began to shepherd the gaggle of excited tourists towards the river. In the midst of the disorder Kurt followed at a slight tangent as if heading in a different direction. Using the garden's foliage as cover he joined the rear of the group. When they reached the open area at the top of the path that led to the almost vertical drop into the gorge, everyone was ordered to squat down in the dirt and listen to the safety briefing. Kurt kept on going down the steep path leading into the echoing gorge. At first the track was no more challenging than a steep flight of stairs but he soon encountered steps which had been cut into the rock. As Kurt descended, the drop became more precipitous where ropes had been slung across the more hazardous sections. As he lowered himself into the booming chasm the undergrowth thickened and the canopy of overhanging trees grew denser. In places thick tree trunks – growing out of crevasses in the rock wall – had been used to assist those making the dangerous descent. Underfoot was green algae and the rock was slick with water. Kurt made his way down into the gathering gloom cautiously. As he reached the halfway point he heard loud voices echoing from below and for a moment stiffened. Suddenly several bobbing heads came into view as they made their ascent up the path. The porters who had carried the flotilla of rafts down to the river at first light where they had assembled and inflated them, were making their way back up to the top. The men eyed him curiously as he greeted them but they did not ask why he was making the descent alone or attempt to stop him. At the bottom Kurt found himself at a narrow beach tucked away in the bed of the gorge. In mid-stream and beyond, the water swirled and boiled as it raced away. Here, the ancient rock formation had created a shallow, natural horseshoe-shaped harbour where the water was placid. In this widening of the gorge a shaft of sunlight glinted on the river. As the clear morning light danced and flickered on the choppy water Kurt saw ten large inflatable rafts pulled up inshore and lashed together with strong cord. Farther around the curve in the bank several small yellow kayaks were tethered to the base of a tree trunk. At first Kurt thought he was alone, but then he spotted a solitary figure at the far end of the line of boats casually smoking and tossing pebbles out into the flowing water. Without pausing Kurt darted to the boat at the far end of the line from where the guard was stationed, hopped aboard and untied the painter and grabbed the paddle. He was soon clear of the other boats and seconds later was swept out into the flow. As he rounded the first curve in the fast-flowing water he heard a strangled cry from behind. The guard had seen him but was too far away to intervene. Kurt could hear the distinct increase in the volume of noise made by the crashing water and could see the river disappearing from view over a small precipice only to re-emerge – in a plume of pitching white water – a little further downstream. He was about to enter Morning Glory, the first rapid. Squatting on his haunches in the centre of the sturdy craft he felt a sense of apprehension as he saw for the first time in years the sheer force and power generated by the vast river as it hurtled towards the Indian Ocean. Quick as a flash, he took the precious bag from his shoulders and secured it to the aluminium frame which formed the backbone of the boat. Just as he was satisfied it would remain in place even if the boat was tipped upside down, the front end of the flexible craft slipped over the leading edge of the rapid. He readied himself with his single oar and prepared to do battle with the river. The raft slid smoothly and slowly down the apparently motionless bulbous face of the rounded wave which formed the leading edge of the rapid. Somewhere underneath, the flow was blocked by a rock obstruction in its path and the water was instantly broken up into a careering mass of white water which pitched back almost vertically upwards in front of him. As the raft hit the face of water its smooth journey was abruptly halted. The front end was immediately swamped with a great weight of foaming water and wallowed alarmingly as the back end bucked upwards towards the white water. Kurt was soaked to the skin and lost all sense of direction as he dipped inside the wave. At the last moment, as the boat reared below him, he gripped the safety line with one hand and endeavouring not to lose his paddle, prepared for a rollercoaster ride. Seconds later the sun was blotted out and he was immersed in fast-flowing green water. For a moment the raft was held fast in the undercurrent. Just when Kurt thought that his lungs would burst it broke free and was launched into the raging torrent downstream beyond the first wave. Kurt lay in the bottom of the boat, unable to offer any resistance to the merciless river, and was carried at high speed downstream. It was only the innate buoyancy of the hull which lay between him and disaster.

* * * * *

Oblivious to the curious gaze of those enjoying their leisurely breakfast on the hotel terrace Rusty tore across the neatly-cut grass and dropped down on to the path that led to the gorge. When he reached the rafters he slowed down and stopped, but a swift appraisal showed him exactly what he had expected from the moment that he had seen the figure on the lawn: the murderer was no longer within the group. Walking briskly around the edge of the huddled people he found the continuation of the path and hurriedly clambered down the steep incline. Just as he started to pick his way down the first of the steps the gang of porters arrived at the top, clearly thankful that the climb was over and that their exertions were at an end for a few hours. Rusty pushed past them. A little further down the steep slope he was suddenly jostled by another figure making the ascent as quickly as he could, in a state of considerable anxiety. Rusty almost lost his balance.

'Take it easy, man. I nearly lost my footing. What's all the hurry for?' he shouted in exasperation.

'Some crazy guy has stolen one of the rafts. He doesn't stand a chance out there. The river is really rolling today. He'll never get through Commercial Suicide and Oblivion is a real killer at the moment. Man! Oh Man! The boss'll skin me alive for this.'

With that the agitated guard continued on his way up the steep climb, to report the unwelcome news to his superiors. Now certain of events, Rusty hurried down the slope. He was moving far too quickly on the dangerous descent and it was more luck than judgement that he finally reached the bottom having caused himself no more damage than slightly grazed knees and elbows when he had slipped on a particularly treacherous spot. As he came out into the bright sunlight at the water's edge his first instinct was to make for one of the rafts but then he saw the kayaks in the middle distance. He had only rafted twice before in his life. Although it was several years since he had last been in a kayak his thoughts went back to two winters in the fast flowing streams in the mountains of Scotland when he had become more than proficient in piloting the flimsy fibreglass boats. As he hurried towards the cluster of tethered boats he did not hesitate. A skill once mastered always remained with you. With that thought uppermost in his mind he put on a life preserver and a helmet from the heap that had been left above the high water mark and pushed off into the swirling angry waters of one of the world's greatest rivers.

* * * * *

Well before he hit the rough fast flowing water Rusty was in deep trouble. As soon as he dipped the paddle into the water he made the cardinal error of the novice and he over-steered. The bow of the kayak reacted instantly and swung round to the left. Rusty found himself facing back the way he had come. In this position, broadside to the flow, he entered the turbulent current. The effect was spontaneous. He was tipped upside down. As he felt the small craft complete the one hundred and eighty degree rotation he did all he could to right the boat. Despite several desperate attempts he failed to get himself upright. As swirling green water raced about his head he realised that he was being swept towards the first rapid and was in danger of being battered to death against the rocks. He knew instinctively this was no position in which to enter the churning water. When the oxygen in his lungs finally gave out he had no option but to slip out of the seat and out of the boat. As he did this he was well aware that it was vital that he did not lose either the craft or his paddle if he were to have any chance of survival further down river. The force of the driving water was too much for him and within a second of leaving the comfortable and secure interior he felt the flimsy kayak torn from his grasp and he knew it had been swept away. At that moment his head once again bobbed up into the bright sunlight and he urgently refilled his tortured lungs. He had an instant to look up and saw he was on the verge of being swept into Morning Glory, its imposing wall of white water rising up in front of him. In a desperate move he rolled over on his back and stuck his feet out. He then crossed his arms over his chest and grimly held onto the paddle along the full length of his body. In that position he would be able to gulp mouthfuls of life-giving oxygen whenever he was above the green water and was also less likely to have his head bashed against the rocks as he raced past them at high speed. Just as he succeeded in getting into the correct position he tumbled forwards down the slope of the face of the rapid and his feet hit the wall of white water in front of him. He felt himself plunging deeper and deeper. All about him green water boiled and the ominous black shadows of submerged rocks flashed by. He was moving with the flow rather than against it. There was a chance he would be buffeted around the rocks in much the same way as the racing water. Although he felt as if he was deeply immersed in the body of the water, his life preserver was in fact doing its job and he was always within a few centimetres of the surface. As he was forced through the long length of the rapid his head came to the surface and he was able to gulp in sufficient air to remain conscious until he reached the smooth water beyond. The Zambezi descends in a series of steps known as a pool drop system. Just as swiftly as Rusty had felt himself flung into the churning grasp of the water so he suddenly felt it release its grip on him. As his head bobbed up to the surface he looked about and could see the rapids cascading behind him. Swivelling quickly he looked downstream just in time to see his kayak disappear over the edge of the next set of rapids which lay a couple of hundred metres ahead. He was in no condition to attempt to ride the next roller given what he had just experienced so he splashed clumsily towards the shore on his left. Swimming was difficult with the encumbrance of the life preserver and the paddle firmly grasped in his left hand further hindered his progress. As he successfully reached a narrow rock ledge and dragged himself on to it, he was grateful for the life preserver which had probably saved his life.

The Zambezi continued its relentless journey to the sea, and behind him the rock face soared up into the bright blue sky. From where he was sitting, recovering his senses and his strength, there was no alternative except to go back into the water. His best chance would be to wait for the flotilla of tourist rafts which would soon come down the river. Cursing his impetuosity, the narrow rock ledge on which Rusty was perched gave no room for movement and he was forced to sit in an awkward position which caused the muscles in his upper legs to ache. Gingerly, he stood up to let the blood flow through his legs. He could see a lot further and his eyes were immediately drawn downstream. The next set of rapids – Stairway to Heaven – foamed and writhed ahead although it was far less severe than the one that he had just survived. He caught sight of a flash of yellow in amongst a pile of medium-sized rocks that lay to the right of the flow, downstream from the rapid. It was the canoe which had escaped him. Although he could not see clearly from this distance it appeared to have survived its solitary journey through two sets of rapids and was now held fast against the rocks. Taking one long look at the water below him as it increased in tempo in response to the narrowing in the gorge that led to the Stairway to Heaven, he leapt out. As he plummeted towards the water his loud cry, a mixture of fear and exhilaration, was drowned out by the sound of the rushing water. As he bobbed back up to the surface he gripped the paddle against his body and adopted the safety position. A few seconds later he felt the water gathering speed as it channelled towards the rapids. As he was swept into the flow, although he was not submerged for any great length of time, he did not enter the mainstream and as a consequence found himself crashing against the rocks as he passed. Once he hit a large rock with his outstretched legs but a deft touch was enough to deflect him away from it before the sheer weight of the water could dash the rest of his body against it. In what seemed like a fleeting instant he was through the maelstrom and after taking a moment to adjust his bearings was swimming purposefully towards where the kayak was trapped. As he reached it he pulled himself ashore adjacent to it and inspected it for damage. Although the trim was dented and the fibreglass scuffed it did not appear to be holed. There was a medium-sized lagoon of placid water just below the rapid and for a few minutes he paddled this way and that, getting the feel of the pliant craft. With a little practice he quickly felt the skills return and although he was by no means certain that he could beat the big river he decided that he would give it his best shot. Paddling quickly and confidently out into the main channel he was soon slicing through the water in the direction of the next rapid. The Devil's Toilet Bowl was a series of eddying currents and swirling whirlpools rather than one large drop and would be a good test of his returning canoeing skills. Rusty knew he would be tested to the full in the huge cascades further down the big river. As he began to remember all of his old tricks he pointed the boat's prow in what he considered to be the best line for negotiating a route through the turbulent water to the far end of the rapid. This time as the churning white water took hold, Rusty did not feel fear, just the sheer excitement and exhilaration of being out on the tossing water. His paddle flashed this way and that, dipping into the water, making minor, but telling, adjustments to the little kayak's passage. In the instant that a large rock would appear in front of him he would flash the blade and a split second later the danger would be past and he would skip effortlessly towards the end of the rapid. Another skilful touch would divert him away from the path of a huge wave that threatened to engulf him or trap him underwater until his breath gave out. The sheer speed and elegance with which the craft danced its way through the powerful torrent gave the impression of simplicity and ease. Rusty hardly had time to think about how well he was progressing before he shot out of the wave at the bottom of the rapid into another placid pool. Taking a few minutes to recover his breath and to allow his racing heart to steady, the river swept him towards Midnight Diner.

* * * * *

Further downstream Kurt had survived the first rapids and had learnt much from the experience. As he had popped out from under the water like a cork from a bottle of champagne, at the end of the run through Morning Glory he had realised that there was no way he could use his paddle to deflect the path of the heavy, ungainly rubber dinghy when he was in the grip of the rapid. It would have required the strength of at least six people and even then it was arguable that their efforts would have made little difference. He had therefore adopted the strategy of attempting to enter the rapids at the point where he thought he would get through with the least amount of damage being inflicted either to himself or to the boat. Once he was into the white stuff he took the simple expedient of throwing himself into the bottom of the boat and gripping the safety rope as firmly as he possibly could. The technique worked admirably as he made his way through Stairway to Heaven and Devil's Toilet Bowl and he soon found himself in the long stretch of placid water leading to Midnight Diner. The prevailing wind on this part of the river normally blew back upstream in the direction from which he had just come. For those paddling the dinghies it was the most unpleasant part of the day: high-sided craft had a tendency to be blown back in the direction it had come. Today, however, the wind was blowing strongly from the opposite direction. All Kurt needed to do was dip the paddle in occasionally to guide it on a suitable course which led him onwards towards possible safety. It was in the heart of Midnight Diner where it all went wrong. This rapid divided into two parts: the first was a series of long pitching waves and the second a short, deep trough into which the river plummeted. Kurt negotiated the initial section successfully but as he entered the trough the boat turned full circle and was buried under the avalanche of water that was dropping into the trough. As that happened the stern was pushed downwards into the green water below. The bow flicked upwards at great speed and, as the raft crested the top of the wave, it turned right over, end on end, like a tossed coin. Kurt was thrown up in the air and the only points of contact between him and the raft were his white-knuckled hands which maintained their strong grip on the safety rope. Unfortunately, as he was thrown upwards at high speed, his arms were turned over, against the angle at which he was moving and as a result, tremendous pressure was put on his shoulder joints. If he had held on any longer there was the distinct probability that he would have dislocated one or both, so great was the force exerted by the crashing river. He relinquished his grip and was immediately released into the crazy white water. Down and down he went, hurtling out of control, his body spinning madly in the turbulence like a rag doll. As he went down deep, the lack of a life preserver nearly caused his death. His body was not sufficiently buoyant on its own to resist the unrelenting downward thrust of the weight of water. He was almost out of breath when his jumbled brain caught a glimpse of sunlight shimmering through the crystal clear green water. It gave an inkling of which way to swim, and with a few powerful thrusts, he resurfaced at the far end of the rapid just as his lungs were on the verge of giving out. Treading water for a moment while he regained his breath he saw the large raft moving slowly upside down in the water about fifty metres away. He was a good swimmer and without a life jacket to slow him down soon reached it. Hopping aboard the upturned hull of the boat he caught hold of the strong rope tied across the width of the underside of the hull, amidships. Leaning back from the edge of the hull he used his body weight to lift the heavy craft out of the water. At first he could only lift it a few centimetres but this was enough to send the water which had collected on the underside coursing back into the river. The boat suddenly flipped over, throwing Kurt back into the flow. He swam close inshore with it and, climbing aboard from the bank, set off downstream, this time in the direction of one of the great monsters that lay in his path, the rapid known as Commercial Suicide. White water rapids are classed by those who know and love them on a scale of one to six for difficulty. Five is considered to be the hardest that it was possible to pass through without the certainty of capsizing. Most of the rapids on the Zambezi Kurt had been through that day were either a four or a five. Commercial Suicide was considered a six. Only the most foolhardy would attempt to raft it and none of the commercial enterprises which ran the magnificent river would consider it. For that reason it was a mandatory portage for all the companies which used the river. There was a space available on the Zimbabwean bank where rafts could be hauled across while nervous customers looked in awe at the mountainous waters, secretly relieved that, however briefly, they were on dry land. Occasionally one or two of the safety kayaks which follow the rafts to pick up those who were thrown overboard would make their way through it and receive rapturous applause for their bravery. The rapid measured a couple of hundred metres in length and the flow was restricted to only twenty metres in width. The water shot through the constriction at breakneck speed rolling and crashing against the rocks beneath. The shape, size and majesty of the magnificent spectacle affected all who saw it but few would choose to pit themselves against it. For Kurt there was only one choice: to run the great rapid. He was lucky he did not have time to consider the enormity of what he was about to attempt as he raced towards the mighty, powerful obstacle.

* * * * *

Rusty was making good progress. He had successfully negotiated Midnight Diner and was now paddling towards Commercial Suicide. All the old skills had returned to him and he was making considerable speed on the flat water that lay in the calm stretch which lay between the two sets of rapids. As he rounded the next sharp bend in the river the crescendo of noise told Rusty that the next rapid was not far distant. Less than a couple of hundred metres ahead and, still some distance from the rapid, was the unmistakable shape of a lone raft, with a single occupant, who was steering it in midstream with his paddle, while staring intently in front of him.

Having come this far Rusty did not hesitate. He powered his slim craft through the water with strong thrusts of the paddle hoping to intercept the raft before it entered the dangerous rapid. As he streaked across the smooth surface it was apparent that they would be together in a matter of minutes. Shortly afterwards, just before the kayak drew alongside the rubber dinghy, Kurt, as if possessed by a sixth sense, looked over his shoulder. As Rusty drew level with the ponderous raft his exertions got the better of him and he paused momentarily. He had been planning to abandon the canoe and to join his adversary in the raft. The lone figure huddled in the centre of the raft gave him one quick glance but for the moment his concentration seemed to be focused on the river. Despite appearances Kurt was well aware of what was happening at the side of his raft and as he realised that his pursuer was not about to jump aboard immediately, he could not believe his good fortune. He feinted as if to dip the sharp edge of the paddle into the water but instead brought it high into the air and crashed it firmly against the head of the man in the kayak as he drew alongside. There was a satisfying thud of metal on something solid and, even more gratifying, the kayak pitched over on its side and its occupant was lost to view. Kurt turned his attention to his descent of the rapid, which now lay less than a hundred metres distant.

Rusty was fully alert under the water: the paddle had given his face a glancing blow, rather than inflicting serious injury. Most of the impact had been taken up by the fibreglass helmet he was wearing. Aware that the rapid was approaching fast he flicked the paddle across himself and then downwards while at the same time arching his back and tensing the strong muscles in his torso. This time the small boat righted itself, just in time for Rusty to see the raft ahead disappear into the first section of Commercial Suicide. Rusty dipped his paddle strongly a few times and soon made the beach about fifty metres above where the river dropped into the abyss. After pulling the kayak well above the waterline he ran higher up the rock shelf in order to try and observe the passage of the inflatable raft. As he watched, it pitched and rolled down the long length of the rapid. On occasions it was underwater for what seemed like an age but he watched in fascination as it continually righted itself. Sometimes the violent power of the water turned it full circle only for it to be swung round again by the next wave. There was no doubt it was swept clear at the other end and soon afterwards could be seen disappearing around the next bend in the river. For a few minutes Rusty stood there, breathing heavily. There was no way he could paddle the small boat back upstream so he might as well just keep on going. Back at the water's edge, he thrust the paddle up inside the hull, picked the kayak up and slung it over his shoulders. He only had to carry it for a couple of hundred metres, but it was a surprisingly difficult task. The rocks were uneven and he had to take care not to stumble into the circular cavities that had been drilled into the rock floor by swirling pebbles in times of flood. The sun was now high in the sky and the boat, although light, was cumbersome. Sweat ran down his face in rivulets. After almost fifteen minutes of hard exertion he reached the pool into which the spent power of the rapid was throwing itself. It was a delight to hurl himself headlong into the cool, invigorating water. Looking ahead there was no sign of the raft before the river turned in a sharp bend and out of sight. Rusty jumped smartly into his craft and once again set off doggedly in pursuit, knifing through the water at high speed. As he paddled downstream Rusty tried to remember the sequence of the rapids on this stretch of the river. He remembered the smooth curve of the one called Creamy White Buttocks and the short sharp shock that was Carnage Maker. Neither were likely to cause him any problems and indeed this proved to be the case for, as he reached each in turn, he was swept through with an increasing degree of proficiency and professionalism in his oarsmanship. He knew though it would not be long before he would have to face Oblivion. This was another monster and although not a complete impossibility like Commercial Suicide was still considered the ultimate challenge by serious rafters. It was a lengthy rapid and consisted of three parts, each dominated by a great wave. It was the last of the three that was the threat. It had not won its awesome reputation lightly. Rounding another bend in the river, the increase in the pitch of the booming water in front of him told Rusty that he was approaching another rapid and that this was a big one. If he had doubts previously he was now certain that this was Oblivion. And once again he saw the raft ahead of him. The hunched figure was still there, in the centre of the boat. There was no doubt now that he had survived Commercial Suicide. This time Rusty did not intend to let the opportunity pass him by and he redoubled his efforts with the paddle. Kurt was feeling the effects of his battering by the river. He had hung on through Commercial Suicide and the rapids which had followed it, but his hands were blistered and raw. He had also swallowed great gulps of water on more than one occasion and although he had managed to spit this out and clear his lungs, the overall effect of the stress had left him weakened and punch drunk. He was however aware that this was the last rapid he needed to negotiate and once through he would be able to slip away into the impenetrable forests on the Zimbabwean side of the river. He was certain he would be able to get his bearings and given time would be able to find one of the outlying camps where he would be able to use his charms to beg, steal or borrow some form of transport. As he approached the treacherous rapid he was able to summon something from deep inside his tired body for one more ordeal. As Rusty bore down on the slower moving dinghy he hoped he would reach it before it entered the rapid. He soon realised that was not to be the case and for a moment felt a twinge of misgiving as he saw it enter the first section. This was his chance to divert to either side and not take up the challenge. This time he dipped his shoulder and pointed the kayak at the very heart of the rapid. As he rode the first gigantic wave he felt his stomach turn over and he crested it, only to be pitched forward and into the trough in front of the second part. Up ahead he could see the raft in the turbulent water that offered a brief respite before the third wave. In a flash he was lifted up and over the top of the second wave and with a deft flick of the paddle reached the lumbering raft. Just as he was about to throw himself aboard, the river helped him by lifting the whole front end of the kayak upwards. Rusty dug his paddle in for the last time and crashed the fibreglass boat right on top of the wallowing dinghy. Kurt had been completely unaware of the impending pursuit and had almost been hit when the kayak suddenly appeared alongside him in the bottom of the boat. As he saw the muscular figure slip out of the cockpit of the kayak he let fly with a hefty, well-aimed kick which caught the other man squarely and firmly in the groin. He watched with satisfaction as he saw him fall into the bottom of the boat with a cry and a look of intense pain on his face. Kurt did not hesitate. With a blood curdling shriek that Rusty heard above the din of the river Kurt fell on top of him with the clear intention of throttling the life out of him. Rusty was in severe pain as a result of the kick but was still able to lift his knees at the crucial moment as the other man dropped on top of him for the kill. He had done enough to deflect the attack for the moment and the two of them were locked together for one long instant. There was no need for words. The look in the eyes of the man above him told Rusty all that he needed to know, that no quarter would be given. This was a fight to the death in the grip of the mighty river. For what seemed like an age the two of them wrestled in the bottom of the boat. Both had lost their paddles in the struggle and the kayak had long since been swept away. They were well-matched and it was not easy for either to gain the upper hand in the confined space at the bottom of the boat, as it pitched and rolled and the water spilled all around them. At one point Rusty managed to smash his forearm against the chin of his adversary but there was no real power in the blow and it had little effect. It seemed that Kurt was the more desperate of the two and his well-aimed kicks, punches and bites forced Rusty up against the bulkhead at the back of the boat. Seizing his advantage, Kurt was able to fall upon him and this time Rusty did not manage to get his legs in the way in time to fend off the attack. Quick as a flash, Kurt was upon him and Rusty felt the strong hands of the other man grip his throat and close his windpipe. As Kurt maintained the deathly embrace he screamed.

'Die you bastard, just die.'

Rusty could feel the blood pounding in his head as the arteries were constricted and the supply of blood to his brain began to dry up. It seemed for a moment that for him, Oblivion would mean just that. Just then they hit the third wave and they hit it all wrong. The whole boat catapulted straight up in the air and then fell backwards into the deep trough in front of the mass of heaving water. Everything went mad. The boat span away out of sight and the two combatants were dragged down to the bottom of the river. This time Rusty was unprepared for the plunge into the cool water. His body flailed as he made a desperate fight to stay alive. They spun this way and that as Rusty did his utmost to escape the grip of the other man in the swirling water. Kurt had by now lost all reason. He was uncaring about his own survival. There was but one thought on his mind and that was to bring the life of his adversary to an end. Only then would he worry about his own chances in the frightening grip of the river. If anything he increased his grip on his victim. His efforts began to pay off and he began to detect that the other man's reserves of strength were diminishing. Rusty still had his eyes open and could clearly see the hideous grimace through the green water, on the face of the man who was trying to kill him. Gradually a sense of calm began to overwhelm him and he felt the pain lessen and his vision begin to blur. At the last, Rusty reached out his flailing hand and in one last attempt to hang on to life, grabbed on firmly to the clothing of the other man. Just then the river decided to join in the fray. As the two struggling figures rolled this way and that in the heaving water they were pitched in among a great pile of rocks at the bottom of the river. Rusty felt them graze by as if in a dream but then, all of a sudden, he felt a jarring impact through his arms and realised the other man had lost his grip. Just before he lost consciousness he saw a puff of crimson blood in the water coming from the head of the other man. Kurt had felt Rusty weaken and had been about to release his grip and make a break for the surface when he hit the rock obstruction square on, with the back of his head, at speed. He was not wearing any protective head gear and he took the full impact. All he felt was a sickening thud and then nothing. He was instantly unconscious with a great gash in his head where his precious blood gushed out.

* * * * *

Rusty came to in the water. They had been at the last part of the rapid when Kurt had received the almighty blow to the back of his head which had caused him to release Rusty. As soon as that happened the life preserver had done its job and despite the fact that he was unconscious he bobbed to the surface where it supported him until he opened his bewildered eyes a few minutes later. As his senses returned, Rusty looked about. The raft was floating just a few metres away and he swam over to it slowly and grasped hold of the safety rope. As he did that he became aware that he was holding something in his right hand. Lifting it out of the water he realised it was the murderer's bum bag which he must have grabbed during the fight. Throwing it into the raft he kicked for the shore. Just then he heard voices and the sound of splashing. Looking up he could see two black guys wading out to meet him. They pulled the raft inshore and helped him to the bank.

'Boy, am I glad to see you,' was all Rusty could say as he collapsed on the beach.

After a surprisingly short amount of time Rusty was almost back to normal. He stood up and scanned the surface of the smooth water for any signs of his adversary. Out in the middle of the pool he could see the floating remains of his kayak which had been dashed to pieces in amongst the rocks. There was no sign though of anything else in the water. Just then he saw a fleeting glimpse of movement on the other bank.

'Any idea what that was, on the other side?' he asked the two locals.

'Man, there are some big mean crocs on the Zambian side. You were lucky you ended up with us, brother,' came the reply.

It transpired that the two men lived in the township on the edge of Victoria Falls and came down here every day to fish in the calm water of the pool. It was also the place where the Shearwater rafts finished their day on the river and the two men were sometimes employed as casual labour if not enough of the porters turned up for their regular stint. When Rusty asked if they would take him into town they readily agreed, especially as he promised them fifty dollars for the ride. Before making the precipitous climb out of the gorge, Rusty went over to the raft and took out the bum bag he had thrown aboard and untied the canvas bag that was still securely in position in the centre of the raft. As they made their way up the steep path he refused in no uncertain terms their kind offer to carry his baggage for him. When they reached the top the two men led him to an ancient Toyota Corolla that was parked in the shade.

'And where would you like us to take you, sir?' asked one of the men, with a big grin on his face.

'The Victoria Falls Hotel, please,' Rusty responded simply.

'Man, oh man, if you're staying there brother, the fare will be a hundred bucks.'

At this both men laughed heartily and Rusty readily agreed to this doubling of the fee.

Soon afterwards they left the rutted track and pulled out onto the tarred road leading back towards Victoria Falls. The two guys sat up front and as the little car wheezed its way into town they smoked and chatted to each another. Rusty had placed the two bags at his feet and took the opportunity to open both and examine them. As he stared down at the gleaming contents he could hardly control his breathing as he gazed at the riches that were in his possession. He had never seen anything so utterly fantastic in his life. At one point he looked up and realised they were approaching a police road block. Almost guiltily he closed the two bags and fastened the bum bag around his waist. The road block was not searching anyone entering town and they were waved through. As they drove on Rusty could see the long queue of parked vehicles and the exasperated faces of those who were unable to go about their legitimate business. Shortly afterwards they pulled up in front of the splendid hotel. The bellhop rushed out briskly from his station under the canopy and was about to send the dishevelled car packing when he saw Rusty emerge. If he was surprised to see a hotel guest get out of such a contraption he showed no sign of it.

'Good afternoon, Mr McKenna, and a lovely day it is to be alive, sir.'

'You can say that again. Would you allow these two splendid guys to wait here for a moment? They have done me a tremendous favour this morning and I just need to get something from my room by way of reward.'

'Sure thing, Sir, I'll give them the best spot in the car park.'

Rusty went into the cool reception area. Without hesitation he took an item from the stationery rack on the counter top and went over to one of the sofas in the corner of the room where he busied himself for a minute or so. Returning to the desk he spoke to the receptionist.

'Good morning, could you deal with this for me please? And could you ring up to my room and check if anyone is there.

'Certainly, Mr McKenna. I would be glad to help.'

With that the receptionist picked up the phone and dialled the number. A moment later there was a response from the other end.

'One moment please, I have a call for you.'

Rusty took the offered handset and put it to his ear.

'Hello, hello, who is that please.'

Rusty at once recognised Polinah's voice and a lump came to his throat as he heard the sound of evident anxiety.

'Polinah, darling, it's me. Everything is okay now. It's all over.'

'Rusty, my God, Rusty, where are you? I've been so worried.'

'I'm downstairs in reception. Can you bring my wallet down with . . .?'

Rusty stopped talking because he realised Polinah had dropped the phone. He could hear it clattering against the table. A moment later she was in his arms. Smothering him with kisses and crying all at the same time.

'Rusty, oh Rusty. Please don't put me through that again. It's been ghastly this morning, not knowing where you were or whether you were dead.'

Rusty just held her and hugged her.

'It's okay, lovely lady, never again. I promise you, never again.'

All about them, life had come to a standstill in the foyer. Both staff and guests looked on in admiration at the young couple. Some were surprised at what they saw. Others saw the look of love that passed between them and could only wish they had such passion and vibrancy in their lives.

'Rusty, I told the police what we saw this morning in the garden and that you chased after him. They said they would go down to the river and for me to report to them if I saw you again, or anything else for that matter.'

'Yes, I think that we had better get hold of them straight away. I've got a lot to tell them and to give them.'

With that Rusty threw the canvas bag to Polinah and went over to the reception desk and asked the girl behind the counter to contact Inspector Moloi and ask him to send a car round. It did not surprise Rusty when the girl told him that the Inspector had been pleased to hear that he was all right and that he was sending a car around right away. Rusty and Polinah returned to their room and collected his wallet. A few minutes later as the police car drew up he was out in the car park where the two fishermen were out of their car and were laughing and smiling and slapping Rusty mightily on the shoulders. Rusty had just handed them two crisp new fifty dollar bills. They would not need to worry about carrying heavy rafts, for a while at least. Shortly afterwards Rusty and Polinah were seated in the spacious office where Inspector Moloi conducted his more important business. The heavy canvas bag was on the table in front of him and Rusty had just reported the events of the morning in full. The Inspector responded.

'We have already contacted the Zambian authorities about all of this and have our own men out on the river,' Inspector Moloi explained. 'If your friend is alive he will be picked up in the fullness of time. In the meantime we had better get these back to their rightful owners as quickly as we can.'

The Inspector picked up the bag from the table and taking it from the room, asked them to bear with him for a short while. He returned a few minutes later with the, now empty, bag.

'As soon as it became clear that this might all come to a head in our little town, Debswana sent two of their senior execs to oversee things from their point of view. They are next door and want to ask you a couple of questions. I have had to tell them that you are under my jurisdiction and that I will do the asking.'

'Fire away then,' said Rusty.

'They have been through the contents of this bag and they want to know if you have opened it or in any other way interfered with it.'

Rusty was quick to respond.

'Yes, I have opened it. I knew all along what was likely to be in it. I have not, however, in any way interfered with its contents, much as I would have liked to.'

With that answer, the Inspector thanked Rusty for his candour and left the room. A few minutes later he returned with two well-dressed officials who sat on either side of the policeman on the other side of the table.

'Rusty, may I introduce you to Tom Robertshaw and Kogtla Segadika of the Debswana Mining Corporation of Botswana.'

'Mr McKenna, we have been instructed by the President of Botswana to thank you for the part that you have played in the return of these diamonds to their rightful owners. The haul that was stolen and which you have recovered for us represents nearly three months production of one of our most productive seams. The loss would have had a very damaging effect on the economy of our country. We are deeply in your debt.'

Rusty sensed the two men were keen to enter into further discussion about the events of the past few days but the Inspector Moloi was not going to permit them to make enquiries on his patch. Having allowed them to make their statement he ushered them from the room.

'So where does that leave us now?' Rusty asked the genial policeman.

'Why, you and Miss Mabina are free to go. It's a pleasure to have such a hero of one of our neighbours as our guest. Please feel free to stay until you have recovered. And then I wish you both every happiness for the future.'

The Inspector had noticed the way that Polinah held Rusty's hand and was pleased that events had turned out as they had. When Polinah had told him that Rusty had bolted out on his own in pursuit of the killer he had spent the early part of the day anticipating the worst. He had also enjoyed sparring with the two officials from Botswana who were not pleased with the way things had turned out, and who would not reveal the full facts. Given that they were clearly keeping something from him he felt he had done as much as was appropriate to assist them, in the circumstances. After shaking hands with them both, the Inspector watched the young couple leave the building, hand in hand. They had declined the offer of a car, adding that they were going down to enjoy the Falls.

* * * * *

Rusty and Polinah spent the best part of a week enjoying the relaxing and pleasant surroundings of the hotel. During that time they went out on the river for a cruise and took a guided tour into the Zambezi Game Reserve. Rusty eventually persuaded Polinah to take the trip up above the Falls in the seaplane. It was quite a spin for a first flight and she had squealed with delight as she stared in wonder at the magnificent views during the spectacular ride. She clung tightly to Rusty as the plane banked and turned above the spray. In the evenings they enjoyed the sunsets as they danced on the terrace. Afterwards, best of all, they retired to the privacy of their room. Polinah applied for some leave from her job which she was duly granted and Rusty wrote to the Training Centre in Hukuntsi to find out what the situation was, now that Mats had been lost to them. He asked them to reply to his English address, explaining that he was returning for a short holiday, but that he would take up his post if they still wanted him. Rusty booked some airline tickets through the hotel's travel agent and emailed his younger brother, Martin, to ask him to meet him at John Lennon Airport in Liverpool the following Sunday morning. When they were both good and ready they bade their farewells to Victoria Falls. When they telephoned Inspector Moloi to say goodbye, he rather dolefully reported that there had been no sign of the killer and that they had no real idea as to his identity. They had found out where he had been staying and that he had also hired a car in the town, but it had transpired that his papers had been false. It appeared that the search was at an end. Rusty and Polinah took the Air Zimbabwe commuter flight up to Harare, from where they caught the twice weekly KLM flight to Amsterdam's Schiphol Airport via Nairobi. After a brief stopover, they were soon aboard an Easyjet flight and were on their way through the leaden skies to the north of England. Polinah was by now dog tired and lay fast asleep with her head in his lap throughout the whole of the flight. As the small aircraft banked in preparation for landing, Rusty saw the River Mersey on his left and noticed the familiar sight of Speke Hall as they passed low over its towering chimneys. As they bumped down onto the tarmac, Polinah awoke and looked out of the window with a baleful expression as she took in the slate grey sky and the drab colour of the river.

'You've never been anywhere like this before, that's for sure,' said Rusty as he kissed her awake.

An hour later, after they had done battle with Immigration, who were unfamiliar with Batswana arriving by air in Liverpool, they made their way tiredly out into the arrivals lounge. As this was Sunday lunchtime on Merseyside it was not desperately busy and Rusty was quick to spot his little brother standing on one side. They both hugged in genuine pleasure at seeing one another.

'You are some crazy guy, Rusty. Only three weeks after a fond farewell at Lime Street for two years and I'm out here at Speke welcoming you back. And I thought you were in Botswana. Your email said you were in Zimbabwe. How do you do it? All I ever get to do is sit here on the dole in Liverpool.'

'Oh Mart. Can I introduce you to Polinah Mabina. We are going to . . . well . . . we're getting married. That's why I've come home, to tell everyone.'

Martin was dumbstruck. He shook hands with Polinah as if in a daze and stared at her in complete awe.

'Getting married? Getting married! You total bastard. Wait till I tell the rest of them.'

With that he picked up their bags and led them out to the car park. There he opened the door for Polinah and shoved their luggage into the boot. He then drove them away in his battered red Sierra, with Rusty sitting alongside. As they wound their way north through the city and onwards to the family home in Bootle, Martin kept looking in the rear view mirror at Polinah who was drifting off to sleep once again.

'Are you really marrying her, you swine? You swine. God, she's utterly lovely, she makes Naomi Campbell look like the back of a bus.

How many sisters has she got? Next time you go, bring back two of them for me and Chris. You total lucky bastard.'

Martin kept up this banter all the way. Rusty sat half-listening and glowing inside. He truly loved this small African woman sitting behind him and he could not wait to break the news to his Mam and Dad. When they arrived he did not get the chance. Leaving the car parked at a drunken angle in the street, Martin raced up the drive shouting.

'Mam! Dad! Rusty's here! He's got Naomi Campbell with him and he's bloody well going to marry her.'

The family did pretty well in the circumstances. They had been expecting Rusty to appear at some point in the day but they were well used to his comings and goings and they had not allowed his arrival to disrupt their day. Of course they had not known he was bringing company and had such momentous news. Rusty's elder brother was there, as were all of his sisters and they had all eaten a thoroughly good lunch.

When Martin burst in they were all sitting in front of the fire. On the television a cup semi-final was in progress and Liverpool were currently three up against Manchester United with only twenty minutes to play. Given that the allegiance of everyone in the room was Liverpudlian through and through, they were initially disinclined to switch it off just because the prodigal son had returned. In fact they would have expected him to crack open a tin of beer and sit down with them and enjoy the rare opportunity for fun at the expense of their neighbours from up the other end of the East Lancs road. As Rusty led Polinah into the small packed living room all that changed. The television was switched off and Polinah was led to the sofa by Rachel, his eldest sister, who immediately tried to make her at her ease. It was clear that the young African woman was slightly off balance in these unusual surroundings and everyone wanted her to feel at home. A cup of tea was brought to her into which she dumped six large teaspoons full of sugar, much to the amazement of the family. As she sat there quietly sipping her drink Rusty was bombarded with questions by his mother and father and his two brothers whilst the girls looked on, mildly jealous of Polinah's perfect brown skin and attractive features.

'So you two are getting married, are you? That's wonderful, Rusty. Your girl looks to be a beauty and it's time someone settled you down a bit. I think it's marvellous news.'

'I don't know about settling down, Mum. I've promised Polinah a traditional African wedding. We're planning to get hitched in Botswana. You'll have to mortgage the house because I want you all to come and join in the fun.'

His Mum visibly blanched at the idea of flying to the dark continent. She had never been abroad in her life so this was not something she could contemplate with ease. Still she did not wish to miss the wedding of her most troublesome but most cherished son. It had not surprised her that he had come home with someone like Polinah. Rusty's sisters were all a flap with the idea of the journey to Africa and Martin was clearly already counting his chickens as regards Polinah's sisters. For the next half an hour or so the room buzzed with questions and answers and Polinah was soon drawn into the heart of the family. There was much hilarity and laughter and once there was a great cheer when Dad turned on the Sky box and discovered that at full time the result in the big game had been five nil to the Scousers. Liverpool were on the road to Wembley once again. Just then Martin came back into the room. He had slipped out a few moments earlier. He threw a small package across the room which Rusty neatly caught.

'Oh, this came for you the other day, Rusty. What on earth are you doing sending things to yourself and then emailing me telling me not to open them under any circumstances?'

Rusty had been itching to find out if this little item had arrived but had decided not to say anything until Martin remembered it. He felt a quick surge of excitement when he saw that it was apparently intact. Throwing it across the room to his little sister, Annie, he said.

'Here, little treasure, you open it and see what you will see.'

Annie happily obliged and tore open the brown paper packet. It bore Zimbabwean stamps and the logo of the Victoria Falls Hotel. Rusty had secured it with tape and the receptionist had dutifully posted it for him. As Annie finally got through the protective barrier of the tape, she pulled out what appeared to be an advertising brochure for a safari company. As she looked up at Rusty with a puzzled expression on her face, five shiny objects fell out from between its pages and came to rest on the living room carpet. Polinah instantly recognised what they were. She had been suspicious for a couple of days or so that Rusty had been up to something but she had not been sure what. Now she knew.

'Rusty you wicked, wicked man. How could you do that?'

As she spoke, a big smile played on her lips and she bounded across the room and sat squarely and without embarrassment in his lap. First of all she kissed him full on the lips and then she hugged him to her, laughing loud and long. Rusty's Mum was the next to react and picked up one of the fantastic gems.

'Rusty, they're diamonds. And all of them are bigger than any in the Crown Jewels. Where did you find them?'

'That, Mam, is a long, long story. Maybe I'll write it all down one day,' replied Rusty, as he hugged Polinah to him.